Large Print
HEA

Heath, Lorraine.

Always to remember.

$25.95

Large Print
HEA

Heath, Lorraine.

Always to
remember.

$25.95

DATE	BORROWER'S NAME	

D1496372

Always to Remember

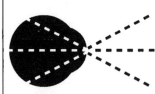

This Large Print Book carries the
Seal of Approval of N.A.V.H.

Always to Remember

Lorraine Heath

Thorndike Press • Thorndike, Maine

Published in 1998 by arrangement with The Berkley Publishing Group, a division of Penguin Putnam Inc.

Thorndike Large Print ® Americana Series.

The tree indicium is a trademark of Thorndike Press.

The text of this Large Print edition is unabridged.
Other aspects of the book may vary from the original edition.

Set in 16 pt. Plantin by Juanita Macdonald.

Printed in the United States on permanent paper.

Library of Congress Cataloging in Publication Data

Heath, Lorraine.
    Always to remember / Lorraine Heath.
        p.   cm.
      ISBN 0-7862-1520-8 (lg. print : hc : alk. paper)
      1. Large type books.   I. Title.
    [PS3558.E2634A79   1998]
    813′.54—dc21   98-22571

To my parents,
Lily Elizabeth and Curtis Rayburn
Heath

Your love gave me the courage
to believe in my dreams.

I wish to express my sincerest appreciation to:

Tavia Fortt, writer/editor at The Museum of Modern Art, New York, for explaining the structural design of stone sculpture. Any flaws in the design of Clay's statue rest with me.

Laurie Grant, writer and registered nurse, for helping me gather the medical information. Any misinterpretation of that information is mine.

Carmel Thomaston, critique partner and dear friend, for believing in the story as much as I did.

As always, the librarians and staff of the Plano Public Library system for sharing a wealth of information.

And the many readers who have taken the time to write me. Your kind words always brighten my day. I hope my stories will brighten yours.

Lorraine Heath
P.O. Box 941673
Plano, TX 75094-1673

Prologue

Autumn, 1862

Beyond the stone walls, the days melted into twilight.

But within the dark void that the walls created, Clayton Holland knew only the inky blackness of a starless night. Days contained neither dawn nor dusk but were filled instead with the monotonous slow passage of time as he waited, his conscience his sole companion.

Kneeling beside his cot, he pressed his forehead against his clasped hands and rested his elbows on the thin mattress. The foul odor of the men who'd come before him wafted around him. In a raw voice, he prayed for his trembling to cease, for courage and, most of all, for the strength to stand firmly by his convictions in these final hours.

After so many repetitions, the prayers should have come easily, but each prayer was different from the one that came before it. With each passing moment, the lingering doubts surfaced, taking on different shapes:

the love in his mother's eyes turning to ravaged grief; his father's guiding hands drifting
away and leaving him to journey along his
own path.

His latest prayer went unfinished, his body
involuntarily jerking as someone jammed a
key into the lock of his cell door. As the door
squeaked open, a sliver of light spilled into
the blackened abyss.

Raising a hand to shield his eyes from the
pale glow, Clayton struggled to his feet. The
door closed, a key grated, but the light remained. Slowly, as his eyes adjusted, he lowered his hand, and a stout man carrying a
lantern came into focus. "Dr. Martin?" he
rasped.

The man cleared his throat, the harsh
sound filling the dismal silence. "Yes, it's
me, Clay."

"Is it time?"

"No, not yet. I just thought you could use
a little company for a spell."

Clutching the waistband of his threadbare
woolen trousers with one hand, Clay extended the other toward the man who had
brought him and most of the boys of Cedar
Grove, Texas, into the world. He almost
wept as the doctor's hand warmed his.
"Thank you for coming, sir. Do you want to
sit? It's not fancy." He released what he

hoped was a laugh and not a sob. "I'm not even sure it's clean."

"It'll do fine," Dr. Martin said as he sat on the wobbly cot and set the lantern on the floor.

Clay eased onto the cot, leaned against the wall, and studied his visitor. Even in the obscurity of the shadows Clay could see the wrinkles that the doctor's kindly smiles had carved into his face over the years.

As a boy, whenever Clay had been ill, he'd always felt better once he heard Dr. Martin was on his way. He found comfort in the man's presence now even though he knew the doctor could do nothing for him. "Do you think it'll be a clear morning?"

"Appears it will be."

"Do you know if I'll be facing east? I sure would like to see the sunrise before I —"

"I don't know."

"Why do you think they execute people at dawn anyway?"

Dr. Martin's shrug was lost in the shadows. "I truly don't know."

A strangled laugh escaped Clay's lips and wandered around the cold cell. "Hell of a way to begin the day." He scratched his bearded chin. "Sir, do you know what became of Will Herkimer?"

"He . . ." Dr. Martin released a harsh

breath. "He died. Pneumonia set in shortly after they brought you here. I'm sorry."

Clay nodded, unable to speak for the emotions clogging his throat. He bowed his head in a silent moment of remembrance. "He had a wife," he said quietly. "And two boys. I always wanted a son." A sad smile crept over his face. "And a daughter." He searched the gloom for anything to take his mind off the dreams that would never come to pass. "Dr. Martin, how come you never married?"

"Never could find a woman willing to put up with the life I had to offer, gallivanting around the countryside in the middle of the night to tend sick folks. That's hard on a woman."

"Have you . . . have you ever been with a woman . . . through the night?"

Self-consciously, Dr. Martin cleared his throat. He never disclosed personal information about his patients' lives that he unwittingly discovered in the course of their treatment. Until now he'd always applied the practice to himself as well. "Yes, yes, I've been with a woman."

"What'd she smell like?"

Dr. Martin heard the deep longing mirrored in a voice that should have reflected the vibrancy of youth. "Lavender," he replied.

"Lavender. I don't recall ever smelling lavender."

A keen sense of loss whispered across the small expanse separating the old man from the young one. Dr. Martin felt the loss as though he'd experienced it himself. He wanted to ask Clay what the hell he had smelled so he could lie and tell him the woman smelled of it. "Honeysuckle," he said after a time. "Once I slept with a woman who smelled like honeysuckle."

"Honeysuckle," Clay repeated in reverence, relief coursing through his voice. "I can imagine a woman smelling like honeysuckle. Was she soft?"

"Very."

"And warm?"

"As warm as a Texas summer."

Silence eased in around them, and Dr. Martin was saddened to think that in this young man's final moments, he was thinking of a woman he'd never met and never would meet. He reached into the deep pocket of his coat, withdrew an apple, and gave it to Clay.

Wrapping both hands around it, Clay relished the fruit's smooth skin against his unnaturally frigid fingers. Bringing the apple close to his face, he cupped his hands over his nose and mouth, blocking out the odors

11

mingling in the cell, as he inhaled deeply. The apple smelled so sweet, so deliciously sweet. As sweet as life.

He swallowed his sob and ground the heel of his hand into the corner of his eye. He refused to walk out of this room with tears trailing down his face.

Leaning forward, Dr. Martin planted his elbows on his thighs. "Clay, all you have to do is hold the damn rifle. You don't even have to shoot it. They're gonna fight those damn Yankees any day now. Wouldn't it be more honorable to die on a battlefield? I could talk to Captain Roberts, have your sentence revoked —"

Slowly, Clay shook his head. For months Captain Roberts had insisted that he must follow orders and carry a rifle. For months Clay had steadfastly refused. "I will not take up arms against my fellow man."

"What am I to tell your father?"

"That I died with honor, fighting for what I believed in."

Dr. Martin sighed heavily. He couldn't deny that the boy had fought. His body carried the wounds from his battles. "Are you in much pain? I could give you some laudanum."

"My misery will end soon enough. You'd best save your medicine for those boys whose

12

misery will just be beginning." He extended the apple toward the doctor. "Don't think I'd be able to keep this down. Imagine you'll be able to find someone who could appreciate it a little longer than I could."

The key grinding in the lock caused Dr. Martin's heart to slam against his ribs as though he were the one about to be placed before a firing squad. He took back the apple because he didn't know what else to do with his hands. His noted bedside manner had deserted him.

The door swung open, and a sergeant, with two privates in his wake, stepped into the room. The sergeant's deep voice bounced off the stone walls. "It's time."

Standing, Clay extended his hand toward the doctor. "Thank you, sir, for coming."

Clasping the young man's hand, taking note of the slight tremor, Dr. Martin wished he could offer more than a handshake. Clay stepped toward the open door.

A rope dangling from his hand, a private moved to block his path. "You need to put your hands behind your back."

Despair flooded Clay's face. "I've lost weight," he stammered. "My trousers —"

The private turned to the sergeant who was already shaking his head. "He's gotta be bound."

"I'm not gonna run," Clay assured him.

The sergeant appeared on the verge of relenting when he suddenly barked, "Orders is orders! Bind him."

"Wait a minute," Dr. Martin said as he shrugged off his coat. The young man had clung tenaciously to his dignity throughout his ordeal, and now they had the power to strip him of it. They'd fed him nothing but bread and water for so long that Clay was little more than a shadow of the robust man who'd once farmed the land in Texas. "He can use my suspenders."

For the first time in his life, Dr. Martin fought a strong urge to strike someone — anyone — when gratitude filled Clay's eyes as he attached the suspenders.

Clay placed his hands behind his back, fighting off the helplessness consuming him as the private wound the rope around his wrists. He wished they'd given him an opportunity to bathe, to make himself presentable. He reeked to high heaven and no longer remembered the feel of freshly laundered clothes against his skin.

He followed the sergeant out of the room and along the dim corridor. Squinting as they stepped into the bright sunlight, he took a deep breath of outside air. He smelled horses, leather, and gunpowder. The world had turned brown, orange, and gold. Autumn had come without his knowing.

The men had gathered at one end of the compound. He could feel their eyes boring into him. They knew he was a man who refused to become a soldier, who refused to carry a rifle. They thought he was a coward. They'd branded him a deserter.

The small procession approached the wall. Clay smiled. It faced east. He didn't look into the faces of the six men standing before the wall, but moved into position silently.

Captain Roberts, a West Point graduate who could trace his family's military history back a hundred years to the Revolutionary War, stepped forward. "Do you have a final request?"

"A prayer," he croaked. "I'd like to say a prayer."

Roberts nodded his approval of the request.

As Clay bowed his head, his voice became clear, strong, and certain. "Heavenly Father, please forgive those who stand before you today for they know not what they do. Amen."

He lifted his brown gaze to the blue heavens.

"I'm sorry, son," the sergeant said quietly before he stepped away to stand beside Captain Roberts and issue his first order. "Ready your rifles!"

Clay's mouth went dry.

"Aim!"

He felt the wind caress his face, heard the leaves rustle —

"Fire!"

One

Spring, 1866

Clayton Holland jerked awake. Trembling and bathed in sweat, he ran a shaking hand through his hair.

The thunder again resounded, and he took a deep, shuddering breath. The nightmares always came during thunderstorms when the rumbling in the sky wove itself through his dreams.

He threw back the covers, clambered out of bed, and made his way to the window. Unlatching the shutters and pushing them open, he breathed deeply, inhaling the scent of rain. Reaching out, he relished the stinging raindrops as they pelted his palm. Lightning flashed and thunder called out against the darkness.

Thunder always reminded him of the volley of rifle fire — the volley that never came. Even now, years later, he still waited for the crack of rifle thunder to disturb that quiet dawn so long ago.

The sergeant had bellowed his final command. Clay drew his last breath and held the precious air deep within his lungs, waiting for the bullets to slam him against the wall, to force the life from his body.

He waited what seemed a lifetime . . . and beyond.

He lowered his gaze to the soldiers standing before him, wondering if they were waiting for him to look at them before they carried out their orders. But as he met the troubled gaze of each man, so each man lowered his rifle and studied his boots.

Oddly, he could remember clearly the color of each man's eyes: brown, brown, blue, brown, green, blue.

The sergeant conferred with Captain Roberts. Then he escorted Clay back to his cell.

Later, Clay learned that his prayer, his concern for their souls and not his own, had touched the hearts of the soldiers and officers in attendance.

A simple prayer had saved his life and prolonged his misery. He had spent nine months shackled, serving time for his refusal to carry a rifle.

After his release, he had found one reason after another not to return to Cedar Grove. Until the war ended.

He had arrived home at Christmas and

discovered that the only peace within his life resided within his conscience. Beyond that, the war had followed him home.

He watched a pale light float toward the barn. A streak of lightning outlined his two youngest brothers as they trudged toward their predawn chores. Entering the world on the same day, Joseph and Joshua were inseparable, and few people could tell them apart. They'd been but five when the Confederate Army had come for Clay. They were nearly ten now. Clay sometimes wondered if it wouldn't have been kinder to stay away, as his other brother, Lucian, often suggested.

He closed the shutters and turned up the flame in the lantern on the bedside table. Self-consciously, he rubbed his bare chest as he picked his clothes off the chair and tossed them on the bed. As was his habit, he dressed carefully, taking time to button every button. He pulled on his socks before shoving his feet into his boots. Standing, he stomped his feet into place.

He'd turned the cheval glass so it faced the wall, saving himself the agony of confronting his reflection. He'd gained little weight in the three months since his return. He couldn't get credit at the mercantile, so the meals he provided his family were dependent on the wild game in the nearby hills and the few assorted vegetables they grew in their small garden. He told his brothers things would improve once they harvested the crops in the fields. He had to believe those words in order to survive to the next day.

He'd learned that small trick during the war. Don't think about tomorrow or what horrors it might hold, just cling to today.

He picked up the lantern and unbolted the door of his bedroom. He walked through the small living area where his family had long ago shared abundant meals and conversation, where a fire had burned in the hearth while his mother quilted as she wove tales to delight her children. His father would whittle, occasionally interrupting to add his own bit of thread to the story. Laughter had filled the room and smiles had been as abundant as the food.

Now, the room served as little more than a place to eat a somber meal in silence. He pulled his slicker off the hook by the door and stepped into the storm.

With his head bowed, he trudged toward the dilapidated barn. The entire farm needed repairs. His parents had passed away before the war ended. Lucian had managed to hold onto the farm and keep the twins from becoming wild. As a young man of sixteen, he had shouldered the responsibility without complaint.

Lucian's complaints had only surfaced when Clay returned home to lift the burden from his brother's shoulders. Their parents had dictated that they wanted the farm passed down to their eldest surviving son. Clay was the eldest, and he'd survived.

Walking into the barn, he inhaled the familiar scent of hay and livestock along with the disappointing smell of rotting wood. He couldn't get credit at the lumber mill either.

He heard the tinny echo as the milk hit the galvanized pail. The sound didn't have time to fade before another took its place. He knew his brothers sat, one on each side of the cow, working together as one. He'd noticed that their being twins had created a certain bond. Sometimes it seemed the brothers didn't even have to voice their thoughts to each other.

"I know what you're thinkin', and it ain't gonna work."

Clay slowed his steps at the sound of Josh's voice.

"It might," Joe shot back defiantly. "It would for sure if you pretended to be sick, too."

"I don't want to spend the whole day in

21

bed. If this frog-chokin' rain stops, I aim to go fishin'."

"We'd just be sick till church was over."

"Nah, Clay'd make us stay in bed all day just to make sure we wasn't sick tomorrow. Ain't worth it, Joe."

"But I hate goin' to church! I hate the way everybody looks at us."

"They ain't lookin' at us. They're lookin' at Clay. 'Sides, if you do catch 'em lookin' at you, you just gotta cross your eyes at 'em, and they'll look away."

"Is that what you do?" Joe asked, disbelief resounding in his young voice.

"Heck fire, yeah! Sometimes, it's even fun. Did it once to old Pruneface, and she started wobblin' her head like a rooster that was tryin' to decide whether or not it wanted to crow."

"And did Widow Prudence crow?" Clay asked quietly.

Startled, both boys jerked back in unison, toppling off their respective stools, their legs flying out, kicking the bucket over and spilling milk over the straw.

"Oh, heck!" Josh cried as he picked up the bucket too late to save much of their effort.

Clay grabbed the stool the boy had vacated, moved it to the corner, sat, and drew his legs up so he could cross his arms over his thighs.

"Joe, Josh, come here and sit down."

With their brown eyes focused on him, the boys dropped before him. He resisted the urge to tussle their red hair. Living with his family often made him feel as though he lived with strangers. The boys accepted him because he was their brother. He'd mistakenly thought that was enough.

He continued to see them as they were the day he left, clutching their mother's apron and crying. They hadn't asked any questions that day because they'd been too young to understand what questions needed to be asked. They were older now, but they'd kept their questions and their doubts to themselves. He wondered if they feared the answers. Before he'd left, they'd loved him. He wanted desperately for them to love him again.

"I want you to tell me the truth because the truth never hurts as much as a lie." He met each boy's wide-eyed stare and waited until both boys nodded. "Does it embarrass you to be seen with me in church?"

The boys slid their gazes toward each other, communicating silently what each felt in his heart. Josh returned his gaze to Clay. "It don't embarrass us none to be seen with you. We just don't like the way people stare at us."

"Do you know why they stare?"

" 'Cuz you're a coward," Joe said without hesitation.

Clay felt as though all six rifles had just fired into his heart. He bowed his head, clasping his hands together until they ached and the knuckles turned white. "Is that what you think?" he asked solemnly. "That I'm a coward? Or is it just what you've heard?"

"It's what they say at school," Josh told him.

"And what Lucian says," Joe added.

"Is that what you say?" Clay asked.

"I tell 'em it ain't so," Josh said.

Clay lifted his head, his gaze not reflecting the hope cautiously soaring within his heart. "Do you really say that?"

Slowly shaking his head, Josh screwed his mouth. "I don't tell 'em nothin'. Just let 'em think what they want."

A bullet slamming into his chest could not have hurt more. "Do you know what a coward is?" he asked.

"Someone that runs away."

"Did I run?"

The boys exchanged troubled glances. "Did you?" Josh asked. "Did you run?"

"No."

"Then how come they think you're a coward?"

"Because I didn't fight either."

"How come?"

Clay heaved a sigh. Knowing they would one day ask this question didn't make it any easier to answer now. "It's hard to explain, but my conscience wouldn't let me."

"What's your conscience?"

"It's a meeting place for the things your heart feels and the things your head knows. Then they decide what you should believe and how you should live in order to be happy."

"But you never look happy, Clay," Joe said.

He offered his brothers a somber smile and laid his palm over his heart. "I'm happy here because I believe — I know — what I did was right for me. I didn't believe in slavery. I didn't believe Texas had the right to secede. I didn't believe we should fight the Northern states, and yet, I could not in all good conscience take up arms against the South, my home, and my friends. But more than that, I would not fight because I believe it's a sin against God to kill another man."

"They don't say it's a sin in church. They don't think all those soldiers were sinnin'."

"Different churches believe different things. We've only got one church in Cedar Grove, and I think it's better to attend a church that doesn't believe everything I do than not to go to church at all."

"Were you the only one who believed all that?" Joe asked.

Clay shook his head. "No, there were others. One man had more courage than any man I ever knew. We talked about what we believed, and we promised each other we'd stand by our convictions no matter what."

"What happened to him?"

Clay swallowed the lump in his throat that always formed when he thought of Will. "He got sick and died."

"You oughta tell people you ain't no coward," Josh suggested.

"It's not the kind of thing you can tell people. They'll believe it only if you show them. That's why, even though I hate the way people watch me when I go to church on Sunday morning, I still go. I didn't do anything I'm ashamed of, and I won't run from their opinions. Someday maybe they'll understand."

"What if they never do?" the twins asked in unison.

Clay sighed. He'd have a damn lonely life, but the loneliness should belong to him, not them. A man lived or died according to his decisions in life, and Clay had made his decision. The twins were old enough now to make their own decisions. "You don't have to go to church with me this morning, and when the rain stops, you can go fishing."

The boys looked at each other, their initial relief quickly giving way to family commitment. "Nah, we'll go," Josh said. "Won't we, Joe?"

Squaring his small chin, Joe gave a quick nod.

Daring to ruffle their hair, he expected them to flinch at his touch. Instead they smiled. "Then I guess you'd better practice crossing your eyes before we leave."

The twins laughed as only children can, with an innocence and joy, as they anticipated honing their skills.

Unfolding his body, Clay walked out of the stall, out of the barn, and back into the storm.

Sitting upon a raised dais to one side of the pulpit, Meg Warner pressed the keyboard. The haunting melody of the organ touched the church rafters, waltzed along the stained-glass windows where the sunlight cast a myriad of rainbows, and whispered across the congregation.

Meg knew every face. The old and weathered faces of the men, the aged faces of the women. Noticeably absent were the faces of the young men with whom she'd grown up. With pride, they'd ridden off to war. Never losing courage, they had been vanquished. They had marched into battle side by side, and Yankee guns had leveled them as though they were little more than wheat growing in a field.

Meg watched Lucian Holland wander down the aisle and ease onto the edge of a pew. An awkwardness had settled around Lucian when his brother returned, as though he no longer knew where he belonged.

She lifted her hands off the keys and folded them in her lap. A reverent silence filtered through the church as Reverend Baxter stepped up to the pulpit.

Meg gazed at her brother, Daniel. Like Lucian, he'd been too young to enlist when the war started. Almost seventeen now, he worked hard to fill his brothers' boots — all three pairs. She could see her older brothers reflected in Daniel's strong jaw, his thick black hair, and his deep blue eyes. His jaw tensed as the church door opened.

Balling her hands into fists, Meg slid her gaze toward the back of the church. Two boys wearing the same wary expression slipped into the last pew. Meg's heart went out to the boys, dressed in trousers that were a shade too short. Then the door closed, and their oldest brother took his place beside them.

If Meg had been struck blind at that moment, she still could have told the world what Clayton Holland would do, for he'd done it every Sunday since he'd returned to Cedar Grove. He would bow his head as though in prayer. Then he would lift his gaze to the minister. His eyes would stray only when the twins fidgeted. And while he never took his eyes off the minister, so Meg never took her eyes off him.

It fueled her anger and hatred to watch him, to be reminded once a week that he lived and breathed while her dear husband and three brothers lay cold in their graves. They had fought valiantly and died bravely defending the honor of the Confederacy while Clayton Holland had bared the yellow streak racing down his back. She knew it was childish to think that one more man on that battlefield would have made a difference, but she resented Clay for turning his back on the South and being rewarded with his life.

Reverend Baxter's words droned on with Meg paying scant attention to their meaning. Her thoughts darkened until they resembled the storm that had blown through in the early hours before dawn. The nightmares always came with the storms and lingered for days like the puddles after a rain.

With her dreams reverberating with the roar of guns and Kirk's agonized screams, she would awaken bathed in sweat. She imagined that the last thing Kirk had heard before he died was the sound of rifle fire or the blast of a cannon, when he should have heard her voice reaffirming her love. The last thing he had felt was the hard ground when he should have felt her gentle touch comforting him. Hundreds of men had surrounded him, but without her at his side, he had faced death alone.

"Meg?"

She snapped her gaze up to Reverend Baxter's. He bestowed upon her a congenial smile and nodded toward the organ. She transferred all her heart to the music as the congregation lifted its voice in song.

From the corner of her eye, she glimpsed Clayton Holland and his brothers as they quietly rose and walked from the church. She poured her energy into the keyboard, allowing the force of the song to wash over her, cleanse her in ways Reverend Baxter's sermon never could.

As the final note died away, she bowed her head for the closing prayer. When Reverend Baxter's voice fell into silence, people scuffled out of the church, and Meg closed her music book.

"That was lovely, Meg."

She bent her head back to meet Reverend Baxter's amber eyes. He was a towering man. A sparse mustache topped his warm smile. She returned his smile. "Thank you."

She started to rise and found his hand beneath her elbow, assisting her.

"I suppose you have a fine meal planned for this afternoon. Will you have your apple cobbler on the table?" he asked.

"Of course. We'd love to have you join us."

His smile broadened. "Wonderful. I'll ride over after I've visited with my parishioners. In an hour or so. Will that be all right?"

"That'll be fine." She skirted him and walked from the dais. Her steps echoed through the church as she continued along the aisle. She stepped into the sultry heat, avoiding the puddles dotting the ground.

She stopped numerous times to visit briefly with old friends, girls with whom she'd grown up, wives and mothers of men who would never come home. They shared a bond that a war had forged. She worked her way through the gathering until she finally reached her father's wagon.

" 'Bout time, girl," her father said as she approached. "Thought I was going to have to go into church and get you myself."

"I invited Reverend Baxter to join us for dinner," she said as he helped her onto the seat of the wagon.

"You invited him? Or did he invite himself?" her brother asked from the back of the wagon.

Turning slightly, she slapped his arm. "Daniel Crawford, you have the manners of a Yankee. I invited him, just as I said."

"I bet he did some powerful hinting, though," Daniel teased, his blue eyes sparkling. "I think he's sweet on you, Meg."

"Don't be ridiculous. He's twice as old as I am. Besides, I don't ever plan to marry again. I could never love anyone as I loved Kirk."

Her father glanced at her, his bushy white eyebrows shifting up over blue eyes that greatly favored hers. "You can't spend your life in mourning."

"Why not? You have."

Thomas Crawford tipped his hat back off his brow. "It's different with me. Me and your ma had fifteen years to make memories and five children. Those memories will carry me through until I join her. You were left with much less than that, girl."

"It's not the number of memories a person has, but how wonderful they are. My memories of Kirk will sustain me."

Sadly, he shook his head. "Still, you might consider the reverend. You have a good heart, Meg. You'd make a fine preacher's wife, and it wouldn't be such a bad life."

She couldn't imagine that it would be such a good life either. She didn't get that warm melting feeling inside her whenever she looked at Reverend Baxter. "I'm thinking of planting petunias around the boys' graves," she said to change the subject.

"Damn it, Meg! They ain't boys!" Daniel cried.

Thomas glared over his shoulder. "Don't use profanity around your sister."

"But she keeps calling 'em boys. They were soldiers."

"You're right, Daniel," she said kindly, trying to soothe the guilt she knew still filled his heart. "But in my mind, I still see them as they were the day they left. Remember how Kirk and I came over for breakfast, and we all had to go into the kitchen and watch Michael shave for the first time that morning?"

"I wish I'd been old enough to fight with them. If only I'd been born sooner . . ." Wistfully, his voice trailed off.

"You wanted to go," Thomas said gruffly. "That counts for a lot."

"Wantin' to go don't count for nothing,

Pa. I should have lied about my age. I should have gone —"

"*He* should have gone!" Thomas bellowed pointing a finger toward the far horizon and a wagon rolling off into the distance. "By God, he should have gone."

Meg heard the bitter edge in his voice, unusual in the man who had held her on his lap when she was a child and laughed until his burly body shook. She couldn't remember when she'd last heard him laugh, and she knew she wouldn't hear him laugh today.

The war had cut deep wounds into the hearts of her family and the whole town of Cedar Grove. Every Sunday, Clayton Holland reopened those wounds when he stepped inside the church.

Sighing into the night, Meg buried herself beneath the quilts. After Reverend Baxter finished his meal and left, her father grabbed his bottle of corn whiskey and headed to the barn. She knew exactly how long it took him to drink himself into oblivion because he did it every night. At just the right moment she'd walked to the last stall in the barn and draped a blanket over the man who had once tucked blankets around her.

Daniel was nowhere to be found, and she was certain he'd run off to meet with his friends and talk about a war that had ended long before they were ready for it to end.

Meg wished it had never started. She longed for the days before the war, for the father who had held her on his lap, for the brothers who had teased her.

She longed for the man who had loved her.

Touching her breast, she remembered Kirk's caress. When they became man and wife, she was seventeen, he an older and wiser nineteen. For less than a year, they shared the pleasures of marriage.

She'd loved Kirk with all her heart and soul. She'd wanted to grow old holding his hand. She'd wanted to bring his children into the world, but they had not been blessed with children. Now, alone in her bed at night, the emptiness was often a searing pain that engulfed her.

She let her hand whisper across her stomach as his had so many nights, but she dared go no farther. Her hand was not his, rough and callused from working the farm. Her hand was not his, gentle and patient with love.

"Always wear your hair down for me, Meg love," he whispered as he fanned her ebony strands across his chest.

Then his mouth took possession of hers, and she threaded her fingers through the thick pelt covering his chest.

"Touch me, love, touch me," he rasped. Slowly, he glided her hand along his stomach, lower, lower still until he groaned, "God, I love you, Meg." Then he showed her, in all the ways a man could, how much he loved her.

Her tears slipped onto the pillow. She'd been afraid whenever those around her talked in quiet voices about the possibility of war. The small word conjured stark images of blood and death. Kirk consoled her, calmed her fears. Then, just as quickly as lightning flashes through the sky, people no longer mentioned the word in hushed whispers, but yelled it across the land.

It never occurred to them that he would not enlist. When the South asked her people to give their sons, Meg gave her husband. Willingly. Proudly.

And three of her brothers.

That last morning, when they gathered in town, the men had looked dashing in their hand-sewn gray uniforms. Full of confidence. Full of life. Perhaps death had come to them because they dared to laugh in its face and believe they were invincible. They were certain their presence alone would vanquish the enemy.

With pride, she had presented a large Confederate flag to the company, a flag she and the other ladies of Cedar Grove had worked day and night to complete in time for the soldiers' departure. The men accepted the silk offering with a whoop and rebel yell that still echoed across the land.

Meg's heart swelled with devotion as they reared their horses before galloping away to face the bitter foe.

Her heart broke with their deaths.

Rolling to her side, she studied the granite figurine that graced her bedside table. A doe protectively shielded her fawn beneath an intricately carved bush. Kirk had given her the statuette because they had seen the deer the day he asked her to become his wife.

But Clayton Holland had sculpted it.

Clay and his father had cut the words into most of the headstones in the cemetery beside the church. Sometimes they carved small statues, particularly for the children's resting places. She had been tempted to ask Clay to carve granite markers for Kirk and her brothers, but she could not bring herself to ask anything of the town's coward.

The Union army buried Kirk and her brothers where they'd fallen, along with so many others. As the months rolled into years, she remembered them through a misty gray fog, their features veiled by the passage of time. She could no longer remember the exact shade of Kirk's eyes. Were they the blue of a sky at dawn or sunset?

Crudely, she'd carved Kirk's name and her brothers' names in wood and set the markers in the family plot. Her action constituted a vain attempt to hold onto them, a desperate need to have something by which to remember them. But her makeshift memorial didn't stop their images from slipping away or ease her pain.

With trembling fingers, she touched the fawn. How could Clay have returned? How could he hold his head up knowing he was a coward? He owed the young men of Cedar Grove, owed them something for not standing beside them. She wanted him to suffer as much as they had before death, as much as she did now in life.

Daniel often said he wanted to pound Clay into the ground, but Meg wanted more. In time, the pain from a physical beating would recede, heal, and scar, but wounds inflicted to the heart left scars that never stopped hurting.

She wanted Clayton Holland to experience the kind of invisible pain that cut thoroughly. She wanted, needed him to face his cowardice, to have it carved into his heart so deeply that he would feel it with every breath he took for as long as he lived.

TWO

Meg halted her mare beneath the shade of a pecan tree that bordered the Holland property.

His bare bronzed back glistening with the sweat of his labors, Lucian toiled in the field using a hoe to shift the soil over the seeds. Clay, with damp splotches circling the back and sleeves of his shirt, was guiding the plow through the field as the mule dragged it. Somehow she was not surprised that Clay wore a shirt while he worked. She'd not forgotten how quiet and soft-spoken he'd been in his youth.

As she prodded her horse through the furrowed field, Lucian spotted her. He straightened, propped his elbow on the hoe, and smiled. "Good day, Mrs. Warner!"

Irritated that Clay continued to plow the field as though company had not come to call, she drew her horse to a halt beside Lucian. "How are you, Mr. Holland?"

"Hot. And you?"

"A bit warm. I need to speak with your brother."

He raised his eyebrows in disbelief. "You're here to see Clay?"

"I have some business to discuss with him."

"Business?" He chuckled. "The last person to discuss business with Clay did it with his fist. Is that what you're planning?"

"No, it is not."

"Too bad." He gave her a sheepish grin. "Guess I'd best let him know you're here. He dreams while he plows the field." He turned on his heel. "Clay!" Lucian peered at her when his brother failed to respond. "See what I mean? I'll get him for you."

He ran across the field, caught up with Clay, and spoke words Meg couldn't hear. Clay drew the mule to a halt and glanced over his shoulder. The brim of his hat shadowed his face so she had no idea what he was thinking. He ambled toward her while Lucian politely stayed with the mule.

As he neared, he removed his hat and squinted against the harshness of the sun. She hadn't seen Clay up close since his return. The abundant streaks of white feathering through the brown hair at his temples astonished her. He and Kirk had been of the same age, and yet he looked considerably older than she imagined Kirk would have looked at twenty-five.

"I'm sorry for your loss."

His solemnly spoken words caused her to realize she'd been staring at him for some time. Thrusting up her chin, she narrowed her eyes. "Are you indeed?"

"Yes, ma'am, I am. Your husband and brothers were fine men."

"They died with courage and honor."

"Yes, ma'am, they did. Kirk came —"

"How dare you!" she hissed, her fingers tightening on the reins. "How dare you speak his name!"

Despair flashed through his eyes. "I meant no disrespect."

"No disrespect! Your very presence here is a disrespect."

Slowly, he shook his head and slid his gaze past her. "Shall I gather up the stones?"

"What?"

"Nothing. Just say what you came to say and be done with it."

He met her gaze, and she wondered when his brown eyes had grown so aged.

"I didn't come here to fight." Preparing to dismount, she swung her leg over the saddle. He took a step forward to help her. She stopped his movements with a cold look of disdain. Sighing, he stepped back. She placed her feet on the ground, holding the reins loosely threaded through her fingers.

Yesterday morning during the church service while she watched Clay as he sat in the last pew, she'd planted the seeds for retribution in her mind. The idea had blossomed by the end of the day and kept her awake most of the night. When she had made the final decision in the hours before dawn to come here, she'd decided she would not address him. "Mr. Holland" showed a measure of respect for which she felt none, and "Clay" indicated an intimacy, a friendship that she would never share with this man.

Gently, she slapped the reins against her thigh. "Do you remember the small figurine you made for my husband?"

The memory of a happier time flitted across his face and lit his eyes. "The one with the deer?"

"Yes. There have been times when I've wanted to smash it against the wall and watch it crumble into a thousand pieces because your hands touched it. I haven't because it was a gift from my husband. I tell you this because I don't want you to have any doubts as to what my feelings for you are. Do you understand?"

Her words effectively snuffed out the light in his eyes. "Perfectly."

Meg swallowed, wondering if she'd been

too harsh. She'd meant to lash out at him, but now that she had, she felt little satisfaction. Deep creases lined his weathered face. At first, she thought they'd surfaced because he was squinting at the sun, but even now, when his eyes had adjusted to the sunlight and he was no longer squinting, the grooves remained.

She heaved a frustrated sigh, needing his help but sickened at the thought of asking for it. She decided her best approach was to ignore her abhorrence of this man and simply state her reason for being here. "I want a memorial built to honor the fine young men of Cedar Grove who gave their lives with courage during the war, and you're the only person I know with the skills to make it."

"A memorial?"

"Yes, a statue of some kind that we could put in the center of town."

"And you want me to make it?"

"Yes. I realize —"

Presenting his lean back to her, he slowly raked his fingers through his hair. She thought he was going to walk away, but he stood, gazing at something she couldn't see. He turned back around, worry and concern etched across his features. "I haven't cut any stone in a long while."

"Are you as afraid of this task as you were of the war?"

Narrowing his eyes, he scrutinized her. She tilted up her chin.

"What kind of material did you want to use?" he asked.

"I don't know."

"What did you have in mind for it to look like?"

"I'm not sure. The only thing I do know is that within the base, I want you to carve the name of every man who died."

"That would be twenty-two names."

Startled, she blinked, her fingers tightening on the reins. "You know how many men died?"

"I can recite their names for you if you like."

"All of them?"

"All of them."

"Oh . . . I see," she mumbled.

"You seem disappointed."

"No, I . . . I just didn't expect it, that's all."

"What did you expect?"

His knowledge had caught her off guard. She herself hadn't known the exact number of young men who had perished. She'd mourned them as a whole, focusing her deepest grief on the loss of Kirk and her brothers. Pulling back her shoulders, she regained her composure. "I didn't expect you to be quite so willing to help. As to the fee —"

"I don't want payment."

Meg felt her shoulders slump. She'd wanted the satisfaction of telling him he'd do it because he owed them that much, that she wasn't going to pay him anything. He shifted his stance as though suddenly uncomfortable and studied the ground.

"There is the matter of the materials." He lifted his gaze to hers. "I haven't the means to purchase them."

Feeling the control slip back into her hands, she tilted her chin. "I have."

He nodded and something akin to hope plunged into the dark depths of his eyes. "I could sketch out some ideas tonight."

"I'll want to look at them, of course. To put it bluntly — while you're working on this project, I'll be looking over your shoulder. I want it done to my specifications."

"On one condition."

In disbelief, she stared at him as though he'd suddenly donned a blue uniform. "I beg your pardon?"

"I have one condition —"

"Impossible. I'm providing the materials —"

"I'm providing the labor."

She crossed her arms beneath her breasts, her foot packing the recently loosened dirt back into the earth. "What's your condition?"

"The base will be a block with four sides. Three sides will carry the names of those who fell in battle — seven names on each side, eight on the front. On the fourth side, I'll carve whatever I want."

"No, that's impossible, completely out of the question. You might put something entirely unsuitable."

"Then I won't do it. It was a pleasure visiting with you, Mrs. Warner, but now if you'll excuse me, I need to get back to my field."

Meg watched in dismay as he dropped his hat onto his head, spun, and began walking toward his plow. "Wait! You can't refuse!"

"Last I heard this was a free country!" he yelled, not bothering to glance back at her.

She rushed after him, unable to catch up to his long strides. "Stop!"

He quickened his pace.

"Stop! Please!" she called out.

Halting abruptly, he turned slowly to face her. Short of breath, she was angry by the time she reached him, but he had skills possessed by no other man in this area. "What did you want to put on the fourth side?"

"I don't know yet."

"Can I at least have a say in what you put there?"

"No, ma'am."

She stomped the ground. "Damn you! You owe —"

"I don't owe anyone anything. They made their choice, and I made mine. They paid their price, but I'm still paying mine and getting mighty damn tired of it. If you want the memorial, I'll make it, but I'm not going to pour my sweat, my heart, and my soul into it and not claim a corner of it as mine." A deep sadness filled his eyes. "I give you my word that when I'm done, nothing engraved on the memorial will detract from its meaning."

"And what do you perceive as its meaning?"

"To honor those who fought and died for their convictions."

She met his gaze, studying him, surprised by his words. How could he understand what he'd never experienced? She fought the tears glistening within her eyes. "This is important to me," she whispered hoarsely.

"I realize that."

She turned away, working to regain her emotions. She needed something more than wooden markers casting shadows over empty graves to keep the memory of those she loved from fading. She wanted Clay to make the memorial so he would be constantly reminded of his own cowardice. Before dawn, it had seemed the perfect punishment for him, more lasting than any beating her brother could give him.

Yet nothing had gone as she'd expected since she'd dismounted. Every sentence she'd practiced had been altered by his response. She spun around — balling her hands at her sides, thrusting her chin upward — and met his gaze. "All right. You can have your side of the base to do with as you wish, but I have two conditions of my own."

"And they are?"

"You're to tell no one what you're working on. It's to remain a secret until it's displayed."

"And the other condition?"

"Under no circumstances are you to ever think that this forced partnership makes us friends. If our paths cross in town, I will ignore your presence, and I would appreciate it greatly if you would ignore mine."

"In other words, you don't want anyone to know you have any association with the likes of me."

"Precisely. Are we agreed?"

"Agreed." He gave her a sad crooked grin. "I don't guess you want to shake on it."

She gazed at his hands, dirty from toiling in the fields, but it wasn't the soil beneath his fingernails that caused her to wrinkle her nose. "No, I have no desire to shake your hand."

He shoved his hands into his pockets. "When do you want to see those sketches?"

"I'll come by late tomorrow afternoon. The sooner we get started, the sooner we'll finish."

He nodded as silence wove around them. She wouldn't thank him for doing what she considered his duty. He wouldn't thank her for fear she'd rescind the offer.

"I'll have Lucian help you mount," he said after several long moments.

Nodding, she turned and tromped to the mare, not nearly as confident with this plan as she had been earlier. Perhaps everything had seemed to fall into place at dawn because she wasn't completely awake.

She glanced over her shoulder. Lucian was walking toward her while Clay stood in the middle of the field, his back to her, his hat clutched in one hand, his dark head bowed.

Sitting at the table, Clay worked diligently to capture the statue on paper. He wanted

Meg to see the monument as he saw it.

Meg.

His hands stilled as thoughts of her filled his mind. Dear Lord, but he'd forgotten how pretty her eyes were. How pretty any woman's eyes were. It had been so long since he'd looked closely into a woman's eyes. He wondered what made a woman's eyes seem so much prettier than a man's when they were the same color.

Meg Warner's eyes were a cornflower blue corridor that led to her tortured soul. Had he ever seen so much suffering in anyone's eyes? He had, but none of the suffering he had seen in the army hospital touched him as hers had today.

How many years younger was she — two or three? He couldn't remember. Not that it mattered. Her youth had died on the battle-field with her husband. She'd buried her smiles and her laughter with Kirk. That was one of the greater tragedies of war that he hadn't recognized until he returned home.

The *not knowing* experienced by those who sat by the home fires was worse than any-thing the soldiers felt. Soldiers knew if they were alive or dead, but those away from the battle could do little more than worry, and it took a toll on them.

He didn't think the memorial would give

Meg back her youth, but he hoped it would help put the war behind her. She was too young and beautiful to spend her life in mourning. She needed to loosen the tight bun that held her hair captive so her glorious ebony strands could blow freely in the wind. He imagined a woman's hair felt softer than a man's. He couldn't remember ever touching his mother's hair, but he remembered nights when she came to tuck him and his brothers into bed, and her hair wasn't braided. On those nights, his father stood in their bedroom doorway waiting for her. As a boy, he hadn't thought much about it. As a man, he thought about it a great deal, wondering how it would feel to wait for a woman, seeing her hair flowing around her and knowing she sought to please him.

Just before he'd gone to fetch Lucian, the breeze had touched Meg, then moved on to touch him, bringing her scent with it.

Honeysuckle. She smelled of honeysuckle.

He thought about her pert little nose. He'd wanted to smile every time she tilted it to demonstrate her disdain toward him. If her obvious hatred for him hadn't been so great, hadn't hurt so badly, he might have smiled.

The lantern on the table cast a yellow glow over his work. The house was quiet except for an occasional board creaking as it settled and an infrequent hiss of the lantern.

He didn't mind the quiet. What he found difficult was hearing people talk and knowing that none of the words would be directed his way. This afternoon, having someone talk to him had been pure heaven. The anger in her voice, the curtness of her tone hadn't bothered him nearly as much as it would have if he hadn't been starved for conversation.

Tomorrow he'd receive a little more conversation when she returned. To prolong her stay, maybe he could explain the sketches. He never drew sketches as finely as his father had. Clay saw the images in his mind, and his hands could carve what his mind saw, but they were too big and clumsy to draw what he saw.

He studied the drawing as he envisioned the statue from the front. The lines gave him all the information he needed, and he hoped Meg would understand what the monument would reflect when he was finished. He moved the top sheet of paper aside and bent over the unmarred white paper that remained. Two sides of the memorial would be equally important. He set to work sketching what he was certain would be his favorite portion of the monument.

Hearing the door to his brothers' bedroom

open, he lifted his gaze. Scratching his backside, Lucian stood in the doorway as naked as the day he was born.

"You still up?" Lucian asked through an open-mouthed yawn. "It's gotta be after midnight."

"I wanted to finish these sketches."

Lucian shook his head. "You think she's bestowing upon you some honor?" He snorted. "God, you're so damn gullible. She was tempting you today. She's not gonna have you make a monument. Why would she ask the town's coward to make a tribute to its fallen heroes?"

Clay slipped his fingers between the buttons on his shirt and rubbed his chest. "I don't know why she asked. I haven't figured it out yet. I'm not even sure I care. I'll be carving again, and this time, I'll create something that's not going into a graveyard."

Lucian ambled to the sideboard, dunked the dipper into the bucket of water, lifted it, and poured the water over his dark head. The water fell to his shoulders, then slid down his body to create a small pool on the puncheon floor. "It's so damned hot tonight I don't know how you can sit there with all your clothes on."

He sauntered to the bedroom door, halted, and glanced over his shoulder. "You're wasting your time. She won't come tomorrow."

She didn't come.

With his fingers wrapped around the paper that he'd rolled into a scroll, Clay sat on the porch. The sun had long since disappeared over the horizon. The stars dotted the blackened sky like minuscule diamonds thrown haphazardly onto velvet. The heat of day faded into the warmth of night.

She wasn't going to come.

He unfolded his body and tapped the paper against his thigh. He inhaled deeply, wanting to smell honeysuckle. He listened to the crickets, wishing their cadence resembled a woman's voice.

He walked into the silent house. His brothers had gone to bed earlier, leaving a lone lantern on the table beside the meal Clay hadn't eaten. He picked up the lantern and went to the room that had once belonged to his parents, the room where Lucian had slept until Clay returned.

Closing the door, he tossed the scroll onto the bed, then knelt before the oak dresser and set the lantern on the floor. He pulled out the bottom drawer. The scent of gunpowder from long ago wafted out through the opening. He removed a worn and frayed canvas knapsack and carried it to the bed.

Sitting on the bed, he carefully untied the braids of thin rope that held the flap closed. Lifting the bag, he dumped the envelopes onto the red-and-white quilt his mother had made. Reverently, he picked up an envelope, held it beneath his nose, and inhaled.

Honeysuckle.

Slowly he trailed his fingers over the delicate script. During the time the army had held him as a prisoner, when the loneliness had consumed him until he felt it as a gnawing hunger in his gut, these envelopes had sustained him. He pulled them out, smelled them, and touched them.

He pretended the woman who sent them had written his name instead of another's across the envelope. Although he never read the letters housed in the envelopes, he knew they contained words of love and longing, perhaps a little loneliness, and a great deal of pride. A wife's letter to her husband would reflect all those things . . . and more.

One by one, he placed the envelopes back into the bag. Reaching across the bed, he picked up the rolled sketches and slid them into the bag before lacing the braided ropes.

Stretching out on the bed, he stared at the ceiling and wondered if Meg Warner had drifted off to sleep with memories of her husband.

★ ★ ★

The bench swing squeaked as Meg pressed her bare toes against the porch and gave a lazy push. Drawing comfort from the gentle swaying, she tucked her foot beneath her.

Late in the afternoon, Reverend Baxter had stopped by unexpectedly, hinting at and receiving an invitation to supper. She tried to convince herself that it was his presence alone that had prevented her from returning to the Hollands' farm as she'd promised. But if that were the sole reason she hadn't gone, she'd go to the farm tomorrow to look at the sketches.

And she already knew in her heart that she wouldn't go tomorrow either. It wasn't Reverend Baxter that stopped her. It was Clayton Holland. She couldn't fathom the difference between the man Clay was before the war and the man he was now.

The wind whispered a lover's rhapsody through the trees, carrying her back to a time when love and joy filled her heart . . . a time when laughter and smiles were wrapped around confidence.

Her wedding day.

Everyone came to share her joy — even Clay. He stood by Kirk's side as Kirk pledged himself to Meg until death. She paid scant attention to Clay or anyone else that day. She only had eyes for Kirk, with his blond hair, blue eyes, and a smile that promised a lifetime of happiness.

After the ceremony, Kirk teased Clay and told him he had to dance with the bride. Clay shook his head, his face burning a bright red, until finally he relented and asked her for a dance. They waltzed, but Meg could recall nothing else. Distracted, she searched over Clay's shoulder for Kirk among the guests, wanting to be back in his arms.

She slipped her foot from beneath her now and pushed against the porch again. As lazily as the swaying of the swing, her mind wandered to the day Kirk left. He had talked with Clay at the edge of town. She thought it odd because everyone knew Clay had not enlisted. They shook hands, then Kirk embraced him. A manly embrace. Two men. One leaving, surrounded by family and friends. The other standing alone on the edge of town.

She hadn't understood how Kirk tolerated being so close to Clay, but no time had remained to ask inconsequential questions. Their final moments came too swiftly, filled with pledges of undying love and remembrance, the promise to write, and the promise to return home soon. She kept her promise to write. He was unable to keep his promise to return home.

Along with her neighbors, she rejoiced when the army came for Clay, glad that at last he would serve the Confederacy. Rumors that he had still refused to join his company on the battlefield were whispered on the wind and chilled Meg's heart. Clay and Kirk had been friends. Clay had not only betrayed the Confederacy, he'd betrayed Kirk.

But for the first time, she wondered what price he'd paid to return home. Did he wake at night to the screams of dying men as she so often did? The depth of despair in his brown eyes seemed to indicate that he might.

Her request for a monument had put a spark of hope in his eyes, which was the last thing she intended. How had he managed to find her request an honor?

The memorial was meant to be Clay's punishment as much as a tribute to the heroes of Cedar Grove. The sooner he began working, the sooner he'd finish — and the sooner his punishment would end.

Slowly. She must proceed slowly. She'd give the hope in his eyes time to die before going to his farm to look at the sketches. Sighing, she drew her legs up beneath her on the swing. She had nothing else to do with her time.

Three

Meg finished playing the hymn, folded her hands in her lap, and tried to focus her attention on Reverend Baxter's words.

The church door opened and distant footsteps resounded. She held her breath until they fell into silence.

Slowly, almost imperceptibly, she allowed her gaze to wander toward the back of the church. Her heart slammed against her ribs when she discovered Clayton Holland's intense gaze riveted on her.

He sat alone, his face solemn. He lifted some sort of cloth pouch so she could see it over the congregation. Then he lowered it, stood, and walked out of the church empty-handed.

Meg balled her hands in her lap, refusing to feel guilty about not having returned to his farm as she'd promised. Clay was a man without honor, and as such, he deserved no respect.

The pouch, however, was another matter. She could no longer see it, but knowing that he'd brought it for her and left it — whatever it held — on the last pew made her feel as though she were sitting on a cactus. She'd never squirmed so much in her life.

When Reverend Baxter finally signaled her to begin the final hymn, her hands itched to touch the canvas bag instead of the organ keys. She'd never realized how slowly people walked from the church. Did she always play this hymn three times before the church was empty?

When the only movements within the sanctuary were the dust motes waltzing in the sunlight, Meg rose from the bench, walked down the steps from the dais, strolled as calmly as she could to the last pew, and slid onto the hardwood bench.

With feathery touches, she stroked the silken threads she had embroidered to form Kirk's initials in the pouch. Lifting the soiled flap, she peered inside the canvas bag, then poured the contents onto the bench. Gunpowder overpowered the scent of honeysuckle.

Ignoring the rolled paper, she gathered the letters together, pressed them against her bosom, and wept. An immense grief swept over her, tearing open the wounds of her heart, wounds she thought had begun to heal.

Sometimes, she felt as though whatever

weaponry had struck Kirk down had sent its death knell across the miles to Texas and embedded its anguish in her heart.

Clutching the canvas bag, her palms sweating, Meg guided the chestnut mare through the trees that bordered the river. Within her heart, molten rage simmered because Clay had possession of Kirk's pouch and her letters these many months and hadn't returned them to her. Her hatred intensified as she considered the possibility that he may have read the letters, read the intimate words she meant to share only with her husband.

Determined to get answers, she urged her horse toward the bend in the river where Lucian had told her she'd find Clay. She ducked beneath a low branch, the sweat on her palms increasing.

She drew her horse to a halt beneath the branches of another tree. Ensconced in shadows, she forgot her anger as she took in the scene unfolding before her.

Deep and vibrant, Clay's laughter rumbled as he stood in the brown river, the gently flowing water lapping at his hips. His back was to her, but with his clothes drenched and plastered to his body, she could see that he was extremely slender; she could even detect the barest rippling of his muscles beneath his shirt as he scooped the water and tossed it toward his brothers. The twins had discarded their shirts, and their bare shoulders displayed a host of freckles.

Without warning, they yelled and lunged for Clay. The force of their combined assault took him under the water. The twins emerged first, holding their stomachs and throwing their heads back to send their guffaws toward the blue sky above. Clay came up, sputtering, shaking his head, and sending a spray of water toward his brothers. Then moving quickly, he plucked one boy out of the water.

Meg gasped. The child was as naked as a blue jay. She knew she should avert her gaze, but she hadn't seen anyone so enjoy life in years.

Clay tossed the boy in the water. Then, laughing, he turned to his other brother. Taunting the boy, he tried to wave him nearer. When the boy refused to approach, Clay plunged under the water. The boy screamed as he came out of the water, cradled in his brother's arms. Then he hollered louder and struggled harder. "Put me down!"

"Not until you say I won!" Clay yelled.

"Gawd Almighty! She's watchin' us!"

Clay spun around, the naked boy dangling in his arms and kicking. His broad smile disappeared like sunshine vanishing as a dark cloud passes before the sun. His chest heaving from his efforts, he released his hold, and the child splashed into the water.

She dismounted and walked to the edge of the riverbank. "I need to speak with you."

"You boys, stay here," he ordered as he plowed through the river.

"Heck fire! We ain't got no choice!" one twin yelled.

"You swim in your clothes?" she asked as he neared the muddy bank.

He offered her an uncertain smile. "They unexpectedly lured me in." He stepped onto the grass.

"You didn't even take your socks off?"

"I don't like the way mud feels between my toes." Absently, he combed his fingers through his wet hair, lifting it off his brow. "You wanted to talk?"

She lifted the pouch. "About this."

He nodded as though her words came as no surprise, then jerked his head to the side. "Mind if we sit on the boulder so I can dry in the sun and keep an eye on the twins?"

"That'll be fine."

She followed as his long legs ate up the short distance. He hoisted himself with ease onto the large boulder at the river's edge. Then he reached down to help her.

Ignoring his hand, she waited until he withdrew it and scooted to the far edge of the rock. Hampered by her skirt, she awkwardly scrambled until she gained her seat. She hadn't bothered to change into suitable riding clothes. She'd just wanted to find him as soon as she could and get this dreaded confrontation over with.

She wiggled her bottom on the rough, warm surface until she was as comfortable as she thought possible. Then she turned her attention to Clay. As he stared at the river, his face resembled the rock, hard and implacable. She cleared her throat. He didn't give her the courtesy of an acknowledgment, and she refused to call him by name.

"This is Kirk's bag," she finally said, not disguising the irritation in her voice.

"I know that."

"I want to know how *you* came to have it!" she spat, her anger rising to the surface.

He snapped his head around, his brown eyes dark and stormy. "I tried to tell you the other day when you came to the farm, but you gave me holy hell because I dared to mention your precious husband's name."

It seemed to surprise him as much as it did her to hear the crack of her palm against his cheek. Then the astonishment changed into a deep sadness before he turned his face away from her.

"Your husband brought it to me a few months before he was killed," he said quietly.

She balled up her hand, still throbbing from the blow she'd delivered. "Why?"

"Said he had a premonition, didn't think he was gonna make it home. He was afraid in the chaos the letters would get lost. He thought they'd be safe with me."

"Because there wasn't a chance in hell that you'd be killed, was there?" she asked, contempt adding a sharp edge to her words. "Can you even begin to understand how much courage it took for them to march onto that battlefield knowing they *might* be killed? How could you not stand by their side?"

"If you have to ask, there isn't any explanation in the world I can give you that would satisfy you."

Shaking her bowed head, she clutched the pouch to her breast. "I don't understand why he wasn't revolted by the thought of your hands touching these precious letters."

"Because he understood."

Swiveling her head, she scrutinized his profile, stark against the blue sky. "He understood what?"

Slowly, he turned his intense gaze on her. "Why I wouldn't fight."

"I don't believe you."

He rolled his slender shoulders into a careless shrug. "Believe what you want. That's what everybody around here does anyway."

She lowered the pouch to her lap and peered at him, dreading his answer. "Did you touch them?" She watched as truth warred against deception, and she knew the answer even before his eyes filled with regret.

"Yes."

She squeezed her eyes shut as pain consumed her heart until it was a physical ache, and tears trailed down her cheeks.

"I'm sorry," he said hoarsely.

Slowly, she shook her head. No apology on earth could atone for what he'd done. She felt utterly and completely violated.

"I . . . I never took the letters out. I only touched the envelopes. I was just so damn alone, so damn lonely . . . sometimes I just needed to have some kind of —"

Opening her tear-filled eyes, she stared at him. "You didn't read the letters?"

He shook his head. "You could take the letters out, burn the envelopes —"

"You only touched the *envelopes?*"

Remorse washed over his face. "And smelled them. They always smelled so sweet

. . . like honeysuckle."

Lifting a letter, she wondered how he managed to notice the honeysuckle when the acrid scent of gunpowder practically drowned it out. She'd been disappointed when she opened the pouch and discovered how distant the honeysuckle smelled. A smile of remembrance graced her lips as she brought the letter to her nose and sniffed. "Kirk liked the smell of honeysuckle," she said softly. "I always slipped a few honeysuckle petals between the folds of the letters."

"It probably reminded him of you."

Blushing, she turned her face away. No conversation with this man ever went the way she planned. His sad eyes, his honesty always took the fight out of her. She wiped away any trace of previous tears and forced all softness from her eyes before she dared look at him again. "Why didn't you *touch* your *own* envelopes. Didn't your family write you?"

"My ma wrote me."

"Then why didn't you read those letters?" she snapped.

"Because they wouldn't give them to me."

His answer startled her. She assumed that an unwritten code guaranteed that a letter be given to the person for whom it was addressed. She shuddered at the thought of Kirk not receiving her letters. "If they didn't give them to you, how can you be sure she sent them?"

"Because they showed them to me just before they burned them. They'd —" Despair contorted his face as he closed his eyes.

Meg's hand was almost resting on top of his before she realized that she was about to offer this man comfort — the last thing she wanted to give him. She jerked her hand back, but her curiosity had been piqued. "What did they do?"

Opening his eyes, he glanced down the river, slipped his fingers between the buttons on his shirt, and rubbed his chest. "Doesn't matter now."

"But why did they burn your letters?"

"Because they hated me as much as you do and weren't real keen on seeing me happy." He heaved a deep sigh. "Then Ma and Pa died while I was gone."

She watched his throat work convulsively as though he were struggling to keep his emotions tamped down.

"I don't even know what she wrote in all those letters she sent," he said in a hoarse, ravaged voice. "I don't know if she understood or if she was worried. I'll never know."

Meg caught herself before she voiced her

sorrow over the loss of his mother's words. She could imagine the devastation she would feel if she discovered that every word she had written Kirk had been burned without his reading them.

As though he'd revealed too much, he ran a finger along a tiny fissure in the boulder, his eyes straying toward the distant horizon. "Did you read the letter he wrote you?" he asked.

"The letter he wrote me?"

"Your husband. Did you read the letter he wrote you?"

"He wrote me more than one and, yes, I read them all. Many times in fact."

He shifted his gaze to her, giving her the sad smile she'd come to recognize. It was almost as though he thought she'd hate him all the more if he gave her the kind of smile he'd worn for the boys in the river. "I was referring to the letter he left you in the pouch."

Meg's eyes widened as her hands began to tremble. In the church, she'd gathered the letters together but hadn't looked at them individually. "He left me a letter?"

He nodded, and the sadness momentarily lifted from his eyes. She threw back the flap on the pouch and spilled the letters and scroll into her lap. She dropped the pouch by her side and sifted through the envelopes until she spotted one that didn't have her handwriting on it. She snatched it up, tears filling her eyes as she touched the scrawled words — her name, sharing his name. Even unread, Kirk's final letter was a bittersweet reminder of all she'd once possessed, all she'd lost.

"I don't know if I can read it. Not now. Not after all this time. I don't understand why you didn't bring it to me sooner, before I came to you."

"I tried. The day I got home I went to your farm. Your brother — Daniel, isn't it?"

She nodded.

"He swore he'd kill me if I didn't leave. From the look in his eyes, I figured he meant it. I didn't dare send it with one of my brothers because I didn't know how deep his hatred ran. I didn't want one of them to take a bullet that should have gone to me."

Slowly, Meg put all the letters into the pouch. If she read Kirk's letter, it would be when she was alone. She couldn't bring herself to thank Clay, although she knew she owed him for bringing Kirk's letter to her. She picked up the rolled paper. "I want to talk to you about the memorial."

"That was just the first thing that popped into my head. It doesn't have to look like that. I can sketch out some other ideas."

She gave him a guilty grimace. "To be honest, I haven't looked at it. I was too upset over the letters."

"You should probably look at it before you make a decision. It's rough. I don't have much talent for sketching."

Unrolling the paper, she laid it on the rock, anchoring one end beneath her ankle so one hand was free to touch the charcoaled drawing. She had expected to see men charging into battle, but not this. She'd never expected this.

The drawing contained only one man. Within the shades of gray that comprised his face, she could see a fierce pride. He sat confidently upon his horse, which had its forelegs raised as it reared back on its haunches. One hand held the reins and the other reached out to a young woman holding a flag that was blowing in the wind.

She brought her trembling fingers to her lips. "It's Kirk," she whispered.

"It will be when I'm done."

With tears brimming in her eyes, she looked at him. "And the woman?"

Careful not to touch her, he pulled the first sheet of paper away to reveal the statue as it would be viewed from a different angle.

The woman's face reflected the pride,

mingled with anguish, that women had felt for generations when they sent their men off to war. Her face mirrored love, courage, and knowledge. Eloquently, in silence, the woman knew she was gazing upon the man she loved for the last time.

Meg didn't realize she was openly weeping until she saw the paper wither where her teardrops splashed upon it.

"The woman," he said quietly, "will be you."

Four

Cursing, Clay removed his hat and wiped the sweat beading his brow. Meg had promised to meet him on the road leading away from town, on the road leading to Austin.

Shifting his backside on the wagon seat, he wondered how many times he was going to let the woman make a fool of him. She'd said dawn. He'd arrived an hour before the sun peered over the horizon. Well, the sun glared at him now.

He jammed his battered hat onto his head, released the brake, and lifted the reins. Hell, he'd go without her. He wasn't certain if Schultz would have anything available at the stone quarry he mined near Austin, but Clay wanted to look. Then when Meg Warner showed her face in a week, or a month, or a year, he could tell her what he'd seen.

Flicking the reins, he knew the prospect of judging the quality of stone hadn't kept him awake most of the night. His inability to sleep had resided in the scented promise of honeysuckle surrounding him as he journeyed to Austin.

He was damn insane to anticipate something as simple as a woman's scent. Maybe he had lost his mind while he was a prisoner. After the execution that never came, they'd sentenced him to hard labor. On days when they couldn't find anything useful for him to do, they made him pound rocks for no good reason except that it caused his back to ache and his hands to blister. He was certain his jailers never realized how difficult it had been for him to see the potential within a rock just before he had to smash it into white powder.

Now Meg was giving him the opportunity to shape a hunk of rock into something of value.

And it scared the hell out of him.

He'd been cutting into wood, stone, and his own fingers since he was a boy. He'd gathered his informal education at his father's knee whenever his father found time to show him the craft that *he* had learned from his father before him. But his father's tutelage had never satisfied Clay's hunger. It always left him craving more knowledge, yearning to create the images that filled his mind.

He'd discovered his own technique through trial and error, nurturing his innate skill, learning from his failures, reveling in his few successes. He knew he'd drawn

74

something on paper that he probably couldn't create with his hands, but, damn, he wanted to create it for all the reasons Meg had stated . . . and more.

He heard the galloping hooves and glanced over his shoulder to see the dirt rise and swirl around the horse and rider as they barreled down the road.

Without an apology or explanation, Meg slowed her horse until it was walking beside the wagon. She was wearing Kirk's faded flannel shirt, woolen trousers, and crumpled brown hat. Beneath the hat's wide brim, Meg's pert little nose strained to touch a cloud. He wondered if he'd imagined the gentleness of her tears the day before as she'd studied his sketches, wondered why he'd thought the tears were strong enough to melt away her hatred. With his thumb, he tilted his hat off his brow. "Morning."

She slid her gaze over to him as though she'd just seen a snake slither under a rock. Her nose went up a fraction higher, and this time he couldn't help himself. He smiled.

Her eyes widened just before she averted her gaze and fidgeted with something on the other side of her saddle. "I am not here to provide you with company. I simply want to make certain you make the best choice."

"Know a lot about rocks, do you?"

She swung her gaze back to his. "I know what I like."

He eased the smile off his face. "And what you don't like."

She gave a brusque nod. "Especially what I don't like."

Heaving a sigh, he stared ahead at the dirt road he'd traveled a dozen times with his father. He had a sinking feeling this trip would be the longest he'd ever taken, and he sure as hell couldn't smell any honey-suckle. "Did you bring the money?"

"Certainly."

Against his will, he found his gaze returning to Meg's slender form. She sat on a horse with a measure of grace and confidence that came from weathering life's storms and bending so naturally with the force of the wind that it could never conquer her. Maybe he should have sketched her and not Kirk, sitting astride the horse.

Only he wanted to capture her as she was before the war had destroyed her innocence and hope. He wanted to capture her resilient spirit, a spirit that had survived even when the war snatched away the dreams she shared with another. "Is it the money your husband was saving to purchase his farm with?"

Her blue eyes widened until he thought they rivaled the sky in beauty. "He told you about the farm he wanted?"

"We were friends. He told me a lot of things."

She wiggled her backside in the saddle, and Clay was tempted to toss a blanket over her lap. They were probably safer with her traveling dressed in her husband's clothes, but she looked decidedly different in trousers than Kirk had looked. Without a doubt, however, she'd made alterations to the clothing so that it fit. Kirk had been straight as a board from his shoulders to his toes; he'd never possessed those curves. But the clothes didn't seem to mind one bit. As a matter of fact, the trousers were hugging her as though they cared for her deeply.

"What did he tell you?" she asked.

He wrenched his eyes up to her face where they should have been all along. He had no business letting his gaze wander to her hips. Since she hadn't slapped him, he figured his hat was shading his face so she couldn't see exactly where he'd been looking. "What?"

"What exactly did Kirk tell you?"

"Lots of things."

"Like what?"

He shrugged. "He told me if I dug a hole when the moon was full I'd have enough dirt to fill it back in."

"Why would you dig a hole at night?"

"I wouldn't."

"Then why did he tell you that?"

"For some reason, when you dig a hole you never seem to have enough dirt to fill it back in. He said digging during a full moon would make a difference."

"I don't see why it would."

He rubbed the side of his nose. "It doesn't."

She leaned over slightly. "Did you dig a hole when the moon was full?"

Her eyes carried a spark of interest, and he was glad he could give her the answer he was certain she wanted. "Yes, ma'am. He always seemed to know everything so I gave it a try."

"And discovered he'd pulled one over on you," she said smugly.

He nodded, astonished that she still took enormous pride in her husband's pranks.

"So he just told you silly things," she said.

Tipping his hat farther off his brow, he smiled lazily. "Mostly."

Looking away, she again fiddled with something on the other side of her saddle. He couldn't see what was happening within the loose shirt she wore, but small waves rippled across her chest with her agitated movements. One day, he'd carve those ripples, but at the moment all he wanted was to look into those blue eyes. "But sometimes we discussed things of a personal nature."

She jerked her head around, her finely arched eyebrows knitting together in consternation. "Like what?"

A corner of his mouth tilted higher as he looked up at the blue sky. The sky should have taken its shading from her eyes. "Things."

"What sort of things?"

He squinted as though thinking hard. "All sorts of things."

She yanked the hat from her head, and the thick braid she'd stuffed beneath it fell along her narrow back. He wondered what it would feel like to unravel that braid and comb his fingers through those ebony strands.

"We've established that you discussed things," she said curtly. "Give me an example of something specific."

He grimaced. "Can't."

"Why? Because it was so trivial you don't remember anything he told you?"

"I remember it all. It's just that I gave him my word I'd never tell you."

She pounded her small fist into her thigh, but he had a feeling she would have preferred to smash it against his nose. "He made you promise not to tell me something he told you?"

Nodding, Clay fought to keep his mouth from forming a smile. "Yes, ma'am."

"What was it about?"

Lifting a shoulder, he feigned innocence.

Her blue eyes darkened. "Was it something about me? Did he talk about me?"

"Of course he did. He loved you."

She shook her head vigorously and tilted up her nose. "I don't believe he ever talked to you about me. You're just trying to make me angry."

"I knew before you did that he was going to marry you."

He didn't know how she managed it, but she looked down on him even though their respective positions on the horse and wagon made their heights even.

"I was fourteen when I knew he was going to marry me," she said haughtily. "I set my sights on him then, and I caught him."

Clay chuckled. "He set his sights on you long before that."

"I don't believe you."

He shrugged. "Believe what you want."

She shoved the hat down over her head, shadowing her face so all he could see was the hard set of her jaw. He supposed that if the woman wanted to believe she was the one responsible for her marriage to Kirk, no harm would come from it. Whereas he suspected that harm might come from her learning the truth.

He and Kirk had been standing on the threshold of adolescence. Girls were no longer the irritants they'd once seemed, but were beginning to have an appeal they were both still too young to understand fully. They based a girl's worth on inconsequential things such as the color of her eyes and the length of her braid.

"I think Meg Crawford has the purtiest eyes I ever saw," Clay told Kirk one afternoon as they watched the clouds roll by. "I'm thinkin' I might marry her."

"You can't," Kirk said. "I'm aimin' to marry her."

"I said it first."

Kirk dug a silver coin out of his pocket. "We'll flip. Eagle you marry her, Liberty I marry her, and loser's gotta promise he won't go callin' on her."

Nodding, Clay drew an X over his heart with his finger. Kirk tossed the coin, caught it, and slapped it down on his forearm. From her engraved position on the coin, Lady Liberty sparkled in the sunlight. Kirk swiped the coin away and shoved it into his pocket. "Reckon I won."

In the intervening years, Clay honored the oath he had taken that day. He'd kept his distance, watching from afar as Meg blossomed into the woman who would hold Kirk's heart.

And now he would continue to keep his distance. Her hatred, far greater than any other's, would keep him tethered to the childish oath. Even when he sat on the last pew, he could feel her eyes boring into him. He disliked sitting through the church service every bit as much as Joe did. Maybe he should take Josh's advice and cross his eyes the next time she looked at him.

But when she did finally turn her attention from the road and meet his gaze, he couldn't bring himself to make light of her feelings toward him.

"What did Kirk say about me?" she asked. "He must have said something you can tell me."

He tugged his hat brim low over his brow. He couldn't very well tell her that Kirk had told him about the soft little sounds she made on their wedding night. He wished now he'd just kept his mouth shut and hadn't tried to get her riled, but she was so durn cute when fury flashed through her face and ignited her eyes so they no longer appeared lifeless. "Well, he talked a lot about the farm, of course, and how he wanted you to have a place of your own."

She relaxed her shoulders, and he wondered if she'd had an inkling as to what Kirk might have told him. "Did he tell you why he wanted us to have our own place?"

He nodded slowly.

"His mother didn't like me," she said, as though he hadn't acknowledged her question.

"I wouldn't take her feelings to heart. She doesn't like anyone."

She rolled her eyes toward the heavens.

"It's true," he went on. "We figured she didn't even like Mr. Warner, which is why your husband never had any brothers or sisters."

She leaned toward him, her eyes wide, her voice barely a whisper even though no one was around to hear. "You truly talked about her like that?"

"Her sour mood bothered him, and it bothered him more when you got married and she didn't treat you kindly."

"He told you how she treated me?"

"We talked about —"

Impatiently, she waved her hand. "I know. You talked about a lot of things."

He offered her a rueful smile. "Yes, ma'am, we did."

"Did you discuss his idea about us living with his grandmother?"

Actually, the day he figured out how long it would take Kirk to save enough money to set up a homestead Clay had suggested they move in with Mama Warner. Hesitantly, he nodded. "He wanted you to be happy."

"I was after we moved in with Mama Warner. She made me feel so welcome."

"She makes everyone feel that way. Do you see her much anymore?" Clay asked, knowing she'd moved back to her father's house after Kirk left for the war.

Meg smiled, the first genuine smile he'd seen on her face since the day war began. He wanted to cut it into stone right then and there so he could keep it forever. He was certain she'd given it to him by mistake.

"As a matter of fact, I went by her house this morning. That's why I was late. I told her if anyone asks, she's to say I'm spending a few days with her, but she doesn't know where I am at the moment. She'll stretch the truth and never ask me why she needs to."

Clay had wondered how she planned to travel with him without her father coming to lynch him. "So your father thinks you're spending a few days with Mama Warner?"

"Yes, only I'm spending the time with you."

As though just realizing that she'd condemned herself to his company, she stopped smiling, hardened her gaze, and turned her attention to the road ahead.

Sighing deeply, he looked at the narrow ribbon of dirt that wagon wheels had cut from the land over the years. The road seemed to stretch into eternity.

At twilight, Clay drew the wagon off the road and guided the mule to a nearby clearing.

Meg dismounted, pressed her forehead against the saddle, closed her eyes, and sighed heavily. Clay's presence irritated her more than she'd imagined it would, in ways she'd never expected. The soft, secretive smile that eased onto his face when he found something amusing caused her to ache for all the smiles of the past, to mourn for all the smiles that would never be in her future.

And apparently he'd found her quite amusing this morning when he'd talked about Kirk. What had Kirk told him?

"Want me to see after your horse?" Clay asked.

Opening one eye, she peered at him. He looked as tired as she felt. "No."

He set a bucket of water within the mare's

reach. "There's feed in the wagon," he said before walking away.

She tended her mare, removing the saddle and bridle, and hobbling her for the night. She retrieved the feed from the large sturdy wagon. She supposed the Hollands had built it specifically to haul stone.

Clay unhitched and hobbled the mule, although Meg didn't think the mule would wander away. In her entire life, she'd never seen an animal move as slowly as that mule. She supposed the army had confiscated the Hollands' horses. Her family had given so many men to the Cause that the army hadn't asked for their livestock, although Meg would have gladly given it.

"I'll fetch some supper," Clay said as he pulled his rifle from beneath the wagon seat.

Meg's first reaction was to say she'd fend for herself, but she felt too weary. She'd compromise slightly tonight: while he hunted, she'd build the fire. As she walked away from the camp, he fell into step behind her. She stopped abruptly, turned, and glared at him. "Where do you think you're going?" she asked.

"I don't think you ought to be traipsing through these woods alone."

She patted the gun handle visible above the waistband of her trousers. "I'm only going to find some dry wood. I can take care of myself."

"I'm sure you can. It's just —"

"I've had enough of your company today. I don't want you to follow me."

"Will you holler if you need me?"

"No. I have no reason to bclieve you'd come. You didn't go when the Confederacy hollered for more men."

He narrowed his eyes to tiny slits, and his jaw grew so rigid she didn't know how he managed to force the word "Fine" out through his mouth. She caught the tail end of a harsh curse as he stalked to the other side of the clearing and disappeared into the thick woods.

She was glad to see him leave. She truly was. With any luck, he'd lose his way, wander through the encroaching darkness, and not return to camp until morning.

Meandering along a virgin path through the wooded area, she gathered fallen branches as her thoughts drifted to the morning. She shuddered with the memory. She had not only spoken with a man she loathed, but she had almost enjoyed the conversation. And she'd smiled at him. A coward. A man who had betrayed those he called friends. For God's sake, what had she been thinking?

He'd lured her into talk of a happier time when Kirk stood by her side. Clay's brown eyes had twinkled with something akin to merriment as he'd baited her. *He and Kirk had discussed things. Had discussed lots of things. Silly things. Things of a personal nature.*

She issued a very unladylike snort. They'd probably discussed nothing.

She picked up a heavy fallen branch and swung it through the air as though it were a club. She could use it to knock Clay right off his feet if he tried to talk to her again. Smiling, she added it to the wood nestled in the crook of her arm.

She reached for another log, and a rattlesnake's rapid tattoo of warning vibrated through the air. Moving only her eyes, Meg searched the undergrowth of brush until her gaze locked onto black eyes that held no life but promised certain death.

As though in a dream, she watched the coiled snake spread its mouth wide, baring its protruding fangs. It lunged toward her. She'd always imagined that death would come quickly, not slowly, giving her time to scream against the injustice. Thunder echoed, and the rattlesnake disappeared.

"You all right?" Clay asked as he grabbed her arm. She stared at him mutely, and he shook her, his voice growing louder. "Are you all right?"

The knowledge that she was alive surged through her simultaneously with the realization that he was touching her. She jerked free of his grasp. "Don't ever touch me."

He shook his head. "Don't know why I was worried. Your hatred probably would have poisoned the rattler if he'd had the misfortune to dig his fangs into you."

Reaching into the thicket, he retrieved the lifeless rattlesnake. "If my rifle blast didn't clear the area of game, your scream did. Guess we'll eat rattler for supper."

Meg stared at the long, thick length of dark brown and gray. Clay held the mangled snake level with his chest, and still its tail brushed the ground. Even in death, the snake's massive body appeared powerful and deadly, and she'd been its prey. She shook violently as her stomach lurched.

"Are you gonna be sick?" Clay asked.

The tingling beneath her jaws increased in intensity. She felt the blood drain from her face and cold sweat pop out on her brow. She clutched the wood to her chest, searching for something to stop the trees from spinning. He knocked the wood out of her arms.

"Grab your knees," he ordered. "Take deep breaths."

She tried to breathe deeply, but the air was beyond reach and eluded her as easily as the calm she fought to maintain. The burning in her stomach rose into her throat, and she began retching.

Clay walked away, and she was grateful that he left her to suffer this embarrassment alone. She was more grateful that he'd hauled the snake away with him.

She heaved long past the time when her stomach was empty. Hearing approaching footsteps, she pressed her balled fist against her aching midriff and slowly straightened her quaking body. Despite the lingering warmth of day, she felt chilled.

"Here," Clay said as he shoved a tin cup filled with water beneath her nose. "Go on. Take it. I didn't drink from it."

She took the cup, filled her mouth with water, and swirled the lukewarm liquid around before spitting it out. She repeated the process while Clay gathered the wood.

"I'll get the fire started," he said just before he walked away.

The sun had fallen beyond the horizon by the time she found the strength and desire to return to their small camp.

Hunkered down before the crackling fire, Clay removed their dinner from the spit. Sitting opposite him, Meg leaned against the tree. She hadn't realized how dark it had grown until she watched the writhing flames create dancing shadows across Clay's features. He'd removed his hat, and the firelight waltzed across the white hair at his temples.

"I thought I was going to die," she said quietly in a quivering voice. "I can't seem to stop shaking."

"You just need to think about something else. You might try looking at the sky and counting the stars."

She gazed at the cloudless black heavens where a full moon glowed brightly. Beyond it, the stars winked. "How many stars do you think there are?"

"Couple of million, I reckon."

Drawing up her legs, she wrapped her arms tightly around them in an effort to stop her trembling. She pressed her chin against her knees. "I didn't realize you were such an expert with a rifle."

"Haven't missed a target since I was twelve."

"Just think about how many Yankees you could have killed if you hadn't been a coward."

His somber gaze met hers. "I did think about it, Mrs. Warner. I thought about it long and hard."

Picking up a tin plate, he stood. "Help

yourself to what's left." He walked to the wagon, dropped to the ground, and pressed his back against the wheel. Rolling to one hip, he dug a small rock from beneath him and hurled it across the clearing.

Meg jumped when the rock hit a tree, and a sharp crack rent the still night air. She removed her hat and flattened it against her face, inhaling deeply so she wouldn't have to smell the aroma of cooked rattlesnake. The hat carried Kirk's fading scent, and she knew a time would come when the hat would smell more of her than it did of him. Until that time, it served as a reminder of the comfort he'd always brought her. When he'd left, she'd slept with his silly hat pressed beneath her cheek.

"Do you want me to try and find you something else to eat?"

Meg jerked the hat away from her face. Clay was crouching before her, his gaze riveted on the fire.

"No, I don't think anything would stay down just yet."

"Your stomach will settle by morning. I'll see to it you have something proper to eat then." He tossed a log on the fire, and orange sparks shot up. "You can sleep in the wagon tonight."

Using the tree for support, she pushed to

her feet. She gripped the bark and forced the hated words past her lips. "Thank you."

He looked up, and she could see the confusion in his eyes. "For killing the rattler," she explained.

He nodded slightly and stirred the fire. On wobbly legs, she walked to the wagon and climbed into the back. Clay had spread several blankets across the wagon bed. She placed a wadded blanket beneath her head as she stretched out and brought another blanket over her aching body.

The night sky was so clear, she felt as though she should be able to touch the twinkling gems that graced the heavens and filled them with tranquillity. She wished she could find a measure of that peace within herself.

She wondered if Kirk had hoped to convince Clay to go with the other men that final day in Cedar Grove. Was that why he had joined Clay on the edge of town? If so, disappointment had ridden at his side, not his friend.

She wondered if he regretted all the years he'd spent in friendship with a man who would one day betray him, a man too cowardly to march where honor dictated.

She was certain that pride had caused him to shake Clay's hand that final morning. He had embraced Clay not to say good-bye to a friend, but to whisper farewell to a friendship.

A soft gentle scratching distracted her from thoughts of retribution. She imagined a small animal scurrying along the ground, foraging for food, stopping to sniff the air, then pouncing on a pecan or moving the dried leaves aside to search out a tasty morsel.

She eased up to her elbows. She could hear the rasping more clearly. Quietly, she sat up and peered over the side of the wagon. She couldn't see any creature, but the scratching grew louder. She looked toward the fire.

Sitting with his back against the tree, one knee raised, one leg stretched out before him, Clay scraped a piece of wood with a small knife. The wind toyed gently with the brown locks covering his bowed head. The rifle rested by his side.

"What are you making?" she asked.

"Damn!" Poking his finger between his lips, Clay glared at her. He removed his finger from his mouth and pressed it against his thigh. "Don't ever do that when I've got tools in my hands."

"Don't ever do what?" she asked innocently.

"Scare me like that."

"I'm sorry. I'd forgotten you scare easily."

"And I'd forgotten you have such a sharp tongue." He plowed his other hand through his hair. "I don't know why the hell I agreed to this."

"I didn't give you a choice."

"A man always has a choice, Mrs. Warner."

"And you chose to be a coward."

"I chose to follow my conscience."

"Same difference."

"I don't think so. Neither did your husband."

"It's not fair to besmirch his character when he's not here to defend himself. Don't you think he would have told me if he didn't think you were a coward?"

"The way the winds of war whipped through Texas, I don't imagine he spent what little time he had left with you talking."

She knew her face flamed red with embarrassment as images from the past rose into her mind. "How we spent our final moments together is no concern of yours, but I'll tell you this. You are goddamned right! We didn't spend a single breath talking about you. We both knew he might not come back, and we crammed a lifetime into what little time we had left. He sacrificed everything for the Confederacy, while you, his friend, sacrificed nothing. Don't you dare speak to me about him again. You lost that right when you watched him ride away."

She dropped onto the wagon bed and curled into a tight ball, fighting back the tears that were suddenly stinging her eyes. Surely, Kirk would have told her if he thought Clay wasn't a coward.

Then again, he had avoided discussing the war or his enlistment because he knew it worried her to think of his leaving.

She squeezed her eyes shut and felt the tears trail down her cheeks. Even in his letters, he had never written about the war. He had described the scenery, or the weather, or the food. He had told her how much he loved her and how much he missed her.

But he had never shared with her his thoughts as a soldier.

Reaching into the waistband of her trousers, she pulled out Kirk's crumpled letter. She had yet to read it. She knew his final farewell resided in the letter. Until she read it, her own final farewell remained in her heart.

Clutching the letter, she pressed it against her breast, trying to hold onto a love that was drifting away into a mist of memories.

Five

The late afternoon sun reflected off the pink granite mound as it stood with majestic pride against the blue Texas sky. As though they were slumbering giants, huge rocks lay haphazardly along the path of stone leading to the hill. Carefully Meg guided her mare around the rocky rubble as Clay rumbled along in the wagon.

He halted the wagon near a stone house. Someone had chopped down the solitary tree that might have provided shade. As though they were desperate fingers, the bare dead branches of the felled tree strained eerily toward the sun. No one worked; nothing created a sound. Even the wind had ceased its whispering.

Clay climbed down from the wagon. The brim of his hat shadowed his face, revealing none of his thoughts, but then he hadn't shared any thoughts with her since dawn. She'd awakened to find the promised meal waiting for her. Silence as heavy as that surrounding them now had permeated the air as they traveled. Much to her dismay, she discovered she missed his teasing banter.

As Meg dismounted, a rock turned beneath her foot. She stumbled before catching her balance. With his hand outstretched, Clay took a quick step toward her.

Their eyes met.

He shoved his hand into his pocket. "You need to be careful."

"I figured that out." She glanced around the area. "There doesn't seem to be anyone here."

He removed his hat and wiped his brow. "I didn't know what we'd find. Mostly Mr. Schultz sells stone to the Germans who settle in the area. They like to build stone houses."

"But you're not building a house."

"No, but the granite is good quality. I was hoping I could find a hunk of rock that Mr. Schultz hadn't started cutting into smaller chunks."

The door to the house opened. A man who looked as though he had been carved from the very land surrounding him stepped into the sunlight. He squinted, then quickly came to greet them. "Young Holland." He took Clay's hand and pumped it vigorously. "Your papa tell me. I'm glad you are safe. My boy, my Franz. Dey kill him."

A lone teardrop, out of place among his craggy features, trailed down his cheek. Meg felt an immediate kinship with the man, understood the devastation of his loss. In a gesture of comfort, she placed her hand on his massive shoulder. A painful ache centered in her chest as she felt his trembling. "My heart goes out to you. The Yankees killed so many."

He stared at her, his eyes hardening. "I not talk about de Yankees. I talk about de Texans. Dey come for him in de middle of de night, people we think are friends. Dey drag him from bed and hang him. Break his mama's heart to see our good boy die like dat. We come from Germany to find peace. Is not our war. I tell him, 'Go to Mexico. Come home when dis war is over.'" He shook his head and wiped his eyes. "But he not listen. Den dey come and hang him."

"Mr. Schultz, I'm so sorry," Clay said raggedly.

The old man patted his shoulder. "Not your doing. I know dat, and you not here to hear my sorrows. You here to get rock." He waved his hand in a circle. "Der is not much here. I have no heart for working the quarry. If you no find what you need, I tell you where other quarry is." He walked away, bent as though he were carrying one of his boulders upon his shoulders.

Clay yanked his hat from his head and

plowed his fingers through his hair. "Damn! His son was only a little older than me." He glared at Meg. "I guess you think it was a just hanging."

"Every story has more than one side to it."

"Too bad we can't have Franz tell us his side."

"Don't use that tone with me. I'm not the one who hanged him."

"No, but you would have. After all, he didn't stand by your precious Confederacy."

She paled at his words. "I was never in favor of lynching. I'd heard stories . . . they sicken me as much as I'm certain they sicken you." She pressed her fist above her heart. "But I do know if you live in this state and reap its rewards, you answer when it calls."

"Unfortunately, Mrs. Warner, for many of us, the answer wasn't quite so simple or easy to give." Settling his hat on his head, he released a long sigh. "We got here later than I thought we would. Let's just look around and see if we can find what we want. Then we'll go into Austin for the night and come back in the morning to pick up the stone."

Before Meg could reply, he started walking with long, even strides. She followed, carefully picking her way through the scattered rocks that littered the ground. "I suppose you need a large piece," she called.

"Yes, ma'am. I'd like to make the statue life-size."

He stopped walking and removed his hat as though he'd suddenly stepped into a place of reverence. Meg quickened her pace, stopping when she reached his side.

Slowly, almost lovingly, he skimmed splayed fingers over a hunk of stone. She tried to imagine it carved into a horse, rider, and woman. She could see nothing beyond what it was: a rock, pure and simple. Huge. Immense. Pink with tiny black specks embedded throughout.

To her it looked just like all the other rocks that stood there as silent sentinels. Rough and hard, it wasn't at all what she had in mind when she thought about the monument.

She glanced around the rocky terrain, and a flash of white caught her eye. Cautiously, she walked to the outskirts of the quarry and placed her hand on the stone that sparkled in the sun.

Smiling, she walked back to where Clay was kneeling, looking at the top of the granite from a different angle. "I found the piece you can use," she said.

Furrowing his brow, he turned his attention to her. "What?"

She pointed to the white rock. "I found a

beautiful piece over there."

He unfolded his lanky body and followed her.

"It's marble," he said as they neared her find. "It shouldn't be here. This is a granite quarry."

"Well, then, that settles it. Fate must have brought it here. I think the statue would look lovely carved out of this."

His face troubled, he ran his hand over the rough surface. "I've never cut into marble before. I don't know how it would respond to my touch."

Meg lowered her gaze to his hands. Long days in the sun had turned them a rich brown. Tiny, thin scars marred his long fingers. He shoved his hands into his pockets. She lifted her eyes to his. "I want the marble."

Removing his hand from his pocket, he wrapped it around the head of a hammer that was barely visible above the waistband of his trousers. He tugged the hammer free and tightened his grip around the handle.

"What are you going to do?" she asked.

He removed his hat. "I need to know if there are any cracks inside the rock."

"How can you tell?"

"Put your ear against the marble."

She laid her ear against the marble. Pressing his ear to the stone, he gently tapped the hammer against the hard surface. She heard a soft ringing. "It sounds like a bell."

He nodded. "That means it's sound. It doesn't have any cracks inside."

"Did you test the granite?"

"Yes, ma'am. I heard a nice little chime." He stepped back and walked around the marble, touching it, studying it as he had the granite, but his face showed no excitement, no reverence. "I think the granite would serve us better."

"I don't like the granite. It's almost pink —"

"Closer to red when the sun hits it just right."

"So it won't do at all. The marble is perfect. It's pure and white like the glorious Cause."

"You can't always tell what's inside a rock by looking at the outside."

"Then they're very much like people, aren't they?" she asked.

His jaw tightened, and he knocked on the rock. "They can be as hardheaded."

"It's my money. I'm purchasing this piece."

"It might not even be for sale. Like I said —"

"Mr. Schultz!" Meg waved her hand in

the air, catching the man's attention. "Mr. Schultz, is this piece for sale?"

He ambled over. "You want it, you have it. My brother bring it from Marble Falls. He think man here want it, but man say no."

"We do want it," Meg said, surprised by the excitement building within her. "We'll come back in the morning to pick it up."

"I have some men here den to load it on your wagon."

"You see," Meg said triumphantly as Schultz walked away, "it was destiny that brought the marble here."

Shaking his head, Clay looked across the way to the granite. "I can't explain it, but I know I can cut the granite into what I sketched out for you. This —" He touched the marble. "It wasn't meant to be a statue. It'd do fine as part of a building, but I think you'll be disappointed if you ask me to carve it into something it was never meant to be."

"Then you'll just have to work doubly hard to make certain I'm not disappointed." She began to walk away, stumbled, and cursed under her breath.

"You don't give a damn about the statue, do you?"

Abruptly, she spun around. "Of course I do."

"If you did, you'd let me pick out the best piece."

"I've explained why I want the marble."

He stalked over until they stood toe to toe, and she was forced to tilt her head back to look him in the eye.

"You want this little project to be as hard on me as you can make it. Fine. Get the marble. I'll cut it, but if you're thinking to torture me with your obstinacy and your pert little nose in the air and your 'we'll do it my way' attitude, think again. I can hold my own against any torture that's handed out."

Torture.

Lying in the soft bed, Meg wondered why Clay had chosen that word. She wanted to punish him, but torture sounded much harsher than what she'd intended.

They'd arrived at Austin near dusk. Clay had secured a hotel room for her, then curtly told her to sleep on her decision, and he'd see her in the morning.

His abrupt departure suited her just fine. She didn't care where he was or where he slept. For all she cared, he could sleep on that hunk of granite to which he was so partial.

Pounding her fist into the pillow, she refused to follow his order and rethink her decision. Since she had commissioned him to make the monument, he should make it to please her, not himself. The marble was the best choice. If he didn't understand that by the light of a new day, he would when he completed the statue.

When he finished cutting it.

When it responded to his touch.

Squeezing her eyes shut did not take away the haunting reminder of Clay's hands caressing the granite. Her mind danced with her memory of the sketches, intertwining them with the granite until the lines disappeared, and she could no longer see the monument.

The monument was inside the rock, and she wanted desperately to see it. She imagined Clay cutting the stone away to reveal the monument. She saw him shape the woman, carving her face . . . carving her throat . . . her shoulders . . . her breasts . . .

Throwing off the blankets, she shot out of bed and nearly tripped on the hem of her nightgown. She scrambled to the window and leaned forward, breathing deeply, relishing the outside air fanning her cheeks.

Pulling quickly back into the room, she peered cautiously into the alley. A man, silhouetted by the lantern hanging outside the hotel, sat with his back against the mercantile. The knife that he was methodically wielding over an object in his hand caught the lantern's glow.

She wondered if that object responded to his touch the way he wanted. Her eyes were again drawn to his hands, weaving in and out of the shadows as he worked. She didn't need to see the hands to know they were scarred. She didn't want to see him set the knife aside and touch his long fingers to the carving as though his flesh and not his eyes could tell him if he'd shaped what he'd intended.

Would he touch the stone in the same manner after he cut it? Would he trail his fingers along her throat after he carved it?

She pressed her fingers against her throat and thought about watching him work. He always caressed what he carved.

She remembered the first time she saw him carve something into stone. His knuckles had been too big for his fingers, but she had loved watching his hands work.

Until that day, she'd never known despair. Clay and his skilled hands had eased her pain.

Why had she forgotten?

She was ten when she went with her father to the Hollands' farm. She stood in the doorway of a large shed, not daring to step inside where they made things associated with death.

"What are you doing here?" a young voice asked.

She turned to see Clay leaning against the building, his hands stuffed into his pockets. "My ma died."

Compassion filled his eyes. Only now, years later, did she realize how he was accustomed to people standing on his land with tears in their eyes. "I'm sorry."

She lifted her trembling chin because her father had said if she kept her chin up, everything would be all right, but the simple act never seemed to make anything all right. "My pa went lookin' for your pa. He's gonna ask him to make Ma's marker." She crinkled her nose. "He wants a lamb and something from the Bible on it."

"What do you want on it?"

She shrugged her small shoulders. "Ma liked birds, and it just seems that we ought to say something about Ma so people will know we loved her mightily."

He shoved away from the wall and stepped into the shed. "Come on."

"Where are we going?"

"To make your ma's marker."

She shook her head. "Your pa's supposed to do it."

"He don't like doin' the letterin'. I been doin' it since I was eight. Ain't never done birds before so I'll do some practicin' first, and you tell me if it's what you want."

She sat on a stool beside him all afternoon, watching him work. When each design he created pleased her, he cut it into the marker. He carved all the small things her mother had loved. He carved her childish sentiment — *We loved her mightily* — because he thought it was beautiful.

In the years since, Meg had never seen a marker with as many etchings on it as her mother's marker. It still brought tears to her eyes when she visited her mother's resting place. Within the stone, Clay had captured the innocent love of a child for her mother.

And he'd only been a boy.

She sensed that as a young man with an old man's eyes, he had a far greater ability to bring the granite to life.

The thought scared the hell out of her.

Damn fool woman!

Clay knew he should curse himself, not her. He'd been lured by honeysuckle into hell.

What did he know about marble?

Nothing except that maybe beneath her clothing, Meg Warner resembled marble that had been patiently polished.

He pressed his head against the building and watched the second window on the third floor of the hotel. The window led into the room in which she slept.

He wondered if she slept on her stomach. Last night, he'd been tempted to crawl across the camp and peer over the side of the wagon to catch a glimpse of her sleeping. He ached for the sight of her without the hatred distorting her features.

He'd gladly give his life for just one ounce of the compassion he'd seen reflected in her eyes when she thought Yankees had killed Franz Schultz.

But she'd never give him compassion or understanding. Aggravation, though, was another matter. She seemed intent on giving him plenty of that. If he hadn't known her before the war, he wouldn't continue to rein in his temper.

But he had known her. Not well. Certainly, not as well as he would have liked, but well enough to know that her wounds were festering.

If he could find a taker, he'd bet the farm she hadn't read Kirk's final letter.

He prayed Kirk hadn't inscribed the date when he wrote that letter. Clay had taken possession of the letter months after Kirk had given him the pouch. If Meg realized that, she would no doubt ask questions Clay didn't want to answer.

He picked up his knife and started carving again. He concentrated on the lines and planes of the wood to keep his mind from wandering too far into the past.

He had his own wounds that refused to heal.

Six

Stepping onto the boardwalk, Meg spotted Clay's wagon in front of the mercantile. Her mare, saddled and waiting, whinnied. Meg ambled over to the mule and rubbed its nose. "Did you sleep as poorly as I did last night?" She smiled. "I'll bet the same thoughts didn't keep us awake."

Walking into the mercantile, she saw Clay standing at the counter. The rotund man behind the counter was inspecting a gold pocket watch.

"Can't give you much for it." He waved pudgy fingers toward a glass case. "Everybody's tradin' their jewelry since the war ended."

"I'll take whatever you're willing to trade," Clay said, his eyes focused on something past the man's shoulder.

The man snapped the watch closed and slipped it into his pocket. "I can spare some flour, some sugar, maybe half a dozen canned goods but that's about it."

"And two sarsaparilla sticks," Clay said.

"You got kids?" the man asked.

"Yes, sir."

"Well, then, take the sweets and a couple more canned goods, but don't go telling anybody I have a soft heart."

Clay's lips lifted slightly as he promised. "I won't."

Meg stood silently as he boxed up his supplies and slipped the sarsaparilla sticks into his shirt pocket. Lifting the box off the counter, he turned and froze, his gaze meeting hers. His face burned a deep scarlet before he walked past her. "Don't suppose you'd get the door for me."

Stepping around him, she opened the door. Once he stepped through, she followed. "He cheated you."

"How do you figure that?" he asked as he placed the box on the wagon seat.

"That watch was worth much more than that piddling amount of food."

"It was only worth what I could get for it, and this is all I could get."

"Mr. Tucker at the general store in Cedar Grove would have given you more. You should have taken your business to him."

"I tried, Mrs. Warner, but he'll only deal with me if I can pay with cash. At the moment, I can't."

"Was that your father's watch?"

He shoved on the box even though he'd

113

already pushed it back as far as it could go. "My grandfather's. We'll need to rent some oxen to pull the wagon. The stone will make it too heavy for the mule. Just outside of town there's a farmer who'll give us a fair price."

Meg wished she hadn't noticed how he'd rushed on as though he didn't want to acknowledge what he'd just sacrificed for his family. She briefly wondered what else he might have sacrificed. "I saw you in the alley last night. Is that where you slept?"

"Didn't sleep."

"Why in the world didn't you?"

"Didn't like the looks of some of the men standing around the hotel. Wanted to make sure you were safe." He rubbed his hand along his jaw. "Even with the oxen, it'll be a slow journey back. We'd best get started, get that marble you want." He began to climb on the wagon.

"I —" She stopped speaking when he dropped back down to the ground and looked at her. She licked her lips. "Last night, I didn't think about the marble."

He gave her half a smile. "I'm not surprised. I let you see how badly I wanted the granite. My mistake."

She tilted her chin. "I thought about the marker you made for my mother. Do you remember it?"

"I remember everything I've ever carved. It's like when I carve something in wood or stone, I carve it into my memory at the same time."

"What was the marker made of?"

"Granite. That's what me and Pa always used."

"That's what I thought. Do you honestly think the granite is the better choice?"

"No, ma'am."

His response startled her. Maybe he had thought things through last night and come to the realization that she did indeed know which rock was better suited for the monument. "You don't?"

"No, ma'am. If you wanted a memorial to stand in silent tribute to those who died, then the granite would be the rock to purchase. But that's not what you want. I don't know what it is you do want, but you won't get it with the marble."

"I asked my question in all earnestness."

He removed his hat, combed his long fingers through his thick hair, and sighed heavily. "I'm sorry. My opinion on the matter hasn't changed since yesterday."

She lowered her gaze and pretended to study her scuffed boots so he wouldn't see the arguments playing havoc with her heart. She preferred the marble. Clay was unfamiliar with the stone. He would be forced to question and doubt each cut he made in the stone just as she wanted him to question and doubt the choices he made during the war. But if he made one error in judgment as great as the one he made when he failed to enlist, all her efforts would be for naught.

An unfinished monument would forever stand in memory of those who deserved more.

Reluctantly, she admitted the granite was the better choice . . . not only for his purpose, but for hers. She lifted her eyes to his and took a deep, cleansing breath. "You can purchase the granite."

Warily, he studied her. "Not the marble?"

She shook her head vigorously. "No, I've decided in favor of the granite."

"You won't be sorry."

She nodded, hoping that he was right and that she hadn't made a mistake. "You'll need the money." She pulled out a drawstring bag she'd tucked behind the waistband of her trousers earlier. She opened the pouch and spilled the contents into his scarred palm. "Will that be enough?" she asked.

He shifted the coins around with his finger. "Should be."

"Oh, wait." She plucked a silver coin out of his palm. "Kirk's tossing coin. I don't want to get rid of that."

He stared at her, his dark brows drawing together. "His tossing coin?"

Holding it up, she turned it so he could see one side, then the other. "It has Lady Liberty on both sides."

"What?" he fairly roared as he snatched it from her fingers and examined it.

"He always used it to win bets against my brothers."

His eyes showed disbelief. "That son of a . . ."

Knowingly, she smiled. "Don't tell me he used it on you as well?"

"A time or two." Handing the coin back to her, he smiled sadly. "But it worked out for the best."

Mesmerized, Meg wore a path around the wagon, viewing the rock from all sides. The glow from the fire's flames washed over one side of the granite, bringing out the red tint. The moonlight spilled across the other side, creating an ethereal quality.

Had Clay envisioned the stone as it would appear surrounded by night shadows, with moonlight whispering across it?

She wished he had brought his tools so he could begin work this evening. "Where will you put Kirk?" she asked as she touched one side of the rock. "Here?"

Clay lifted his head. What was the woman on about now? Since they left Schultz's quarry, she'd been chattering to her horse, the oxen, the damned rock, and now him. She was hopping around the wagon as though someone had set hot coals beneath her feet.

"Which side do you think Kirk will be on?" she repeated.

Slowly, he unfolded his weary body and wandered to the wagon. He touched the side of the rock at the end of the wagon. "I'll probably make this the base, so . . . I guess I'll carve the horse and rider here."

Meg scurried to the side of the wagon away from the fire. "I can't see them."

"You will when I'm done."

He began to walk away. She ran around to the other side. "And I'll be here?"

"I reckon." He rubbed his hand up and down his rough cheek. "If you don't want to sleep on the ground, you're small enough that you ought to be able to curl up on the wagon seat."

"Are you going to sleep now?" she asked.

"No, ma'am, I aim to keep watch."

Meg watched as Clay meandered back to the tree. He dropped to the ground and pressed his back against the trunk. He didn't seem the least bit interested in the granite now that they'd acquired it. She should have purchased the marble. At least their conversation carried a spark to it when they were in disagreement.

She climbed onto the wagon and arranged the blankets on the bench seat. Stilling her hands, she looked at the granite. It was just a piece of stone, and yet she was drawn to it. "Which direction . . ."

She stopped speaking as Clay snapped his head back. He looked around. "What?"

"Are you all right?" she asked.

"I'm fine."

Watching as he rubbed his shoulders against the tree before staring vacantly at the fire, she doubted his words. She'd been so thrilled with the stone that she'd paid little attention to anything else.

Shortly after they'd made camp, he went in search of game. She heard his rifle shot fill the air three times, but he returned to camp empty-handed. She dipped into his meager supplies, cooked some biscuits, and warmed a can of beans. Remembering the manner in which he wolfed down the simple, tasteless meal, she had a feeling that sleep wasn't the only thing he'd done without the night before.

She thought back to the first night they'd

made camp. Had he slept then? She remembered that some time had passed after her outburst before she again heard the knife shave the wood. She'd taken the sound into her dreams. Had it been with her all night? "Have you slept at all since we began this journey?"

"I don't need much sleep."

Meg gathered the blankets and clambered out of the wagon. She marched across the narrow space separating them and dropped the blankets in his lap. "You sleep. I'll keep watch."

Shaking his head, he pushed off the blankets. "You won't call if you need me."

For the first time, she noticed the dark shadows beneath eyes that were fighting a losing battle to remain open. "Is that why you stayed in the alley outside the hotel last night?"

Slipping his fingers between the buttons on his shirt, he rubbed his chest. "I reckon you got cause to think the way you do, but I'd die before I'd let any harm come to you."

Disconcerted by his slightly slurred words, Meg bundled up a blanket. "Here, lie down and go to sleep before you make yourself sick."

"Careful, Mrs. Warner. You might make me think you care."

120

"About you? Not in the least, but I just spent Kirk's life's savings on that hunk of rock you wanted so desperately, so you damn well better take care of yourself until you've turned it into the monument you promised me. After that, I don't care if you drop dead."

"Truth be told, you'd probably prefer for me to drop dead."

"Absolutely."

He gave her a tired grin. "I won't hold it against you if you're not quite so honest with me."

She stopped fussing with the blankets. Why did it tug on her heart when he teased her like that? "I never want you to doubt where you stand with me." She patted the blanket. "Now, get some sleep."

"I can go four days without sleep." He stretched out on the ground, and she shoved the folded blanket beneath his head. He yawned. "Went five days once."

"Why in the world would you want to?" she asked quietly, but she doubted that he heard her question. His face was relaxed, his dark lashes touching his cheeks. His long brown hair had fallen across his brow. He hadn't shaved recently, and his bearded stubble seemed to cast a shadow over his face.

The facial hair on Kirk's face had never been that thick, but then Kirk had never been this old, had never reached this phase of manhood. Studying Clay as he slept, she felt as though she'd been married to a boy instead of a man.

The last time she looked upon her husband, he'd been filled with the exuberance of youth. In her mind, the man who had fallen beneath Union guns was the same man who had kissed her soundly and laughed at the prospect of defeat.

In her heart, he would always remain the confident twenty-year-old who loved practical jokes.

But beyond the hills, he had aged . . . for two years.

Had he changed as much as the man who now slept on the ground?

Like an ancient map, Clay's face was well-worn and lined with paths traversed by sorrow and pain. And perhaps regret.

Tentatively, Meg brushed the hair away from his eyes. She wondered about the circumstances that had shaped those deep furrows.

Against her will, she was intrigued. If Clay, who had fought no battles, had changed to such a degree in the years he was away from Cedar Grove, how much more Kirk must have changed. His face would have carried more lines, shown his deep conviction to the Cause, reflected his true character.

With a deep sadness, she realized the man to whom she'd handed the silk Confederate flag probably wasn't the same man who died at Gettysburg.

Slowly, laboriously, Clay opened his eyes. She was sleeping beside him. Well, she wasn't exactly beside him. If he reached out, he didn't think he'd be able to touch her, but he was close enough to hear her even breathing and see the fire's faint glow reflected on her ivory cheeks.

And she snored, just as Kirk had told him. It was a gentle snore that reminded him of the way a contented kitten purred after its belly was filled with warm milk.

She laughed softly, and her shoulders shook slightly. He lifted up on an elbow and stared at her. Her mouth had formed a sweet tender smile.

Kirk hadn't told him about this. The laughter came again, washing over him in its innocence. The smile eased off her face, and he supposed the dream or whatever had given her a brief moment of happiness had passed.

Sitting up, he unrolled the blanket that

had served as his pillow and spread it over her. She made one hell of a night guard. If she slept through her own laughter, she'd probably sleep through someone wandering into their camp.

Stretching out on his side, he glanced toward the horizon. Dawn would soon lift away the darkness. He knew he should get up and find them something to eat, but he'd never watched a woman sleep. He supposed he should find it boring. After all, she wasn't doing anything.

But even while she slept, Meg fascinated him.

Slowly, she opened her eyes and smiled softly. Clay ached for all the soft smiles he'd been denied in the passing years, and he braced himself for the moment when she realized exactly at whom she was smiling.

"Morning," she said quietly.

Clay's voice knotted in his throat and threatened to strangle him. She was no doubt still dreaming and thought Kirk was lying on the ground beside her. All hell was going to break loose when she did come fully awake.

Rolling, she arched the small of her back. Clay's mouth went as dry as a desert.

Returning to her side, she slipped her palm beneath her cheek. "This used to be my favorite time of day, just before dawn, knowing I had a whole day to enjoy." She sighed wistfully. "Now I don't care if the sun never comes up."

Lord, he wished he were Kirk. He didn't want to see the hatred return to her eyes.

She turned onto her stomach and rested her face on her forearm. Her smile grew. "Kirk told me something about you," she said.

His breath caught. She was talking to him, with dawn easing over the horizon, bathing the earth in a new day. Good Lord, what had happened while he slept? It made him nervous to think about it. "What'd he tell you?" he croaked.

He didn't think her smile could grow any bigger, but it did. "I'd dearly love to tell you, but I promised him I wouldn't."

"He told me you do that," he said.

"Do what?"

"Start talking about something days after he's finished talking about it."

"Kirk really did tell you a lot of things about me, didn't he?"

He nodded.

"I dreamed about him last night," she said, with longing laced through her voice.

"I figured you did."

Her smile eased away.

"You laughed in your sleep," he hastened to explain, wanting to hold onto these moments before she remembered she hated him.

"I laughed while I was asleep?"

"Not loud. Soft. Like you were enjoying something."

Her face took on a hue more lovely than the dawn, and Clay realized she'd probably been dreaming about something that was absolutely none of his damn business. He grabbed his rifle and jumped to his feet. "I'll find us something to eat."

Stalking into the woods, he thought about the yearning in her blue eyes when she mentioned the dream.

He stopped walking, wrapped his arm around a tree, and pressed his forehead against the rough bark. He wished he could find a woman willing to dream about him.

They arrived at the Holland farm at twilight. Clay halted the wagon in front of the house as the door swung open, and the twins bounded out, Lucian sauntering behind them.

"Gawd Almighty!" one twin yelled. "You gonna make Miz Warner somethin' out of that?"

Clay climbed down from the wagon and

ruffled the boy's hair. "I aim to try, but remember, Josh, it's supposed to be a secret."

"We ain't got nobody to tell," Joe said as he climbed onto the wheel and looked into the wagon.

"Geez, Miz Warner, Clay must like you a powerful lot to make you somethin' that big," Josh said as he hauled himself up on the other wheel.

Meg felt her face warm as Clay glanced at her quickly before moving the box across the seat.

"Brought some supplies," Clay said as he lifted the box down.

"What'd you trade?" Lucian asked. "Grandpa's watch?"

"It was mine to do with as I thought best."

"It wouldn't have been if you hadn't been a coward. If you'd gone off to fight like the other men around here, you woulda been killed, and the watch, like the farm, woulda been mine." He hit the box. "I sure as hell wouldn't have traded it for a sack of flour."

He stomped away, hitting everything he passed until he was out of sight.

Josh hopped down from the wagon wheel. "I bet that box ain't too heavy for me and Joe to carry into the house."

"I bet it's not either," Clay said as he

127

handed the box to the boys. "Open your mouths." He took the sarsaparilla sticks out of his pocket and stuck one in each boy's mouth. Their eyes widened as they clamped their lips around the gift, mumbling their thanks before heading for the house.

"You get it from all sides, don't you?" Meg asked quietly.

Clay placed his hand on the granite. "I don't hardly notice anymore."

"Why do you stay?"

"It's my home. I don't think I did anything that took away my right to live here."

Meg disagreed. Everyone in the area disagreed. If her plan worked, Clay would eventually realize that he had indeed lost his right to live here. "When will you start working on the monument?"

"I need to get the oxen back to Austin. Then I have a few chores around here to take care of. Guess I'll start a week from Monday."

"I'll be here bright and early."

"There's not a lot to see at first. All I'll be doing is chipping away what I don't need."

"Regardless . . . I'll be here."

Seven

Cloaked in early morning darkness, Mcg scurried across the Holland property.

Only three days had passed since she'd last looked upon the red Texas granite, but she couldn't get it out of her mind. At home, she was listless and distracted. She'd burned the evening meal two nights in a row.

She was tempted to tell her father and Daniel about the monument, but she feared their reaction. Normally, if a father discovered his daughter had been alone with a man, he leveled his rifle at the man and ordered him to marry his daughter. If her father discovered she'd traveled alone to Austin with Clay, he'd level his rifle at Clay and shoot.

When Clay finished the monument, she could explain everything so they'd understand how wise her plan had been. Until that moment, however, the monument and everything associated with it had to remain a secret.

As she neared the shed, excitement raced through her veins with the lure of the forbidden. Holding her breath, she pressed her ear against the door. She couldn't hear anything move on the other side, but then, she'd expected to hear silence.

She'd planned this excursion with extreme care. She reasoned that Clay needed a day to unload the stone and another to return the oxen to Austin. Perhaps two. He would need at least two days to ride home on the mule. He wouldn't be back until this evening or tomorrow morning.

She was safe.

She pushed on the door. It creaked in protest at the early morning intrusion. She stopped and looked over her shoulder, her gaze darting between the house and the barn.

Nothing stirred.

She slipped into the building.

And couldn't see a thing.

Grimacing as the hinges squeaked louder, she pulled the door open wider. Slowly, her eyes grew accustomed to the darkness still hovering in the shed. As though they were winter blankets, shadows covered everything. She could barely discern the shape of the large object in the center of the shed, but it was the only thing she cared about. It seemed larger with four walls surrounding it. She wanted desperately to see in it what Clay saw underneath the surface.

130

She walked toward it, knocked against something hard, and yelped as pain ricocheted through her shin.

"It helps if you open the windows," a deep voice boomed behind her.

Meg screamed, tripped over the object, and fell flat on her face. Breathing heavily, she rolled over and stared at the man in the doorway, silhouetted against the approaching dawn. She heard him swallow his laughter. "Damn you! What are you doing here?"

Lazily crossing his arms over his chest, Clay leaned against the doorjamb. "I live here."

Meg scrambled to her feet, brushed off her backside, and angled her chin. "You said you were going to take the oxen back to Austin. There is no way that sorry mule of yours could have gotten you back here so quickly."

"You're right about that. Lucian offered to take the oxen back to Austin."

"How generous of him. I wouldn't have expected him to do you a favor."

"I don't think he saw it as doing me a favor. I think he saw it as an opportunity to get off the farm for a few days." He uncrossed his arms. "It does help if you open the windows."

He disappeared from the doorway. She heard him tell someone to help him raise the shutters. She groaned. Obviously, the twins had been waiting nearby to discover who was inside the shed. As though she were a small child, Meg wanted to run home and hide her face beneath the pillow. Moaning and creaking filled the shed as cracks appeared in the wall. Slowly, the morning light filtered through the widening crevice.

Pulling a rope, Clay became visible on one side of the window. Huffing on the other side, the twins strained to raise the window covering.

When they'd opened the shutter fully, they secured the rope on the outside. Then the twins leaned in through the large open window. She wondered if all little boys had grins that reached from one ear to the other.

"We surely are glad to know it was you we saw, Miz Warner. We thought you was a spook. Nearly scared us to death."

Meg wished she was a spook so she could turn into a mist and disappear.

Clay patted the boys on the shoulders. "Come on, let's get the other sides up."

They raised the shutters covering the windows on the remaining two sides. A breeze wafted through the building, and the sun chased away the shadows.

Along one wall, stone peered out from beneath tattered blankets. Shelves lined the lower walls of another side of the building. She could see now that she'd stumbled over an extremely short stool with four broad legs attached to a square top. It came no higher than her knee. She couldn't imagine that it served much purpose.

"Does that help?" Clay asked from the doorway.

She wondered if he was this polite to all trespassers or only those that amused him. She wished he'd release that smile he was fighting to hold back and be done with it.

"It helps immensely." Rising onto her toes, she pivoted slowly, her arms outstretched. "I almost feel as though I'm outside."

"Pa built it so we'd have a place to work. Seems people always die when it rains, and Ma didn't like all the dust that cutting on rock stirs up." He turned to walk away.

"Where are you going?" she asked.

He glanced over his shoulder. "To finish our chores and leave you to do whatever it was you tiptoed over here to do."

"I only came to look at the granite."

His smile broke free. "Yes, ma'am, I figured as much."

He walked away with the twins following close on his heels.

Meg sat on the short stool and stared after

them. Clay had the most beautiful smile she'd ever seen.

His small smiles of amusement had been distracting. His smile of pure joy was devastating. She'd have to pay more attention to her actions and make certain she gave him no further reason to smile.

With that resolution tucked away, she rose from the stool and looked at the rock. It hadn't changed.

She was no longer certain why she'd come or what exactly she'd expected to see. She narrowed her eyes. The monument was buried somewhere within that stone.

She touched the rough surface, anxious to see Kirk again. Maybe Clay was as eager as she was to see the monument completed and would be willing to begin work today instead of waiting for Monday. After all, they were both here.

She strolled to the house, stepped on the porch, and, unnoticed, peered around the open door. Clay was crouching before the hearth. As though they were matching bookends, the twins squatted on each side of him.

"Did Miz Warner's husband kill people?" one twin asked.

Clay took a deep breath. "Yes, he did."

"You reckon he liked killin' people?" the other twin asked.

"He didn't like it at all."

"Did he tell you that?" Meg asked from the doorway.

Clay shot straight up, banged his head on the stone mantel, swung around, jerked off the apron he was wearing, and waved the poker at her. "I had a tool in my hand!"

The twins rolled on the floor as though they were little bugs that curled into a ball whenever they were touched. Their guffaws echoed around the house.

"I couldn't see beyond your back. I didn't know you had anything in your hand. Besides, I thought you were referring to carving tools. I didn't realize I needed to make certain you had nothing at all in your hands before I ever spoke to you."

One twin stopped laughing. "Hey, Clay, you're bleedin'."

Blood trickled slowly along Clay's temple. He touched his fingers to his head and winced. "I'm all right."

Meg walked into the house. "Let me see."

He wadded the apron and pressed it against his head. "I'm fine."

Both twins stared, concern clearly reflected in their young faces. "Let her look, Clay. We don't want you to die on us."

"I'm not gonna die." Scowling, he moved the apron away from his head.

"You're too tall. You're going to have to bend down so I can see," Meg said.

"Maybe you're just too short."

"No one's ever complained about my size."

"No one's complained about my height."

"How many people talk to you?"

He bent his head but not before Meg saw that her teasing had cut him deeper than she'd intended. She'd assumed that he wasn't bothered by people in the area shunning him. He continued to attend church, but other than that he kept to himself much as he had before the war.

Kirk's mother had always used silence as her weapon whenever she was angry at anyone. Meg remembered how much it hurt the first time the woman refused to talk to her. She would have preferred yelling to the ominous quiet. She had assumed that the pain ran deeper because it involved family.

Perhaps Daniel was wrong. Clay didn't need to have their fists pounded into his face to feel their hatred. Their silence pummeled him just as effectively.

Gently, Meg parted his hair until she could see the wound. "That's some gash. Do you have a needle and thread? I could sew it up."

He straightened. "It doesn't need to be sewed."

"You could use the needle and thread Clay was usin' to fix the hole in my shirt," one twin offered.

"It does need stitches," she insisted.

He tightened his jaw. "Fine." He walked across the room, dropped into a chair at the table, crossed his arms over his chest, and sat unmoving as though he'd become one of his statues.

The twin rushed to a sewing basket beside a chair and proudly produced the needle and thread.

"Which one are you?" Meg asked.

"Josh," he said, his face beaming.

"I'll never be able to tell you apart."

"It's easy. Joe's got more freckles."

"I do not," Joe said as he climbed onto the table.

"What are you doing?" Clay asked.

"I ain't never seen nobody sew somebody up before."

"It's no different than sewing cloth so get outta here."

Josh scrambled onto the table. "Ah, Clay, let us have a look see."

"You might make Mrs. Warner nervous, and she'll end up sewing the tip of my ear to my head."

Laughing, the twins punched each other on the arm. Then they grew serious. "Will we make you nervous, Miz Warner?" Joe asked.

She smiled. "No. Do you have any whiskey?"

"No, ma'am," Clay said.

Gingerly, Meg lifted the strands of his hair aside. "Well, the blood probably washed out the wound."

"Probably."

"This may hurt," she said quietly.

"That should make you happy," he said.

He was right. She could jab the needle a little deeper than necessary, pull it through slower than usual, and prolong his misery. She took a deep breath to steady her fingers and poked the needle through his flesh.

He didn't flinch. If Meg hadn't known better, she'd think he'd turned into stone.

"Gawd Almighty! She stuck that needle right into your head, Clay. Look, Joe, all that blood looks like a red river runnin' through a forest of hair. Ain't that somethin'?"

Joe dropped to his backside and let his legs dangle over the edge of the table. "I think I'm gonna puke."

"Do it outside," Clay ordered through clenched teeth.

So he hadn't turned to stone after all.

"Don't that hurt, Clay?" Josh asked. "I'd be a hollerin' —"

138

"Then I'll make sure I never lower the mantel over the hearth."

The boy smiled. "Miz Warner, you gonna eat breakfast with us? We're havin' biscuits again." His eyes filled with delight at the prospect. "Reckon Clay'd fix you one."

"Or maybe I'll just swipe his," she said as her fingers nimbly worked to close the gash.

"He don't make him one."

"Why not?" Meg asked.

"He never eats much lessen he shoots a buck or somethin' big. Then he eats like he's got two bellies to fill."

"Mrs. Warner isn't interested in my eating habits," Clay said sharply, but his tone didn't take the smile off Josh's face.

Meg had a feeling she knew why he ate heartily when the food was plentiful. The man probably didn't eat at all when little graced their table. She had an irrational urge to bop him on the head.

"All done," she said as she snipped the thread.

"I appreciate it."

"I can't have you bleeding to death on me. Who'd make my monument?"

He peered up at her and grinned slightly. "Right."

"What's that gawd-awful smell?" Josh asked. "Did you puke, Joe?"

"Nah, I didn't puke. I swallowed it back down."

Clay bolted from the chair and rushed to the hearth. "Damn." Grabbing a heavy cloth, he pulled the pan of biscuits off a shelf set in the wall of the hearth.

"They look worse than what we had yesterday," Josh said.

Clay thumped the blackened bread. "They are worse."

"I suppose it's my fault," Meg said.

"It's nobody's fault," Clay said. "It just happened."

"Still, I feel responsible. I'll make another batch."

"I'll bet she can make good biscuits, Clay. Will you let her?"

"I reckon." He set the pan on the table and headed for the door. "I've already eaten, so just fix something for the twins."

"Where are you going?" Meg asked.

"I've got chores to finish up." He walked out of the house.

Meg smiled at the twins. "I'm not sure if I remember how to make just two biscuits."

Clay had never known torture could be so sweet.

Meg's fingers brushing lightly across his scalp had sent warmth flowing through his body clear down to his boots.

He wished she'd taken her time instead of rushing through the job, but he knew she hadn't wanted to touch him any longer than necessary.

Part of him wished she'd never touched him at all.

A greater part of him wished she'd never stopped.

He laid his hand against the granite. He was accustomed to the feel of rough rock grating against his palms. He imagined every inch of Meg was unlike anything he'd ever touched. She was probably soft, smooth, and as warm as a Texas summer.

A couple of times while she was stitching him up, her breast had come close to grazing his cheek. He had held his breath, not certain what he'd do if she actually did brush against him. The moment never came, so he could only wonder what it might have felt like.

He hit the stone. He should have been paying attention to Josh, not Meg's curves. The boy had a tendency to run at the mouth, speaking his mind and everyone else's. As a result, he'd told Meg a lot more than Clay would have liked. How many biscuits he cooked was none of her damn business.

He walked around the stone, trailing his fingers over the gritty surface. Every morning he came to the shed and pulled open the windows to let in the first rays of sunlight. Then he touched the granite, getting a feel for the rough texture beneath his roughened hands. He'd spent hours imagining where he would first place his chisel, how hard he would tap his hammer. He thought about the sound of that initial crack and how much to cut away before he actually began shaping the figures.

A dozen times he'd picked up his tools with steady hands. He touched the chisel to the rock, studying the angle, determining how the stone would react to the assault. He could see every movement in his head and had been tempted to begin chipping away the unwanted stone.

But he'd refrained because Meg wanted to watch.

And now his palms were sweating so badly he didn't think he'd be able to get a good grip on his tools.

He walked to a low table where he kept his tools laid out. He wrapped his hand around a chisel and felt it slide through his palm. He closed his eyes. He didn't want to disappoint her. He wanted this monument to be all that she thought it could be . . . and more.

Opening his eyes, he stared across the

fields. That she sat in judgment of him didn't bother him. That she might sit in judgment of his efforts within the shed did.

He lowered his gaze and watched as delicate fingers pushed a plate across the table. He slid his gaze over to Meg. "I said I'd already eaten."

She shrugged innocently. "I'm used to cooking for three. Besides, judging by the weight of your biscuits, I'd say you used a lot more of your staples than I did. I wrote my recipe on a piece of paper and left it on the table in the house." She tapped the plate. "Kirk always liked biscuits with honey. So eat it. You can't afford to waste anything around here."

He leaned his hip against the table and picked up the plate. He bit into the warm honey-drenched biscuit and nearly groaned. "This is better than what you cooked on the way back from Austin."

"It helps to have soda and milk."

"Soda?"

She nodded quickly, and the corners of her mouth tipped up slightly.

He shoved the rest of the biscuit into his mouth. No telling what else he hadn't put in the batter that he was supposed to.

"I don't suppose you'd start working on the monument today?" she asked.

He set the plate aside. "I was thinking about it, since you're here." He scattered a stack of papers across the table. "I've been studying the rock since we brought it home, trying to see it from all sides, from the corners, from the top, the bottom."

She picked up a piece of paper. "And you think this is what it looks like on the inside?"

"It's what I need to make it look like on the inside."

She lifted her eyes from the drawing, and Clay captured her gaze. "Do you understand?" he asked.

"You look at things so hard," she said in amazement. "Whenever you look at something, anything — the rock, the twins, me — you look so intense, it's almost frightening."

"I'm sorry. I didn't know I did that."

"I know. Kirk told me you didn't look at the world like everyone else does. He said when he looked at me, he saw a beautiful girl, but when you looked at me, you saw lines, curves, and angles that were beautiful. You look at things so hard because you try to figure out exactly what it is that makes them look the way they do."

He nodded in agreement. "I stare a lot."

"When we were growing up, I hated it when you stared at me."

He lowered his gaze to the ground. "I didn't mean to offend you . . . or anyone else for that matter."

"It no longer bothers me that you look at things so hard."

He dared to lift his gaze to hers. "It doesn't?"

She shook her head and picked up the first drawing he'd sketched for her. "You remember everything because you study it. This is exactly what Kirk looked like the last time I saw him." She held his gaze. "What did he look like the last time you saw him?"

Clay felt as though she had just slammed a chisel through his heart. He saw her chin quiver, and he couldn't tell her the truth.

"Didn't you see him when he brought you the letters? What did he look like then?"

He combed his fingers through his hair, wincing when he hit the gash she'd mended. "Tired. He looked tired."

"Was he thin?"

"Everyone was thin. They were having a hard time getting supplies through." She looked so damn fragile trying to pretend she wasn't hurting. He'd never expected Meg to look fragile. "He'd grown a beard."

"A beard? I can't imagine Kirk with a beard."

He offered her a small grin. "Well, it

145

wasn't much of a beard."

"Was it as blond as his hair?"

"A little darker."

"Did it make him look older?"

"Considerably," he said, although he knew it was the war that had aged his friend.

Her hands tightened their grasp on the paper until her knuckles turned white. "Did he . . . did he still believe in the Cause?"

Clay nodded. He didn't want to hurt Meg, but Kirk's words echoed through his mind. *You were right. There's no glory to be found in war. I just want to go home, but the damn Yankees won't let us.*

"Do you think he was afraid of dying? I mean, when death came, do you think he had regrets?"

"He believed in a state's right to secede, to govern itself. That's what he was fighting for. He felt his beliefs were worth dying for so I don't think he regretted giving his life as he did, but I imagine he regretted not being able to hold you again."

Tears flooded her eyes, and Clay wondered how he could have said something so stupid. He'd wanted to reassure her, but he didn't know a damn thing about the kind of words women wanted to hear. The tears spilled over onto her cheeks, and he thought he'd drown in them. He took a step toward her, hesitated, then strode from the building.

In disbelief, Meg watched him leave. She walked to the small stool, sat, and buried her face in her hands. She cried with a force that caused her chest and shoulders to ache. Kirk had grown a beard, and she'd never seen it.

She felt a light touch on each shoulder and lifted her tear-streaked face. The twins looked at her with concern reflected in their eyes.

"Clay said you was in need of comfort," one said. He squeezed her shoulder. "Said we was to give it to you."

The other twin dug a soiled piece of cloth out of his pocket and extended it toward her. "Only blew my nose on it once, and it was a long time back. You're welcome to use it. I don't mind."

Meg took the offering and used the cleanest corner to wipe the tears from her cheeks. She forced a tremulous smile as she handed the cloth back to him. "Thank you."

Nodding, he stuffed it into his pocket. "We ain't got much experience at givin' comfort, but when I'm feelin' sad 'cuz I ain't got no ma, Clay makes me close my eyes and do some powerful thinkin' about her. He says there's a touch of heaven in our hearts so our ma's always with us even though we can't see her."

"Your brother says some smart things, doesn't he?"

"Yes, ma'am, but he can't make biscuits worth a damn."

Sitting on an old tree stump beside the house, Clay fought the urge to return to the shed. He wanted to wrap his arms around Meg, lay her head against his chest, and comfort her. Instead, he sent the twins to her.

Perhaps he *was* a coward after all, for it was fear that made him leave, fear that if he touched her, she'd slap him again, and he'd crumble into a thousand pieces of nothing.

He stopped his wood carving.

He had the ugliest damn hands in the entire state. When he was a boy, they'd been too big for his skinny arms, and he'd always felt like a mongrel pup waiting to grow into its big paws. Whenever possible, he'd kept them shoved deeply into his pockets.

Now he was grown, but his hands still looked too large. His palms were rough from years of running them over abrasive rock. When he relaxed his hands, the veins and muscles continued to stick up like an unsightly mountain range.

But they were the ugliest when he carved. When he held tools and tightened his grip, everything in his hands and forearms visibly strained with his effort.

He couldn't imagine that any woman would want hands as big or as rough as his to touch her. He knew his hands repulsed Meg, not only because of the way they looked, but because of what they hadn't done.

His hands had never killed a man.

He saw her small feet come into view and lifted his gaze to hers. "You all right?"

She nodded. "Thank you for sending the twins to me."

"They always seem to know the right thing to say."

"They knew exactly what to say."

"I think it's because children don't weigh their words before they say them." He laid his knife on the stump and stood. "I think it'd be best if I waited until tomorrow to start work on the monument."

She wiped a stray tear from her cheek. "All right. I'll come back tomorrow."

"I'll open the shed early so you don't have to sneak in."

She forced a quivering smile. "I wasn't planning on sneaking. See you in the morning." She turned to leave.

"I —"

Stopping, she looked at him.

He extended the wooden carving toward her. "This is what your husband looked like the day he told me he was going to marry you. Thought you might want it."

She took the offering and studied it. "He couldn't have been any older than twelve."

"That sounds about right."

"Why are you giving me a present?"

"It's not a present. It's just something I carved, and now I've got no use for it. If you don't want it, you can throw it away. Makes no difference to me."

"Is this what you were working on when we traveled to Austin?"

"Yes, ma'am."

She trailed her fingers over the small features he'd carved. Then she extended it toward him. "I can't take it."

"Why not?"

"Because we are not friends. We will never be friends. If I accept this, I'd be —" She shook her head. "I don't know. I just know I can't take it."

"Consider it payment for stitching my head. I know it's not much, considering I nearly bled to death, but it's all I have to trade. The carving for my life. Considering the value you place on my life, it's probably a fair trade."

"Doesn't it bother you that I hate you?"

Shoving his hands into his pockets, meeting her cold blue gaze, he said quietly, "It bothers me a great deal."

Meg stared at the land where Mama Warner's sons and daughters had once toiled and crops had flourished. One by one, her children had left to build their own homes and harvest their own dreams. In abundance, the wildflowers had reclaimed the fallow fields.

Shortly after her return from Austin, with a strong need to tell someone about the granite and the monument, she'd confided in Mama Warner. She knew Kirk's grandmother wouldn't judge her actions and would understand her motives.

She'd come here today to savor and share her first victory, but she'd only shared the carving of Kirk that Clay had given her. She didn't know why, but she couldn't boast about the pain she'd seen reflected in Clay's eyes when he'd answered her question.

Lowering her gaze, she touched the delicate petal of a wooden flower that Mama Warner had planted in a wooden box. Kirk had made the box for his grandmother when he was ten. Clay had carved the flowers from twigs and bits of wood and painted them blue.

Everywhere Meg looked, she ran into their lives, intertwined.

"Do you like my buffalo grass?" Mama Warner asked.

Wiping the tears from her cheeks, Meg turned and smiled at Kirk's grandmother. She'd grown frail since the war. Her grandsons and two of her sons had ridden away in gray. Only one grandson had returned, but it was Kirk's death that had nearly broken the woman's spirit. She'd always been closest to Kirk.

"They look like bluebonnets," Meg said.

"Years ago, when I was young and filled with dreams, I watched the buffalo forage on the blue weeds that coated the hills. I haven't seen a buffalo in a good long while, but I always have my buffalo grass." She pressed the wooden carving against her breast. "And now, I almost have my grandson again."

Quickly, Meg crossed the room and knelt beside the rocking chair. "I didn't mean to upset you with the carving."

The older woman touched a gnarled finger to Meg's cheek. "Ah, child, memories don't upset me. They're all I have in my winter years to keep me warm." She trailed her finger along Kirk's likeness. "I can almost see his freckles. Kirk hated them so, and Clayton knew it, but he still put the shadow

152

of them here. He always carves what he sees. Honest to a fault that boy is. Did you notice the freckles?"

Meg smiled. "No, ma'am, I guess I didn't look that closely."

"It's just a little difference in the shading. Over the years, Clayton has become skilled at carving. When he was a boy, he'd bring me things and ask me to guess what they were. Got to the point where I hated to guess. I said a cloud once, and it was a pig. Nearly broke his heart. Not that he'd let me know that, of course, but his eyes don't just see more than most. They also tell more than most. But you gotta look closely. Have you looked closely, Meg?"

"I try not to look at him at all. I hate him and all he stands for."

"You said that too strongly."

"Because my hatred for him is strong."

"Or is it not strong enough? You accepted his gift —"

"I only took it because he didn't want it, and I thought you might like to have it. I certainly don't want it."

"But it's a likeness of Kirk when he was a boy."

Standing, Meg held up her hands to emphasize her point. "He made it. I can't keep it."

Mama Warner leaned back in her rocker. "But you've asked him to make you a monument."

Meg walked to the window and gazed at the flowers Nature had created, trying to ignore the flowers that a boy had made. "That's different. The monument isn't for me specifically. It's to serve as punishment for him, and it'll serve as a memorial for the others."

She heard the gentle creaking of the rocking chair. Sometimes, she wished she were small enough to crawl onto Mama Warner's lap as she rocked. She glanced over her shoulder and watched the older woman slowly touch every line and curve of the carving.

"I'd say Kirk was about twelve when he looked like this," Mama Warner said.

Returning to the woman's side, Meg placed her hand over one disfigured by years of fighting to survive. "That's what he said."

"He? Will you not even say his name to me?"

"Speaking his name sickens me."

"And yet you plan to spend the coming days in his company."

"So I can witness his suffering."

"Revenge has a way of turning on itself, sweet Meg." Mama Warner gently touched the tip of her finger to a tear that clung tenaciously to Meg's eyelash. "Are you not the one who will suffer?"

Roughly, Meg swiped the tear away. "I made the mistake of asking him about Kirk. In the future, I won't speak to him at all."

"In silence you'll watch him work? Sometimes, silence can be so very loud. Remember how you cried when Kirk's mother wouldn't talk to you?"

"Which is why I know it'll be an additional punishment for him."

"You feel strongly about this, don't you?"

"Yes, ma'am. They were all so young, so brave, filled with conviction. They were men of honor. He betrayed them when he didn't stand by them."

"And you think he'll come to recognize his failings as he works on this monument?"

"If he doesn't, he will by the time he's carved every name into stone. He'll have to face each man's memory again."

"And when he's finished?"

"Then we'll have a tribute to those who gave their lives for the Cause."

"A tribute steeped in revenge. It'll be interesting to see if this monument will become what you envision, to see how deeply your punishment will cut into his soul. Will you bring me my box?"

Meg knew the box. It sat in a corner beside the window. Kirk had made it, using cedar. The scent circled Meg as she shoved the box across the floor to the rocking chair.

Leaning forward, Mama Warner rubbed her fingers over the bluebonnets that Clay had carved in the lid. Her wispy white hair fell across her cheeks and along her shoulders as though it were delicate lace. She lifted the lid and carefully placed the carving of Kirk inside the box. "There will come a day when I'll tell you to take this box home with you. You do it without questioning me. This box and the things inside it are for you."

"I don't want the carving he made."

"A day will come when you will want it. When you're young, you wish for things in the future, but when you grow old . . . you wish for things from the past."

"This box should go to your children."

"Had Kirk not died, this box would have gone to him. He loved you. He'd want you to have it. I want you to have it, and I'll ask you to take it before I die so my children won't be fighting over it. I'll be leaving them enough around here to fight about. They're Texans, and Texans surely do enjoy their fights."

"Not all Texans."

"We can't seem to steer the conversation

away from Clayton. Why is that? What did he say to make you cry?"

Meg felt fresh tears well within her eyes. "He told me Kirk had grown a beard." She laid her cheek against Mama Warner's knee. "It hurts. It hurts to know he saw Kirk after I did and knows things about Kirk that I don't."

Mama Warner gently brushed her fingers over Meg's hair. "I know, child."

"I hate him all the more because his memories of Kirk are fresher than mine."

"Memories don't age, Meg."

Lifting her face, Meg met the older woman's blue gaze, a gaze that very much resembled Kirk's. "No, but they fade."

Eight

Meg set the plate of bacon on the table and took her seat. Her father sat at the head of the table. To his left, two chairs remained empty. To his right, set another empty chair. Each served as a reminder of the young men who had once toiled in the fields beside Thomas Crawford.

Meg sat across from Daniel at the end of the table closest to where their mother had sat. In the thirteen years since her mother's death, only dust and the gentle caress of a dusting rag had touched her mother's chair.

Waiting quietly while her father and Daniel scooped food onto their plates, she missed the banter that had once been as abundant as the food. Enjoyable conversation during meals had ridden away with her brothers.

Daniel moved the bacon around on his plate before lifting his blue gaze to hers. "Burned it a bit, didn't you, Meg?"

She tilted her nose. "I like it crisp."

"Thought I heard you moving around in the middle of the night," her father said.

She began filling her plate. She'd risen an hour earlier and thought she'd been quiet as she moved through the house. "I wanted to get my chores finished early. I thought I'd visit with Mama Warner today."

Her father leaned back, chewing his food as intently as he seemed to be studying her. "You've been spending a lot of time with Mama Warner of late."

"She's aging. I'm not certain she'll be with us that much longer, and I want to glean some of her wisdom."

Nodding, her father returned to his meal. With shaking fingers, Meg picked up her fork. She didn't like lying to her father, but she feared he'd grab his rifle if she told him she was planning to spend the day in Clay's company.

"We'll be working Sam Johnson's fields this week if you need us."

The shortage of able-bodied men to work the fields was a hardship that the local families had overcome by gathering to work each other's fields. With her father and Daniel working other farms, they seldom came home before dusk.

As Kirk's wife, she'd grown accustomed to her independence. It had been an adjustment when she moved back home, but now her father expected no more from her than a meal at dawn, a meal at sunset, clean clothes, and a tidy house. Although it would no doubt wear her out, she was certain she could maintain all her chores and still spend a good part of the day watching Clay work.

"You need a husband."

Meg snapped her head around and stared at her father.

"You need a husband and children to occupy your day, not an old woman," he said.

"Who would she marry?" Daniel asked. "She don't want to marry Reverend Baxter. He doesn't even bother to invite himself to dinner anymore. All the other men around here are either years older or years younger, except for the damn coward, and I know Meg ain't interested in him, not the way she glares at him during church service. I'm surprised he hasn't burst into flames."

The table shook as Thomas pounded his fist down on it. "By God, I don't want talk of that man in my house." He glanced at the empty chairs on either side of him, his jaws clenched. "He turned his back on my sons. By God, we should have hanged him the day our sons rode away." Rising from his chair, he stalked out of the house, the door slamming in his wake.

Accustomed to his father's outbursts, Daniel simply shoved his plate forward and laid his forearms on the table, leaning forward slightly. "Some of us are thinking maybe we ought to tar and feather the coward."

"What would that accomplish?" Meg asked, tearing her gaze from the vibrating door.

"Might make him leave this area. Every time there's a good wind, it brings the stench of his fear blowing across the fields."

"That's not enough," Meg said quietly. "Daniel, do you remember when you took Michael's harmonica without asking?"

Daniel dropped his gaze to the table and nodded. "Yeah, and I lost it."

"Did he tar and feather you when he found out?"

"No, he just gave me that puppy dog look of his and made me feel guilty as hell for losing his most treasured possession."

"And you still feel guilty about it because you came to understand what you took from Michael. The town's coward needs to understand that he betrayed my husband and our brothers so he can carry the knowledge and pain with him for the rest of his life."

"How can we make him understand that? I sure as hell ain't gonna give him a puppy dog look."

Gazing into his earnest face, she was

tempted to tell him about the monument, but Daniel hadn't yet acquired the patience that came with age. She didn't think he'd understand the motives behind the monument. She didn't want to take a chance that he or her father would try to stop her from watching Clay work. "I don't know," she said quietly. "But I'm sure there's a way."

Meg felt the familiar ache in her heart as she watched the twins race toward her, each trying to outdistance the other. She didn't know how she could miss something she'd never had, but she did miss having her own children. Dismounting, she smiled and waited for them to reach her.

"Mornin', Miz Warner!" they cried as they ran past her, circled, and loped back, breathless from their efforts.

She ruffled their red hair. "Good morning."

"Want us to see after your horse?" one asked.

"Do you know how to care for a horse?"

"Yes, ma'am." The boy's eyes brightened. "Clay taught us last night. It ain't that much different from takin' care of the mule. Clay said lookin' after a lady's horse was the gentlemanly thing to do, and he wants us to grow up to be gentlemen. Says it's important to know how to treat a lady."

She handed the reins to the twins, and they started walking toward the shed.

"We had biscuits again this mornin'," the twin continued. "Clay musta used your recipe 'cuz they was better than what he cooked before. 'Course, they still wasn't as good as yours, but they come pretty close."

"Did he make three?"

"Yes, ma'am. He surely did. Course, he'll probably stop eatin' one if Lucian comes home."

"When will Lucian be home?"

"Maybe tomorrow. Maybe never. Before he left, he hit Clay."

Meg stared at the child. "He hit him?"

"Yes, ma'am. You know what Clay did?"

She shook her head.

"He just got up off the ground, wiped the blood away from his mouth, and asked Lucian if he felt better."

"Did he feel better?"

"No, ma'am. We think he felt a sight worse. He moped around the barn all day. Then Clay asked him if he wanted to get away for a few days. Lucian jumped on that idea like a fly on a cow chip, and off he went with the oxen." He shrugged. "But we don't know if he's comin' back."

"I'm sure he'll come back," she said, trying to instill conviction in her words when she wasn't at all certain. Lucian's hatred of Clay rivaled her own.

"We surely do hope so 'cuz we're gonna need him come harvest time. We planted us a cash crop this year. Lucian only ever planted enough for us to eat 'cuz we didn't have no help with the fields. But Clay said if we all worked a little harder, we could have some extra to sell. So we planted some extra acres of corn. When it comes up, we'll be pert' near rich, and we'll have biscuits every mornin'."

Meg glanced over the furrowed fields. The Holland acreage had always paled in comparison with everyone else's. Clay's father had more interest in stone than in soil.

The twin stopped walking and the entourage halted. He tilted his face back so he could meet Meg's questioning gaze. "You ain't gonna tell Clay that I swore yesterday when I was talkin' about his biscuits, are you? He says we can't swear till we're sixteen. If we swear before then, he'll wash our mouths out with soap, and we ain't never supposed to swear in front of a lady. Yesterday, that 'damn' just sorta slipped out of my mouth, and then I couldn't shove it back in."

"I don't imagine I'll be telling him about your swearing."

"Well, if you decide you gotta tell him, just remember that I'm Joe."

"You sure as heck ain't!" the other twin yelled, voicing his thoughts for the first time.

"I am, too. You can even count my freckles. You'll see that I got the most."

He stretched so he stood on the tips of his bare toes, and she could see his freckles more clearly. From the corner of her eye, she watched the other twin struggle with his dilemma: to prove he was Joe without confessing to having the most freckles.

"I'm not going to tell him," she said.

"Cross your heart?"

Meg drew a cross over her heart. "Cross my heart."

"See, Joe. I knew she wouldn't want your mouth to get washed out with soap."

"And what if you'd been wrong? You were the one that said 'damn,' not me," the quieter twin stated.

"But I wasn't wrong. Come on, Miz Warner. Clay's in the shed waitin' on you. He's been there since dawn. Reckon he thought you'd be early again this mornin'."

She'd wanted to be here at dawn, but she'd waited until her father and brother had left for the fields. They seldom returned home before dusk so she wasn't concerned with their noticing her absence during the day. "Has he started carving on the stone yet?"

"No, ma'am, but I think he was sorely tempted to. He keeps pickin' up his tools, but then he just puts 'em back down."

They neared the shed, and the twins veered away from her. "Don't worry about your horse none," Josh said, smiling.

She watched the twins and horse disappear around the corner. Taking a deep breath, she stepped into the shed.

Clay stood beside the low table. The wind ruffled his hair, dragging it across the collar of his worn flannel shirt. He wiped his hands on his trousers. "Morning."

Pursing her lips, holding her return greeting captive, she tilted her head slightly.

"Thought I'd start this morning," he said.

"That's why I'm here."

Nodding, he turned his attention to the table. He picked up a tool and set it down.

He gazed out the window.

He touched the tools.

He looked out the window again.

Meg wasn't familiar with the implements. Tools that plowed into stone were a little different from those that plowed into earth, but she did know that in order for Clay to use them effectively, he had to hold them longer than it took to sneeze.

She crossed her arms and shoved them beneath her breasts. The man must have taken lessons in moving from his mule.

He walked slowly around the granite, studying it as though he'd only just seen it. He stopped and looked at her standing in the doorway. "I'll get you a chair."

With long strides, he quickly left the shed. Stupefied, Meg glanced around. She could have sat on the empty stool nestled in the corner.

He returned moments later and set a hard-backed wooden chair beneath the threshold. Meg picked it up, carried it closer to the stone, and sat.

"It'd be best if you sat by the door," Clay said.

"Why?"

"Because when I start working, dust and stone are gonna fly everywhere."

"I'll take my chances."

"Fine."

He stomped out again, leaving Meg to stare at the door. She wiped her sweating palms along her skirt.

Clay walked in carrying a piece of red cloth. "This was my pa's. It's clean. You can tie it around your face, cover your nose and mouth so you're not breathing in all the dust."

"Do you have one?"

Nodding, he pulled a similar cloth out of his pocket.

"Then I guess we're all set," she said.

"Yes, ma'am." He walked to the table and picked up an instrument with a blunt end.

"What's that?" Meg asked.

"A chisel." He held up a tool which looked similar to a large nail. "This is a point."

Meg cursed her curiosity, but couldn't resist it. She rose from the chair and walked to the table. "Why do you have them in different sizes?"

"I use the larger ones in the beginning when I'm chipping away the stone I don't need." He touched smaller tools that had finer points or smaller blunt ends. "I use these when I'm working on the details."

"You even have different hammers."

He held a hammer with pointed grooves in both ends. "I use this one to pound the granite into shape." He set it down and waved his hand over the remaining hammers which had flat ends. "I use the heavier hammers at first, then I'll use the lighter hammers."

"How did you learn when to use each tool?"

"By making mistakes." He wiped his palms on his trousers. "Are you thirsty? I can draw you some water from the well."

She shook her head. "No, I'm just fine."

"Let me know if you want some water."

"I will."

He touched the largest chisel. "Think I'll have a drink of water before I get started."

Clay strode out of the shed and crossed the yard to the well. With rapid-fire motions that resembled those of a Gatlin gun, he turned the crank and brought the bucket from the bottom of the well. He set it on the stone ledge and dunked his head in the cool water.

All night, he'd planned the moment when he'd chip away his first bit of stone, and he certainly hadn't expected to be distracted by honeysuckle. The damned fragrance floated around Meg like a low cloud on a misty morning. He knew she hadn't worn the scent for him. She was just in the habit of bathing in it or throwing it on her body or whatever the hell she did to tease a man's nostrils.

He kept his head submerged until he thought his lungs would explode from lack of air. He jerked his head out, took a deep breath, and threw his head back, tunneling his fingers through his hair, careful to avoid the spot she'd stitched the day before. He rubbed his hands over his face, wondering how long it'd take his hair to dry so he didn't look like a drowned cat. He hadn't even considered that he'd have to explain —

"Are you nervous?" she asked quietly behind him.

Clay nearly jumped over the well. He spun around.

She held up a finger to silence his protest. "You didn't have any tools in your hands."

With a rueful smile, he sighed and sat on the edge of the well. "I've never done anything this big before, or something that was so important."

"I disagree. My mother's headstone was just as important."

"It was a little different and a lot smaller."

"But you're accustomed to carving granite. You know how the rock will respond to your touch."

She gazed at his hands, and he fought against shoving them into his pockets. He couldn't work with his hands in his pockets, and he couldn't work wearing gloves. She'd spend a lot of time staring at his large ugly hands. The sooner he accepted that, the better.

She lifted her eyes to his. "How do you know where to begin?"

"You ever make a quilt?" he asked.

"Of course. What woman hasn't?"

"Well, you know how you take all the little

pieces and sew them together? It's like you're building something. I do the opposite. I take something that's finished — like the rock — and scrape away its covering to reveal what it is inside." He plowed his hands through his hair. "That doesn't make sense."

"Yes, it does. You're trying to get to the batting."

He smiled. "Yeah, I reckon so, although that doesn't make it sound very exciting."

"Which figure will you work on first?"

"In the beginning, I'll work on the whole monument."

"I don't understand how you can work on the whole thing when it's so big. I thought you'd work on it in sections."

"I work on it in layers. See your shadow?"

She glanced at the silhouette stretching out behind her.

"It's not your true shape, but it's close enough that a person could tell from looking at your shadow that you were a woman. I try and imagine what the monument's shadow will look like from every side, and I concentrate on those images. Then I'll use the larger chisels and points to create the monument's shadow in stone. When I have everything shaped so it resembles a shadow, I'll switch to the smaller tools and work on the details."

"How do you know if you're doing it right?"

He dropped his gaze to the ground. He didn't know; he wouldn't know until the monument was finished. "I've had a lot of failures." He lifted his eyes to hers. "Do you want to see them?"

Her eyes widened in wonder. "Your failures?"

He nodded.

"You kept them?"

"Most of them, so I could figure out what I did wrong."

"Where are they?"

He smiled. "In the graveyard."

"It's not your typical graveyard," he said as they walked past the house to an area where pecan trees provided a cool morning shade. "It's just a place where my ideas died."

Meg stepped carefully around odd shapes of stone that peered through the wildflowers.

"Pa used to bring the stone out here when he was finished with it so what I started with wasn't the best quality anyway." He knelt in the tall grass and moved the weeds aside. "This was the first thing I ever tried to carve. Reckon I was about eight." He peered at her.

"What do you think it is?"

She hoped an eight-year-old boy wasn't buried deep inside him expecting her to guess what he'd created. She didn't care if she hurt the man, but she didn't want to hurt the child. She grimaced. "A cloud?"

He smiled broadly. "A turtle. It was a good thing to start with because it's flat and close to the ground so I didn't have to worry about it supporting any weight."

"What did you learn from your turtle?"

He trailed his finger along a fissure in the rock. "When I started carving the lines on his shell, I set a narrow point so it went straight up and down and its tip touched the rock. When I hit the flat end of the point with the hammer, the metal cracked the turtle's back. I learned to always work at an angle so I don't crack the stone." Leaning over, he pulled another rock into a standing position. "This —"

"A rabbit!" Meg smiled triumphantly as she knelt beside him.

He released his hold on the rabbit, and it fell, buried again within the tall grass. "The rabbit won't sit up because his weight's not distributed evenly."

"It might have helped if you'd given him two ears."

"I tried." He reached into the grass and

173

picked up a broken piece of stone. "I made the top of his ear pointed, and then I flared out so it would look like he was listening. Then I came back in, to where his ear would join his head."

He outlined the ear with his fingers as he talked. Even when he didn't have tools in his grasp, he carved the images with his hands. She could envision an alert rabbit sitting in the field listening for the sound of a predator.

He wrapped his thumb and forefinger in a circle around the base of the ear. "But I got carried away with the carving and made this part too narrow. It couldn't support the weight of the ear above it. It's a deafening sound when you hear the crack of rock, and you aren't holding tools."

"How are you going to keep that from happening with the monument?"

"I'm not going to give anyone ears."

Meg didn't know why she laughed. Perhaps it was the image of two people and a horse without ears, or perhaps it was the way Clay fought to appear serious. He grinned, and she shook her head. "I'm serious. It seems as though the monument could crumble very easily."

"It could, but since your husband didn't have big ears, I think we'll be all right."

"What's going to stop the horse's legs from snapping under his weight?"

A smile of appreciation lit his face, and Meg felt the pleasure flow through her.

"You're right. The legs are the problem." Using both hands, he touched the tips of his fingers together to form a steeple and spread his palms apart. "It won't be apparent, but the monument will look like a pyramid from all sides. It'll be narrow and more detailed at the top. As I near the base, I'll leave more stone in place. I don't plan to hollow out the area between the horse's hind legs. I'll keep the stone there so it can act as support for the weight above."

"Won't that look odd?"

"I don't think so. Hopefully, the rider and the woman will capture everyone's attention, and no one will care about the horse. I'll carve the horse's flank and the outside of his legs. I'll carve the details in his tail, but it'll serve as support, too. I'll bring it up from the base so it'll look as though the horse is rising out of the stone. I'll do the same thing with the flag. Your arms will be raised, but the flag will drape down to the base, so you're not actually holding the flag. The flag is supporting your raised arms."

"Do you foresee any problems in carving me?"

"None at all since you don't have big . . ."
— his gaze flitted to her breasts just before
he averted his eyes and turned scarlet —
"ears."

He picked up the rabbit's ear and tossed
it aside. It grated across the turtle.

Watching Clay's cheeks turn crimson,
Meg felt a wickedness grow inside her. "Is
that why you're using me in the monument?
Because I have small . . . ears?"

She thought he was going to hop over
some stones. He scrounged around until he
located a small rock. He threw it toward the
trees. "Your ears are perfect. Your form . . ."

She watched him struggle to speak without
drawing images of her in the air with his
hands.

"Is perfect. That's why I'm using you as
the model."

"You don't think my . . . ears are too
small?"

His cheeks turned so red, Meg was surprised they didn't ignite into flames.

"No, I don't think they're too small."

"So you won't have any trouble carving
my . . . ears?"

"No, I won't have any trouble carving your
ears."

"I wouldn't want to end up here."

He met her gaze. "I'll do all in my power

to see that you don't."

She studied the abundance of stone. Each piece was imperfect: a fallen angel without a nose, a dog without a tail. Yet, each stood in silent tribute to determination. Each had provided a lesson, so none were truly failures.

"It seems as though it would have been less work to go to school and learn to be a sculptor," she said.

"No schools in the area."

"Kirk told me that you wanted to go to Europe."

He studied his hands. "That was a boy's dream."

"Didn't the man have the same dream? Why didn't you go?"

"The timing wasn't right. War was in the air." He shrugged. "I had this stupid notion that if I left, people would think I'd gone to avoid the war. Thought they wouldn't welcome me back when I was ready to return. Thought if I stayed, they'd at least respect the stand I took." He released a mirthless laugh. "Guess the past few years didn't turn out the way any of us thought they would." He stood. "Let's see if I can at least do justice to this monument you want."

As she rose and followed him away from the field, Meg realized he'd shown her more than a graveyard of broken stones and a place where his ideas had died. He'd shown her a place of broken dreams.

She watched as Clay walked with more confidence to the shed. His graveyard of stone wasn't that much different from other graveyards. She always drew strength from her visits to her mother's resting place. Perhaps he drew strength from his past carvings.

He tied the bandanna over his nose and mouth, walked to the table, wrapped his fingers around a large chisel, and hefted a hammer. "Reckon I'll get started. You'll want to cover your nose and mouth."

Sitting in the chair, Meg brought the bandanna around her face and knotted it behind her head. She felt the excitement mount until it was almost a physical presence. He shoved the stool she'd tripped over the day before to one side of the granite and climbed onto it so his eyes were level with the top of the rock.

He ran his hand over the corner. Then he leveled his gaze on her. "This is when you have to be quiet."

Nodding in understanding, Meg shifted her backside in the chair. She wanted to stand on that stool with him so she could watch the stone from his perspective. Unfortunately, she didn't think the stool was wide enough for both of them. She would have had to wrap her arms around him for support.

Reluctantly, she admitted she'd have to be content with her present vantage point.

He set the chisel so it touched the stone at an angle. Then he swung the hammer so it slammed against the flat end of the chisel. A clang and a crack resounded around her. He shifted the chisel slightly and swung again. Meg heard another ring and a crack. She held her breath. He swung the hammer with another fluid movement, and the sound of cracking granite drowned out the metal ping. She watched the corner of chipped stone sail through the air and land near her feet.

Clay jerked his bandanna down, hopped off the stool, bent, and retrieved the fallen stone. He held it toward her. "You can keep the first chunk as a memento."

Meg lowered her scarf and studied the rock that barely covered her palm. "It's so small. I expected you to knock it off in huge chunks."

"Once I take it off, I can't put it back on, so I only take off a little bit at a time."

She stared at the huge hunk of granite sitting in the middle of the shed. Then she stared at the small piece of stone resting in her palm. "It'll take you forever to finish the monument."

"Not forever. I figure a couple of years."

"Years!"

He furrowed his brow. "How long did you think it would take?"

"Two or three months."

Leaning against the rock, he crossed his arms over his chest. "Why should the amount of time make a difference to you?"

Meg stood and began pacing between her chair and the door. "I just hadn't expected it to take so long. I'm anxious for people to see the monument."

"You could tell them about it."

"No!" She came to an abrupt halt. "People wouldn't understand."

"They wouldn't understand you wanting a monument to honor their fallen sons?"

"They wouldn't understand my talking to you, my presence in this shed, my putting foot on your land. They'd think I'd forgiven you for your cowardice, and I certainly haven't done that." She tromped over to the chair and sat. "Just get back to work."

"You want to tell me the real reason you asked me to make this monument?"

Clutching the granite, Meg felt it dig into her palm. "Please, just go back to work."

He set his tools on the stool, walked to the

chair, and knelt before her. "Just tell me what it is you want, Meg, and I'll give it to you. I'll work until my hands bleed. I'll work until my soul bleeds, but it won't bring him back. It won't give you the life you had before the war."

Meg squeezed her eyes to shut out his intense gaze. She didn't want to look into brown eyes that said he'd already suffered. She didn't want to know about his dreams, or his failures, or rabbits with only one ear.

"The war weakened the South," he said quietly. "Don't let it weaken you."

Opening her eyes, she tilted her chin. "I'm hardly weak. I just hadn't expected to spend the next two years of my life in your company, but if that's the price I have to pay in order to have the monument, I'll pay it."

A corner of his mouth tilted up, and she thought she'd probably hit him if he smiled again.

"Ah, so it's being in my company for such a long time that's bothering you." He unfolded his body and walked to the stone. "It's an awfully big piece of stone. I hope I can do it in two years." He peered at her. "Might take three." He picked up his tools. "Maybe four."

"If you say five —"

The teasing glint left his eyes. The half

smile withered away.

"For you, Mrs. Warner, I'll finish it in a year."

Clay sank into the hot water. The steam rose and misted his face.

He was a damned fool.

The stiffness was already settling into his neck and shoulders, and he dreaded waking in the morning. He'd pushed himself harder than he'd intended, certainly harder than he was accustomed to. He hadn't swung a hammer with such a steady rhythm in a long time, and tomorrow he'd pay for it. He hadn't worked faster, but he'd worked longer.

Closing his eyes, he listened to the fire crackle in the hearth. A bath before a blazing fire was a luxury he hadn't indulged in since his return home. When he bathed, he did it in his room behind a locked door because too many people lived in this house.

Tonight was an exception. Taking care of Meg's horse had worn the twins out, and they'd fallen asleep early. Lucian hadn't returned from Austin.

Clay had decided to pamper himself.

Besides, he needed to celebrate.

Meg Warner had teased him.

Lord, he'd been so embarrassed by what

he'd almost said that he nearly missed the fact that she was teasing him. He didn't think he'd ever be able to look at her ears or her perfectly shaped curves again without turning red.

He supposed since she'd been married, she knew how a man's mind worked. He supposed since she'd been married to Kirk, she was comfortable with the way a man's mind worked.

He wished he understood how a woman's mind worked.

One minute she was teasing him, and the next she was worried because she was going to spend time with him.

Lifting his foot from the water, he scratched the memento from the leg irons he'd worn as a prisoner. He kept his scars to himself, especially those that weren't visible even when he stripped down.

Slipping his foot back into the water, he rested his head against the wooden tub and watched the firelight play against the wall.

What did Meg want?

She wanted more than the monument from him. Of that, he was certain. He supposed she'd tell him when she was good and ready. Until then, he'd enjoy the few moments of happiness he stole from her: calling her Meg when she was too upset to notice;

teasing her until she teased back; being near enough to touch her.

The front door hinges squeaked as the latch rattled. Clay sprang halfway out of the tub as the door swung open. Momentarily he froze, then dropped into the water until the undulating waves his actions created lapped at his chin. "What are you doing here?"

Lucian closed the door. "I live here."

"I mean what are you doing back tonight?"

He shrugged. "No money. Nothing to do in Austin. Didn't see any point in staying when I at least have a bed here." He grabbed a chair, pulled it across the room, and sat beside the tub. "Didn't realize I'd been gone so long. Is it Saturday already?"

"I started working with the stone today. Got covered in dust. Felt the need for a bath."

"You're not gonna bathe every night, are you?"

"What business is it of yours?"

Lucian shrugged. "Just wondering. I ain't never heard of a man taking as many baths as you have since you got home. It's a wonder we got any water left in the well." He dipped his finger into the water. "Damn, that water's hot."

Clay slapped his hand away. "I like it hot."

184

"That could scald a man."

"Why don't you go on to bed and leave me in peace?"

Lucian stretched his long legs before him and crossed one foot over his ankle. "I'm not tired."

"Then why don't you leave so I can wash up and get out of the water?"

"I ain't stopping you from washing up. Besides, I've seen your bare ass." He flicked the water toward Clay's face. "When did you get so damn modest?"

"I didn't have any privacy while I was away. I'd like to have some now that I'm home."

Lucian scraped his boots across the floor, planted his feet firmly on either side of the chair, leaned forward, and braced his forearms on his thighs. "You never talk about what happened while you were away."

"There's nothing to talk about."

"What'd you do while you were gone? You didn't sit on a tree stump and whittle."

"No, I didn't whittle."

"You didn't fight."

"I didn't pick up a rifle and kill men if that's what you mean."

"So what'd you do?"

Clay sighed deeply. Since his return, no one had asked what he'd done during all the years he was away. So much had happened, and he wanted to forget most of it. "They held me prisoner at a fort for awhile, doing anything the officers considered 'hard labor' to fill up the days and nights."

Lucian studied the puncheon floor between his feet. "You think they'd have let you come home sooner if I'd written them that Ma and Pa had died?"

"Probably not."

Lucian glanced up, then dropped his gaze. "I thought about writing —"

"I don't think it would have made a difference."

Slowly, he nodded as though giving himself time to contemplate his next words. He spoke cautiously in a voice that reminded Clay of a child trying desperately to avoid a well-deserved whipping. "I wasn't afraid. I would have fought, but I had things to take care of here. I couldn't leave the twins, and I didn't have time to write —"

"You stayed where you were most needed. Nobody questions that."

Lucian bolted from the chair. "That's right. I'm not like you. I'm not a coward." He swung an arm through the air as though he were lost in a dark cave and couldn't find his way to the sunlight. "Hell, you don't even fight back. You could at least have hit me."

"I thought I did."

"Hell, no. You didn't lay a finger on me."

"Then why are you hurting?"

Plowing his hands through his hair, Lucian stormed toward the door. "Christ, I don't know. I'm sleeping in the barn tonight." He slammed the door behind him.

Clay groaned as the twins opened their bedroom door and peered out.

"What the heck's goin' on?" Josh asked.

"Lucian's home. Go on to bed."

The boys padded across the room to the bathtub. "Why the heck are you bathin'?" Josh asked. "It ain't Saturday."

"I felt dirty after working with stone all day."

"We feel dirty all the time. That ain't no reason to bathe. People bathe when they want to look nice for somebody. You sweet on Miz Warner?"

"Did you say you were feeling dirty?" Clay asked.

The boys exchanged glances.

"Because if you are, I'll put you in this water as soon as I get out."

"Nah, we ain't feelin' dirty. Not tonight."

"You feeling sleepy? Because if you're not, I'm gonna put you in this water anyway."

Both boys opened their mouths wide and yawned.

"Get on to bed," Clay said.

The boys trudged back to their room and closed the door.

Clay grabbed the lye soap and scrubbed briskly. Leaning to the side, he reached for the towel. The front door opened, and Clay slid back into the water.

"I came home to sleep in my bed," Lucian growled. "By God, I'm gonna sleep there."

He slammed the front door, then slammed the door to the bedroom he shared with the twins.

Clay waited until silence filled the house, the water turned cold, and the fire died in the hearth before he ventured from the tub.

Celebrating was a risky undertaking in this house.

Nine

It was torture to sit in silence as Clay worked.

A thousand questions surfaced within Meg's mind as she watched him chip away the stone, piece by piece. She held her curiosity and tongue in check because she knew if she interrupted his concentration, he could turn the chisel at an incorrect angle, hit it harder than he should, or slam the hammer where he shouldn't.

But it was torment to sit perfectly still while he moved with that steady, fluid rhythm that never faltered. His lean body emanated a controlled strength as he repeatedly swung the hammer and adjusted the angle of the chisel.

He'd rolled up his sleeves, exposing his forearms. Meg watched in fascination as his muscles tightened until his arms looked as hard as the stone into which he cut. His large hands held the chisel and hammer with a death grip.

Only his brown eyes were visible above the red bandanna. His gaze never strayed from the chisel. His thick, dark brows met above the bridge of his nose to form a deep furrow in his brow.

He ignored the sweat trickling along his temple. His attention was focused solely on the stone and the tools he wielded with the expertise of a marksman.

Just as early morning dew gathered on clover, beads of moisture coated the back of his neck. She imagined that it covered his throat as well, but the bandanna prevented her from seeing if it pooled within the hollow at the base of his throat. She watched as wet streaks appeared on his shirt.

Heat permeated the shed. Even with the windows open and a slight breeze blowing through, the air was still hot. Meg pressed her bandanna against her upper lip to blot the moisture that tickled her face.

Every day she sat in the sweltering warmth watching him work. Every day she expected him to remove his shirt and give his body some release from the baking heat. She had on occasion thought of suggesting it to him. She didn't want him to collapse.

But more, she wanted to see his entire body tense and carry the strength that was so evident in his hands and forearms. She had the impression that his craft had carefully molded his entire body over the years until it was as finely tempered as his tools.

His shirt hung loosely off his shoulders, his trousers were a shade too short. He'd grown taller and thinner since the day he'd stood on the outskirts of town watching his friends ride away. Yet his clothes could not conceal the intensity with which he worked. From the white hair at his temples to the worn soles on his boots, he gave himself up to what he was doing: he was merely an extension of his tools, using his mind, his imagination, and every muscle he possessed to take Nature's work of art and turn it into his own.

Sometimes, she thought she might feel a keen sense of loss when he finally did complete the statue. She wasn't altogether certain that the finished monument could possibly cause the swelling emotions that she felt as she watched the fabric of stone unfold.

Clay was a master at unraveling Nature's quilt, and Meg often wished the townspeople could see the making of the monument because its creation seemed as significant as its completion.

The clanging of metal against metal ceased. The furrows in his brow lessened, and he pulled down the bandanna. He took a deep breath and touched his fingers to the portion that remained after his latest efforts.

She never could tell if he was pleased with

the progress he was making. He stepped down from the stool and walked to the low table where he kept a bucket of water.

Every question Meg had wanted to ask escaped her mind. She jerked her bandanna down, jumped up from the chair, and clambered onto the stool so she could look closely at the silhouette. "This will be Kirk's head, won't it?" She swiveled her head around to meet Clay's gaze. "If you're going to make that silhouette the horse, you must intend for this one to be Kirk. Am I right?"

A smile of appreciation slowly eased onto his face. "Yes, ma'am."

She turned her attention back to the stone, and Clay watched her fingers touch the stone with reverence. He wondered how many times she'd touched her husband in the same manner.

"His head wasn't this big," she said.

"It won't be that big when I'm done. I like to leave plenty of stone to work with."

She nodded in understanding. Clay lifted the wooden lid off the bucket and brought the dipper to his mouth. He let the water trickle slowly down his throat.

With each passing day, he stopped working more often just so he could watch her hop up from that chair, climb onto that stool, and touch the stone.

He returned the dipper to the bucket and covered it so the dust and stone couldn't get into the water. Then he leaned one hip against the table and crossed his arms over his chest. He so enjoyed watching her excitement. He could hardly wait to begin working on the details.

"Are you going to start carving his face?" she asked.

"No, ma'am."

"Why not?"

"Because I want to wait until I have all the forms cut out."

She didn't like his answer. He could tell by the rapid tapping of her foot. Kirk had warned him about that. *When her foot starts tapping, I head for the hills till she cools down.*

He didn't think she was angry, just frustrated. In the past couple of months since he'd begun the project, he'd learned that his patience greatly exceeded hers.

She stopped tapping her foot and tilted her chin. "I don't see why you can't work on his face. You know this is his face. It would be nice to go ahead and have it finished."

Slowly, he shook his head. "I'll admit I'm tempted, but I know I need to get all the shadows shaped out before I start working on the details. When I'm working on the shapes, I have to keep the whole monument

193

in my head, the relationship of each piece to the other. I don't want to lose that feeling before I've got everything cut down."

"I don't think it would hurt to make one exception."

"When you're making a quilt, do you start quilting as soon as you've finished sewing that first block?"

She stuck out her tongue, and Clay chuckled. The action made her appear so young, almost like the girl she'd once been.

"Want to make yourself useful?" he asked.

Wrinkling her nose, she looked at the stone littering the ground. "You need the area cleaned?"

"No, ma'am. The twins haul the stone out every evening. I need you for something more important." Picking up his tools, he walked over to the stone. "I have to create the horse and rider from memory, but the woman . . ." He glanced up at her and smiled — "will be much easier to carve because I have a model. If you're willing."

Her face flushed. "You're going to start working on me? But you haven't finished the horse and rider."

"I told you I work on the whole monument. I begin at the top and work my way down. Right now, I'd like to get the size and shape of the woman just right and mark her distance from the rider."

"What would I have to do?"

"Stand where I can see you and pretend you're holding a flag."

She clambered down from the stool. "Where should I stand? Here?"

He stepped onto the stool and tilted his head. "Move a little to your right."

She took a step as small as a piece of chipped stone.

"A little more," he said.

She inched over, and Clay rubbed his eyes. They'd be here until evening. He climbed down from the stool and drew an *X* in the dirt near her feet. "Stand here."

He stepped onto the stool and looked at her. "Now, raise your arms so your hands are just below your chin."

"Shouldn't I raise them above my head? I was handing Kirk the flag. I didn't want him to have to reach far for it."

"I don't want anything to block the view of your face. It's more important than the flag."

Blushing, she began to fidget.

"You're gonna have to stand still."

She stopped squirming, but she looked as nervous as she had the first Sunday she played the organ in church.

"All right, I need you to turn just a little

to your left. A little more. A little more. Perfect."

"Is this so you can see my ears better?"

He pointed toward the silhouette she'd identified as Kirk's head. "It's so he can see your ears better."

She smiled. "Would it help if I brought some calico from home that I could drape down and pretend was the flag?"

"It might. If your arms get tired, you can lower them. I'm not doing anything right now that will be messed up if you move, but it's easier if you're still."

"I'm ready."

Clay had always liked the natural look of stone. Plain and unadorned, it possessed a simple beauty. At this moment, though, he wished he had material that could hold the blue of Meg's eyes and the rosy glow of her cheeks. No matter how hard he worked, he'd never be able to capture her beauty in the granite.

"You can blink," he said.

"Oh." She released a light laugh. "I don't even think I was breathing. I don't know why I'm so nervous."

"Maybe because I have to watch you so hard." He tapped the silhouette of Kirk's head. "Just look at this and ignore me."

"Ignoring you is what I do best."

She tilted her chin and focused her gaze on the stone. Clay took his own sweet time in *not* ignoring her. He allowed his gaze to travel freely from the top of her head to the tips of her toes. He studied every curve and line, and he wondered how he was going to concentrate on creating Meg's silhouette when he couldn't keep his mind focused on the task. It kept drifting away from her image cut in hard stone, and imagining her soft body against his palms instead.

If God had given him a hunk of flesh and told him to carve it into any shape he wanted, he would have carved it so it looked exactly like Meg — with her tiny waist and her narrow hips and those small . . . ears.

He wiped his sweating palms on his trousers.

"Are you going to chip the stone away?" she asked as she leveled her gaze on him.

He nodded. "I'm just adjusting my thinking since I don't have to rely on my memory."

"Your thinking seems to be a mite slower than your memory."

"I'll see if I can remedy that." He set the chisel against the stone and brought the hammer back.

"Oh my God!" Meg cried.

He jerked his attention from the stone and

stared at her. She skittered to the other side of the stool and pressed her back against the stone. "It's Tom Graham."

Clay glanced through the open door and saw a man walking toward the shed.

"I can't let him find me here," she whispered harshly.

He hopped off the stool and set his tools aside. "I'll see that he doesn't come inside." He strode past her, resisting the urge to shake her and ask what difference it would make if people discovered that she talked with him. Hell, she did more than talk with him. Sometimes, he suspected that she actually enjoyed his company. He was a damn fool.

He stepped outside and squinted against the sunlight. "Afternoon."

Tom Graham merely nodded. Slightly older than Lucian, he had a prominent Adam's apple that bobbed as he avoided Clay's gaze. The peach fuzz covering his chin looked as though it hadn't been shaved in a while. Holding a large piece of wood pressed against his side, he ran his finger over the raggedly curved edge that extended past his arm.

"Lucian is out in the fields," Clay informed him.

"Didn't come to see Lucian."

Clay shifted his stance. "Well, the twins aren't about."

"Didn't come to see them neither."

Clay was about to tell Tom the mule was in the field, but he narrowed his eyes and studied the wood more closely. Tom had cut it into the shape Clay disliked most. "What can I do for you then?" he asked quietly.

Tom wiped his eyes. "Our baby girl died. Dr. Martin said she was just born too soon. Weren't nothing he could do for her. Sally ain't stopped crying since. She wants a proper marker, but her pa says if I get one from you, he'll break it up. Hell of a thing when a man's hatred for another is greater than his love for his grandchild." He wiped his eyes again. "Anyway, I been trying to make a marker, but Sally wants special words on it, and I keep running out of room. Thought maybe you might show me how to cut the words in this here piece so I don't run out of room."

"What words were you wanting?" Clay asked.

With a shaking hand, Tom reached into his pocket and brought out a crumpled piece of paper. "She wants 'Here lies the sweetest bud of hope that ever to us was given.' " The young man's face reddened as he met Clay's gaze. "I don't know where Sally got that, but it's what she wants."

Clay nodded solemnly. "My pa carved some headstones before he died. I think there's one with those words on it."

Disbelief washed over Tom's face. "He did?" Then another somber truth hit him. "But it won't have our little girl's name on it. Sally named her, wants her name on the marker."

"I can have Lucian carve the name and dates."

"Didn't know Lucian did any carving."

"He can carve lettering."

Tom rubbed his scraggly chin. "Sally's father couldn't object to that, could he?"

"I wouldn't think so," Clay said.

"How much would I owe you?"

"My pa didn't take money for headstones he made for children. We won't either. When is she to be buried?"

"Tomorrow morning. In that little cemetery beside the church."

"I'll place the headstone on the church doorstep at dawn."

Tom extended the crumpled paper toward Clay. "Here's all the information Lucian will need."

Clay took the paper and turned to walk back into the shed.

"I'm obliged to you," Tom said. "You

didn't have to tell me about them headstones your pa made."

Clay looked over his shoulder. "Wouldn't make me much of a neighbor if I hadn't, now would it?" Stepping into the shed, he stuffed the paper into his pocket.

"Your father made some headstones before he died?" Meg asked.

He gave her an unappreciative stare as she cowered behind the door. "What were you doing? Listening?"

Meeting his gaze, she straightened her stance and angled her chin defiantly. "Well, I had to make certain he wasn't going to come in here."

"I told you I'd see to it he didn't come in here."

"And you're a man of your word."

"I'd die before I went back on my word."

Turning away from her, he walked to his table and fingered the smaller instruments. "I won't be working on the memorial anymore today so you can go on home."

"Where are the headstones? I don't recall seeing any."

"I've seen them and I'll find them," he said as he stared out the window.

"Everything is such a mess in here. Do you want me to help you find them?"

He spun around. "I want you to go home."

She tilted her nose. "Maybe I don't want to go home."

"You've got no choice. Your condition was that you'd look over my shoulder while I worked on the memorial. Now, I'm not working on it, and I'm not inviting you to stay."

"I didn't realize my company offended you."

His eyes captured hers and shackled them to the truth. "I'm not the one who was afraid Tom might see me here."

Her cheeks flamed red as she lowered her gaze. "You have to understand that the hatred people feel toward you goes beyond your shadow to touch those around you."

"I do understand that — only too well, as a matter of fact."

"Then you can't blame me for not wanting to be seen in your company."

He turned his attention back to the fields beyond the window. "No, I don't blame you."

"Do you want me to let Lucian know you need him?"

"No, I'll take care of it."

"They'll need me to play the organ at the memorial service. You can work on the monument tomorrow without me. I'll try to stop by in the evening to check on your progress."

"You do that, Mrs. Warner."

His father never took money for children's markers. Meg shook her head. Little wonder they still lived in a house made of rough hewn logs while other folks had bought lumber and rebuilt their homes once the sawmill had opened.

She stared past the wooden buffalo grass to the darkening sky. "A storm's rolling in," she said quietly. "He said it always rains when someone dies. I never noticed. He notices everything."

"We really need to give Clayton a name," Mama Warner said as she rocked slowly in her chair. "It takes this old brain of mine too dadgum long to figure out who you're talking about sometimes."

Sighing, Meg turned away from the window. "Sally Graham's baby died."

Mama Warner ceased her rocking. "A sad thing to lose a child. Lost four myself. You'd think it wouldn't hurt losing a little one but the pain is as great as if they'd been with you all your life. You can't remember what it was like before they touched your heart, and you can never forget them."

Meg walked across the room, knelt, and took the aged hands into her own. "Do you want to hear something amazingly wonderful?" She smiled. "Before he died, his father carved a headstone for a child and inscribed the exact words on it that Sally wanted for her daughter. Can you believe that?"

Mama Warner worked her hand free of Meg's grasp and cradled Meg's chin within her palm. "Do you believe it, child?"

"Of course."

The older woman smiled. "Then that's all that matters."

The knowledge reflected in Mama Warner's eyes drove Meg to ride through the moonless night with the rain pelting her back. She drew her mare to a halt near the Holland homestead.

Darkness encased the house. She'd expected it to look that way, as though everyone inside were sleeping.

Markers weren't made in the house.

She guided her mare toward the shed. Someone had lowered the shutters against the force of the wind and rain. The door was partially open, spilling pale light into the night.

Meg dismounted beneath a tree to give her horse some protection from the rain. She sloshed through the growing puddles until she reached the shed. Standing in the doorway with the rain dripping off the brim of

Kirk's hat, she learned what Mama Warner had already surmised.

Clay's father hadn't made any headstones before he died.

Hunched over so he was almost parallel with the tablet of stone, Clay sat on a stool at his low worktable.

As though she were a wraith, Meg moved silently toward him. The thunder rumbled. Clay stilled momentarily, then continued with his task.

With the windows closed, the room was stifling hot. No breeze blew through to cool him. The sweat drenched the back of his shirt, and he wiped his brow. He worked by the flame of a solitary lantern.

Halting at the edge of the shadows, Meg watched as he used the small chisel and hammer to create an abundance of delicate detailing on the tiny headstone. With a gentle breath, he blew the dust of his labors away from each letter and design as he completed it.

An eternity seemed to pass before he set his tools aside, rolled his shoulders, and bowed his head.

"It's beautiful," Meg said quietly.

"Christ!" He leapt off the stool and stared at her. "How long have you been here?"

"Long enough to know Lucian doesn't do

lettering." She trailed her trembling fingers over the perfectly carved script. "You created a beautiful headstone for a child, and you're giving the credit to your father and brother."

"Then why don't you tell everyone tomorrow so they can crush it into dust, and Tom's wife can have something else to grieve over?"

He stepped away from her. Without thinking, she grabbed his arm. He stopped, but didn't look at her. "Do you truly believe they'd destroy a child's headstone if they knew you made it?"

"Yes, ma'am."

The uncompromising briskness in his voice caused her to release her hold on him. He walked across the room to a corner where he kept an assortment of odds and ends. He picked up a blanket and ripped it in two. He brought one piece back to the table and wrapped it around the headstone with the same gentleness that a person may have used to wrap a blanket around an infant.

Meg walked to the hunk of granite and placed her hand on the rough stone. She could almost see Kirk in the shadows, could hear the neigh of his horse, his promises, and his courageous yell. "Do you think they'll destroy this monument?" she asked.

"No, ma'am."

Over her shoulder, she watched him

smooth out the wrinkles in the blanket as though it mattered how he delivered the marker to the church. "Why don't you think they'll destroy this monument?"

"Because we're not going to tell them I made it."

She stepped away from the granite. "What?"

He turned from his task and met her gaze. "I haven't thought through the particulars yet, but we'll find a way to get it to town without anybody knowing. You can tell folks you had some fellow back east make it."

"You're not going to put your name on the backside?"

"I thought we'd agreed this memorial would reflect the names of those who died fighting for their convictions."

"We did."

"Well, now I didn't die, did I?"

"And you didn't fight either," she reminded him.

"You think the only battles fought are done so with rifles, and the only wounds that kill draw blood. You think courage is loud, boisterous, and proud. Mrs. Warner, I don't think you have a clue as to what this memorial truly represents."

Ten

Sitting on the porch swing, Meg watched clouds drift across the moon as her thoughts slowly wandered to Clay.

With his gaze always riveted on the granite stone that was slowly materializing into three distinct shapes, he worked from dawn until dusk with the steady determination of a man who wanted to rid himself of a despised burden. His rare smiles and occasional teasing no longer surfaced. He seldom stopped chiseling to rest, and when he did, he walked out of the shed.

Meg suspected he dunked his head in a bucket of water drawn from the well because he always returned with water dripping from his hair and his shirt collar soaked as though it alone had stood in a storm.

Each day, he acknowledged her presence with a "Morning" when she walked into the shed. At the end of the day, he stepped off the stool, walked to his low table, set his tools down, stared out the window, and spoke to her once more. "I'm done for the day."

Meg loathed the days that dragged by more than she hated the days when she'd waited in dread for news of Kirk. She felt as though she resided in a prison, a prison that she herself had built, using hatred for bricks and revenge for mortar. She had wanted to punish Clay, but she too ended up suffering.

She didn't want to sit in that shed where silent voices loomed and the steady clinking of hammer to chisel echoed, but she couldn't stay away.

Every day, his hands revealed more of the shadows. The muscles along his neck, back, and arms strained with his efforts. Then they gradually relaxed, and he touched the stone as though to apologize for his harsh treatment and to promise it would all be worth it.

He hit the stone with enough force to send the sound of a crack ricocheting around the shed. Then he glided his palm over the granite creating a rasping whisper.

The whisper stayed with her long after she left the shed. It haunted her dreams, along with the memory of his hands creating mesmerizing shapes from simple stone.

Sometimes, she felt an apology rise in her throat, and she'd clamp her lips to keep them from filling the shed with remorse and regret. She wasn't the one who had hurt him. It was his cowardice and his failure to recognize it that caused his pain. He thought she should stand by his side even though he had been unwilling to stand beside Kirk.

She'd laugh at the irony if it didn't hurt so badly.

She watched a silhouette move through the night.

"What are you doing out here, Meg?" Daniel asked as he stepped onto the porch.

"Just thinking. Where have you been?"

Shrugging, he combed his fingers through his dark hair and dropped to the porch, pressing his back against a beam. "Me and Sam Johnson had some talking to do. Where's Pa?"

"He fell asleep in the chair."

"I reckon that's better than the barn."

"I suppose." She sighed. "I guess we all grieve in our own way."

"I want to do more than grieve, Meg. I want to do something for my brothers. I should have gone with them. I could have been their drummer boy."

"Drummer boys died, too, Daniel. Then who'd help build the Wrights a barn tomorrow?"

He gave her a wry smile in the darkness. "You think Stick would approve of Caroline marrying John?"

Everyone called Caroline's first husband Stick because he'd been so tall and thin. They teased him about it, claiming that as long as he marched into battle sideways, the bullets would whiz right past him. But the bullets hadn't missed him.

John Wright had spent two years in a Union prison. In a tattered gray uniform, he had been heading home to a little fork in the road west of Cedar Grove. Weary from his journey, he stopped beneath the shade of a tree on Caroline's property. He never reached the fork in the road.

He had married Caroline two weeks ago, and now the community had a reason to celebrate and a barn to raise.

Meg held fond recollections of Stick, memories she'd never shared with Kirk. "Yes, I think he would have approved."

Shortly after dawn swept the dew from the ground, Meg arrived at the Wright homestead with her father and brother. Helen Barton, who took charge of anything that needed to be taken charge of, assigned Meg the momentous chore of keeping the children away from the desserts.

Having risen long before dawn to make many of the pies and cobblers that now adorned the table, Meg should have welcomed a task that required nothing more of her than to wave tiny, dirty fingers away from cakes and cookies.

Instead, she discovered that the chore left her hands with little to do and her mind with less than that. She tried to enjoy the gentle breeze wafting among the trees surrounding Caroline's house, but then she would find herself imagining that same breeze blowing through three large windows of a shed. She wondered if it had stirred Clay's hair before it traveled to work her own strands free from their netting.

She'd captured her hair in a delicate chignon instead of wrapping it into a tight bun. She wasn't accustomed to the weight of her hair brushing along her neck and shoulders.

The hammers echoed in the distance as the men worked to build the barn, and she compared the staccato beat to the steady rhythm Clay used to hammer the stone. She knew she should enjoy the sound of men working together on a common project, but she longed to hear the solitary strains that one man produced as he worked alone, expecting no praise for his efforts.

She glanced at the long table of desserts. Watching desserts held no appeal. She'd rather watch Clay.

Yesterday, when she told him she planned

to spend the day at the Wrights' farm, he merely nodded and shoved his hands into his pockets. They both knew the need for willing hands to build a barn did not include his.

She wondered if he had begun cutting the stone at dawn — or had he waited? Kirk's shoulders were a visible silhouette in the stone now. She wondered if he'd work down to Kirk's waist first or carve her shoulders.

The desserts weren't going anywhere. She could sneak away for a few hours, and no one would notice. She'd just peek inside the shed and see how much progress he'd made —

"Hello, Meg," a solemn male voice said, vibrating behind her.

Spinning around, she stared at Kirk, her heart thumping so loudly she no longer heard the distant hammers. He had the same blond hair, but deep crevices resembling fur-rowed fields touched the corners of his blue eyes. He appeared much older and more mature. His beard, darker than his hair, was thick. Not at all the way she'd envisioned it.

"I don't know if you remember me," he said. "I'm Kirk's cousin, Robert."

She felt her breath rush out and pressed her hand to her throat. "Of course. We met at the wedding." Against her will, her gaze flitted to his empty sleeve.

"Left my arm at Shiloh," he said with a sad smile that implored her not to pity him.

With tears in her eyes, she tilted her chin and returned his smile. "But you're safe now, and that's all that matters." She wrapped her arms around his neck and felt his arm go around her waist. "You reminded me of Kirk," she whispered in a raw voice.

"I'm sorry he didn't come home."

Releasing her hold, she wiped away her tears. "So many didn't. None of the young men who went with Kirk returned. It's left so many fathers without sons, wives without husbands, and children without fathers. We're extremely grateful for those who did come back."

"Yeah, well, nothin's the same. That's for damn sure." He blushed. "Pardon my language."

"How's your farm? It was somewhere north of Austin, wasn't it?"

"It was, but I didn't have the money to pay the taxes on it, so I had to give it up. Came here to help my uncle with his farm."

"Are you living with Kirk's parents then?"

"With that mean-spirited mother of Kirk's? No, ma'am. I'd rather be in a Union prison than inside the walls of their house when she gets a bee in her bonnet. I'm living with Mama Warner."

"I visited her recently. She didn't tell me you were there."

"I've only been here a few days, and she didn't know I was coming until I showed up on her doorstep. She told me you frequently stop by. I was looking for you."

He uttered his words with such sincerity that Meg almost wept.

"I hope my being there won't stop you from coming by to see Mama Warner," he said. "She enjoys your company."

Meg knew Mama Warner enjoyed any company since her legs had grown weak and she was confined to her house. "Of course I'll continue to visit. I love her dearly. She seems to understand people so well."

"Reckon that's because she's met such an odd assortment during her life. I wasn't going to come here today. Didn't figure a man with one arm could do much to help build a barn, but then she did some low talking —"

"Low talking?" she asked.

He spread his lips in a smile so similar to Kirk's that Meg wanted to touch her fingers to each corner of his mouth.

"Yeah, when she wants to impart some wisdom on you to ponder, she talks low so you have to strain to hear her. Guess she figures that way you're paying attention."

"It must work. You're here."

"Yeah, but I haven't figured out what I can do to help."

"Well, if you're up to the excitement, you can help me watch the desserts."

He laughed, and Meg realized she hadn't heard a man laugh since the day she saw Clay playing with the twins in the river. The pounding of rushing feet gained Meg's attention.

Breathless, Helen stopped and grabbed Meg's arm for support. "I can't believe *he* came."

Meg didn't have to ask who he was. The red tinge covering Helen's face and the fire in her blue eyes spoke of a hatred that stretched as far as her husband had journeyed. Meg followed Helen's gaze and watched Clay climb down from the wagon as the twins clambered out of the back.

"Lucian didn't come?" Meg asked.

"He's been here since dawn. He helped Taffy's father bring the lumber from the mill."

Briefly, Meg wondered if Lucian was sweet on Stick's younger sister. She remembered the summer long ago when Mary Lang had suddenly grown as tall as her brother and taller than any of the boys her age. Teasingly, Lucian said she looked as though she'd been stretched out like taffy. Soon everyone was calling her Taffy.

Helen huffed and stomped the ground as though she could cause the earth to open up and swallow Clay whole. "I just can't believe *he* had the nerve to come here."

"Maybe he just wanted to help."

"We can do without his help, thank you very much."

Meg watched Clay walk toward the barn. The men had already raised the frame. The hammering stopped, and a heavy silence hovered over the crowd. She wished he hadn't come, but her reasons were far re-moved from Helen's or anyone else's.

She didn't want him to get hurt.

Clay discovered that for some ungodly rea-son it had been easier walking to his own execution than walking toward the men gathered beside the unfinished barn. He could feel the men glaring at him. He wished he had left the twins at home. He didn't want them to see the beating he figured he was about to receive. He heard someone bellow, "This is neither the time nor the place!" He thought the commanding voice belonged to Kirk's father. Slowly the men turned their backs on Clay and walked away. Their action should have lessened his anxiety, but it didn't. By the time he reached the side of the barn, Lucian was the only one who remained, and the hatred that his brother directed his way was palpable.

"What the hell are you doing here?" Lucian asked.

"I heard strong backs were needed. I've got a strong back."

"Strong enough to support a yellow streak, but that's not exactly what we need here."

"The Wrights asked the community to help them build a barn, and I'm part of the community."

"But we don't want you."

Clay met his brother's hard glare. How simple it would be to turn around and go home. "I'm going to help build the barn."

"And what's that gonna prove?"

"To you, probably nothing. To me, everything."

Lucian shook his head. "Stay if you want, but don't expect me to stand by your side." Turning on his heel, he walked away.

Clay gazed down on the twins' anxious faces. He gave them a smile that he figured probably looked as hollow as he felt. "Well, reckon this is our side to finish up."

"All by ourselves?" Joe asked.

"Reckon so."

"Lucian ain't even gonna help us?"

"Reckon not."

"You ever wonder if maybe Lucian ain't family?" Josh asked. "I'm thinkin' maybe somebody left him on the doorstep 'cuz he was so ornery they didn't want to put up with him."

"I thought all babies was left on the doorstep," Joe said.

"Heck fire, no. There's some kinda magical bird that drops babies down the chimney. Ain't that so, Clay?"

Clay had little doubt that Joe believed babies were left on the doorstep, but he was certain that Josh, with his challenging grin, knew the truth. "I think we'd best see to getting our side of the barn finished."

As the boys walked toward the pile of lumber, Clay heard Joe ask what the bird looked like. Josh stopped walking and waved his arms, probably describing in great detail every feather of this imaginary bird. Clay sighed. He'd no doubt just lost his helpers.

"Howdy, Miz Warner."

Meg gazed at the identical faces, knowing Clay could tell them apart, wondering how he did so. "Hello."

With their hands stuffed behind the bibs on their coveralls, the boys rocked back on their heels. "Fine spread you laid out here," one twin said. "Clay said we could look, but we wasn't to ask for nothin'. So we're just lookin'."

Smiling, Meg teased, "Well, the vegetables are on that table over there."

"Yes, ma'am, but me and Joe like to look at the cakes and pies. Been a powerful long time since we ate a piece of cake or pie. 'Course, we ain't askin'. We're just lookin'."

Helen flicked a cloth over the table to chase the flies away. She'd run Robert off just as easily so she and Meg could gossip as they had when they were young girls trying to decide at whom they should direct their warmest smiles. Meg was grateful Helen had avoided talking further about Clay's arrival. Instead, they'd discussed the apparent blossoming courtship between Dr. Martin and Widow Prudence.

Smiling, Helen leaned across the table. "Would you boys like a piece of cake?"

"Obliged, ma'am," Joe said as he reached for a piece of cake smothered in chocolate icing.

"Can we take a piece to Clay?" Josh asked.

The smile eased off Helen's face. "No, I don't think that would be appropriate."

Josh nodded with an understanding that belied his years. "Then I reckon we'll pass on the offer."

Joe froze, the cake nearly touching his lips.

He slid his gaze over to his brother. "Surely does smell good."

Josh laid his hand on his brother's shoulder. "You gotta stick with family."

"Lucian don't."

"I done told you somebody left Lucian on the doorstep. He ain't really family. You eat that cake, and I'll start thinkin' somebody left you on the doorstep, too."

Slowly, Joe set the cake on the table. With woeful eyes, he looked at Meg. " 'Preciate the offer but reckon I'd best not." The boys shuffled away from the table.

"That's pitiful," Helen said.

"It wouldn't have hurt to let them have an extra piece."

Helen's eyes nearly popped out of her head. "It would have been like giving a peace offering, and I'm not about to forgive that man for what he didn't do. Not now, not ever."

"There was a time when you saved your warmest smiles for him."

Helen's face burned a deep crimson. "Thank God, he was too shy to notice. I can't imagine anything more humiliating than having that man for a husband." She visibly shuddered. "It makes me ill just to think about all the times I smiled at him."

"Still, it seems a shame for his brothers to

suffer for something they had no control over." Meg glanced at the abundance of food and hoped her next words didn't betray her. "I suppose they're fortunate your father extends them credit at the mercantile."

Helen looked at Meg as though she had no more sense than the Hollands' mule. "He doesn't extend them credit. My father told him if he ever set foot in the mercantile, he'd shoot him as a thief. Said he robbed this town of its honor."

"That hardly seems fair to Lucian and the twins," Meg said.

"Then they should run him off."

"I think he owns the farm. What can they do? And those twins look so thin."

Helen held up a finger. "Don't do that. Don't make me feel guilty about the decision my father made."

"I don't want you to feel guilty, but surely your father could work out an arrangement with Lucian that will give them credit as long as his older brother doesn't partake of the offerings."

"Why do you care?" Helen asked.

"Because they're children, and if I had been blessed with children, it would break my heart to think they were going to bed hungry."

Helen picked up a ginger cookie and took

a bite. "I'll think on it."

"The twins have such big brown eyes —"

"All right. I'll talk to him. He just hates Clay—" She stopped herself with a groan. Not saying Clay's name was a game they began when the war started because women weren't supposed to care about politics or talk about war. "He just hates him so much, he made his decision without thinking how it would affect the others."

"I'm sure Lucian would be agreeable to an arrangement. He seems to dislike his brother as much as we do."

"I can't say I blame him." Helen shoved the rest of the cookie into her mouth. "The men have stopped working. Guess we'd best see to filling their plates."

Looking toward the barn, Meg watched the men wander toward the makeshift tables, which had been set within the shade of the trees to provide some respite from the heat. They'd eat. Then they'd nap or go to the river, waiting for the day's heat to pass. They'd finish the barn in the late afternoon.

From the corner of her eye, she watched Clay walk to his wagon, where he'd find no shade.

Isolated.

Alone.

How simple it would be to prepare him a

plate and walk to the wagon to give it to him.

How difficult to step into his world of loneliness.

Clay liked bluebonnets because they were well suited to carving. Any thick twig, with the gentle application of his knife, could become the delicate stalk with the dainty petals.

"Damned hot today!" Dr. Martin barked.

Shooting off the back of the wagon, Clay pressed his hand to his chest, trying to calm the rapid thudding of his heart.

"Where were you, boy?" Dr. Martin asked.

Clay grinned. "Lost in my thoughts, I guess." He held out his hand. "Thanks for walking over."

Dr. Martin shook his hand before dropping onto the back of the wagon. Clay sat beside him. "People aren't gonna like that you're over here talking to me."

Dr. Martin withdrew an apple from his pocket and held it toward Clay. "You keep people well, they don't mind what you do, and I've kept most of these people well."

Clay took the apple and brought it to his nose, inhaling deeply. So sweet. He and the twins had already eaten the food they'd brought from home, but their meal hadn't included anything this sweet. With his carving knife, he cut the apple in two. "Joe! Josh!"

The boys stopped their game of leapfrog and rushed over. "Dr. Martin brought you an apple."

Grins filled their faces as they took the offering. "Thanks, Dr. Martin," they said before running off.

"They're good boys," Dr. Martin said.

"Yes, sir, they are."

"What were you thinking before I disturbed you?"

Picking up the small branch, Clay started whittling again. "Trying to figure out when walking away isn't running."

"Thinking of heading home before the barn's finished?"

Clay peered over at the doctor. "No, sir. Thinking of heading a little farther than that."

"Away from Cedar Grove?"

"Yes, sir. I'm beginning to see that Lucian was right. I didn't realize the hatred ran so deep. I don't like it touching the twins. It's one thing for people to avoid me. I made my choice and was willing to accept the consequences. My brothers shouldn't have to suffer because of it."

Dr. Martin sighed. "I never cottoned to hatred, never understood the way it flowed

225

or how to dam it up."

Clay held out the flower he finished whittling. "You can give this to your girl."

"My girl?" Dr. Martin turned as red as a sunset. "Is it that obvious?"

Lifting his eyebrows, Clay nodded and smiled. He'd noticed Dr. Martin trailing after Widow Prudence most of the morning.

Dr. Martin removed his hat and wiped his balding pate. "I'm set in my ways, never figured to take a wife, but Pru . . . well, she's got three boys, and that oldest one needs a firm hand applied to his backside. And it's gonna take more than one application."

"I'm happy for you, Doc."

Dr. Martin shoved his hat over his brow and slid off the back of the wagon. "Well, I gotta ask her first. Haven't figured out how to do that yet."

"By God, we could still hang him. Plenty of strong trees around here," Thomas Crawford said.

Meg dropped the ladle into the pot of beans she held and stared at her father as he plowed his hands through hair that had once been as black as hers and was now as white as newly fallen snow. Women were heaping portions of food onto the men's plates, but the men didn't appear to notice.

The younger men were looking at her father. The older men had turned their attention to Kirk's father. He sat at the end of the table, opposite Meg's father. As the eldest son of one of founding fathers, Mr. Warner and his opinion were held in the highest esteem. His blond hair had lightened over the years, but his blue eyes and the intensity of his gaze had yet to fade.

"Four years ago we all agreed —" he began.

Meg's father slammed his hand onto the table. "We agreed to wait and see what the army would do. Well, we've seen what the army did — nothing. I say we hang him now."

Mr. Warner shook his head. "I gave my son my word that I'd be no part of lynching. I'm not going back on my word now."

Meg felt her knees quake with the realization that her father and the other men had planned to hang Clay four years ago. No one had told her then what they'd planned. Did men think that war and everything about it was their domain alone? She wondered at all the things Kirk might not have told her.

Daniel shrugged shoulders that had begun to broaden as his voice had started growing deeper. "If you don't feel right about hanging him, then we could just shoot him."

227

Daniel jumped to his feet yelling, "God, Meg, you're supposed to put the beans on my plate not in my lap!"

"I'm sorry. You're just growing so much I can hardly see around you," she lied, wishing she could change the course of the conversation.

Scowling, he sat down again, then leaned forward, addressing the man sitting across from him. "What do you think, Robert? You're a war hero."

Briefly, Robert lifted his gaze to Meg before studying the food on his plate. "I'm hardly a war hero."

"But you fought. You gotta have some feelings on this matter. Don't it curdle your gut to know we got a coward living among us?"

Robert glanced at the faces surrounding him. "Most Texans ignored the conscript laws —"

Meg's father slapped his broad palm on the table. "By God, we're not talking about the conscript laws. I was against the damn things myself. You don't tell a Texan he has to fight." He slapped his hand on the table again. "You just tell him where the battle's to be fought, and by God, he goes. Our sons didn't wait for no law to come around telling them they had to go. Soon as the call to arms

228

sounded, they enlisted. All but that one out there!" He shook his fist in the air. "Our sons were men of honor, and they paid the ultimate price. It don't sit well with me at all to see that one still breathing."

The men had invited Lucian to sit with them, but he was staring at his food, shifting his backside on the bench. He clenched his jaw so tightly that Meg didn't think he'd be able to eat if he tried.

"What do you think, John?" Meg's father asked. "This is your land now that you're married to Caroline."

John shook his head. "I saw enough men die in prison to last me a lifetime. I don't want to see blood shed on my land."

"It seems to me," Robert said quietly, "that you've lost enough men. I don't see that you'll gain anything by losing one more."

"Peace of mind," Meg's father said as he shoved his plate forward. "By God, it'd give me peace of mind."

"Anyway, I thought when the army came for Holland, he went with them," Robert said.

"He went, but he didn't fight. He ain't even ashamed of that fact," Meg's father said. "He'll tell you if you ask him."

"Had a fellow in my outfit that didn't want to fight," Robert said. "They branded him a deserter and made him sit on the edge of his coffin. Then they shot him."

"I could build a coffin," Daniel said.

Meg dropped the pot on the table and beans splattered every man in the vicinity. With hands on her hips, she tapped her foot and glared at their slack-jawed expressions. "I thought today was supposed to help John and Caroline celebrate a new beginning. If I'd known you were going to spend the day mourning the past, I'd have stayed home."

She trudged toward the dessert table. "Joshua and Joseph Holland! I need you!"

She reached the table, picked up three spoons, and buried the round ends in one of her apple cobblers.

Gulping for air, the twins stopped short of ramming into her side. Their brows were creased with concern. "What do you need, Miz Warner?" they asked at once.

"I need you to eat this cobbler," she said as she handed the bowl to them. "And you can share it with anyone you want to."

"Even Clay?" one twin asked.

"Anyone," she repeated with a brisk nod.

"Thank you, Miz Warner," they said before walking away, holding the bowl between them, and taking such small steps that she wasn't certain they'd reach their destination before nightfall.

She crossed her arms beneath her breasts. It wasn't much. It probably wasn't enough. Watching as the twins approached the large wagon where a man sat alone, she suddenly felt as though nothing would ever be enough.

Meg watched Helen pour water over the dirt. Her four-year-old daughter, Melissa, plopped on the ground.

"Give her a mud puddle, and she's happy," Helen said as she sat beside Meg and Sally Graham beneath the shade of the tree.

"Dr. Martin said there's no reason Tom and I can't have lots of children," Sally said quietly.

Reassuringly, Meg took her hand. "I'm sure you'll have more children."

Sally blushed. "Tom is so good to me. I don't know what I'd do without him. I don't know how all you widows survived. You're only a little older than me, but you all lost your husbands."

Tom appeared with a glass in his hand and knelt beside her chair. "Here you are, Sally, honey. I brought you some lemonade."

Tom's tender expression caused the loneliness to surround Meg. Only a few years difference in ages had carved out different lives for the women in the area. While Daniel bemoaned the fact that he'd been born too late, she wished she and Kirk had not been born quite so soon.

As though her thoughts conjured him, Daniel strode toward them. "Tom!" he yelled.

With fire raging in his blue eyes, he glanced briefly at Meg before turning his attention to Tom. "Holland took the twins to the river. While he's gone, some of us are gonna take down the boards he nailed up. You wanna help?"

"Why are you gonna do that?" Tom asked.

"So he'll know he's not wanted and he'll leave."

"I think he probably figured out he wasn't wanted when we all walked away this morning. He's not stupid."

"No, but he's a yellow-bellied coward. Hell, Tom, you enlisted as soon as you were old enough."

"Yeah, but my regiment never left the state. We just sat at the Louisiana border waiting for the Yankees to come. They never did. I never even fired my rifle at a man."

"That ain't the point," Daniel said. "The point is you were willing to do your part. He wasn't."

"Tom's right, Daniel," Meg said. "Just let him finish his side, and he'll go home."

"Damn it, Meg, I think you're getting soft. Are you forgetting it was your husband and our brothers he didn't stand by? I can't believe you gave him your cobbler."

"I didn't give it to him. I gave it to his brothers."

"Knowing full well they'd share it with him. I told you last night I wanted to do something to preserve the memory of my brothers. Well, this is it. You coming, Tom?"

"Nope, I won't help him, but I'm not gonna undo his work."

"Then we'll do it without you."

Meg watched her brother storm back toward the barn. She knew he harbored feelings of guilt because he hadn't been old enough to enlist alongside his brothers, but until today she hadn't realized the full extent of her family's hatred. If they discovered she'd spent time with Clay . . .

She closed her eyes, not wanting to think about what they might do. This land had too many trees growing on it.

Someone took her hand. Opening her eyes, she smiled at Robert as he knelt beside her.

"I wanted to ask a favor of you," he said. "I feel pretty useless now that the desserts are gone, and I no longer have to stand guard over them. It occurred to me that if I had someone to hold the nail, I could hammer it into place. I was wondering if you'd be willing to be that someone."

Eleven

"Gawd Almighty!" Josh shrieked. "What happened to our wall?"

Clay came to a dead stop as though he'd just slammed against the wall he had erected earlier that morning. The side of the barn they'd been walking toward looked as though no one had touched it all day.

He jerked off his hat and plowed his fingers through his hair. Taking the twins to the river so they could cool off hadn't been such a good idea after all.

"We gonna go home now?" Joe asked.

Clay settled his hat on his head and narrowed his eyes. "Nope. We're gonna finish our wall."

Both boys released baleful sighs.

"You can work with Lucian if you want to," Clay said.

"Nah, we'll work with you," Josh said.

"In that case —" Clay knelt and placed a hand on each boy's shoulder. "Remember that rule we have about no swearing until you're sixteen?"

The twins exchanged suspicious glances

and nodded.

"Today's an exception. Until the sun sets, you can say any swearword you want as often as you want."

"We can?" Josh asked, excitement at the prospect reflected in his eyes.

"Yep."

"But we only know one," Joe said.

"Stay by my side," Clay said, "and I'll teach you a few more."

Meg looked through the opening in the frame at what had once been a partially completed opposite wall. She gazed beyond it to where Clay and the twins had come to an abrupt halt. Around her, the hammers fell into silence as everyone waited to see how Clay would react.

The litany of *go home* raced through her mind. He had but to turn and walk to his wagon. *Take the twins home,* she thought. *Please take the twins home.*

He knelt in the field. The next thing she knew the twins were whooping, hollering, and running toward the wall that was little more than air.

With a broad smile, Clay swaggered to the pile of fresh lumber, hefted a board, and carried it to the frame where the twins waited.

Of all the things Clay could have done, the last thing she'd expected him to do was smile. He drove the first nail into the board with such force that Meg felt the frame vibrate where her fingers were touching it.

Tom started whistling and put his hammer into action. One by one, other hammers took up the beat.

"Well, I'll be damned," Robert said quietly.

"I suppose we could build that wall," Meg said, tilting her head toward the wall where Clay worked.

Robert gave her a sad smile. "I'd rather be at Shiloh again than have this town's hatred directed my way. I have hopes of settling here, Meg, and having a family. I don't want my children playing alone."

An unspoken hope touched his eyes, and Meg knew he wanted his family to include her. He was young, strong, and resembled Kirk to such a great degree that she wanted to hold his promise in her heart.

He tapped the board he'd set against the frame. "Want to see if we work well together?"

Nodding, Meg knelt and placed her palm flat against the board to keep it in place. Then she positioned the nail. Turning her head slightly, she saw Clay crouching on the other side of the barn. His hat brim shaded his eyes, but she could feel his penetrating gaze riveted on her. She wanted to tell him she wasn't responsible for what they had done to his side of the barn. She wanted to tell him —

She cried out as a sharp pain shot through her hand and raced up her arm. She saw Clay straighten and step through the opening in the frame. She closed her eyes, willing him not to come to her. If anyone knew how to handle a thumb that had been hit with a hammer, it would be Clay, but she couldn't explain to the people surrounding her why she wanted Clay's help instead of theirs. She couldn't even explain it to herself.

She opened her eyes and sighed with relief. Clay had returned to his side of the barn. She could see his knee jutting beyond the board he'd nailed in place. She knew he was squatting down, his back against the board, his head undoubtedly bowed as he fought not coming to help her. How had she come to know him so well in such a short time?

"Meg, I'm so sorry," Robert stammered. "I thought I was watching."

Cradling her hand, Meg forced a smile she didn't feel. "It's all right. It doesn't hurt that badly."

"Let's find Dr. Martin and make sure I

didn't break anything." He slipped his hand beneath her elbow and helped her rise to her feet.

"I'm sure nothing's broken," she said, although she wasn't certain at all.

"Anyone seen Dr. Martin?" Robert asked as they neared the house.

"Last I saw him, he was on the back porch," Helen said. Robert guided Meg around the corner of the house. Prudence was stomping the earth while Dr. Martin stared at her in bewilderment.

"Why would I want something he made?" she cried. She pressed her finger against Dr. Martin's chest. "I just wanted to die of embarrassment when I saw you talking to that coward."

"I talked to a lot of men today, Pru. I don't recall talking to any coward."

"That Clayton Holland. You went right over to his wagon —"

"If you see a coward when you look at that young man, then you stop by my office tomorrow, and I'll fit you with a new pair of spectacles. I wouldn't weather the hatred of the people in this town even if they promised to make me a rich man, and they're giving him a hell of a lot less than that."

She pushed her spectacles up the bridge of her nose and thrust up her chin. "You

239

needn't bother to call on me any longer. I won't be answering your knock."

She strutted away like an enraged hen. Dr. Martin picked up a mangled twig. "I guess there's no point in asking her to marry me now."

"Give her a couple of days," Meg said. "Everyone seems to have short tempers today."

"It sure ain't like the old days. When we gathered, we had a good time and were glad to see one another." He smiled lightheartedly and slipped the twig into his coat pocket. "Were you looking for me?"

"Yeah, Doc. I slammed a hammer against Meg's hand," Robert said.

"Now, why did you do that?" Dr. Martin asked as he gently took Meg's hand and examined it.

"I was stupid enough to think I could help build the barn if I had someone hold the nails for me."

"That doesn't sound so stupid to me, but I'll confess I can think of things I'd rather do with a pretty girl than build a barn." He winked at Meg. "You're gonna have a little bit of bruising, but it shouldn't stop you from dancing tonight."

As twilight neared, Clay heard the hammers fall one by one into silence. He didn't need to look to know that he was being left to put the final boards into place. He'd had the unrealistic hope that maybe he'd finish first. He'd certainly had the incentive. Finish up his side and be gone, but he wouldn't leave before he finished what he'd started. Even if it took him past midnight.

He set the board against the frame. As he had most of the afternoon, he turned slightly, pressed his backside against the board, reached down, and tapped the first nail into position. Straightening, he moved the board a fraction of an inch, making certain it was level with the other boards. Out of the corner of his eye, he saw Lucian striding toward him.

"At the pace you're working, you'll be here till midnight," Lucian said just before he slammed his hammer against the nail Clay had used to set the board into place.

Both men heard the wood split and watched as a tiny fissure raced up the center of the board. Raising a brow, Clay looked at his brother. "I'll be here till dawn if you help me."

Lucian wrapped his hand around the head of his hammer. "They made bets on whether or not you'd stay the whole day."

"How much did you lose?"

Lucian dropped his gaze. "Why didn't you leave?"

"I suppose that's what a brave man would have done."

Lucian snapped his head back. Clay captured his gaze and said, "But a coward might have stayed, hoping if he built one wall, he might knock another one down."

"Lucian?" a soft feminine voice asked.

Lucian spun around. Clay'd never seen a hat come off a head so fast in his life.

"You shouldn't be over here, Taffy," Lucian said quietly.

Smiling softly, she extended a dipper of water. "I thought you might be thirsty."

Lucian grinned. "How could I be thirsty when you been bringing me water all day?"

She shrugged slightly, her cheeks pinkening. "You just looked thirsty."

"Then I reckon I am."

Lucian took the dipper and drank the water, his eyes never leaving Taffy. He handed the empty dipper back to her. "I appreciate the thought."

In the distance, the tuning of a fiddle sounded. "You gonna stay for the dance?" Taffy asked.

"I haven't decided yet."

"I was hoping you might. I thought maybe you'd ask me to dance."

Lucian sighed deeply. "I talked to your pa." He shifted his hat to the hand holding the hammer and touched his thumb to her cheek. "Taffy, honey, he doesn't want me calling on you."

She studied the ground, then nudged Lucian's foot with her toe before meeting his gaze. "I don't see that it's his decision to make. I'm almost seventeen, nearly fully growed, and he doesn't know what I look for in a man."

Lucian chuckled. "Girl, you're gonna get me a good sound beatin'."

"I'm worth it," she promised before she walked away.

"Just between you and me," Clay said, "if I had to choose between a pretty girl wanting a dance and pounding nails into boards, I'd pick the pretty girl."

An appreciative smile eased onto Lucian's face. "She is pretty, ain't she?" He crossed his arms over his chest and leaned back before Clay could remind him the wall wasn't finished. He fell through the frame and hit the ground.

Clay threw his head back and laughed until his sides ached.

Standing within the twilight shadows, Meg heard the deep laughter rumble, the first sound of pure unexpected pleasure she'd heard all day.

She watched Clay extend his hand and pull Lucian to his feet. Lucian walked away, and Clay pounded the nails into the one wall of the barn that was not yet completed.

She heard the bittersweet strains of the fiddle wrap around the echoes of the solitary hammer.

Why had he stayed?

Why had he stayed to suffer the wrath and scorn of people who would prefer to lie among snakes than speak with him?

And why did she feel so guilty for not acknowledging his presence? They had a pact, a gentlemen's agreement, which he'd honored today.

Why did she wish he hadn't?

He didn't silence his hammer until night fell. In the dark she watched his silhouette walk to the wagon where the twins had gone at dusk.

He'd spent his entire day giving his neighbor the wall of a barn, and no one had thanked him. He'd spent a stormy night carving a child's marker for which no one would ever thank him. In the name of honor, he had sacrificed his dream of going to Europe.

She wondered how many other things he

may have done in his life for which he had received no praise or consideration.

The gentle strains of "Greensleeves" filled the night. Closing her eyes, she allowed the melody to bring forth memories of dancing within Kirk's arms.

"Meg?"

She opened her eyes. "Hello, Lucian."

"Would you honor me with this dance?"

They walked to an area where lanterns hung from tree limbs. "Thank you for asking me to dance. This is my favorite song."

They began to waltz. "Clay asked me to dance with you if they played this song, and you weren't already dancing."

"I'm sorry for everything my father and Daniel said during the meal today —"

Lucian shook his head. "For the most part, I feel the same way they do, or I thought I did. I don't understand him, Meg. Why'd he stay?"

"I don't know, and I don't know why it hurt to see him stay, but it did."

They lost the rhythm of the music, their steps becoming little more than two people swaying in place as people danced around them.

"When we were younger," Lucian began, "he used to give me his dessert at suppertime if I promised to sit still for him the next day so he could carve my likeness."

"He showed me his graveyard," Meg said. "I saw an angel that looked familiar."

Lucian smiled. "That was supposed to be me. You have to be quiet when he's carving because he thinks so hard he forgets other people are around. If he's got a hammer and chisel in his hands . . ." He shook his head at a memory. "I was sitting for him, and he was working to carve my face. I saw this deer slipping through the trees. I said something to Clay about it, and my nose went flying off that piece of stone. He got so upset, he threw down his tools and ran to the house. Don't know what he said to Ma, but the next thing I know, she's running outside hollerin' for Pa to go get Dr. Martin because Clay cut off my nose."

She laughed at the image his words created. She could imagine Clay saying he'd cut off Lucian's nose. To him, stone was as important as a person.

"Why did you ask him to make the monument?" Lucian asked quietly.

The music drifted into silence, and Meg answered with the truth. "I don't know anymore."

Sitting on the porch, Clay felt the night wind ruffle his hair. As far as miserable days in his life went, today ranked right near the top.

He'd gone to the shed at dawn and stared at the granite. He'd chipped off a piece here and there, but he'd found no joy in his actions. He hadn't enjoyed working on the monument since he'd made the headstone for Tom's baby girl. The statue was just something he wanted to finish now. Finish it and be done with it.

And move on.

He wanted to live someplace that didn't have the scent of honeysuckle in the air. He wanted to live someplace where women didn't have blue eyes.

Stretching out his legs, he leaned back on his elbows. It'd probably be best if he lived someplace that didn't have women at all.

He'd gone to the Wrights' farm because as much as he hated the way Meg watched him work, he hated the thought of a day without her in it even more.

From his distant vantage point, he thought she'd been the prettiest woman there. He'd wanted to walk up to her just to see if her blue dress made her eyes look as blue as he thought it might. He'd caught her laughter on the wind and held onto it to ease his loneliness, a loneliness that deepened when he noticed how much attention Robert

Warner bestowed upon her, how much attention she gave Robert.

A shadow moved through the night. He sat up as Lucian came into view. "Wasn't expecting you home so early."

Lucian shrugged. "Danced a couple of dances with Taffy, then thought I'd best head on home and not push my luck."

"Did you dance with Meg?"

"Yep."

"I appreciate it."

Lucian leaned against the beam that ran from the porch to the eaves. "Tucker from the mercantile offered to extend me credit." He shifted his stance. "As long as I give him my word you won't eat any of the supplies I pick up."

Slowly, Clay nodded. "Does he want it in writing? I could sign a statement —"

"God damn it!" Lucian tore his hat from his head, stepped away from the porch, and glared at Clay. "Why the hell won't you fight?"

"What do you want me to do? Go into town and beat him up? What would that gain us?"

"Some respect."

"If I went into town and beat up a man over twice my age, people would respect me? I can do without that kind of respect."

"At least they'd stop thinking you were a coward, and me and the twins could start walking with our heads held high."

"The only one stopping you from walking with your head held high is you. What I do with my life shouldn't affect your pride."

"You're my brother. If people think you're a coward, then they'll think I inherited the same yellow streak. Why the hell couldn't you have caught some disease and died like so many others did? It sure would have made my life simpler."

Clay studied the shadows between his feet. He'd only been a little older than Lucian was now when he made his decision not to enlist along with his friends. He supposed at Lucian's age, every young man thought the decisions he made affected the world. "Think Taffy's father would let you call on her if I hadn't come home?"

"He might."

He peered at his brother. "Want me to go talk to him?"

"Hell, no, I don't want you to talk to him."

"So what are you going to do about Taffy?"

Lucian ran his fingers through his hair. "Hell, I haven't decided yet. If she can sneak away tomorrow, we're going on a picnic. I'll talk to her about it then."

"You start sneaking around now, you'll always be sneaking around."

"Those are fine words of wisdom coming from a coward."

"I never sneaked around. Everyone knew exactly where I stood."

Lucian leaned down so his gaze was even with Clay's. "You would have been sneaking around if you'd known they had plans to hang you the day their sons rode away."

"I did know," Clay said quietly. "Kirk told me before he left."

Twelve

"If you're gonna do it, you'd best get it done."

Lucian snapped his head around and glared at Clay. "That's easy enough for you to say. You don't know what this feels like. Hell, I feel like I'm gonna walk to my own execution."

Clay unwrapped the reins from around the brake handle. "Just take a deep breath, look straight ahead, and start walking."

Lucian turned his attention to the people wandering from the church. "A deep breath?"

"A very deep breath."

Lucian was halfway across the churchyard before he realized he hadn't breathed at all. He breathed deeply, but his legs still shook as though he walked on unsteady ground. Nearing the Lang family, he yanked off his hat. "Taffy?"

She spun around, her gray eyes wide. He figured the South had dressed her men in gray because of Taffy's eyes.

"Taffy, about that picnic we were planning. I know this real nice spot, but it's too far to walk to so I thought I'd pick you up in the wagon in about an hour."

A smile lit her face, and Lucian figured the pain her father was about to deal him was going to be worth every blow. "Mr. Lang, you might as well pound your fist into my face now because I aim to call on your daughter."

"Oh, Pa wouldn't hit you. Would you, Pa?"

When Taffy touched her father's arm, Lucian thought he could actually see the man's heart melt. "I reckon not."

Taffy's smile grew, and she squeezed Lucian's hand. "I'll be waitin'."

Lucian nodded and hoped his smile didn't look as silly as it felt. Jamming his hat on his head, he walked backward. He bumped against someone. "Sorry, Robert."

Quickening his pace, he headed toward the wagon. Clay flicked the reins, and Lucian started running. The twins were laughing and yelling by the time he dove into the back of the wagon.

"Well?" Clay asked over his shoulder.

Lucian looked at the blue sky. "I'm gonna spend the day near heaven."

Meg had not lost her mind.

Last night while her father guided the wagon home, she'd lain in the back staring at the stars. Somewhere along the rough road, her good sense had tumbled out.

After her father and Daniel went to sleep, she tiptoed to the kitchen and baked until dawn. Carefully, she packed all but one cake into a wicker basket. The cake was her decoy so her family wouldn't wonder why the warm kitchen smelled of cinnamon, sugar, and butter at dawn.

She hid the basket in her room. When they returned from church, she feigned a headache, went to her bedroom, climbed out the window, and saddled her horse. Picnic basket tied precariously behind her, she headed toward the stream where she hoped Clay would again spend the afternoon with his brothers.

She knew she was courting danger, but the twins' loyalty to Clay had touched her deeply. She dismounted within a copse of trees near the river's edge. She heard no gaiety or laughter. She heard only the birds and the wind whispering through the branches overhead, teasing the leaves. She heard a small splash, the sound of a fish returning to the water before it was ready.

Clay had left Cedar Grove before he was ready; he'd returned before the people of

Cedar Grove were prepared to accept him.

Silently, she wended through the trees until she saw the riverbank clearly. Beyond it, no naked boys rollicked. No grown man fully clothed, soaked to the skin, made threats, then proceeded to carry them out.

She sighed heavily. If they weren't here, where could they be?

"Howdy, Miz Warner!"

Meg jumped, spun around, and pressed her palm against her chest, grateful to find her heart could still pound. "You frightened me," she said to the grinning twin.

His grin widened. "Yes, ma'am, I could tell. You pert' near looked like a bird tryin' to protect its nest." He glanced around. "You got a nest round here?"

She planted her hands on her hips. "Which twin are you?"

He studied the ground for a moment, then peered up at her, suspicion showing clearly in his brown eyes. "Joe."

"Well, Josh, are you alone out here?"

"I said I was Joe."

"And I think you're afraid I'm going to tell how you frightened me so you gave me your brother's name."

He scrunched up his face. "Are you gonna tell? Clay said we was always to treat ladies kindly, even when they was bothersome.

Reckon scarin' you wasn't treatin' you kindly. You gonna tell?"

"Are you Josh?"

Slowly, he nodded.

"Should I tell him?"

He shook his head. "Nah, I'll tell him. He says we gotta own up to the things we do — good or bad."

"Well, I don't think it's truly necessary to tell him anything. Is he out here?"

"Yes, ma'am. We was fishin' down yonder, but the fish ain't bitin' so I come lookin' for some pecans." He withdrew his hand from a pocket to display his finds. "We didn't bring nothin' with us, figurin' we'd have fish for our noonday meal, and my belly done started rumblin'. Clay said it was so loud, it was scarin' the fish away."

"Actually, I was looking for a place to have a picnic."

"You can share our spot if you don't mind shelling your own pecans."

"I sure as heck hope Josh brings back a bunch of pecans," Joe said as he toyed with his fishing line. His stomach growled, and he glanced over at Clay. "They can't hear that."

"You'd be surprised what they can hear." Lying on his back, his hands folded beneath his head, Clay watched the clouds roll by. Like Josh before he went in search of pecans, Clay had stuck his fishing pole in the muddy bank.

"I think Josh is right," Joe said. "I don't think Lucian is family, else he woulda invited us along on his picnic with Taffy."

"Lucian is family. It's just that he didn't want his brothers butting in while he was courting."

"He's really and truly courting her?"

"Reckon so."

"Is he gonna marry her?"

Clay shrugged.

Joe stuck his pole into the mud, scooted back, and rolled onto his stomach, his elbows perched so he could rest his chin in his hands. "You ever gonna marry?"

Clay pointed to a bank of clouds. "Look, there's a buffalo."

Joe twisted his head and squinted against the sunlight. "I don't see it."

"Just to the left of that cloud that's a little darker."

"You reckon Pa's up there carving them clouds?"

"I wouldn't be a bit surprised. Seems like a good thing to do. Reckon I might do that when the time comes."

"I bet you'll carve out some fancy clouds."

Clay smiled. "Yeah, I imagine I will."

Joe dropped his elbows, pressed his palms flat on the earth, and rested his cheek on his hands. "So are you?"

"What?"

"Gonna get married sometime."

The emptiness engulfed Clay. He respected honesty and was trying to teach the twins to be honest in their dealings with people. He just wished he hadn't taught them to speak quite so much of what was on their minds. "No, I don't reckon I will."

"On account of you not fightin' in the war?"

"That's got something to do with it."

Joe scooted over until his arm knocked against Clay's shoulder. He lifted up on his elbows and looked down on Clay's face, locking his brown eyes onto Clay's. "If you had it to do over, would you fight?"

"No."

Joe grinned. "I'm glad." He flopped to his back and looked at the sky.

Clay rolled over to his side and rose up on an elbow. "Why are you glad?"

"On account if you'd do it different now, it'd mean you made the wrong choice the first time. And you didn't."

Shaking his head, Clay gave his brother a rueful smile. "I think you and Josh think things too old for your age."

They heard a commotion behind them and glanced over their shoulders.

"I found somethin' better than pecans!" Josh yelled as he thrashed through the trees. "Miz Warner was lookin' for a place to have a picnic. Told her she could share our spot. And guess what? She said we could call her Miz Meg."

Clay scrambled to his feet as Meg emerged from the trees. Sweet Lord, but her blue dress did deepen the hue of her eyes. She'd caught her hair in some sort of lacy thing that made her hair look thick and heavy, and he wondered why it didn't break free and tumble down her back.

She gave Joe one of those rare smiles that needed to be carved for posterity. "Do you mind if I have my picnic here?"

"No, ma'am," Joe said, with an answering smile that could have blinded her if the sun reflected off it.

Her smile grew smaller as she looked at Clay. "Is it all right with you?"

He nodded, wishing he hadn't changed out of his church clothes. They weren't fancy, but she saw him in his worn work clothes every day.

"I brought a quilt," she said.

"The boys can spread it out for you."

"Why do we need a quilt?" Josh asked.

"Because ladies don't sit on the ground," Clay said.

"We ain't never had a picnic with a lady before," Joe said. "What else do ladies do?"

That beautiful smile returned to her face. "They bring lots of food."

Grabbing her hands, the boys pulled her to her horse. Her laughter filtered through the air as Clay yanked their fishing poles out of the mud. His pride wanted to tell her they didn't need her charity, but his love for the twins was greater than his pride. He'd heard all about the desserts that graced the table the day before. The twins had dug into her apple cobbler with such enthusiasm that he'd just sat and watched. He hoped Meg had thought to pack a small piece of cake for them today.

"Gawd Almighty!"

Clay swung around and wished he had a heart of stone. Leaning against the tree, he watched the delight in Meg's face as she spread her picnic over the quilt. He didn't know how she'd managed to pack all that food in that small basket, but she'd already set out three cakes and an apple cobbler. The boys' eyes grew as large as the two pies she was now lifting out of the basket.

Then she brought out fried chicken, and

Clay felt the juices flow like a raging river within his mouth.

She brushed her hands together, then folded them in her lap. "That's it."

"Gawd Almighty. Can we have a piece of cake first?" Josh asked.

"That's up to your brother," she said softly.

Josh turned to Joe. "Can we have a piece of cake first?"

Laughing, she tapped Josh on the shoulder. "Your older brother."

"Clay, can we eat a piece of cake first?"

"I reckon."

She sat back on her heels and picked up a knife. "I have buttermilk cake, spice cake, and chocolate cake. Which do you want?"

The boys glanced at each other, then looked at the cakes, then looked at each other. Clay rolled his eyes. They'd be here all day.

"How about a small piece of each?" Meg suggested.

"Yes, ma'am!"

If the woman called those pieces she was cutting small, Clay didn't think he wanted to see what she called big. She handed the plates to the boys, and they were stuffing the cake into their mouths before the thank you's had completely escaped.

Meg spread a napkin over her skirt. It never would have occurred to Clay to bring a napkin to a picnic. She picked up a plate and, with dainty fingers, plucked a piece of chicken out of the pot and dropped it on her plate. Wiping her fingers on the napkin, she peered over at him. "I made enough for everyone."

"Come on, Clay," Josh said. "Bet you ain't never had nothin' this good before."

If he had, it was too long ago to remember. Clay shoved away from the tree, ambled over, and sat on the ground beside the quilt.

She handed him a plate. "Just help yourself."

Like the twins, he found the choices too many, the decision as to where to begin impossible to make. He supposed he was too old to begin his meal with a piece of cake so he dug a chicken leg out of the pot and bit into the succulent meat. He chewed it slowly, savoring the flavor. Swallowing, he glanced at her. "How's your hand?"

Meg rubbed the area just below her thumb. "It's just a little bruised."

"I've hit my hand enough times to know it can smart. You're lucky he didn't break something."

"I think it hurt Robert's pride more than it hurt me."

He grimaced. "If he's like most in his family, I reckon yesterday was hard on him. They're used to doing for themselves."

Meg wanted to point out that yesterday had probably been hard on Clay as well, or hadn't he noticed?

He set his plate on the quilt, and she watched his gaze flick over the desserts. She wished she knew which was his favorite so she could just cut him a piece and slap it on his plate.

"Can I have a piece of your cobbler next?" Josh asked. "It's the best thing I ever ate in my life."

"Certainly," she said as she spooned out a generous helping.

"You ever gonna get married again?" Josh asked.

"It's none of your business," Clay said.

"How come?" Josh asked.

"Who do you think I should marry?" she asked, intending to aggravate Clay, but instead regretting the words the moment they slipped past her lips. She knew who the twins admired most, knew they'd think she held the same admiration for him.

Josh scrunched up his face. "Me and Joe will have to set our minds to thinkin' on that. We'll let you know when we figure it out."

Clay picked up his plate and walked to the

river. He knelt at the bank, and Meg saw his hand glide over the plate as he dipped it in the water. He carried the plate back to the quilt and set it down. "I appreciate the meal. You boys, be sure and clean up when you're done."

Meg watched him walk away. All this food, and he'd eaten one chicken leg. The man was impossible to understand.

"Don't pay him no never mind," Joe said. "We was talkin' about him gettin' married before you got here. Reckon it bothered him to be talkin' about it again."

"Who's he going to marry?" she asked.

"No one."

Meg set her plate down. "Eat as much as you want while I'm gone." She rose to her feet and walked away from the picnic area.

She hoped Clay had walked in a straight line and not wandered off and gotten lost. She had no earthly idea how to follow a trail. She thought the twins could probably help her find him, but she was in the mood for some of Mama Warner's low talking, and she didn't think the twins could talk in a low voice if she gagged them.

She saw Clay hunkered down in a small clearing, as still as any statue he'd ever sculpted. Quietly, slowly, she walked past the trees until she obtained a clearer view of him.

He was leaning over slightly, his elbow resting on his thigh, his hand poised near the ground.

She saw a bushy tail shoot up through the tall grass, then a squirrel was sitting on its haunches and sniffing. It scampered toward Clay, stopped, studied its surroundings, then scampered again. It came to a quick halt, lifting its gaze to the soft brown eyes of the man, then dropping its gaze to the pecan nestled within his palm.

The squirrel snatched the pecan and darted away. A slow contented smile eased across Clay's face before he reached into the pocket of his shirt and withdrew another pecan. He slipped the pecan up his hand until it was nestled between his thumb and forefinger, his eyes never leaving the area into which the squirrel had disappeared.

"Want to give it a try?" he asked. He twisted slightly and gazed at her. He tossed the pecan into the air and caught it without taking his eyes off her.

Meg strolled into the clearing, knelt in the tall grass, and held out her hand, palm up. "I'm not sure he'll come to me."

Clay turned his palm so the pecan rolled out of his hand into hers. "Just pretend you're a statue and be quiet. He'll come."

Leaning over, Meg rested her elbow on

her thigh just as Clay had. It occurred to her it might be easier to feed the squirrel than it was to feed Clay.

"Did Kirk tell you 'Greensleeves' was my favorite melody?" she asked quietly.

"He might have mentioned it."

She peered at him. He stared ahead as though he could will the squirrel to return and take the pecan from her palm. "Do you remember everything he told you about me?"

"I imagine I forgot a thing or two."

"I remember very little of what he told me about you. Yet you probably know which of those cakes is my favorite."

A ghost of a smile appeared on his face as he pulled a stalk of grass out of the ground and slipped it between his lips. He covered his mouth when he worked so she never had an opportunity to study his lips as she did his hands, but she imagined his mouth could create haunting whispers as tenderly as his hands did.

"Spice," he said quietly.

Disbelieving, Meg blinked. "Did he tell you everything about me?"

His smile broadened as he turned his gaze on her. "He didn't tell me which cake was your favorite, but when you were cutting pieces, you weren't as generous with the spice cake. Figured you wanted to make sure you had a piece left over for yourself."

Shaking her head, Meg smiled. "You're right. The spice is my favorite, and I am stingy with the pieces."

"I'd hardly call you stingy. Not with the feast you brought today." He removed the grass from his mouth and tossed it aside. She watched his throat work as though he fought for the words. "I appreciate that you brought the twins a picnic. When I made the plans for yesterday, I didn't consider that they'd do without."

"It didn't seem to bother them."

"Well, it bothered me."

"I don't think there's much you can do about it as long as they stick to your side the way they do."

"It ought to get better once we harvest the crops, and I finish the monument."

"Why will it get better then?"

"Because I'll be moving on."

Meg felt as though he'd just hit her in the chest with his hammer. "Where will you go?"

"I don't know, but I figure sitting on top of a mountain by myself would be better than being here." Plowing his hands through his hair, he sighed deeply. "God, I'm so damn lonely."

Meg's heart lurched. He was lonely, un-happy, and miserable. All the things she'd wished on him, he'd acquired without com-pleting the monument. He hadn't admitted he was a coward, but she was certain he would before he finished carving the names into the base.

She should feel like dancing. Instead, she had a strong urge to ask him what kind of cake was his favorite.

He pointed to the center of the clearing. "You need to be quiet now. He's coming."

Cautiously, Meg slid her gaze forward and watched the squirrel scamper toward her. The squirrel stopped shy of Meg's hand and sat on its haunches.

"He won't take it," she whispered.

"Shh. He will."

She held her breath. Her nose itched. She crinkled her nose and the itching increased.

The squirrel dropped its front paws and stretched out, sniffing the air around her hand. Then he snatched the pecan from her hand and scurried away.

Closing her hand, Meg cradled it against her chest and laughed. "I can't believe he took it."

She heard a noise and glanced over her shoulder to see the twins sauntering toward her, rubbing their bellies. They dropped to the ground in front of her.

"I ain't never ate so much in my whole entire life," Josh said.

Leaning forward, Meg scratched their stomachs. "I'm glad you enjoyed it."

"Clay, it don't hardly seem enough to tell Miz Meg that she cooks the best food in the whole state. We was wonderin' if we could share the bats with her."

"I'm sure Mrs. Warner has seen the bats," Clay said.

"The bats?" Meg asked.

"Yes, ma'am," Josh said. "They look like smoke risin' out of the hills when the sun goes down."

Meg looked at Clay. "Did Kirk know about the bats?"

"Yes, ma'am. We found them when we were about twelve."

"He never showed them to me," she said, feeling a sense of loss.

"There's a particular spot we have to go to so we can see them," he said as his hands formed the shape of a mountain. "It's not easy to get to, and he probably didn't think you'd enjoy bats."

"I'd like to see the bats," she said.

"Miz Meg," Joe said solemnly, "we should probably tell you that we've got one rule when it comes to goin' to see the bats. If you decide to come with us, you gotta follow that rule."

"And what's the rule?"

"No matter how scared you get, you can't turn back."

Fear, as Meg soon discovered, could lope along beside her like two whistling twin boys. She jumped every time they hopped on a twig, broke a small branch off a tree in passing, or hollered, "Watch out!"

But she refused to turn back. As the shadows grew longer and they traveled farther, she hiked up her skirt and marched along with them.

Clay followed at an easy gait, leading her horse.

The twins stopped. "That's it, Miz Meg."

Meg searched the twilight sky. "Where? What does a bat look like? I don't know if I've ever seen one before."

"Not the bats," Josh said. "What we gotta climb to see the bats."

Meg lowered her gaze and followed the trail of his pointing finger. The mountain loomed before her.

Clay might call it a hill, but it was a mountain.

"Sun's goin' down, so we gotta hurry!" Josh cried as he and Joe ran toward the mountain.

"You don't have to do this," Clay said quietly behind her.

She angled her chin. "Of course I do. That's the rule." Bending, she reached between her feet and grasping the back of her skirt, brought it up and tucked it into her waistband so she had a makeshift type of trousers. She didn't know why she hadn't thrown on Kirk's clothes before she crawled out her bedroom window. Probably because she hadn't realized she'd be out searching for bats.

She walked to the foot of the mountain and stared at the twins scrambling up its side. Grabbing the bushes as one went seemed to be the secret. She took a deep breath.

"I know you're not fond of my touch," Clay said, "so I think I'd better warn you. If you start to fall, I'll do all in my power to catch you."

She glanced over her shoulder. "Then I'd best not fall."

She flexed her fingers before wrapping them around the low branch of a bush. She stepped onto the slope.

"Test your weight on that spot before you go any farther," Clay said.

"I can do this without your help," she said as she glared at the high rocky ledge from which the twins were already peering down at her. She tried to test her weight on the spot without letting Clay see she was following his advice. She heard him move in behind her. "You're not coming up with me, are you?"

"No, ma'am, I'll follow a good distance behind."

Meg released her stranglehold on the bush and lunged for another one. She pulled up inch by inch. She'd be at least a year older before she saw the bats.

The twins urged her on. She reached for another branch and scooted farther up the side of the hill. She had nothing to fear.

She glanced down. Clay still stood on the ground. He'd hiked one foot up so it rested on the hill, but his arms hung at his sides as though he were waiting for her to climb farther before he followed.

She moved her foot to a large rock protruding out of the dirt. She knew how strong rocks could be, so she shifted her weight to that side. The rock broke free of the earth and fell down the side of the hill. Losing her footing, she dangled from the bush.

Then she heard a crack. Clay was right. The sound of a crack when you weren't wanting one was deafening. Almost as deafening as her scream as she slid down the hill.

271

She came to an abrupt halt with the hard, prickly side of the hill pressed to her stomach, and a strong, firm man pressed against her back.

He'd kept one foot firmly planted on the ground. He'd dug the other one into the side of the hill. She was practically sitting on his hard thigh with her body nestled against him so her head fit snugly against his shoulder.

"Are you all right?" he asked quietly, and his breath whispered along the nape of her neck.

She turned her face to tell him that she was fine and he didn't need to hold her. He furrowed his brow, and sorrow filled his eyes.

"Ah, you scratched your face," he said in a low voice as he gently touched the tips of his fingers to her cheek.

He gazed at her cheek, and Meg wondered how badly she was cut. Her cheek smarted, but it wasn't the small ache that brought tears to her eyes. It was the expression of wonder on Clay's face.

"Dear God, but you're soft," he said in a raw voice.

He lifted his fingers away from her face and stepped back. Meg stumbled before catching her balance.

Averting his gaze, he shoved his hands into

his pockets, reminding her of a lost little boy. He looked as though he'd just discovered something he'd have been better off not knowing.

He cleared his throat and scuffed the toe of his boot against the ground, turning up the roots of the grass and weeds. "You gonna try again?"

Meg brushed her raw hands together. "Is that the only way up?"

He nodded solemnly. "I could go up right behind you. Stop you sooner if you lose your hold."

"Isn't there a chance that we'd both just tumble down the side of the mountain?"

He gave her a lopsided grin. "Yeah, but I'd be softer to fall on than the ground."

She wasn't completely certain about that. From what she'd just felt, his body was as rock hard as the stone into which he cut. She breathed deeply. "All right. I don't want to disappoint the twins."

She grabbed the bush that had served her well during her first attempt to climb the hill, and she placed her foot on a scraggly bit of earth. Clay moved behind her, and she pressed her body against the earth.

She eased her way up. He swung his arm over her and grabbed a bush above her head. His body brushed against hers. Kirk had always smelled of bay rum. Clay smelled of the earth, strong and musky. He didn't attempt to cover his male scent. He was as natural as his rocks.

She pulled up to the next bush. As close as her shadow, he stayed with her. She imagined that the positioning of his body over hers gave the appearance of a compromising situation, which prompted her to move a little more quickly.

"Don't rush," he said.

"I'd like to get to the top before I'm an old woman."

Her foot slipped. His hand clamped around her waist.

"Slow and easy will get you there," he said.

"Patience is not one of my strong suits."

He chuckled. "I know."

She jerked her head around. "What did Kirk tell you about my patience?"

"Nothing. Now reach for the roots of that tree."

Meg did as instructed, over and over, reaching for the limbs and roots he indicated, pulling herself up, gaining ground slower than she would have liked, but losing very little. He began to slip his foot beneath hers, giving her additional support. More often, he only used one hand to hold onto the side of the hill. With his other hand, he held her waist or splayed his fingers across the small of her back. She thought he probably had the largest hands in the entire state. And perhaps the strongest. And in an odd sort of way — the gentlest.

It also occurred to her that he seemed extremely skilled at helping someone climb the hill. She wondered with how many other ladies he might have shared the bats.

"Just a little more, Miz Meg!" Josh yelled.

Meg scooted up and felt small hands grab her wrists.

"That's it, Miz Meg," Joe said. "We won't let you fall."

She smiled as she eased over the edge of the hill. Then she shrieked as Clay pushed against her backside and sent her sprawling over the top.

She scrambled to her feet and glared at the man as he worked his way over the edge. She was tempted to place her foot on his shoulder and send him back down the hill.

Rubbing his hands on his thighs, he turned as red as the sun-banked horizon. "I'm sorry. It just seemed the best way to get you over the edge."

Meg dusted off her skirt and flicked her hands over her backside. "No harm done, but I think I could have gotten over without assistance."

"Come on, Miz Meg," Josh said. "It's pert' near time."

The boys grabbed her hands and pulled her toward the far side of the plateau. When they reached it they released their hold, fell to their stomachs, and peered over the ledge.

"Oh, don't do that," she said. "You'll fall."

"No, we won't," Josh assured her.

"It bothers Mrs. Warner for you to be so near the edge," Clay said. "You won't miss anything if you scoot back."

Joe glanced over his shoulder. "How come we can call her Miz Meg and you can't?"

"Because she and I have a business arrangement. It wouldn't be proper."

"She call you Mr. Holland?"

"No. You need to be watching for the bats now."

Meg was grateful the boys turned their attention back to the view before them. She didn't want to explain why she wouldn't say their brother's name. Carefully, she walked to the edge and eased onto her stomach beside Joe. Clay stretched out beside Josh, and she was glad they had the buffer of the twins between them.

"Gawd Almighty! Look at the sky," Josh said.

"Yep, it's beautiful all right," Clay said.

The deep blue sky melted into wisps of pink weaving among streaks of lavender and orange. Meg couldn't remember the last time she'd actually watched the sun set and appreciated its majestic farewell. The moon was already a faint glow as though anxious to bring on the night.

"Do you come here often?" she asked.

"Yes, ma'am," Josh said. "As often as we can. It's a good place to be glad for all the things we have."

For all the things they had: an occasional biscuit, a brother who was shunned by the community. She didn't know if their innocence was a blessing or a curse.

"Look, Miz Meg. There they are."

She peered over the edge at the hills fanning out over the countryside. She saw a small spiral of smoke rising into the fading sky. "Where do they come from?" she asked.

"We don't know," Josh said. "We figure there's a cave or somethin' down there, but it's one of those things where the not knowin' makes it special."

Josh scrambled over Clay's back. Quickly, Joe followed him. Josh reached across Clay and patted the spot he'd vacated. "Move over here, Miz Meg, so you can see better."

She wanted to tell them that she could see just fine where she was, but she could tell from their expressions that the twins thought they were offering her the most wonderful gift in the world. How could she possibly face them tomorrow if she hurt their feelings now?

She scooted over until she was as close to Clay as she could get without actually touching him. The twins nestled beside Clay as though settling in for a long night's sleep.

The spiral of smoke widened and reached higher. The flurry of activity blackened the sky. Meg heard high-pitched squeaks and the rustle of wings. She'd never experienced anything like it.

Moments passed, and no one spoke, as though each was mesmerized by the incredible number of bats soaring toward the distant horizon.

"Where do they go?" Meg whispered.

"Got no idea," Clay said.

"When do they come back?"

"Near dawn."

"How do you know?"

"We stayed here all night once waiting to see when they came back."

"You and the twins?"

"No, me and your husband. Only he wasn't your husband at the time."

Meg intertwined her fingers. "I won't get upset if you say his name."

He slid his gaze over to hers. "I wouldn't want you to think I was being disrespectful."

"I won't think that."

Sagely, he nodded before turning his attention back to the flying creatures.

"I guess you've shared the bats with a lot of people," she said, wishing it didn't bother her to think about all the women with whom he might have shared this unique place.

"Just you and the twins. Invited Lucian once, but he wasn't interested."

The smoky haze of bats disappeared, leaving an audible silence in their wake. Meg wished she could stay here forever, away from the bitter words and hatred that filled the world below.

"He doesn't know what he's missing," she said quietly.

Thirteen

"Miz Meg!"

Meg dismounted the next morning and hugged each twin before handing them the reins. "Thank you for yesterday evening," she said.

"Our pleasure, ma'am," Josh said. "And guess what? We figured out who you should marry."

Meg stopped walking, not certain she wanted to hear this announcement. How could she explain that she would never, could never marry their brother?

"We decided you ought to marry Robert Warner."

"Robert?"

"Yes, ma'am. He seems nice enough, and you wouldn't have to change your name."

Meg laughed self-consciously. "I thought you were going to say I should marry your brother."

"Clay?"

She nodded.

"Ah no, ma'am." Josh said. "It wouldn't do at all for you to marry Clay. If you married him, he'd no doubt want to kiss you from time to time, and we figure kissin' is unpleasant enough when you like the person you're kissin'. It'd be downright miserable to kiss someone you hated."

Meg felt her heart lurch. It bothered her that the twins realized that she hated their brother. The words coming from their innocent mouths sounded so ugly.

They walked toward the shed. Clay stood in the doorway, waiting for her. Yesterday had changed something between them, and she had a feeling that the following days would more closely resemble the days they'd shared before Tom had needed a marker for his daughter.

When they neared the shed, the twins led the horse away. Clay gave her a cautious smile. "Morning."

She laced her fingers together. "Good morning."

"I like the way you're wearing your hair now," he said.

Meg touched the chignon. "This is less trouble than trying to imprison it in a knot at the back."

"Looks prettier, too." He stepped back. "It's been a couple of days since I did any cutting. Hope I remember how."

"I would think it's not something you'd

easily forget."

Tying his bandanna over his face, he walked to his table. Meg picked the bandanna off the chair. "Will we need to wear these when you're cutting the details?"

"No," he said, his breath causing his bandanna to billow away from his mouth.

She remembered the feel of that warm breath last night on her flesh. Sitting, she wrapped the bandanna around her face. She was as anxious now to watch Clay work unmasked as she was to see Kirk's features take shape in the stone.

Clay began to work, and clouds of dust materialized. Before she went home each evening, she stopped along the river to wash off the stone powder coating her skin. She supposed Clay felt even grimier than she did at the end of the day. Even now, his hair was sprinkled with the fine particles.

Her thoughts drifted to Robert. He would make an exceptional husband, but the image didn't appeal to her as much as it had two days ago. His unspoken promise lay heavy on her heart.

Clay stepped down from the stool and walked to the table. He no longer felt the need to step outside and dunk his head in a bucket of water when the scent of honeysuckle became too strong.

He'd taken it personally when she didn't want Tom to see her here, but in the past few days, he'd learned he'd rather have her here than not. "I'm stopping for awhile."

"Oh, yes, of course." She rose from the chair, walked to the stone, and placed her hand on the granite.

"I carved on the other side," he said.

"Of course." She moved to the other side and touched the shaved stone.

"Is something bothering you today?" he asked.

She sighed. "Did you tell the twins I hate you?"

"No, but they tend to notice a lot more than they should, and sometimes they sound like eighty-year-old men thinking about life."

She smiled weakly. "They think I should marry Robert."

"He's a good man."

"He fought at Shiloh."

"Then I'd say he was close to perfect."

She pressed her forehead against the stone. "I loved Kirk so much. I can't imagine someone taking his place."

"And no one ever will, but he was the kind of man who'd step aside and make room for someone else. He'd want you to find happiness."

"Sometimes, it seems impossible. Watching the bats was the closest I've come to being happy in years. The twins look at the world the way I used to, the way I always thought I would."

A dull ache throbbed through his chest for all she'd lost. Brave Meg. She'd watched the man she loved ride away, never to return to her side. He picked up a small chisel and hammer. "Want to chip off a piece of the stone?"

She pulled her head back with such force he was surprised she didn't snap her neck. "What?"

He held out the tools. "Thought you might like to cut on the rock a little bit."

"I could ruin it. Then all your efforts would be for nothing."

"I don't think you'll ruin it. You can chip a small piece off this corner that I haven't touched yet."

Her eyes lit up as she walked to the corner and examined the stone, running her fingers along the edge. "I'm probably not strong enough."

"Won't know unless you try."

She wiped her hands on her skirt. "All right." She started to draw the bandanna over her face.

"You don't have to wear that. I don't think you'll create enough dust to bother us." He handed her the tools.

"Oh, they're heavier than I thought," she said as she moved her hands up and down, testing their weight.

He placed his finger on the stone. "Hold the chisel in your left hand and put the blunt tip right here." She did as he said. "Now you want to have a firm grip on the chisel because you don't want it to go flying when you hit it."

She nodded.

"Relax the arm holding the hammer. You want the hammer to do the work. And never take your eyes off the chisel."

She slid her gaze to him. "Never?"

He didn't realize how close he was standing to her until she turned her head. A man could drown in the blue pool of her eyes. He'd spent most of the night thinking about how soft and smooth her cheek felt. Her lips looked even softer.

"Never," he said in a raspy voice. "You'll get distracted and start thinking about things you shouldn't."

"Like what?" she asked.

It had been a mistake to tell her not to cover her face. Her face was a perfect oval, her eyes a perfect blue. Her lower lip was so full it gave the appearance she was pouting when she wasn't. The tip of her tongue moistened her lips, and he wondered what it would feel like to have those glistening drops touch his own lips.

"You'll wonder . . ." — he lowered his head slightly — "wonder if . . ." He brushed his lips lightly over hers.

She jerked her head back.

Clay straightened and swallowed the lump that had formed in his throat. "I'm sorry. I'll stand still if you want to slap me."

"I don't want to slap you, but I think I need to leave."

He felt the trembling in her hands as she gave him the tools. "I don't think my carving is such a good idea."

She untied the bandanna from around her neck and dropped it on the chair before walking out of the shed. Clay fought against picking it up and tying it around his neck so he'd still have the scent of honeysuckle with him.

"What'd you do to make Miz Meg cry?" Josh asked.

Clay looked around the stone at the twins' concerned faces. "Was she crying?"

"Not like she did that day when we had to comfort her, but her eyes was full of tears."

"God damn it!" Clay slapped his hand against the granite and banged his forehead against the stone. The pain bellowing in his head wasn't loud enough to drown out the pain cutting into his heart.

"What'd you do?"

"Kissed her."

"Why the heck did you do a fool thing like that?"

Clay moved his head from side to side and felt the abrasive rock chafe his skin.

"You reckon she'll come back?" Joe asked.

Clay heaved a deep sigh. "No."

"Then who's gonna make us smile?"

Clay squeezed his eyes shut. Who was going to give him a reason to anticipate the dawn?

The world encompassed her, quiet, warm, and silky. The sensual sensations gave Meg a freedom she hadn't experienced in almost five years, but the freedom was fleeting, lost the moment she broke through the moon-glistened surface of the water.

Shortly after they were married, Kirk brought her here. It was their special, private place. The pool was a circle of deep water with large boulders running along a portion of it, and land and trees gracing the remaining edges.

She had no idea where the water came from. She supposed it somehow seeped through the earth and passed through crevices in the rocks. She really didn't care. She only cared that the pool had been waiting for her tonight when she needed it.

She had come here hoping to bring back the feel of Kirk's lips upon hers, but the attempt was proving futile. She could only feel Clay's lips upon hers, a light tentative brushing of his mouth over hers, and yet, warmth had shot through her. She'd felt the desire to lean into him, to press herself against his body, to twine her arms around his neck, to return the kiss with a fervor that far exceeded his.

She sank into the depths of the pool. She had loosened her hair because she enjoyed the way the water seemed to turn the strands into wisps of clouds floating freely through a black sky. But even here, where the water cut off the night sounds, it couldn't cut off her memories of Clay. He haunted her thoughts, and she feared that if she slept, he'd haunt her dreams.

When her lungs felt near to bursting, she rose to the surface of the pool. The night sounds had changed. The insects had taken refuge, their silence palpable in the night. It seemed that even the water had ceased its lapping against the shore.

The mournful strains of a song whispered

from a harmonica filled the night. She eased away from the center of the pool to an area where tree branches shielded her from moonbeams. She glanced toward the boulder. A lone figure sat upon the rock, his shoulders hunched, his hands near his face. Moon shadows hid the harmonica that she was certain he held, and they concealed the expression on his face. Yet the sound he created told all that needed to be known about his feelings and thoughts.

A lonesome wail, a soul crying in the night.

She wanted to yell that he wasn't alone, but the ground she walked upon was shaky. She had already offered him far more friendship than she'd intended.

The music stopped, and she watched in amazement as he stripped out of his clothes. He stood, a myriad of shadows and moonlight dancing over his body. She only had time to notice how tall and lean he appeared before he leapt from the boulder.

She screamed.

Clay heard a woman's shrill cry rend the stillness of the night just before he plunged below the surface of the water. If it hadn't been for that, he might have thought his foot had struck an unusually long and silky fish. As it was, he had a feeling his sole had run the length of a woman's leg.

He shot straight up to the surface, his breathing labored as he flung his hair out of his eyes. "Christ! What are you doing here?"

Even as Meg struggled to stay afloat in the water, she tilted up her chin. "Me? What are you doing here? This was our private sanctuary."

"Our? Did Kirk tell you about this place?"

"What if he did?"

"Damn his worthless hide. We all swore an oath we'd keep this place a secret."

"Who's we?"

"Kirk, Stick, your brothers. Hell, everyone that was around our age."

"I don't know why you're so angry."

Clay didn't know either. Her warm, bare foot touched his, and he glided away from her. She was no doubt wearing as much as he was . . . which was nothing. He thought the water around him might boil if he thought about that too long. "I'm getting out."

He swam to the bank where the shadows lay thick upon the water. "Can you see me?"

"No!"

"Good." He scrambled up the bank and headed to the boulder.

"I'm getting out as well!"

He stopped walking and wondered where she'd left her clothes. For the sake of the statue he should look over his shoulder and see if her curves were all he thought they were. He balled his hands into fists and stormed to the boulder. Seeing those curves in his dreams was bad enough. He didn't need to see them in the flesh.

He snatched up his clothes. Damn Kirk! The man was turning out to be more of an enemy than a friend.

Clay yanked his trousers up his legs and shoved his arms into his shirt. She couldn't have gotten a good look at his body, not in the darkness.

A button on his shirt went sailing through the night. He cursed and took more care with the other buttons. He didn't need a gaping hole exposing his chest. He pulled on his socks and jerked on his boots.

He plowed his hands through his wet hair. At least he was covered from shoulder to toe. Lord, how close he'd come —

"Are you decent?" Meg asked in a soft voice behind him.

He nearly jumped back into the water. "I'm dressed," he barked.

She stepped out of the shadows and sat on the ground beside the boulder. She set her shoes beside her, and he could see the faint outline of her toes peering out from beneath her skirt. She bent her head, draped her hair over her face so the thick strands pooled in her lap, and began brushing her hair.

Her ebony hair, shining in the moonlight, reminded him of silk. His fingers ached to glide through it. He'd made a mistake working with stone all his life.

"Why did you and the others need to keep this place a secret?" she asked.

He leaned against the boulder. "We wanted a place where we could discuss things in private."

"What sort of things?"

"Men things."

She parted her hair down the middle and peered through the silken crevice at him. "Men things? Like war?"

He rubbed his chest. "Not exactly."

She gave him an impish smile. "Women?"

He had a feeling she knew exactly what they'd discussed. Hell, Kirk had probably told her every conversation word for word. "We discussed things that concerned us."

She laughed. "Women!" She patted the ground. "Why don't you sit down?"

She went back to brushing her hair, and Clay slowly eased to the ground. He wondered if he could find a way to touch her hair without her noticing.

She flung her head back and her hair cascaded around her. She wasn't gentle enough when she brushed her hair. He wanted to show her how she ought to brush it. She pulled her hair over one shoulder and began to attack the ends.

"Who was the first girl you ever kissed?" she asked.

Clay stared at her. She stopped brushing her hair and looked at him. "Did you promise her you wouldn't tell?"

He dropped his gaze and started picking at the worn sole of his boot.

"Stick was the first boy I ever kissed."

Clay jerked his head up. "Stick? Did he take you to the sawmill?"

"What do you know about the sawmill?"

"He told us he'd take girls on a tour of the sawmill after everyone left for the day. He had three kinds of tours: the kissing tour, the touching tour, and the —" He cleared his throat.

"The lots-of-touching tour?" she asked.

"Is that the one you went on?"

She shook her head. "The first time, he kissed me behind the schoolhouse, barely touching my lips. A couple of years later, he took me to the sawmill and surprised me by sticking his tongue in my mouth when he kissed me."

"He stuck his tongue in your mouth?"

She nodded. "I was about thirteen. I wasn't expecting it. I bit him."

Clay laughed. "I remember when he couldn't talk for a week. He wouldn't tell us what happened."

"So who was the first girl you kissed?"

His laughter abruptly died. He rubbed his hands on his thighs. "You," he whispered.

"I don't remember kissing you. Was it during one of the hay rides we had at harvest time? I kissed a few boys then, but I don't remember —"

"No." He studied the small patch of ground between her knees and his. Damn honesty. "Today."

"You never kissed a girl before today? Don't you kiss women when you make love —"

"I need to go." He started to get up and froze when she grabbed his ankle.

"Please stay. It's none of my business."

Reluctantly, he dropped back to the ground. Before the war, he'd had no one special in his life, and a bought woman hadn't appealed to him. Now, he didn't have the money for the only women who would suffer through his touch.

"What's your favorite kind of cake?" she asked as she parted her hair into thirds and began braiding it.

"I like pies."

"What kind?"

"Pecan."

"I hate shelling pecans."

He shrugged. "I don't mind shelling them."

She tossed the thick braid over her shoulder. "Shell me a bowl of pecans sometime, and I'll make you a pie."

"You don't have to do that."

"Shell me two bowls of pecans so I can keep one pie. That'll make it fair."

The quiet eased around them like a comforting blanket. Clay glanced around a place he'd once enjoyed. "God, I miss them," he said in a ragged voice. "Kirk, Stick, all my friends. It hurts to think about them sometimes."

"But you wouldn't stand by their sides."

"The war wasn't about us standing together. It made each of us take a stand for what we believed. Kirk didn't believe in slavery, but he believed a state should have the right to secede."

"And you didn't believe we should have seceded."

"No, ma'am, I did not. Neither did Governor Sam Houston, but no one hung him by his thumbs when he opposed secession."

"Did someone hang you up by your thumbs?"

"No, I was spared that indignity, but I

know plenty who weren't."

She picked up her shoe, and he figured she was going to throw it at him. She dropped it. "The morning Kirk left . . . what did he say to you?"

"He asked me to ride with him."

She bowed her head and clenched her fists. "I knew it. I knew he wanted you by his side. Damn you. Damn you, for betraying his friendship."

Clay chuckled.

She snapped her head up, anger blazing in her eyes. "What's so damn funny?"

"It's just odd that the thing I admire most about you is the very thing that makes you hate me so much."

"What's that?"

"Your loyalty. To Kirk. To the men who fought with him. You never question their motives. Few of the men who went with Kirk could have explained to you what he was fighting for. Some believed in slavery. Most just wanted to partake in a good fight. But you stand behind them, you support them, you want a memorial to honor them."

"And I think you should have ridden at his side."

"He only wanted me to ride as far as the border."

"What?"

"He'd heard that some of the older men planned to stretch my neck because I didn't enlist. He wanted to give me an armed escort to Mexico, but I wasn't interested in leaving."

"What'd he say when you told him that?"

"Most of what he said I can't repeat to a lady. Basically, he called me a fool and said I'd end up dying for my beliefs. I asked him if he was willing to give less than his life for what he believed."

"He wasn't," she whispered.

Within the shadows created by the moon, he held her gaze. "The only difference between us was that your husband was willing to kill for what he believed in. I wasn't."

The flowers slept, their petals folded in slumber, yet their scent lingered on the air. Meg hadn't noticed it as she walked to the swimming hole, but she noticed it now as she walked home.

Over her shoulder, the full moon lent its light, creating soft shadows in the night. Her shadow reached out and dared to touch what she would not: the man walking beside her. Their shadows joined until she could no longer tell where each began.

Just as she could no longer distinguish her feelings for Clay. In the beginning, they'd been as the rock he now carved — clearly defined, hard, unforgiving. Somehow, in the passing days he'd chipped away her hatred as easily as he seemed to chip away the granite. In rare moments, she felt as though he were shaping her into someone different. She wondered if anyone in Cedar Grove would look upon the monument Clayton Holland created . . . and remain the same.

When they reached the edge of her family's land, where the furrowed fields began, he stopped. Her house was visible in the distance, a lone lantern hung on the porch to guide weary travelers to a place of rest.

"I'll wait here till I see you open the door."

"I crawl in through the window."

"Ah," he said, taking a long slow nod. "Which window?"

As she pointed, he leaned to the side. "I'll be able to see you going in." He smiled. "Should be interesting to see."

Studying him as he stood before her, bathed in moonlight, she remembered a time when he would have been welcome on their land, a time when he wouldn't have stopped at the furrowed fields but would have walked to her door. His hair had dried and the dark locks fell over his brow. She resisted the urge to brush them back.

"Are there" — he rubbed his chest — "are there particular nights you go to the swimming hole? I mean if there are, I'll be sure and not go those nights."

"Actually, tonight's the first time I've gone since Kirk left. How about you? What nights do you go?"

"Tonight was the first time for me, too. Do you want to pick a couple of nights so I don't bother you there anymore?"

Slowly, she shook her head. "I'll take my chances."

He nodded. "Well, then, you'd best go on in. I'll just stay here to make sure you get there safe."

His eyes caught and held hers in the moonlight. The last thing she wanted was to crawl into an empty bed alone. Like a moth drawn to a flame, she took a step closer. "I won't slap you if you kiss me again."

"What if I kissed you the way Stick did?"

"I won't bite your tongue."

Lifting his hand, he came within a whisper's breath of touching her cheek before dropping his hand to his side. Reaching out, Meg wrapped her fingers around his rough hand and pressed it against her cheek. He drew small circles on her cheek with his thumb, then trailed his thumb down to touch the corner of her mouth. She parted her lips in silent invitation.

As though offering her the opportunity to

change her mind and run, he moved slowly toward her, his eyes searching hers. She lifted her face to his.

Groaning deep within his throat, he closed his eyes and settled his mouth over hers.

The kiss was tentative, unsure, causing Meg to ache for all the stolen kisses he should have had in his life. He brushed his tongue over her lower lip. She placed her hand on the back of his neck, threading her fingers through his hair. Then she touched her tongue to his and drew him in.

Moaning, he clamped his free hand on her waist and drew her against his body while the hand holding her cheek continued to caress her. His tongue moved slowly through her mouth as though savoring the taste.

He explored her mouth as cautiously as he carved stone, bit by bit, touching each nook and cranny, leaving his mark before moving on. She couldn't remember a time when anyone had been so tender, so seemingly appreciative of what she had to offer. Even Kirk, for all his gentleness, had never been this tender.

Ending the kiss, he trailed his thumb over her lower lip. "Did I do it right?" he asked quietly.

Meg moved her hands away from his neck and glided them along his chest. "I have to go now," she said in a hoarse whisper.

She ran to the house, keeping the answer to his question locked inside her heart.

Fourteen

Before dawn, Clay was standing in the doorway of the shed, waiting.

She didn't come.

Throughout the day, he chipped on the stone, hit his thumb more often than he hit the chisel, gazed out the windows, walked to the door, stared in the direction of her farm, and released a sigh stronger than the wind.

As twilight filtered through the windows, he sat in the chair, his hope that she'd come dwindling to an aching loneliness. Holding the bandanna she usually wore, he inhaled the scent of sweet honeysuckle and studied the granite.

The shadows looked as though they were rising from a sea of stone. If he were generous, he could have said he'd cut away at least half the stone that he needed to.

What he was contemplating was wrong, and he knew it. He knew it would be a mistake to work on the details of Kirk's face before he completely carved out the silhouettes.

But he wanted Meg to come back to the

shed and watch him work.

Kirk was the only one with the power to bring her back.

Sunday morning Clay awoke unable to remember a time in his life when he'd felt more alone. If he'd known kissing Meg would mean he'd never see her again except in church, he wasn't certain he would have kissed her.

Hell, he would have kissed her. He just would have kissed her longer and more tenderly until she made those little sounds Kirk had told him about.

He'd kissed her wrong. That's why she hadn't come back. Maybe he'd held her waist too tightly and hurt her. Maybe he'd scratched her face with his rough hand. He should have kept his fingers still instead of touching every inch of her face that his fingers could reach.

And he hadn't shaved before he went to the swimming hole. Maybe a day's growth of beard had chafed her delicate skin.

In retrospect, he could think of a hundred things he'd done wrong when he kissed her.

He couldn't think of a single thing he'd done right.

Sitting at the back of the church, he knew that the days since he'd seen Meg at the swimming hole had been equally long for her. She sat at the organ, staring at the keyboard, her eyes drifting closed from time to time, her shoulders slumped. She didn't even seem to come to life when she played.

Did she regret letting him touch her, letting him kiss her? Did her regrets keep her awake at night? Did his kiss give her nightmares?

He wanted to tell her he'd begun working on Kirk's features. He wanted to tell her he'd never kiss her again or touch her. He wouldn't even talk to her if she'd just come back and watch him work.

The reverend called for a prayer. Usually Clay bowed his head, but today he kept his eyes open and focused on Meg. If he was only going to see her one day a week, he needed to gather as much of her into his memory as he could.

When the prayer ended, Robert stood and addressed the congregation. "As you know, Mama Warner has taken ill. Our dear Meg has been at her side almost constantly. My uncle is with Mama Warner now, but as you go on with your lives, I hope you'll keep my grandmother in your prayers."

Clay bowed his head and prayed. He was the most selfish man he knew. All week he'd only thought about how much he wanted

Meg. It had never occurred to him that perhaps someone else needed her more.

She began to play the organ, and he lifted his gaze. He wished she'd look at him, just once, but she didn't. He got up and walked out of the church.

"If you're gonna do it, you'd best get it done."

Clay glared at Lucian as the people wandered out of the church. "That's easy enough for you to say."

Lucian laughed. "Yeah, it is."

Clay turned his attention back to the churchyard. Holding onto Robert's arm, Meg walked toward the wagon, with people swarming around them like bees to honey.

Clay took a deep breath. She was going to hate him all the more for what he was about to do, but his heart gave him no choice. He settled his gaze on her and started walking.

He ignored the gasps, curses, and stares that pummeled him as people moved aside. He didn't like the way Robert shielded Meg as Clay neared the wagon, but then there wasn't much that he did like lately.

He swept his hat off his head, and his gaze caressed her face while she stared at a button on his shirt. She looked so tired that all he wanted to do was carry her home and rock her in his arms until she fell asleep. "I was sorry to hear Mama Warner has taken ill. I hope you'll tell her that she's in my prayers."

Meg nodded slightly, a tear glistening in her eye. "I will."

It wasn't much. It wasn't enough, but it was all he dared under the circumstances. He nodded toward Robert, returned his hat to his head, and walked away, cursing himself for the coward he was.

Standing in the shed doorway, Meg couldn't take her eyes off the man who was carefully chipping away small bits of stone. He looked as tired as she felt, and she wondered if he'd slept as little as she had this week.

She tended to Mama Warner's needs all day. In the evening, when Robert took her home, she was too exhausted to do anything but fall into bed, but even then she seldom slept. Her body ached, and it felt as heavy as stone.

In her dreams, Clay chipped the stone away and glided his hands over her body. While she dreamed, she longed for his touch. While she was awake, she longed for the safety of her dreams where she could have what she wanted without suffering through the scorn of her family or neighbors.

Robert had been unusually quiet on the ride back to Mama Warner's, and Meg wondered what her face had revealed when Clay had walked up to her. She'd tried to keep her expression impassive, but all she'd wanted was to fall into his arms.

Clay stopped carving and wiped his brow. Then his gaze fell on her, and he became as still as the stone.

Meg walked to the stool and looked up at him. "I didn't think you were going to work on the details until you'd cut away all the stone."

"I felt a need to carve Kirk's face. Do you want to touch it?"

She nodded, and Clay stepped off the stool. He transferred the chisel to the hand holding the hammer. Then he held out his hand to her.

She slipped her hand into his and felt his strong fingers close around it as he helped her climb on the stool. When he started to release her hand, she stopped him, clinging to his fingers. Slowly, she trailed the fingers of her other hand over the edge of a triangle that would one day be Kirk's nose.

"I still have a lot of work left to do," Clay said.

"I know. I didn't think I'd ever see him again."

"I'm hoping in another week or so I'll have his face as it should be."

Nodding, she squeezed his hand and stepped down from the stool. "Robert went to see his uncle. Mama Warner would like to see you while he's gone."

"I'll go clean up."

Silently, Clay stood in Mama Warner's bedroom and studied the withering body. Mama Warner's request to see him had not come as a surprise. He had known that as death approached, she would want to discuss her marker with him. She wasn't one to let others handle her affairs.

Meg eased onto the bed and took Mama Warner's hand. "Mama Warner?" Gently, she shook the older woman's shoulder. "Mama Warner? I brought him. Remember, you asked to see him?"

"Him. Him. Him." She opened her eyes. "Before I pass to the next world, I want you to say his name." She waved her hand. "Let Clayton sit here."

Rising from the bed, Meg smiled uncertainly at Clay before moving into the shadows. Clay sat on the bed and took the frail hand within his larger coarser one. He wished he had worn gloves.

The aged woman smiled and patted his

hand. "You didn't come to see me when you got home."

"I thought it best."

"You never was a smart one." She touched his hair. "You've grown older . . . older than you are. I remember the last time I saw you. You were with the army. They'd stopped here for some water. Remember?"

"Yes, ma'am."

"I asked that nice young lieutenant if you could come into my house and hang a picture over my fireplace." She chuckled. "I didn't have a picture for you to hang. I brought you inside and took you to my kitchen door. You and Kirk used to play in the woods behind my house. No one would have been able to find you if you'd hidden in the woods, but you told me you wouldn't run. A coward would have run. Ever wish you'd run, Clayton?"

"No, ma'am."

"They treated you kindly, did they?"

He didn't want to talk about his past, especially with Meg standing in the room. She seemed on the verge of forgetting the past. He didn't want the fires of hatred rekindled. "That's all in the past. Can't dwell on it."

"You can't because you're young. I'm old. I've earned the right to dwell on whatever I want. My grandson, Robert, told me about

Gettysburg. Told me the Union army dug a few big holes and dropped our boys into them."

Meg gasped from the shadows, and Clay wondered if the war would ever leave these people in peace.

"A mass grave for our men who fought with honor. Do you know if that's true?" Mama Warner whispered hoarsely, tears welling in her eyes.

Clay enfolded his hands around hers. "Mostly."

"There's no such thing as mostly. It's either true or it ain't."

He sighed heavily. "A mass grave was dug, but the men from Cedar Grove weren't buried there." He closed his eyes against the memory. Meg's hatred would grow. The people in town would probably hang him at dawn, and this dear old woman would wish she'd never welcomed him into her house. Opening his eyes, he cleared his throat. "Because I wouldn't fight, I spent some time as a prisoner at a fort. When they released me, I went to find Kirk, to see if he wanted me to bring any messages back. I got there too late. They'd fought the battle. Bodies littered the ground." He shook his head. "So many bodies."

"My grandson died there."

He squeezed her hands. "Yes, ma'am, but I found this little clearing away from the battlefield. It was so green. It looked as though it had never been touched by war, as though it never would be. I dug the graves and made markers. I buried Kirk and the others beneath the shade of the trees." He didn't see any reason to mention that he was unable to locate everyone. He'd given them markers and a place anyway.

"So my grandson has a proper resting place?"

"Yes, ma'am."

She closed her eyes as though too weary to keep them open.

"I'm sorry," he croaked.

She opened her eyes. "Sorry?"

"Yes, ma'am. I'm sorry I didn't bring them home. I didn't have a wagon. I didn't have a horse. I didn't know how I was gonna get myself home. I know I should have found a way to bring them home. I shouldn't have left Kirk there. He wouldn't have left me."

"Do you know that, Clayton? Do any of us know what we'll do when the time comes?"

"I should have brought them home."

"You dug them a grave. You made them a marker. Did you say a prayer for them?"

"Yes, ma'am. Twenty-two prayers."

"We all pay a price when war comes to call. You've paid more than your share. As have I. My dear husband died at the Alamo so we would be free to join the Union. His grandson died so we could be separate from the Union. Which one died in vain?"

"Neither," he said without hesitation. "They both died fighting for what they believed in."

She gave him a warm knowing smile. "Maybe you're a smart one after all." She patted his cheek. "I have a favor to ask."

"I'd do anything for you."

"I know. Meg, bring me my Bible."

As Meg leaned over the bed, the flame from the lamp cast a yellow glow over her face, and Clay saw the trail of her tears. Without looking at him, she gently placed the worn book in Mama Warner's hands.

"I want a marker made of stone," Mama Warner said. "I want the words cut deep so the rain and wind can't take them away any time soon." She folded back the cover on the Bible, and a small piece of paper slipped onto the quilt. "Those are the words I want."

Clay picked up the paper and read the words inscribed in unsteady script. "I lived a life filled with Texas tears and sunshine and never regretted a moment of either."

"Will you do it for me?"

"Yes, ma'am."

She placed her hand over his, and Clay thought she meant to squeeze it, but her touch felt more like a shadow passing in the night. "You make my son pay you for it."

Clay felt the tears sting his eyes and burn down his throat. "No, ma'am. You always treated me like one of your own. I consider it an honor. . . ." He squeezed his eyes shut to stay the tears. "I won't do it for money."

Her fingers slipped from his hand. "I'm tired now. Meg, give this boy some pie before he goes."

"Yes, ma'am."

Clay picked the Bible off the bed and set it on the table beside her bed. He stood, leaned over, and placed a kiss on the wrinkled brow. "I love you, Mama Warner."

"Love you, too, Clayton," she whispered without opening her eyes.

Straightening, he watched her drift into sleep.

Meg lifted the lamp off the table. "Come on," she said in a low voice.

Clay followed her to the kitchen, a kitchen he'd visited many times in his youth. It smelled of flour, cinnamon, and sugar. It smelled of Mama Warner even though she'd probably not entered the room in a good long while. He thought she'd spent so many years in this room that it would always carry a part of her with it. Just like his life. She'd always be there, in his heart, even after she left this world.

Meg walked to the table. Clay walked to the door and stopped, turning his hat in his hands. "I won't be staying."

She turned her head quickly, the knife she'd picked up hovering over the pie. "But Mama Warner wanted you to have some pie."

"You can tell her I did. Tell her I enjoyed it." He settled his hat on his head and reached for the door.

"But she wanted you to stay for a while."

He studied the glass doorknob, remembering the day that several such knobs had arrived. He and Kirk had helped Mr. Warner put them on the doors. They'd given one to Clay, and he'd taken it to his mother — something fancy for her house. She'd put it on her front door so it could greet her guests. He wrapped his hand around the knob. "I'm not up to dealing with your hatred this evening, Meg."

"Please stay," she whispered, a slight tremor in her voice. "It's pecan."

He glanced over his shoulder. She looked vulnerable and so damned tired. She'd been honest in the beginning about her feelings and how she would treat him in town. It was unreasonable to think a couple of kisses could destroy a wall built on a foundation of hatred. Reluctantly, he nodded. "One piece."

She turned her attention back to her task. "Would you like some coffee?"

Placing his hat on the table, he sat in the chair. "Buttermilk, if you got it."

She set the plate and glass before him.

"You gonna join me?" he asked.

"I'd rather just watch."

"I don't like being watched. I get enough of that in town." Ignoring the fork she'd set before him, he picked up the piece of pie and took a healthy bite. While he chewed, she pressed her finger to the plate, picked up a crumb, and carried it to her mouth. With great difficulty, he swallowed. He was jealous of a damn crumb because it had touched her lips.

He cleared his throat. "I, uh, I was concerned when you didn't come to watch me work. I thought . . . I don't know . . . I just thought . . ."

"What did you think?" she asked softly, holding his gaze.

He returned the pie to his plate before the sweat on his fingers made it any soggier. "I thought maybe the kiss upset you."

He brought the glass to his lips, drinking deeply, then wiped the back of his hand across his mouth.

Briefly, she placed her finger against the corner of his mouth. "You missed some."

In awe, he watched as the white liquid on her finger disappeared into her mouth, and he wondered if she had any notion what her actions did to his insides.

Smiling softly, she placed her hand over his. "I never much liked buttermilk before."

He turned his palm up and laced his fingers through hers. "Actually, I did miss having you watch me work this week." He touched his other hand to her cheek. "I thought about you a lot, about that kiss. I wish to God you'd slapped me."

"I wish I'd slapped you, too."

"Why didn't you?"

"I don't know."

"You wouldn't even look at me today."

"I was afraid if I did, people would see how glad I was that you walked over."

"Would that have been so bad?"

She squeezed his fingers. "I'm not up to explaining to the people of this town or to my family what I feel for you. I can't even explain it to myself."

The kitchen door burst open, and Meg

jumped to her feet. "Robert."

"What the hell's going on here, Meg?" Clay shoved away from the table and stood.

"Mama Warner wanted to see him about a marker."

"She seen him?"

She angled her chin. "Yes. She wanted him to have a piece of pie for his trouble."

Clay felt as though he were a damn dog sitting under the table waiting for a morsel of conversation to be tossed his way. He placed his hat on his head and brought the brim down low. "I'll be leaving now." He walked to the door. "It's good to see you, Robert."

Robert stepped aside. "My uncle would rather not see your shadow crossing this threshold."

"I'm sure that's true, but if your grandmother asks to see me again, only a bullet will stop me from coming into this house."

Maybe it was crazy for a lonely man to want to be alone, but Clay hadn't wanted the company of his brothers after visiting with Mama Warner.

He stared at the swimming hole. No ripple disturbed the dark water, which resembled a mirror reflecting the pale light of the moon.

During moments like this, Clay wished he were a painter.

Stone captured a strength that wasn't always there. Stone contained no softness. Over the years, it had roughened his hands. He wished it had roughened his heart.

"I thought I'd find you here," a voice as soft as silk whispered through the night.

Clay turned from the water and leaned against the boulder. Pressing his boot heel against a worn spot in the rock, making his knee jut out, he fought to appear calm.

Meg walked to the boulder and gazed at the pond. "It occurred to me that you lied to me," she said softly.

"When?"

"When I asked you what Kirk looked like the last time you saw him."

"That's not the question I answered. You changed the question and asked what he looked like when he brought me the letters. I told you."

She placed her hand over his where it rested on the boulder. "What did he look like the last time you saw him?"

Turning his palm up, he squeezed her hand. "Don't do this."

She tilted her face toward him, her eyes filled with tears that made them seem as deep as the water on the other side of the boulder. "Ah, Meg."

Moving around his knee until she was nestled between his thighs, she placed her cheek against his chest. "What did he look like?"

Clay brought his arms around her. She was so small. He didn't think he'd ever realized how small she was. "He looked . . ." — closing his eyes, he swallowed, swallowed the truth — "he just looked as though he'd fallen asleep."

She lifted her gaze to his, the moonlight reflected in her tears. "I kept hoping someone had made a mistake, that somehow he'd been spared, and one morning I'd look out the window and see him walking home. But he's not going to come home, is he?"

Clay shook his head. "I'm sorry I didn't bring Kirk home. I should have at least brought him home, even if it meant carrying him on my back."

"They were his friends, his men. He organized them and had them all enlist together so they could fight together. He was their leader. They fought and died at his side. He wouldn't have wanted to leave them. Why didn't you tell us you'd buried them?"

"I didn't figure anyone around here would appreciate the fact that I'd touched their honored sons. You can't take a man off a battlefield without touching him. You can't

319

bury him without touching him. I did what I did because those men had been my friends, and they deserved more than a mass grave. I didn't do it to please their fathers. The day you came to see me about making the monument, you didn't even want me to say Kirk's name. How would you have felt then if you'd known I'd held him in my arms and wept over him?"

"I would have hated you more." Touching her fingers to the white hair at his temples, Meg wondered if his quest at Gettysburg had aged him. She tried to imagine the horror he'd faced, wading through a field littered with bodies, searching for those he knew, smelling the stench that must have risen higher and higher with each passing day, and carrying mangled bodies to a place where they might rest in peace. Despite Clay's words that Kirk looked as though he'd fallen asleep, Meg could not imagine that death ever came silently during war. Kirk would have fought death as diligently as he'd fought the Union soldiers. Pressing her face against Clay's chest, she released the agony of her grief, no longer certain if the tears she shed were for Kirk . . . or for Clay.

Clay felt the small tremor travel along Meg's back. He tightened his hold on her. "Meg?"

Her trembling increased in intensity.

Where were the twins when he needed them? What had they said to her? What could he say to her to ease her hurt?

She cried hard mournful sobs that rose from the deep well of her heart. He gazed at the stars. He supposed if she needed or wanted more from him than his arms around her, she'd tell him.

She sniffed inelegantly. "Do you have a handkerchief?"

"No, ma'am."

She lifted her skirt and blew her nose before wiping the tears from her cheeks. He caught a glimpse of white cotton and closed his eyes against the sight. He'd never realized how alluring white cotton could be.

"It hurts to cry," she said, her voice raspy.

"It hurts worse not to."

"Did you cry?"

"For four days straight."

"Is that how long it took you to bury them?"

"Yes, ma'am," he said in a voice that sounded like stone grating against stone.

She looked to the heavens. "The moon's pretty tonight."

He wanted to tell her she was pretty tonight, but he didn't know how to phrase the words so he wouldn't sound like some lovesick schoolboy.

She pressed her finger to his lips. "You said you spent a lot of time thinking about our kiss. I thought about it as well." She wrapped her hand around the back of his neck and threaded her fingers up into his hair.

"Meg —" He wasn't certain what he'd planned to say, but he knew it couldn't have been important because the words drifted from his mind as soon as her lips lighted upon his. Her mouth was as warm as the shade in August and as soft as a piece of velvet that his mother had sewn into one of her quilts.

She touched the tip of her tongue to one corner of his mouth, then to the other. She nibbled on his lower lip, and he felt as though she were pulling him through the keyhole of hell into heaven.

He cradled her face between his hands, angled his mouth over hers, and welcomed the bliss she offered. Boldly, she gave her tongue the freedom to roam within his mouth. She sighed. He moaned.

He thought a man could become spoiled touching a woman. He might never want to touch stone again. Stone wasn't warm. It didn't alter its shape with the gentlest of pressures. Stone didn't breathe so he could feel its moisture on his face. Rocks didn't make soft sounds that he'd carry with him until the day he died.

She drew her mouth away from his, and he forced himself not to follow and reclaim what he wanted.

Her eyes were dark within the shadows of the night, but he felt the intensity of her gaze as strongly as he felt her fingers tighten their hold on his neck.

"I hate you," she whispered hoarsely.

He lowered his hands from her face. "I know."

"So why am I here?" She trailed her fingers over his face, touching every line, crease, and crevice. "Robert kissed me tonight." She rubbed her thumb over his lower lip. "And all I could think about was kissing you."

She returned her mouth to his. If this was hate, he'd probably die if the woman ever loved him. His heart beat so hard he was certain she could feel it thrumming through his shirt. Each breath he took carried with it the scent of honeysuckle. Her hands, so small, slipped beneath the collar of his shirt. Her slim fingers moved gently, creating small circles on his neck that seemed to travel clear down to his toes. Then she parted her lips and gave him the greatest treasure of all: hot, moist, and silky, her mouth invited him home.

Meg felt Clay's hesitancy to follow her lead. She teased his tongue, suckled it, then drew it into her mouth. He groaned, and she felt a shudder run the length of his body. She found his uncertainty endearing. When it came to matters of the heart, he had maintained an innocence that she had seldom seen since the war.

She knew Kirk had kissed an abundance of girls before he ever kissed her, knew he had bedded others before he took her as his wife. He had taught her the pleasures to be found with a man, had given much more than he'd taken. He'd been a skilled teacher, she an apt student.

Yet now, she found Clay's lack of experience as intoxicating as she'd found Kirk's abundant knowledge. He moved his hands back to her face, his fingers lovingly tracing the curves of her cheeks, the lines of her brow, and the jut of her chin. He touched her as though she were as delicate as fine-spun glass. He touched her as though she were more precious than gold.

Drawing away from the kiss, she placed her hands over his. "Are you trying to memorize my lines so you can carve the stone accurately?"

Slowly, he moved his head from side to side. "I could carve your likeness in stone if

I were blinded. I've just never touched anything as soft or as smooth as you are. I can't
get over how incredible you feel." His hands
fell away from her face.

"What's wrong?"

In the moonlight, she could see the barest
of smiles touch his lips. "Wish I had diffcrent
hands. Mine are so damn ugly, they
shouldn't be touching you."

Wrapping her fingers around his hands,
she lifted them to her lips and pressed a kiss
to his knuckles. Releasing one of his hands,
she turned the other over and skimmed her
fingers over the roughened surface, a palm
that was as unpolished as the stone it had
caressed over the years. She placed a kiss in
the center of his palm. "I like your hands."

"Why?" he asked, and she heard the disbelief mirrored in his voice. "They're so big.
They look and feel like stone."

She rubbed her cheek along his hand. "But
they don't touch like stone. I watch the way
you chip at the stone, and then you touch it
as though you're apologizing for treating it
so harshly, as though you don't realize you're
doing it a favor and turning it into something
of beauty. I've missed watching you work
this week to the point that I've resented every
thoughtful neighbor who stopped by to visit
Mama Warner because I had to play hostess

and couldn't sneak away for a few minutes. I don't mind caring for Mama Warner, but it wears me out to care for all the people who come by to see her."

"I've never felt lonelier in my life than I felt the day after I saw you here, and you didn't come to watch me work. I started carving Kirk's features because I thought it would bring you back to me."

"Will you stop working on his face now that you know why I didn't come?"

He shook his head. "No, I'll go ahead and finish it now that I've begun. Might have to carve your features as well, just so I won't feel so dadgum alone."

"I'd watch you work if I could, but Mama Warner has always been there when I needed her. I can't leave —"

"I know."

She pressed her cheek against his chest. "Don't stop working on the monument."

"I won't," he promised.

Fifteen

By unspoken agreement, they met at the swimming hole every night after that. Lying on a quilt, Meg gazed at the stars. Stretching out beside her, Clay looked at her.

She told him about her day, caring for Mama Warner. She never talked enough to satisfy him. He could have listened to her soft voice all night, well into the morning, if she would have stayed with him that long, but he always escorted her home around midnight, watching while she climbed in through the window, wishing he could boldly escort her to the front door.

The days were shorter when he had the nights to look forward to, but the nights were never long enough.

Perched on an elbow, he lifted the end of her braid.

"What are you thinking?" she asked.

"Wishing I was a painter. I'd use your braid as my brush, dip it in the colors, and create the most beautiful paintings in the world."

"And what would you do if I wasn't near you?"

"Ah, there's the secret. I'd have to keep you near me."

She wrapped her hand around his neck and pulled him toward her waiting mouth. With no doubts, she initiated his favorite part of the night.

Rolling onto his stomach, he braced his elbows on either side of her to keep his weight off her, grazed his knuckles along her cheeks, and lowered his mouth to hers.

Words he dared not speak drifted through his mind, questions with answers he'd rather not hear taunted him. If she hated him, why did she meet him here every night? If she hated him, why did she welcome his touch? If she loved him, why did she meet him secretly?

If he loved her, why didn't he leave her alone instead of luring her into his world where hate overshadowed love, and battles were still fought over a war long over?

Moaning softly, she pressed her head back against the quilt, arching her throat. Clay had learned that she liked it when he used his mouth to blaze a trail along the ivory column of her throat. Each night he learned more what she enjoyed because each night, she gave a little more of herself to him.

Gliding her hands along his shoulders, she kneaded his muscles. "You feel so tight, you must have worked extra hard today."

"Worked extra long." He lifted his face, his gaze holding hers. "I want you to come and see what I've done before you go home tonight."

"I wish you could work at night."

"Lanterns wouldn't give me enough light. I need the sun."

"You carved a headstone during a storm at night."

"That was different. It's smaller. I have to keep all the monument in sight. Shadows at night would distort the stone. No telling what I'd end up carving."

She threaded her fingers through his hair and rubbed her thumbs in circles over his temples. "Have you made Mama Warner's marker?"

"I made it the day after I saw her."

"Is that what you want to show me?"

"No, making markers never brings me joy."

"What you did today —"

"I think it'll bring you joy."

Walking through the moonless night, her hand wrapped firmly within his, Meg wanted to tell Clay that he brought her joy.

Watching Mama Warner grow weaker with each passing day, knowing she could do nothing but offer comfort and company, Meg went home exhausted each evening. Only the knowledge that she'd see Clay carried her through the long hours of the day.

She didn't know why she'd denied herself the pleasure of his company that first week or why she thought she was too tired to crawl out the window and run to the darkened swimming hole.

She enjoyed listening to his voice as he talked about his day. Carving, she discovered, was very much like plowing a field, only the crops he hoped to harvest grew from seeds planted in dreams. Mesmerized, she'd watch his hands create shapes in the air as she was certain they'd created shapes in the stone. He talked low, his voice a caress in the night. She took the sound of his voice, the feel of his kiss into her dreams, drew strength from the small amount of time that they had together each night.

They neared the shed, and he gripped her hand harder as he slowed his steps. He opened the shed door.

"You oiled it," she whispered.

"Yeah, sometimes I just come out here and sit, long before dawn. I prefer not to wake the twins when I do."

They stepped into the shed, and he released his hold on her hand. She heard scratching, then a flame flared, and he lit a lantern. Lifting it over his shoulder, he walked toward the statue.

Meg eased around him and lifted her gaze. "Oh, my."

He held out his hand. Slipping her hand into his, she stepped onto the stool. With trembling fingers, she touched the stone face.

"What do you think?" he asked quietly.

"It looks just like him," she said in awe. She worked her other hand free of Clay's grasp and touched both palms to Kirk's cheeks. She ran her fingers over the stone brow, along the eyes, and down the nose. "It's perfect."

"It's hardly perfect."

"You captured so well the man he was before the war. Look at the pride reflected in his face. He has no doubts. He believes in what he's doing." She sighed wistfully. "I wish Mama Warner could see this."

"Why can't she?"

"She's so weak, she can't even get out of bed, and you certainly can't drag the monument to her."

"I could bring her here."

"She's too frail. I don't think she could travel this far."

"She could if we used the wagon. I'll put

a couple of mattresses and several blankets in the back. We'll go slow. I'll carry her to the wagon. Then I'll carry her in here."

"When would we do it?"

"Tomorrow?"

Meg knew it was unlikely that Mama Warner would live long enough to see the monument completed, but Clay had finished carving what she would care about most. "People are traipsing in and out of her house all day. All we need is for one of them to tell Robert or Mr. Warner, and after you dared Robert to shoot you, what's left of the family would probably come after you with all guns loaded."

"We could do it in the evening."

Meg planted her hands on her hips. "So Robert wouldn't have to come looking for you? He could just shoot you as you cross the threshold?"

"Not if he doesn't know I'm crossing the threshold. The man's gotta sleep some time."

"You mean go late at night?"

"Why not? She's never put locks on her doors."

"And if we get caught?"

"I'm willing to risk it."

The following night Meg sat in the wagon,

hoping she wouldn't regret what she and Clay were about to do. Their good intentions could easily bring harm Clay's way if they were discovered.

"Take off your boots," Meg whispered as she worked off her shoes.

"Why?" Clay asked.

"So we don't wake Robert when we're walking through the house."

"Does he wake easily?"

Meg snapped her head around. "I don't know, but Kirk did. I assume since they're cousins . . ."

"Wish I'd known . . . ," he mumbled as he jerked off his boot.

The lantern resting at Meg's feet in the wagon cast its light on his large toe as it peered through a hole in his sock. He pulled the bottom of his sock over the hole and wedged it between his toes. Meg bit back her smile. She'd never in her life known a man as modest as this one.

He jumped off the wagon and walked around the mule. The moon was but a silver sliver in the sky, the stars sparkling like a thousand diamonds. She didn't know if they could have picked a better night for their clandestine adventure.

After helping her climb out of the wagon, he reached for the lantern. She laid her hand on his arm, and he stilled. "Promise me if we wake Robert that you'll walk out the door."

"And leave you to face his wrath?"

"He won't get angry at me. In all likelihood, he'll shoot you."

He chuckled low. "I won't run, Meg."

"I'm not asking you to run. I'm just asking you to leave if we wake Robert."

"How will you explain what you're doing in the house?"

"I'll say I couldn't sleep and came to look in on Mama Warner."

Bowing his head, he studied the ground. "Do you think I'm a coward?"

"I just don't want you to get shot in the middle of an act of kindness."

He lowered the flame in the lantern until it was little more than a whisper of light in the dark. "All right. Let's try not to wake him."

As they trudged toward the house, Meg realized for the first time in her life how loudly the grass crunched beneath her feet. She feared they'd wake the entire county. Clay walked in long sure strides as though he'd forgotten that their visit was a secret, as though he wanted to tempt Kirk's father to aim a gun at him.

She hurried to catch him and wrapped her

hand around his swinging arm as they neared the house. "Let me go in first," she whispered.

Clay reluctantly acknowledged the wisdom of her words. If Robert did wake up, he'd be less alarmed if he saw Meg walking through the house. Clay gave a brusque nod.

Meg took the lantern and slowly eased open the door. She peered into the darkened kitchen and listened intently. Slipping the lantern through the opening, she searched the shadows, then tiptoed into the house.

Clay stepped in after her, and Meg could have sworn he stomped the floor. With her finger pressed to her mouth, she spun around and glared at him.

He shrugged.

"Walk on your toes," she said in a low voice.

He grimaced.

"Do it or I won't go any farther," she threatened.

She watched his height increase and lowered the lantern for a closer inspection of his feet. His large toe had escaped through the hole in his sock.

She crept through the kitchen and halted at the hallway. One way led to the room she'd shared with Kirk, the room where Robert now slept. The main room of the house lay beyond it. In the opposite direction, a few steps down the hall, the door to Mama Warner's room stood ajar.

Taking a deep breath, she cautiously tiptoed down the hall. She peered in through the open door.

Smiling, Mama Warner lay in the bed, her hand lifted slightly, and her fingers wiggling in the air. Meg hurried across the room, the lantern swaying and chasing away the shadows.

"I was starting to worry about you," Mama Warner whispered.

Meg pressed her finger to the older woman's lips. "We have to be quiet."

Mama Warner waved her hand as though shooing away an irritating fly. Then she extended her gnarled fingers toward Clay. His larger hand swallowed hers. "Meg says you're taking me on an adventure."

To Meg's surprise the brilliance of Clay's smile shone through the dimness of the room.

"Yes, ma'am. I'm gonna be as gentle as I can, but you tell me if I hurt you."

Meg forgot about cautioning him to be quiet. She forgot about everything but watching the care with which he wrapped a blanket around Mama Warner before gingerly lifting her into his arms and cradling her against his chest.

"Comfortable?" he asked.

"You know how to hold a woman so she feels precious. Makes me wish I was sixty years younger."

Clay laughed, and Meg thumped his shoulder. "Shh."

He rolled his eyes. "She keeps me on a tight line."

"Not tight enough from what I hear."

"Will you two be quiet!" Meg whispered sharply. "You're gonna wake Robert, and then we'll have all hell to pay." She nudged Clay. "Get moving."

"It'd help if the person with the lantern led the way," he said in a low voice.

Meg took the lead, and the whispering behind her increased. These two were worse than maiden aunts at a social. She scurried down the hallway and ducked into the kitchen.

And waited while Clay took his own sweet time following her. She felt as though she were standing on the edge of a deep abyss by the time he finally ambled into the kitchen. She could tell he and the woman in his arms were fighting to hold back their laughter. She trudged through the door, holding it open an eternity.

"You must have trained your mule," she

whispered when Clay finally walked onto the porch. "You move slower than it does. Try and hurry. I'd like for us to be back before sunup."

"She always harping at you like that?" Mama Warner asked.

"She's usually worse."

Meg doubled back. "How can you walk so slow when your legs are so long? Usually I can't keep up with you. Tonight when it matters, you're slower than a turtle."

"I don't want to get reckless and drop my precious bundle here."

As they neared the shed, Meg felt her heart flutter. She was afraid Mama Warner wouldn't like the statue; maybe it was a mistake to show it to anyone before it was finished.

They walked into the shed, and Meg increased the flame in the lantern. As Clay walked by, she lifted the lantern higher and saw the same doubts reflected in his face. She didn't know why it hurt to know that he was nervous about sharing his work. He had a rare gift, and she suddenly wished that he had gone to Europe, that he had developed his art and honed his skills.

Meg moved closer to the granite, and the shadows shifted over the stone. Mama

Warner gasped. With tears filling her eyes, she covered her mouth with her gnarled fingers. "I want to touch him," she rasped.

Clay shot his gaze over to Meg. She saw in his eyes that he hadn't expected Mama Warner's request. She also saw that he wasn't about to disappoint the woman. He glanced at the stool, then looked back at her. "Go get Lucian. He should be in the house."

Meg set the lantern on the table.

"I'm a lot of trouble," she heard Mama Warner say.

She glanced over her shoulder. Cast in faint shadows, Clay sat on the stool, holding Kirk's grandmother in his lap and shaking his head, a tender smile on his face. "No, ma'am. You're no trouble at all."

She patted his cheek. "You should have walked out my backdoor years back when you had a chance. You would have had a lot fewer lines in your face."

"If I'd walked out your backdoor that day, I never would have been able to walk back in through it."

He bowed his head. A lump knotted in Meg's throat as she detected a subtle movement of his arms; she guessed that he was holding Mama Warner tighter. They didn't seem to notice that she hadn't left yet, but she felt as though she was intruding on an intimate moment that belonged only to the two of them.

Creeping out of the shed, she headed to the house. She knocked lightly and waited several moments before slowly pushing the door open. The amber glow of a dying fire in the hearth and the low flame in a lantern on the table threw a pale light over the room. She stepped into the house and picked up the lantern. The wall to her right contained a closed door, as did the wall to her left. She chose the door to her right. She walked across the room and tapped her fingers on the door. "Lucian?"

Carefully, she opened the door and peered into the room. A familiar scent greeted her. Clay.

Entering, she glanced at the bare furnishings. A cheval glass faced the wall, and she wondered why he didn't want to look at his reflection in the mirror. Did he see a coward when he met his gaze?

A smaller mirror did hang on the wall above a washstand. She stood on the tips of her toes. She supposed he looked in this mirror when he shaved, although she didn't think he could see much of his face at one time.

She imagined Clay holding the razor in his large hand, angling his chin, and peering at the mirror as he grazed the sharp edge over his face, removing a night's growth of thick beard.

She touched the brush with which he tried to manage his hair. He didn't have the skills with the brush that he had with a chisel and hammer. He could shape stone, but he couldn't make his hair do anything but fall over his brow.

He'd tucked the quilts neatly into place on his bed. She wondered how far down he sank into the mattress. She wondered if he found sleeping alone as lonely as she did.

Turning to leave, she noticed an object on the dresser as the light of the lantern swung past it. She walked to the dresser and touched the stone.

He had carved a small girl sitting with her elbows on a table and her chin in her hands. The girl looked incredibly sad, as though she'd just lost something precious. One side of the rock was jagged as though whatever Clay had carved had fallen or broken off. She trailed her fingers over the braid along the girl's back. She knew why the girl was sad; she was the girl.

"What are you doing?" a deep voice demanded.

Meg spun around, her hand pressed to her throat. "Oh, Lucian. I was looking for you."

"You won't find me in Clay's room."

"I didn't realize it was his room . . . not at first, anyway. He needs you in the shed."

He ran his hands through his hair. "Let me get a shirt."

He disappeared in the darkness. She walked quickly out of the room and quietly closed the door. Lucian walked through a door across the room. "I'm ready."

"I'm sorry," she said as she set the lantern on the table and walked to the door. "I didn't know where you slept."

"I sleep with the twins, and the little rascals snore."

He held the door open for her, and she stepped back into the night. They walked in silence to the shed.

Meg crossed to the other side of the shed, and Clay snapped his head up, his brow furrowed. "Mama Warner fell asleep while we were waiting on you."

Kneeling, Meg gently shook Mama Warner's shoulder. "Mama Warner, you need to wake up now."

Mama Warner squinted. "I saw Kirk."

"No, ma'am. You saw his face carved in the stone."

"Ah, yes. The monument. It's not gonna be what you wanted, Meg."

"I think it's going to be exactly what I

wanted. You wanted to touch Kirk, remember?"

"Of course, I remember. I'm old. I'm not forgetful."

"Lucian, you hold Mama Warner," Clay said. "I'll stand on the stool, and you can hand her up to me."

Standing, Meg moved aside, and Lucian took Mama Warner from Clay. Clay climbed on the stool and braced his legs. He lifted Mama Warner into his arms and held her toward the statue.

Mama Warner ran her gnarled fingers over Kirk's carved features. Then she slumped against Clay's shoulder. "You done good, Clayton. You done good."

Leaning against the boulder, Meg watched as Clay spread the quilt on the ground. They'd taken Mama Warner home and then come to the swimming hole. With so little moon, the darkness hid most of Clay's actions.

She'd tried to maintain a wall of hatred, but he'd chipped away at the wall little by little. He'd begun innocently the day she saw him playing with the naked twins in the river. She could recall each and every unselfish act that had served as his chisel, each kindness as his hammer.

Now she watched his silhouette stretch and pull the corners of the quilt across the grass. He knelt on the quilt and braced his hands on his thighs. "You've been unusually quiet. Would you rather I take you home?"

Meg walked across the small space separating them, dropped to her knees, and wrapped her hand around the back of his neck. "I'm not certain I want you to take me home at all tonight."

She pressed her mouth to his, and he lifted his hands to her face, the only place he ever touched her. She slid her hand around and began to unbutton his shirt. He moved his mouth from hers with lightning speed.

"What are you doing?" he asked.

"I want to remove your shirt."

"Why?"

She ran her hand along his shirt. "Because I want to touch your chest, your bare back."

Clay looked at his hand touching her cheek. He could see the outline of her face, but he couldn't make out the smooth unmarred surface. He hoped the shadows hid his imperfections as easily as they hid her perfection. He brushed his lips over hers, hoping she'd find the permission she needed.

She did.

She worked the buttons free on his shirt

as he groaned and deepened the kiss. Easing his shirt free from his trousers, she lifted the ends.

Clay didn't want to withdraw from the kiss, didn't want to give her a clear view of his chest, but she tugged on the shirt, giving him no choice. He took one last taste of her with him before leaning away and lifting his arms. He felt the warm night air touch every inch of his chest and back as she slowly pulled his shirt over his head. He wondered if she was taking her time because she was considering covering him up again. The shirt had risen up to hide his face so he could no longer see Meg, and he didn't know if that was a blessing or a curse.

He felt her curves brush against his chest as she worked the shirt free of his arms. He'd never realized how damn long his arms were. His hands gained their freedom, and he dropped them to his side. Then she whipped the shirt off his head, and he found himself staring at her face in the darkness. He couldn't tell a damn thing about what she was thinking. He cursed the blessed darkness. He wished he could see her clearly without her seeing him.

With trembling fingers, she outlined his shoulders. "You feel just as I thought you would," she said softly. "It gets so hot in the shed. I kept hoping you'd take your shirt off so I could watch you work. It's as though when you shape the stone, it shapes you."

She trailed her hands along to his back and pressed her fingers against every muscle and bone he had while he sat like a statue. She had such small hands, such gentle hands. He'd never in his life had someone touch him with such tenderness. He wanted to return the favor, but was afraid she'd stop if he moved.

"I never realized how incredibly strong you have to be to chip away at the stone. You move with such grace, showing so little effort, but I can see the strength in your hands, feel it in your shoulders and back. I could easily spend the rest of my life watching you cut into stone."

He could easily have spent the rest of his life watching her watch him, having her sit in that chair, filling the shed with the scent of honeysuckle. If he slowed his pace on the monument, perhaps he could keep her with him for three years, but he knew once he finished the monument, the chair would remain empty, the honeysuckle would fade away, and all he'd have were memories of a woman who'd touched him one night as though she no longer hated him.

She ran her hands back up to his shoulders

before slowly moving her splayed fingers toward his chest. He wrapped his hands around hers to stop the exploration. He feared, even in the darkness, she'd discover things about him that he'd rather she didn't know. "I like it when you touch my back," he said as he guided her hands around his sides.

Leaning forward, she trailed little kisses along his throat, branding him with the heat from her mouth. "You can touch me, too," she whispered just before she nibbled on his ear.

He flexed his fingers and touched them lightly to her cheeks. He angled her head away from his ear and covered her mouth with his own. She sighed softly, and he held back an answering groan. She'd probably think he was in pain if he continued to sound like an animal every time she touched him.

She shifted her body, and he felt her breasts whisper along his chest. She moved her hands off his flesh, and he felt them working between their bodies. He snapped his head back. "What are you doing?"

She ducked her head as though embarrassed. "I'm hot."

He watched in amazement as the material of her blouse parted and her throat came into view.

She peered at him. "Would you like to do this?"

"I've . . . I've never unbuttoned a lady's blouse before."

"It's not much different than unbuttoning your shirt. You just slip the button through the hole." He could hear the laughter in her voice as she demonstrated with ease and exposed a little bit more of her flesh.

Clay felt as though someone had just stuffed cotton into his mouth. Rubbing his hands along his thighs, he tried to calm their trembling. He reached for the button, and his knuckles grazed the inside swells of her breasts. He jerked his hands back. "Maybe you'd better unbutton that one."

She shook her head slightly. "I want you to."

He took a deep breath and returned his fingers to the button. His hands didn't want to cooperate. They didn't want to push a button through a hole. They wanted to open and cup her breasts. He tried to force them to forget they were nestled between the lush valley of her breasts. Her button went flying out into the night.

"Damn!" He moved his hands away from her blouse. "If we find it, I can sew it back on."

She wrapped her hands around his. "I'm

not worried about my button. I'm worried that maybe you don't want what I'm offering."

He swallowed hard. "What are you offering?"

"All of me."

"Oh, Lord." He bowed his head. "I want you so bad, Meg, that it hurts. I've loved you so long that I can't remember when I didn't." He lifted his gaze to hers. "You won't even say my name."

"I will." She pressed a kiss to the corner of his mouth. "I promise I will."

"When?"

"When it'll mean the most."

"Do you still hate me?"

She shook her head. "No. I haven't hated you for a long time. I tried to hate you. I pretended that I did because it frightened me to have all these feelings again. I loved Kirk. I wanted to die when he did. I didn't think I'd ever fall in love with anyone else." She laid her palm against his cheek and smiled tenderly, with tears welling in her eyes. "But I have."

Taking her hand, he pressed a kiss into the heart of her palm. "I don't know how to show you what I feel without fumbling all over myself . . . and you."

"Then I'll show you," she said in a voice

as sultry as the night.

He didn't know if he'd survive her showing him, but he was willing to chance it. She presented him with her profile as she worked her shoes off. He tugged off his boots and tossed them aside. He'd worry about finding them later. She touched his knee and might just as well have touched his heart, so tender was her caress.

"I'll finish undressing you in a minute," she said.

She hiked her skirt over her knee, and he watched as she slowly peeled her stocking down her calf, over her ankle, and past her toes. Where was a full moon when he needed one? One that would shine on her and not on him.

Abruptly, she spun around and placed her stocking-covered foot in his lap. "You can take this one off."

He wrapped his hand around her calf. "You're so smooth, so soft." He rolled the stocking down, slipped it off, and covered her foot with his hand. "You have such small feet."

"And small ears."

He lifted his gaze to her chest where her fingers were busily giving freedom to her buttons. The valley widened. "I don't think they're as small as I thought."

She eased out of her blouse, exposing her shoulders to the night. He tugged on the ribbon holding her chemise together. The bow disappeared, and the material parted.

She rose to her knees and slipped the straps off her shoulders. "You do the rest."

He fumbled with the buttons, ribbons, lace, and cotton, but she didn't seem to mind. She moved slightly to accommodate his needs, to give him easier access to her clothes. He didn't know how his trembling hands managed to remove her clothes and pile them up beside her, but they did.

Unbraiding her hair and fanning it over her bare shoulders, she laughed lightly. "I've never been quite so bold."

"I've never felt quite so timid. I wish you didn't have any experience at this."

She pressed on his shoulders until his back hit the quilt. "You're not competing with anyone tonight. It's only you and me." She skimmed her hand over the front of his trousers. "No ghosts from my past." She unbuttoned his trousers. He lifted his hips, and she deftly removed his remaining clothes.

Clay was breathing as though he'd just run to the top of a mountain, and she was sitting there as calm as the dawn, trailing her fingers up and down his thigh, touching his knee and moving her fingers closer to his groin with each sweep. The woman was an expert at torture.

"Has any woman ever touched you?" she asked as she splayed her fingers over his thigh.

"No."

"Do you want a woman to touch you?"

"No."

She stilled, and Clay pushed himself up. He cradled her cheek in his palm. "I want you to touch me." He kissed her deeply, with more urgency than he'd ever experienced. The curve of her breast brushed against his chest, and he wanted to crush her against him, to feel her weight on top of him.

Her hand slowly caressed his upper thigh, circling higher. His breathing stopped altogether. Her fingers journeyed across his stomach, trailed along his other thigh, then cut across the pass, and stroked him with an intimacy that caused his body to buck with a series of nearly violent spasms. Lost in the fiery sensations, he buried his face in her hair until his body was replete, and his breathing slowed. "I'm sorry," he rasped.

Cradling his cheek, she moved his face away from her neck. "It's what I wanted."

Slowly as his senses returned, he realized that her other hand was still stroking him. If she'd been repulsed by his body's reaction to her touch, she had a strange way of showing it.

"I'm the one with the experience." She kissed him lightly. "If you've never been with a woman, I didn't think you'd be able to hold out long. My body doesn't react quite as swiftly, so I was hoping to even us out."

"You might have warned me."

"That I'm a brazen hussy who enjoys a man's touch?"

"That you were gonna take me straight to heaven." He gave her what he hoped was a devilish grin. "Now it's my turn to take you to heaven."

Her eyes widened. "I didn't think you had any experience."

"I'm a fast learner."

"You might start by pretending you just finished carving me from stone. I love to watch your hands move over the stone after you've carved it."

Using his fingers, he brushed her hair off her shoulders so her curves were a visible silhouette in the night. Slowly, he skimmed his hands along her shoulders, down her side until he could feel the weight of her breasts nestled in his palms. "You're nothing like stone, Meg. Stone's harsh and rough. Countless times, it's made my palms bleed. It's toughened my hands so I often forget there are soft things in this world. You make me wish I'd never run my hands over stone, that I'd kept them soft for you."

"I've told you before that I like your hands. I like the way they feel on my skin. I feel like they're whispering secrets."

He eased her down to the quilt. "Is there something special I should do?"

Meg studied the shadows of his face. Even in the dark, he appeared older than he was; even his innocence had been tainted by the war. "Just touch me . . . with your hands . . . with your mouth . . . with your body."

He laid his body partially over hers. "I want you to enjoy being with me."

"Then kiss me."

He swooped his mouth down to cover hers. Meg welcomed him with a desperation that unsettled her.

He swept his tongue inside her mouth as he brushed his thumb along the underside of her breast. She felt her breasts swell and the warmth travel through her body. Rolling slightly, she pressed up against his bare thigh.

He was incredibly solid, his muscles firm and tight. She ran her hands along his back and wondered how he could look so lean and be so strong. His touch contained a strength tempered with gentleness.

He trailed his mouth along her throat and dipped his tongue into the hollow at its base. Then he moved lower and his tongue swirled around her nipple. The touch of his hand had hardened it, the promise of his mouth caused it to pucker. He closed his mouth around the tip and suckled gently. Moaning softly, Meg arched her back and turned into him.

"You taste good," he said without moving his mouth from her breast.

"So do you when you're not stingy with your mouth."

He chuckled and shifted his weight so he was nestled between her thighs. He trailed his mouth from one breast to the other, then brushed it along her stomach as he sat back on his heels. Slowly, he glided his hands over her body. "You're perfect, Meg. Did you know that? If I was a real sculptor, I'd always use you as my model."

"You are a real sculptor."

"No, Meg. I dreamed of being a sculptor, thought I could be one, but I'm not. I've already made some mistakes on the monument. They're small, barely noticeable, but I know they exist. Thought you should know before we take this any further."

"The monument has nothing to do with what's happening between us tonight. I love you, Clay."

His name whispered on her lips was something Clay'd yearned for as much as he'd yearned for her love, her touch, her eyes holding his as though she saw nothing about him to be ashamed of.

Sitting up, she palmed his cheek and whispered his name once more before kissing him tenderly.

He gave his heart into her keeping.

Meg kissed his cheek, his chin, the hollow at the base of his throat where she was certain the sweat gathered when he worked. Running her hands along his shoulders and arms, she eased back down to the quilt. "Come to me, Clay."

He laid his body over hers. Sliding her hand between their bodies, Meg opened herself to him and guided him home. He shuddered and stilled. "Oh, God, you feel good. I didn't expect you to feel like this." Braced on his elbows, he lowered his mouth to hers, accepting her offering.

Instinct took over and he rocked his hips against hers, slowly at first, timidly, until his confidence grew and they found their rhythm. No hair covered his chest, and his body rubbing over hers felt like silk upon silk.

Meg felt the warmth between her thighs kindle and ignite into a raging fire. Writhing beneath him, she met his thrusts and dug her fingers into his back.

Clay listened as her soft whimpers filled the night. He'd never heard anything more beautiful in his life. She gasped, and he wanted to ask her what she needed from him. He increased the tempo of his thrusts and delved deeper. She arched her back and called his name to the heavens. It was all he needed to send him spiraling over the edge.

When the storm passed, he could still feel the slight pulsing of her body around his. He kissed her throat, her chin, her cheek, her lips, before burying his face in her hair. He tightened his hold on her. "I didn't think anyone would ever want me," he whispered.

She trailed her fingers along his back, over his shoulders, and took his face between her hands, turning it so their gazes could meet in the darkness.

"You were wrong."

Sixteen

Standing by the wagon, Clay watched closely as the congregation poured out of the church. Meg's father and brother ambled toward their wagon.

Then he saw what he was waiting for: Robert walked out of the church alone. His departure left only one person inside. Clay brought the brim of his hat low over his brow. "I'll be back in a minute," he threw over his shoulder to his brothers before he began walking back toward the church.

To his surprise, Meg had looked radiant playing the organ even though he hadn't taken her home until dawn. He'd yawned through most of the service and would have fallen asleep if it weren't for the fact that he would have been deprived of the pleasure of gazing upon her.

He tried to be discreet as he walked to the church, but the murmurs of people standing in the churchyard rose like locusts swooping down to devour the crops. Removing his hat, he walked through the open door into the sanctuary. The clapboard building echoed his hollow footsteps as he strode down the aisle. Stopping, he smiled as Meg walked toward him. "Morning."

Her step faltered, and she glanced quickly around the empty church.

"Thought I might escort you home or to Mama Warner's . . . wherever it is you're going."

She paled. "Please, don't talk to me here. We had an agreement to ignore each other in town."

She started to brush past him, and he grabbed her arm, spinning her around. "I thought what passed between us last night sent that agreement to hell."

"My father will kill you if he sees you talking to me."

"I'm willing to risk it."

"I'm not."

"Get your hand off her, you yellow-bellied coward." The young male voice reverberated off the church walls.

Clay glanced over Meg's shoulder to see her brother standing in the doorway, legs akimbo, hands balled into tight fists.

"Please," Meg whispered. "I don't want any trouble here."

He released his hold on her. As though she might say something further, she parted her lips slightly. Then she walked out of the church.

"Touch her again, and I'll kill you," Daniel said.

Clay wondered if he should tell her brother that he'd be doing him a favor if he killed him . . . because his heart had just died.

Darkness cloaked Meg. The night before she'd found comfort in it; now she felt as though she'd fallen into a well of loneliness.

She'd waited for hours by the swimming hole, but Clay hadn't come. She looked at his house. Everything appeared serene. Surely if he'd been hurt or fallen ill, she would have seen some sign.

Running toward the side of the house where she knew his bedroom to be, she tripped and fell. Sitting up, she rubbed her scraped shin. In the darkness, she could barely make out the shape of a rabbit with a solitary ear.

She scrambled to her feet and walked carefully through the stone graveyard until she reached the house. A pale light spilled through the uneven cracks in the shutters. She tapped on the wood. "Clay?"

Pressing her ear to the shutter, she heard movement within the room. "Clay?"

Someone blocked the light escaping through the cracks. "Go home, Meg."

"I need to talk to you. Please let me in."

Opening the shutters, Clay was a dark silhouette against the backdrop of the lantern. "You said all that needed to be said in church."

"Please let me explain."

Releasing a deep sigh, he pulled her through the window and closed the shutters. Leaning against the wall, he crossed his arms over his chest. "Explain."

She brushed the dirt off her skirt and smoothed the stray strands of hair away from her face. "You didn't meet me at the swimming hole."

"I didn't see any point in going."

"I know you're angry —"

"I'm not angry."

If he wasn't angry, he certainly did a good imitation. His voice was clipped and as hard as stone. She wrung her hands together. "I love you, Clay."

"No, you don't."

Meg felt as though he'd just slapped her. "Yes, I do. When you leave this town, I'll go with you."

Narrowing his eyes, he studied her. "Will you marry me?"

"Yes."

"Will you give me children?"

"If I can. Kirk and I were never able to

conceive, but if I can have children, I want to have yours."

"In this town that we move to, wherever it is, will you walk down the street with me?"

"Of course."

"Holding my hand?"

"Yes."

"And the hands of my children?"

"Yes."

He unfolded his arms and took a step toward her. She wanted to fling herself into his embrace, but something hard in his eyes stopped her.

"And what happens, Mrs. Warner, when someone you know rides through town and points at me and calls me a yellow-bellied coward? What will you do then? Will you let go of my hand and take my children to the other side of the street? Will you pretend that you haven't kissed me, that you haven't lain with me beneath the stars?" With disgust marring his features, he turned away. "You think I'm a coward. Go home."

"I don't think that. I love you."

He spun around. "You don't believe in that love, you don't believe in me."

"Yes, I do."

He stalked toward her. She backed into the corner and bent her head to meet his infuriated gaze.

"How strongly do you believe in our love?" he asked, his voice ominously low. "If they threatened to strip off your clothes unless you denied our love, would you deny our love?"

He gave her no chance to respond, but continued on, his voice growing deeper and more ragged, as though he were dredging up events from the past.

"If they wouldn't let you sleep until you denied our love, would you deny our love so you could lay your head on a pillow?

"If they stabbed a bayonet into your backside every time your eyes drifted closed, would you deny our love so your flesh wouldn't be pierced?

"If they applied a hot brand to your flesh until you screamed in agony, would you deny our love so they'd take away the iron?

"If they placed you before a firing squad, would you say you didn't love me so they wouldn't shoot you?"

He stepped back and plowed his hands through his hair. "You think I'm a coward. You don't think I have the courage to stand beside you and risk the anger of your father. I'd die before I turned away from anyone or anything I believed in. You won't even walk by my side."

He looked the way she imagined soldiers

who had lost a battle probably looked: weary, tired of the fight, disillusioned.

"You don't believe in me," he said quietly. "How can you believe in our love?"

A shot rang out through the night, followed rapidly by another and the pounding of hooves.

Clay jerked open his bedroom door and stormed into the front room. Meg hastened after him. Lucian and the twins were looking through the slats in the shutters that covered the window to the right of the front door. Clay moved to the window on the other side, peered through the shutter, and bowed his head.

"Get out here, you yellow-bellied coward!" Another shot echoed in the darkness.

Clay captured his brothers' gazes. "Give me your word that no matter what you hear, you won't come outside."

Everyone stood as still as statues.

"Your word!" Clay barked.

Lucian gave one quick deep nod. "You got it."

Clay settled his gaze on the twins, and they rapidly crossed their fingers over their hearts.

"Keep her in here," Clay said with a quick jerk of his head in Meg's direction before he slipped out the door.

"No," she gasped as she rushed after him.

Before she reached the door, Lucian snaked his arm around her waist, lifted her off the floor, and slapped his hand over her mouth. She struggled, fought, clawed, and kicked at him, but he wouldn't release his hold.

Someone fired another shot. The bullet splintered the wood of a shutter, and the ping of its ricochet echoed through the house.

"Gawd Almighty!" the twins yelled.

"Get under the table!" Lucian ordered.

Meg felt her breath forced from her body as he slammed her to the floor and laid his body over hers. The twins, trembling violently, curled up beside her.

She heard horses whinny and more guns fire. She could see an eerie dance of shadows and flames through the cracks in the shutters as though the people outside were carrying torches.

"If you promise to keep quiet, I'll take my hand off your mouth," Lucian whispered.

She nodded. Cautiously, he moved his hand away.

"Please let me go out there," she pleaded.

"It'll just go worse for him if they know you're here."

"Who is it? Who's out there?"

"I don't know. They're wearing flour sacks over their heads."

They heard an agonized wail that sounded as though it rose from the bowels of hell. Meg elbowed Lucian in the ribs and broke free of his hold. She scrambled out from beneath the table. He came after her, grabbed her legs, and brought her back down to the floor.

She kicked him and pounded her fists into his shoulders. "Please, let me go. They've hurt him!"

"I can't, Meg. I gave him my word."

The yells of men, the singing of bullets, and the pounding of hooves faded into the night. Lucian released her. She scrambled to her feet, threw open the door, and rushed outside in time to see the last of the hooded riders disappear in the darkness.

But she didn't see Clay.

She spun around as Lucian and the twins came outside. "Where is he?"

Lucian lifted the lantern, but all they could see was the emptiness. "Did they take him?" he asked.

A low moan, like that of a wounded animal without hope, sounded through the darkness. In long strides, Lucian walked around to the side of the house, with Meg and the twins in his wake. He came to an abrupt halt. "Dear Lord."

The lantern cast a glow over Clay's battered face as he looked up at his brother. Kneeling beside the tree stump, he wrapped his right hand around the hilt of the knife that someone had driven through his left palm into the stump. "Help me."

Meg swallowed the bile rising in her throat and took the lantern from Lucian. "Help him."

With uncertainty, Lucian approached Clay. "Maybe I should get Dr. Martin."

Clay shook his head. "Just help me with the knife."

Lucian placed his foot on the stump and wrapped his hand around the knife handle. "It's gonna hurt like the devil."

Nodding, Clay pressed his free hand against the wrist of his pinned hand. Lucian glanced over his shoulder at Meg, and she saw the anguish reflected in his face. He closed his eyes and pulled the knife.

Clay released a strangled groan as Lucian worked the knife free. Lucian stumbled back, the bloodied knife in his hand. Clay slumped to the ground, wrapped the end of his shirt around his wounded hand, and cradled it against his side. Meg set the lantern on the stump, and the light glistened off the black pool of blood. She knelt beside Clay. "Let me see your hand."

"Go home, Meg. This doesn't concern

you." He placed his good hand on the stump and struggled to his feet.

"I want to help —"

He staggered to the house and leaned against the wall. "You think I'm a coward. Your brother called me a coward in church, and you let the words go unchallenged. I've never —" Closing his eyes, he took a shaky, shallow breath. Opening his eyes, he impaled her with his gaze as effectively as the knife had pierced his hand. "I've never done anything in my life that I had to cover my face to do. Go home to your brave men."

He took an unsteady step toward the door, faltered, and collapsed. Meg hurried to his side and placed his head in her lap. His eyes were closed, and his head lolled in whichever direction she turned it. She lifted her gaze to Lucian. "Help me get him into the house."

He moved swiftly and put his hands under Clay's shoulders. "Joe, you carry the lantern. Josh, you and Meg carry his feet."

"He ain't gonna die, is he?" Josh asked as he picked up his burden.

"Nah, I reckon all the excitement just wore him out," Lucian said as he lifted Clay and walked backward into the house.

Meg's gaze was drawn to the trail of blood as they carried Clay to his bed. Who'd done this? Why? How could they have done this?

Clay groaned as they dumped him on the bed, but he didn't waken.

"Do you have a rag I can use to wrap around his hand?" Meg asked.

Lucian walked out of the room and returned carrying a white cloth. He handed it to her, and she wrapped it around the ghastly wound. "Joe and Josh, I need your help." They came to her side and stood at attention as though they were tiny soldiers. "He has such a large hand that I need both of you to press on it like this to stop the bleeding." She took their hands and positioned them around Clay's hand.

Stepping aside, she looked to Lucian. "Let's take his clothes off and see how badly he's hurt."

Lucian lifted his brows. "Shouldn't I take his clothes off while you wait in the other room?"

"I'm a widow. I've seen a man's body. I'm not likely to faint if I see another one." She moved to the foot of the bed and began to work off Clay's boot. She'd dropped it to the floor before Lucian walked to the head of the bed and began to unbutton Clay's shirt. Meg pulled off Clay's sock and stared at the wide pink scar that circled his ankle.

"Dear God," Lucian whispered.

She jerked up her head. Lucian had un-buttoned Clay's shirt, and the sides had parted to reveal by the light of the lantern what she'd been unable to see by the pale light of the crescent moon. Another scar. Someone had burned a *D* into the center of his chest.

She sat on the edge of the bed and lightly touched her fingers to the scar.

She remembered how Clay had stopped her from running her fingers over his chest as they made love. Now, she understood why he had guided her hands to his back. He hadn't wanted her to feel the scar, to know that the army had branded him a deserter.

"Go get Dr. Martin," she said.

"Yes, ma'am," Lucian said before quickly leaving the room. She wished she could get rid of the twins as easily, but she needed them to keep the pressure on his wound.

"They hurt him somethin' bad, didn't they, Miz Meg?" Josh asked.

"This is an old scar. It doesn't hurt him anymore." She placed her hands on each boy's shoulder. "It might be best if you look away and study the wall over there while I see how badly he's hurt."

"Yes, ma'am." Watching their chins quiver as they turned away, she felt the tears sting her own eyes.

She lifted the bloody end of Clay's shirt. A thin, ragged scar marred his side. She unbuttoned his trousers, pulled them past his hips, and saw what she'd hoped she wouldn't see: more scars crisscrossed his backside. His past words rushed through her mind like a torrential rain:

"I can stand up to any torture that's handed out . . ."

". . . four days without sleep . . ."

". . . bayonet . . ."

". . . only difference between us is that he was willing to kill for his beliefs. I wasn't . . ."

Gently, she removed his clothes. New bruises were emerging and covering old scars. She carried the quilt up to his chin and tucked it around his sides as though it could somehow protect him.

She left the room and returned carrying a bowl of warm water. Using a clean cloth, she wiped the blood away from Clay's mouth. How many times had they hit him? One eye was nearly swollen shut and his cheek was grazed and bloody.

She dropped the stained cloth into the bowl and set it on a table beside the bed.

Sitting on the edge of the bed, she took his hand from the twins, laid it in her lap, and pressed her palms against the wound. "You can go to bed now. There's nothing else for you to do. I'll wake you if he needs you."

Nodding, the twins walked from the room and quietly closed the door.

Meg bowed her head and wept.

Sometime later, Dr. Martin burst through the door like a cyclone. "God damn it! What'd they do to him?" He stalked across the room and yanked the quilt down to Clay's hips.

"He has scars —" Meg began, not certain why she wanted to explain to this man that the undeserved scars were badges of honor.

"I'm familiar with his scars," Dr. Martin said as he prodded his fingers along Clay's ribs. "Some damn private got overzealous with his bayonet, and they couldn't stop the bleeding so they sent for me." He released a mirthless laugh. "They were afraid he'd bleed to death before they got a chance to execute him. Damn idiots."

Meg heard footsteps. She glanced over her shoulder to see Lucian standing in the doorway, his troubled gaze flickering guiltily over his brother. He looked as though he'd been trapped in a storm. His damp hair clung to his face as tenaciously as his sweaty shirt hugged his body. Meg hadn't thought to tell him where he could find her horse, and she realized, with regret, that he'd run to town to find the doctor.

Clay gasped, and his eyes flew open.

"That one hurt, didn't it?" Dr. Martin said.

Clay nodded slightly. "Yes, sir." He looked down at his bare chest, flinched, and struggled to pull the quilt up to his chin with his good hand. Turning his face away from Meg, he said in a hoarse voice, "Make her leave, Doc."

Meg felt a strong need to reassure Clay that her feelings for him were genuine. She met Dr. Martin's intense gaze. "I want to help. His hand is still bleeding."

Dr. Martin wrapped his hands around the bandaged wound. "I'll take care of the bleeding. I think you both can help most by leaving the room."

She opened her mouth to protest, but the expression on Dr. Martin's face told her he'd brook no arguments. "I need some water warmed up and some coffee," he said.

"We ain't got no coffee," Lucian said.

"Well, then, make yourself useful and rustle me up something to eat. I always get hungry in the middle of the night after tending hurt folks. Now, go on. I gave you something to do, get to doing it."

Meg eased off the bed and leaned close to

Clay's face. "Clay?"

"Go home," he forced out through clenched teeth.

"I love you," she said softly. He squeezed his eyes shut as though her words caused him more pain. She looked to Dr. Martin. "Call if you need me."

With one last look at the man lying on the bed, she walked out of the room.

The minutes passed as slowly as hours. Meg sat at the table with her hands clenched in her lap. Lucian sat opposite her, his elbows on the table, his chin pressed against his fists.

A door opened, and the twins padded out of their bedroom. "We can't sleep," Josh said as they approached the table.

"Dr. Martin's here," Lucian said. "Clay'll be all right now."

"That ain't why we can't sleep," Joe said.

The twins looked at each other, their eyes filled with such sadness that at that moment, Meg wished more than anything else that she could have spared them this hurt.

Josh cleared his small throat. "Lucian, was we cowards tonight?"

Lucian snapped his gaze over to Meg. Slowly, he lowered his fists to the table and looked at the twins. "No. Clay told us to stay inside, and we were doing what he told us to do."

"Then how come you say he's a coward when he was just doing what his heart told him to do when he wouldn't fight in the war?"

Lucian bolted out of the chair. "How the hell should I know? You two ask the dumbest questions I've heard in my whole life, and then you give the smartest answers. Why do you ask the questions if you've got the answers? Hell, I'm going for a walk." He stormed out the front door.

With tears in his eyes, Joe said, "Miz Meg, we still don't know if we was cowards. Even if Clay had said it was all right, we don't know if we woulda gone out there."

Meg scooted away from the table and patted her lap. The boys sidled up to her, and she wrapped her arms around them, drawing them close. They were too thin, too small, too young for what they'd witnessed tonight. "I think tonight it was Clay's battle to fight."

"But he lost."

"No, I don't think he did. He's the kind of man who'll never lose because he never strays from what he believes in. He's rare, so rare that even I didn't recognize how much courage he has."

The door to Clay's room opened, and Dr.

Martin ambled out. He dropped his black bag on the table and slowly shook his head. "He's got a couple of broken ribs and that hand's a mess."

"Will he still be able to use it?" Meg asked.

Dr. Martin shrugged. "I don't know. I stitched it up as best I could. Fortunately, the knife went between the bones so nothing in his hand is broken. Only time will tell how much permanent damage was done. But he has a quiet determination unlike any I've ever seen. He's sleeping now, so I reckon I'll head on home. Want me to escort you home?"

Meg shook her head. "No, I'll be staying for a while."

"Reckon your pa don't know you're here."

"No, he doesn't."

Dr. Martin picked up his bag. "Well, he won't hear it from me."

"If you knew how they treated Clay," Meg said quietly, "why didn't you tell us?"

"Because I'm a doctor, not a gossip. People have to know that they can trust me not to repeat what I learn when I'm treating them. Besides, the hatred around here is so thick, I didn't think it'd make any difference." He ruffled the twins' hair. "Clay told me he's never seen anyone as brave as you boys were tonight."

The twins' eyes widened. "He did?"

"Yep. Reckon he'll tell you himself in the morning." Smiling sadly, he tilted his head toward Meg. "Good night."

Meg held the twins close until she heard the door close. "I don't know if I've ever known a night so long. I need to put you to bed."

"Can we have a lantern in our room?" Joe asked. "Lucian don't like having a lantern burning in the room, but seein's as how he ain't here . . ."

"I'll leave the lantern in your room," she promised.

"And could you leave the door open?" Josh asked as he slipped away from her.

"That sounds like a good idea."

Yawning, the boys shuffled to their room, their bare feet dragging along the floor. Josh stopped in the doorway. "Wait here, Miz Meg, and we'll holler when we're undressed and under the covers. We know it don't bother you seein' our backsides since you're a widow and all, but it'd sure bother us . . . even though you've seen 'em before. We kinda like to keep 'em to ourselves."

Meg bit back her smile. In the worst of circumstances, these boys held a view of the world that charmed her. "You take the lantern, and I'll wait here."

Taking the lantern, Josh ducked into the room. She heard the scuffling, the whispers, and a small laugh.

"We're ready, Miz Meg!"

She walked into their room. Josh had set the lantern on the table beside their bed. With angelic faces, they peered at her. She pulled the quilt to their chins. She wanted desperately to lean over and kiss each and every freckle dotting their cheeks and noses, but they weren't accustomed to having a woman in their life, and she didn't know if they'd welcome the affection she wanted to bestow upon them.

Tonight, they'd grown up more than any child of ten should ever have to.

"Miz Meg?"

"What, Josh?" she asked.

"How'd you know it was me talking?" Josh asked.

"I don't know. I guess I've just been around you for so long that you don't look the same to me anymore."

He grimaced. "I got the most freckles."

She smiled. "I know, and I love every one of them."

"Miz Meg, would you mind terribly if we was to give you a hug?"

Sitting on the edge of their bed, she shook her head and held out her arms. They bolted upright and flung into her embrace. She held them close, inhaling their scent of dirt, leaves, and bats at twilight.

"We love you, Miz Meg," one of the twins rasped.

She didn't know which one had spoken, but she knew it didn't matter. "I love you, too."

They wriggled out of her embrace. "You gonna go home now?" Joe asked.

She cradled their chins in her hands; their faces, their eyes were as easy to read as the pages of a favorite book. "I'm going to stay right here until you fall asleep; then I'll sit with Clay until he wakes up."

"Bet we could fall asleep faster if you was to sing to us," Josh said.

She tweaked their noses and folded her hands in her lap. "Do you know why I play the organ at church?"

They sneaked glances at each other before shaking their heads.

"Because I can't sing. I sound like a mule that's had its backside kicked."

Laughing, the boys fell back against their pillows. She brought the quilt over their quaking shoulders, and they snuggled into the center of the bed.

"Don't tell anyone," she whispered. "It's my secret."

"We won't," they promised.

If anyone else had promised her something with that much snickering, she wouldn't have believed it, but she knew the twins understood the value of their word.

They rolled onto their stomachs, and she rubbed their backs.

"I like this better than listenin' to someone singin'," Josh said. "Don't you, Joe?"

Joe answered with a light snore. Josh struggled to keep his eyes open, but soon surrendered the fight and joined his brother in slumber.

So many battles to fight. She combed their fine red hair off their brows. So many battles to lose. She lowered the flame in the lantern. So many battles to win.

She glanced at the rumpled bed where Lucian had no doubt been sleeping before the hooded riders swept into their world. She wondered where he'd gone and if he had his own battles to fight.

Held at bay too long, the anguished sobs rent the still night air. With the dew seeping through her nightgown, Taffy rocked the man curled against her as if he were a newborn babe.

"I need you, Taffy," was all he'd whispered through her window and all she'd needed to hear to climb into the night.

Lucian dragged his hands down his tear-drenched face and took a shaky breath. "He didn't even hesitate, Taffy. He just went out there. I've called him a coward behind his back, called him a coward to his face. I wouldn't have gone out there."

"You can't say that, Lucian. A person never knows what they'll do until the time comes. If they'd called you out, you may have gone."

Moving away from her, he swiped his hand beneath his nose. "No, Taffy, I wouldn't have gone. I told Clay he was a coward so he wouldn't see that I was one. I was glad when Ma and Pa died. I thanked the Lord because their deaths left me as the oldest on the farm. I didn't write and tell Clay they'd died because I didn't want him coming home. I didn't want to go off and fight. I'm the coward, not him. He never was a coward. The day the army came for him, he didn't run. He just stood in that field and waited. I knew then he wasn't a coward. When Ma and Pa died, I hid behind their deaths. Clay never would have done that."

"You can't be sure," she said quietly.

"Yes, I can, and I ain't hiding anymore, Taffy. He's my brother, and I'm gonna stand by him like I should have done from the beginning. I wanted you to know because it'll mean I won't be welcomed in most homes around here."

She intertwined her fingers with his. "You'll always be welcome in my arms."

He laid her on the damp earth and kissed her as tenderly as only a man who'd just conquered the enemy within could. Victory, he discovered, was sweeter when shared.

It hurt to breathe. It hurt to move. It hurt to think.

It hurt to love.

Clay studied the small hand and delicate fingers curled on his chest. They reminded him of a tiny trusting kitten napping in the shade on a warm afternoon.

He'd been wrong to fall in love with Meg, to expect her to stand by his side and weather the gale of a storm that he was no longer willing for even his brothers to endure.

Her avoidance in church had sliced into his heart as easily as a bayonet through his flesh. He'd felt betrayed and, like a wounded animal, had struck out at the one he loved above all others.

Yet here she remained, as though she were a rag doll plopped into a chair. Unable to sit upright, she had spilled forward onto the bed, with her face nestled in the mattress next to his side, her eyelashes tickling his skin, her breath warming his scarred hip where the quilt had fallen away.

Cautiously, he lifted his hand and touched the ebony wisps of hair that were no longer threaded through her braid.

His words following the attack had only deepened the wound piercing his pride. The emotional pain would eventually lessen, and his wounded pride would scar, but he'd rather carry the self-inflicted scar than ever again witness the agony and fear he'd seen in Meg's eyes.

He had a strong desire, a stronger need to wake Meg, pull her into his bed, apologize for his harsh words, and love her one last time.

Instead, he gently moved her hand off his chest and eased out of bed, holding his breath against the shards of pain traveling through his arm, chest, and head.

Getting dressed was no easy task, and he contented himself with getting his trousers over his hips and buttoned. He'd never intended for anyone to know how harshly he'd been treated. Some people in the area would have reveled in the knowledge, some would have pitied him, others would have agonized over the way he had been treated. He wanted none of those emotions directed his way for what he'd willingly accepted and brought on himself.

But gentle, caring hands had exposed the scars. Raising his arms nearly caused him to reel over with the pain, so he knew it would be impossible to pull his shirt over his head. His shirt remained as she'd left it: draped neatly over a chair, the blood removed, the damp ends touching the floor.

Quietly he walked around the bed to where Meg slept. He'd probably never again awaken to find a woman asleep near him. He placed a light kiss on her cheek before leaving the room.

As she awoke, Meg arched her spine to get the knots and tightness out of her back and shoulders. She should have gone with her instincts and crawled into bed with Clay, but she was afraid she'd cause him further pain if she rolled against him in her sleep.

Easing back in the chair, she rubbed her neck, opened her eyes, and stared at the empty bed. She hopped out of the chair and frantically searched the room. Having just awakened, she needed a minute before she realized that the room gave a man no place to hide.

She darted into the living room area. Nothing stirred. She crossed to the other bedroom and glanced inside. The twins were sleeping. Sometime during the night, Lucian had returned, for he was sprawled over his bed, his clothes and boots still on.

She rushed outside. With feathery fingers, dawn was creeping over the land. The door to the shed was open.

Hurrying to the shed, Meg tripped over her clumsy feet. Picking herself off the ground, she brushed the dirt off her hands and continued. Her heart pounding, her breathing labored, she reached the doorway and came to a dead stop. Clay was slumped against the granite, his eyes closed, his mouth turned down. In the dim light spilling in through the doorway, he looked as though something as heavy as the monument weighed upon his heart.

She walked into the shed and knelt beside him. He cradled his wounded hand. The pristine white bandage Dr. Martin had wrapped around his hand was now crumpled, bloody, and loose fitting as though Clay had discarded it and retrieved it without care.

He heaved a melancholy sigh that sounded as mournful as the wind that preceded the first storm of winter. "I wasn't the only one who wouldn't carry a rifle."

He opened his eyes, and Meg fell into the

dark brown depths, which had aged considerably since yesterday. Lightly touching the white wisps of hair at his temples, she understood at last that it was the harshness of other men that had aged Clay, not the passing years.

"They hung some men by their thumbs to convince them carrying a rifle was what they should do," he said hoarsely. "I listened to those men scream, and I prayed they wouldn't hang me by my thumbs. I was afraid if my thumbs were pulled free of my hands, I wouldn't be able to hold my tools, I wouldn't be able to carve when I got home. A damn selfish thing to pray for, but they never hung me by my thumbs."

She trailed her fingers along his roughened cheek. She wanted to shave him, trim his hair, prepare him a nice warm bath, and never let anything harsh touch him again. "They hurt you in other ways," she said quietly.

She watched his Adam's apple move slowly up and down. "They deprived me of sleep, deprived me of my mother's letters, and branded me a deserter."

"Dr. Martin said they'd planned to execute you."

"Changed their minds. They wrapped heavy chains around my ankles and kept me prisoner at a fort instead."

"Is that where Kirk visited you?"

He nodded slightly. "You'd written him that my ma and pa had died. He thought if he showed your letter to the officer in charge, he'd send me home."

She felt the anger swell inside her at the injustice. "But he didn't release you."

"I asked him not to show him the letter."

Stunned, Meg sat back on her heels. "Why?"

"Your letter was four months old. Lucian was coming up on the age when they would have wanted him to enlist. Figured since I hadn't heard from him, that maybe he was content where he was. Our parents' deaths gave him an honorable reason not to enlist —"

"It gave you an honorable reason to return home."

He shook his head. "I wasn't sure how Lucian felt about the war, but I took his silence as a plea not to come home. Maybe that was wrong on my part, but they'd already done all they were going to do to me. After Gettysburg, I stayed with Dr. Martin and helped him tend the wounded till the war ended."

"Why didn't you tell me all this sooner?"

"What difference does it make? You're no

different than the Confederate officers. You want a man who's willing to kill. I won't. I told them I'd tend wounded, but Captain Roberts had gone to West Point with Robert E. Lee's son, and by God, every man under his command would carry a rifle."

"But you didn't."

"No, ma'am. Figured if I held a rifle, the day would come when they'd order me to shoot it, so I never gave them the chance."

She touched her fingers to the scar that marked him as a deserter. "I'm so sorry they did all this to you."

"Are you, Meg?"

She felt as though a frozen river had just traveled along her spine. "Of course I am."

"I'm not so sure. I may have figured out why you wanted me to make the monument."

"What are you talking about?"

"Why did you ask me to make the memorial?"

The reasons raced through her mind: her reasons in the beginning were vastly different from her reasons now. She'd planted the seeds for retribution, and they'd flourished, but the harvest in no way resembled the bitter fruits she'd expected. She knew she'd waited too long to answer his question when his eyes dulled and one corner of his mouth lifted mockingly.

"You place a man's dream within reach, and then you do all in your power to see he never touches it. That's why you wanted the marble instead of the granite, why you came here every day. You didn't want to watch me carve the monument, you wanted to see me fail."

"Perhaps in the beginning —"

"And when you realized I wouldn't fail, you decided to make me suffer —"

"No!"

"You just happened to be here last night —"

"I was here because you didn't meet me at the swimming hole."

"If I'd been at the swimming hole, would they have taken their vengeance out on my brothers?"

"I don't know."

He glared at her. "Is that why you made love with me the other night? So I'd know exactly what it was I'd never have?"

"No!"

"I could have done it, you know. I could have given you a monument to honor Kirk, Stick, your brothers, and all the other men who sacrificed everything in the name of honor."

"You still can. You can finish the monument —"

He shook his head, his dark brows knitting together over the bridge of his nose as he squeezed his eyes tighter. "I can't close my hand."

"Because it's bandaged."

"I took off the bandage."

"The pain —"

"I fought the pain. I can't close my hand."

"Once it's healed —"

"It won't make a difference." He struggled to his feet. "They say you reap what you sow. Well, take a good look at your monument, Mrs. Warner. They took away my ability to finish it, and they left you with nothing but shadows to honor those you loved."

Seventeen

Meg crawled through her bedroom window. She walked to the washstand and splashed the cool water on her face, but it couldn't wash away the dark circles beneath her eyes or the heaviness that had settled in her heart.

She needed to cook breakfast, and all she wanted to do was crawl into bed and cry, long and hard, until she was so exhausted that she'd sleep without dreaming of Clay.

Lethargically, she walked to the kitchen and took a pot off the wall. Her father and brother would have to be content with porridge because she didn't have the energy to fix anything else.

She heard Daniel coming down the hallway whistling "Dixie." Perhaps his hatred toward Clay would be less if her father had let him leave and be the drummer boy for the Confederacy that he'd wanted to be. Unfortunately, drummer boys had died as well.

"Mornin', Meg." He came up behind her and put his hands on her shoulders. "What are you fixin'?"

"Porridge."

"Sounds good."

Smiling, she looked at him over her shoulder. Porridge was his least favorite meal. "You seem awfully happy this morning."

"Yes, ma'am. You don't have to worry about that yellow-bellied coward touching you no more."

Meg's heart constricted so tightly she thought it might stop beating. "What?"

He released her, dragged a chair out from the table, and dropped his body into the seat. "We took care of him last night. Didn't we, Pa?"

Meg spun around. Her father averted his gaze as he took his chair. "That's right," he said quietly.

Daniel planted his elbows on the table. "He won't be touching any of our women any time soon, that's for damn sure. My brothers would have been proud of us."

Meg thought she was going to be sick to her stomach. The room began to spin and tilt.

A hard knock sounded on the door, and Meg took a deep breath, trying to right her world, wondering if anything would ever feel right again.

Robert stepped into the kitchen, and Meg knew from the sadness in his eyes what was coming before he spoke.

"Mama Warner's taken a turn for the worse."

Easing onto the bed, Meg brushed the wisps of silver hair away from the wrinkled brow. "Were you here with Mama Warner throughout the night?"

"Where else would I have been?" Robert asked.

She lifted her gaze to the man standing beside her. "My father, my brother, and some other men attacked Clay last night. They put a knife through his hand. I think they did it because he touched me after church yesterday."

Robert knelt beside her. "What is Holland to you, Meg?"

She felt the tears well in her eyes.

Reaching out with his thumb, he captured a fallen tear. "So that's the way of it, is it?" He smiled sadly. "I suppose I'd be wasting my breath if I asked you to marry me."

"I love him, Robert. I didn't want to. Things would certainly be simpler if I'd fallen in love with you."

"Would it have made a difference if I had two arms?"

She cradled his cheek. "No."

He laid his hand over hers. "I didn't think my loss would matter to you. You're a special lady, Meg. You don't look like you're aware of that this morning, but you are." He stood. "Once word gets out about Mama Warner, we'll have more company than we can shake a stick at. I'll try and keep as many as I can out of here because you sure don't look like you need company today."

"Thank you, Robert."

He walked from the room, and Meg took the frail hand into her own. She leaned over Mama Warner. "Can you hear me, or are you too close to heaven to hear us anymore? I feel like I'm in hell."

She studied the pale features that time had lined with wisdom. "You knew Clay wasn't a coward. If you'd told me, I wouldn't have believed you, but he showed me in so many ways. The irony is that he's the only one among us who isn't a coward. I think that's why we all hated him so much. He is exactly what we believed ourselves to be."

Lucian had a strong urge to punch Clay in the jaw. Not out of hatred, but out of love. He wanted to knock some sense into his brother.

In the days after the attack, Clay took his meals on the porch — alone — and spent his time walking through the fields of corn stalks, pulling weeds.

He never raised the shutters on the shed. He didn't talk about his past or the future. He didn't talk at all unless the twins asked him a question, and then he discouraged them by giving them an abrupt answer.

Sometimes, Lucian would see him staring in the direction of the Warner farm. For long moments, he wouldn't move. Then he'd look toward the shed, shove his hands into his pockets, bow his head, and begin walking through the fields of growing corn.

Lucian walked along the row of corn until his shadow fell across Clay, who was kneeling beside a corn stalk. "I was thinking, next year we could rent those oxen to help us plow the fields, maybe take in an extra acre or two."

Clay tugged a weed out of the soil. "Whatever you think is best." Standing, he removed his hat and squinted against the sunlight. "Once we harvest the crops, I'll be moving on, so any time you want we can go into town and have the deed to the farm put in your name."

"What about the monument?"

"It's served its purpose."

"What the hell does that mean?"

Clay looked toward the shed. "It was never meant to be more than shadows of a dream."

"What the hell are you talking about?"

Clay squinted into the distance. "Do you see that?"

Lucian followed his gaze. Black clouds billowed up from the earth. "Looks like smoke."

"Joe, Josh!" Clay yelled.

The boys stopped hoeing and rushed to his side. "Go to the barn and get some blankets. It looks like Sam Johnson's field is on fire. Hurry."

"You're not gonna help put it out, are you?" Lucian asked.

"How will he make it through the winter if he loses his crop?"

Lucian jerked his hat off his head. "God damn it! Not one of them would come over here and piss on our crops if they were on fire."

"I can't help the way they are, but I'll be damned before I become like them."

Clay began running across the field. Lucian followed. He was beginning to think his older brother was the most aggravating man he knew.

The twins caught up with them, their faces filled with exuberance. Clay yanked a blanket away from Josh. "Don't get too close to the fire and don't breathe in the smoke."

Against his better judgment, Lucian took the blanket that Joe offered him.

By the time they arrived, neighbors were already pitching in, beating back the fire. Lucian took his place beside his brothers, slapping the blanket against the bright orange flames. In their eagerness, the twins kept getting too close to the fire, and he and Clay continually dragged them back to safety.

Lucian glanced at Clay's blackened sweaty face. He probably looked as grimy, but he felt good. It had been a long time since he'd felt as though they were a family, united in a cause. He wished now that he had helped Clay with his side of the barn. His past regrets were many. He was determined to have fewer in the future.

The flames before them died a quiet death, and Clay rubbed each boy's head. "Good job."

They began walking over the charred field. Sam Johnson was shaking hands with his neighbors and thanking them for their help. He came to an abrupt halt when his eyes fell on Clay. Clay met his gaze.

"Clay, your hand's bleedin'," Josh said.

Clay glanced at the blood seeping through the bandage. "It'll be all right. Come on, we need to get home now."

In long strides, Lucian set out to follow his brothers.

"Lucian?"

Stopping and turning, he stared at Sam.

Sam extended his hand. "I wanted to thank you for helping me out here."

Lucian ignored his hand. "Don't thank me. If it'd been left up to me, we wouldn't have come, but Clay's the head of the family, and he was worried you might have a hard winter if you lost your crops."

Sam ducked his head, his face turning beet red. "Look, things got out of hand the other night. He wasn't supposed to get hurt. We were just going to frighten him."

"You didn't do anything to stop them from hurting him though, did you?"

Sam snapped his head up. "I didn't see you out there stopping us either."

Lucian took a menacing step forward and Sam flinched. "No, you didn't, but I won't make that mistake again. You and your friends show up on our land again with flour sacks over your heads, and you'll have to put knives through four of us."

Meg was grateful that Mama Warner had drifted closer to heaven and was unaware of all that had happened the last night Meg saw Clay. The knowledge would have broken the older woman's heart.

It very nearly broke Meg's.

Each day she sat in the rocker beside the bed and read *The Scarlet Letter* aloud. She could not read the words without thinking of the puckered pink scar that Clay bore upon his chest. The army had hurt him. The people in the area had hurt him. Yet she knew she'd hurt him most of all.

"Meg?"

She glanced up and gave Robert a warm smile.

"You have company. The Holland twins."

Rising from the rocker, she set the book on the table and slipped past Robert. She hurried into the kitchen. She'd never been so happy to see anyone in her life as she wrapped her arms around both boys.

"I've missed you," Meg said as she planted a kiss on each boy's forehead.

"Yes, ma'am, we been missin' you, too," Josh said.

"Do you want a piece of pie? I made it fresh this morning."

"No, ma'am, we didn't come here for ourselves. We come about Clay."

"How's his hand?"

"It ain't bandaged no more, but he don't never use it. He just keeps it buried in his pocket like he's ashamed of it or something. Thought maybe you could come talk to him —"

Shaking her head, she stepped back. "I can't."

"But, Miz Meg, he just walks up one row of corn and down the other all day long. We know he said some powerful ugly words the night he was hurt, but that was pain talkin', Miz Meg. Not Clay. He didn't mean none of it. Wish you'd come back and let him apologize."

Placing her hands on their shoulders, she felt the tears sting the back of her eyes. They had such earnest faces. "I wish it were that simple, but it isn't. Nothing would be solved if I went to your farm. Things would only worsen."

The boys released baleful sighs as their shoulders slouched. "Reckon we'll mosey on then," Josh said. The boys shuffled to the door.

"Would you like to take a pie with you?" Meg asked.

"No, ma'am, but thank you. People just ain't eatin' much around our house these days."

When they disappeared through the door, Meg slumped into a chair, buried her face in her hands, and fought back the tears. She heard Robert's footsteps echo through the room. Why wasn't he in the fields where he belonged?

"Meg, I know this is none of my business —"

She dropped her hands and found him kneeling beside her. "You're right, Robert. This is none of your business."

He gave her a disarming smile. "Think you need some low talking, girl. Why didn't you go with those boys?"

"Mama Warner needs me."

"Meg, you and I both know that she's not even aware that you're here. Why didn't you go with those boys?"

She intertwined her fingers and squeezed her hands until they ached. "Because I'm afraid. My brother put the knife through Clay's hand. I'm sure of it, although he didn't say it exactly. If my father discovered that I'd spent time with Clay, I think he'd kill him."

"So you think it's best if you stay away?"

"He wanted me to walk out of the church with him, and I wouldn't do it because I was afraid of what might happen. All these months, I've called him a coward, and I'm the coward."

"Being scared doesn't make you a coward, Meg."

"It certainly makes me feel like one."

He wrapped his hand around hers. "When Kirk left, were you afraid the Union soldiers might kill him?"

"I was terrified. I didn't sleep for weeks

worrying about him."

"So, the morning he left, you stayed in bed under the covers."

"No, sir, I did not. I went to town with him and stood proudly . . ." She searched Robert's serious face. "I stood by his side."

"And they killed him anyway."

Tears welled in her eyes. "And they killed him," she whispered, bringing her hand to her lips.

"How would you have felt, Meg, if he'd died, and you'd stayed home that morning?"

Sitting cross-legged on the foot of her bed, Meg stared at the wooden box. Mama Warner's wooden box.

Meg had brought it home the day after Mama Warner had asked Clay to make her headstone.

But she hadn't looked inside it.

Why did Mama Warner want her to have it?

Easing off the bed, she knelt beside the box. With trembling fingers, she opened it.

The carving of Kirk rested on top. Gently, she removed it, placed it in her lap, and brushed her fingers over his youthful features. Mama Warner was right. She did want the carving. Now that she understood Clay wasn't a coward, she wanted everything he'd ever touched.

She peered into the box, wondering what other treasures it held. Her breath caught at the sight of an envelope bearing Kirk's scrawled script.

She hadn't realized that he'd written to others while he was away. She wondered why Mama Warner hadn't shared the letters. She picked up the letter and turned it slowly in her hands. Mama Warner must have meant for her to read it, or she wouldn't have left it in the box.

Meg opened the envelope and removed the single sheet of paper. She wanted to capture every memory of Kirk that existed, even those that weren't her own. Slowly, she read the scrawled words her husband had written.

March 3, 1863

Dear Mama Warner,

It took some doing, but I finally located Clay. He looks like death warmed over. You know Clay and his quiet ways. He suffers through their punishments without complaint, and I think that only makes them angrier and causes them to treat him harsher.

I've written Jefferson Davis again asking that he exempt Clay based on his beliefs. Every man in my company applied his signature to the letter. We hear that President Davis is not as sympathetic toward conscientious objectors as Abraham Lincoln. Therefore, we hold out little hope for Clay, especially now that the South is in dire need of men.

Of course, Clay would object to our good intentions. He believes he should fight his own battles, and we should fight ours.

Before I left Cedar Grove, he asked me not to get involved in his fight, and I honored his request. And yet, I often wonder if, with my silence, I betrayed him.

I send you Clay's love, as well as my own, and that of the men in my company. Keep us all in your prayers.

Kirk

Meg crushed the letter to her breast. Perhaps only those who faced death daily were able to recognize that courage could be as quiet as a man's thoughts.

And with her silence, she had betrayed Clay as well.

"Hoowee! That woman looks mad enough to spit!" Lucian said as he stepped off the porch.

Halting in the doorway, Clay followed his brother's gaze and saw Meg trudging toward the house. His stomach tightened, and he was grateful he hadn't eaten much breakfast.

The twins worked their way past him and hopped off the porch. "Mornin', Miz Meg. We wasn't expectin' to see you this mornin'."

"I need someone to pull up the shutters on the shed."

"No, you don't," Clay said. "The shed is staying closed."

She quirked a thin, dark brow. "My stone is in there, and I want to have a look at it."

"Your stone?"

"That's right. I purchased it. It belongs to me."

"But it's in my shed, and I don't want you going in there."

"Unfortunately, we can't always have things go the way we want them to. If you won't pull the shutters up, I'll do it myself."

"We'll get 'em up for you," the twins yelled before they darted toward the shed.

"I'll give them a hand," Lucian said as he tipped his hat toward Meg and walked away.

She smiled triumphantly, and Clay felt as though he'd just marched into a battle he couldn't win. He shrugged. "Suit yourself."

"I intend to."

His hand itched, and it had nothing to do with the healing wound. He had an urge to reach out and touch her cheek, press his lips against hers, and invite the softness back into his life. He nodded toward the shed. "They've got the shutters up."

"Are you going to come with me?"

"No, ma'am."

She tilted up her nose. "Suit yourself."

"I intend to, Mrs. Warner."

Spinning on her heel, she walked toward the shed. Clay watched as she ruffled the twins' hair in passing. Judging from the wide grin on Lucian's face, Clay decided she smiled at Lucian along the way.

Stepping off the porch, Clay watched her walk into the shed. Sometimes, late at night, he went into the shed and watched the shadows. They changed with the positioning of the moon, but they no longer changed with the touch of his hand.

"What do you reckon she's lookin' for?" Josh asked as he sidled up against Clay.

"I don't know. What did you tell her to look for?"

Josh's eyes widened. "Didn't tell her to

look for nothin'."

"Mmm-uh."

"Honest."

"After all this time, she just shows up this morning after you two disappeared for a spell yesterday. I find that to be mighty coincidental."

"Clayton Holland!" she yelled from the doorway. "Get yourself in here."

Clay leaned against the porch beam. Joe stepped onto the porch. "We did go see her. Our hearts and minds had a meetin' and decided it was best. Think if you'd let your heart and mind have a meetin', you'd go see what she wanted."

He knew what the woman wanted: trouble. Shoving away from the beam, he walked toward the shed. If he didn't look in her eyes, maybe he could avoid giving her what she wanted.

He'd had enough trouble to last a lifetime. All he wanted now was to live alone. He hadn't gone to church since the night of the attack, and he didn't plan to go any time in the future. He'd abandoned the hope of proving he wasn't a coward. Meg saw a coward when she looked at him, and if she did, so would the rest of the world.

He no longer cared about the rest of the world, and he was fighting the toughest battle of his life trying not to care about her.

He sauntered into the shed. She was tapping her foot with a vengeance and had planted her hands on her hips. He lifted his gaze to hers so he wouldn't be tempted to place his hands on her hips.

Blue fire greeted him.

"It doesn't look any different from when I was last here," she said curtly.

"Reckon because it's not."

"And why not?"

Laughing, he took his hand out of his pocket. "Because, Mrs. Warner, I can't hold tools."

Meg winced at the angry red scar that appeared to be a reflection of the enraged man standing before her. "Does it still hurt?"

He shifted his stance. "It's a little tender."

"Have you tried to hold the chisel since the bandages came off?"

"I try every morning." He curled his hand and held the air. "That's as much as it'll close. Even if I could close it all the way, I've got no grip. I can't hammer at a chisel when I don't have the strength to hold it in place."

"I could hold the chisel."

He looked as though she'd just slapped him. "What?"

"I could hold the chisel. You have one

good hand, and it's the hand you use to hold the hammer. I'll be your left hand."

"Have you gone insane?"

Taking a deep breath, she walked to the table and studied his tools. He'd used the largest chisel when he began. They'd have to go slower, more carefully. She picked up a smaller chisel. "You can position the chisel, and I'll hold it in place."

He plowed his good hand through his hair. "Do you have any idea how hard I have to hit that chisel to crack the stone?"

"If the sound the hammer makes when it strikes the chisel is any indication, then I'd say you have to hit it fairly hard."

He took a menacing step toward her. "I have to hit it damn hard."

"I know I'm not as strong as you are, but if I held the chisel with both hands, and we chipped off smaller bits of stone —"

He picked up a hammer and slammed it against the table. Meg flinched.

"That's how hard I'm gonna hit the chisel. That's how hard I'm gonna hit your hand if I miss the chisel."

She took a shaky breath. "Then don't miss the chisel."

"Didn't you learn anything when Robert hit your hand with the hammer?"

"That it hurts."

"And I'll leave a hell of a lot more than a bruise." He hit the table again, and Meg heard the wood split. "I'll break your bones! I'll crush your hand!"

She tilted her chin. "I'm willing to risk it."

He slung the hammer to a distant corner. "Well, I'm not."

He started to stalk away.

"I read Kirk's letter last night."

He came to an abrupt halt.

"You told me he gave you the pouch of letters a few months before he died."

"That's right."

"He dated his letter June 30 — the eve of the Battle of Gettysburg."

He bowed his head. "I searched his pockets before I buried him. That was all I took."

Hesitantly, she walked across the shed and placed her palm on his back. She felt him stiffen. "The letter isn't very long." She withdrew the letter from her pocket and extended it toward him. "I'd like for you to read it."

He shook his head. "It's not mine to read."

"I'm giving you permission to read his thoughts before he was taken from us."

His jaw tensed, and she watched him swallow. She removed the letter from the envelope and unfolded it. "Please," she said quietly.

Slowly, he took the letter from her. Breathing deeply, he lowered his gaze to the letter. Meg didn't have to see the words to know what he read. She'd memorized the letter during the night.

June 30, 1863

My dearest Meg,

I should be sleeping, but the night sky beckons to me. I look at it and think of you as you were the day I rode away. How proud I was, Meg, to know the beautiful woman waving me bravely on was my love.

I spoke with Clay recently. I told him if he should ever carve again, to carve my beloved as she looked when last I gazed upon her.

I will take you with me now into my dreams. Sleep well, my love, and know that the happiness you have brought me knows no bounds.

Affectionately yours,
Kirk

Dropping his hand to his side, Clay squeezed his eyes shut. She watched his throat work and knew he was fighting the same emotions she'd fought during the night.

411

She'd expected the letter to be different, written as though Kirk knew it was the last time he'd have an opportunity to write her, but he'd written it as though he would write another letter, as though he would again gaze upon the night sky and carry memories of her into his dreams.

"You chose to capture the moment he left because he asked you to carve me. You're not making a monument to honor those who rode away. You're making a monument to honor those who watched them go."

"Courage is shown in different ways. That's what I was hoping to show."

"And it's what you are showing. The monument will be in memory of those who died, and it'll honor so many more. You have to finish it."

He spun around and glared at her, holding up his hand as though it were a claw. "I can't!"

"We had an agreement, an understanding. You gave me your word that you'd make the monument if I purchased the stone. I purchased the stone. Now, you're going back on your word when you told me you'd die first."

"I've got no choice," he ground out through clenched teeth.

"Yes, you do." She walked to the table

and picked up the smaller chisel. "I've been thinking about the monument. I take it this portion you haven't touched yet is going to be my backside when you're done."

He furrowed his brow and took a step nearer. "Yeah," he admitted cautiously.

"Well, I figure it'll take us a while to get used to working together so this is where we'd begin. The worst thing that can happen is that we'll chip away too much, and I'll have a smaller backside. I wouldn't mind that."

"There's nothing wrong with your backside."

"You don't think it's too wide?" she asked, her voice lighter.

Averting his gaze, he blushed. "No, I don't think it's too wide," he growled. "But you're wrong about the worse thing that can happen. I could smash your hand to hell."

She wrapped her hand around his. "If you break my hand, we'll stop . . . until it heals."

He dropped his chin to his chest and slowly shook his head. "Meg, I don't want to give you hands as ugly as mine."

"How can they be ugly if you give them the chance to create something that will mean so much to so many people?"

She retrieved his hammer from the corner and handed it to him. "We'll go slowly and

413

chip off a little bit at a time. Just show me how you want the chisel positioned against the stone."

He gave her a weak smile. "You're crazy. It'll take us years to finish."

"I have nothing else I'd rather do."

"All right. Stand over here," he said as though resigned to her determination.

He set the hammer on the floor, and with his good hand he helped her position the chisel. She wrapped both hands around the chisel.

"Think you can hold it steady?" he asked.

She nodded, although she wasn't at all certain. She didn't want to let Kirk down, but more than that, she didn't want to disappoint Clay now that she'd placed his dream back within reach.

He hefted the hammer and placed his wounded hand over hers. "I can't grip the chisel, but I can at least protect your hands. This is gonna be awkward as hell."

He tapped the hammer against the chisel a couple of times as though trying to get his bearings. He took a deep breath and swung his arm. Meg closed her eyes.

She heard the echo and felt the vibration travel down her arm as the hammer hit the chisel. She opened her eyes and reveled in the sweet victory. "It worked! We can do it!"

Clay walked to the table. He dropped the hammer on the wooden surface and stared out the window. "We'll start tomorrow."

Eighteen

Although Mama Warner was not aware of her surroundings, Robert, bless his heart, told the townspeople that it was too much for her to have visitors traipsing in and out all day, and he restricted their visits to the afternoon. His thoughtfulness left Meg free to spend the mornings working with Clay. Their progress was slow because Clay took long moments to study the rock after they chipped off each small piece.

He told her it was because he found it strange not to hold the chisel himself, and he didn't feel as close to the stone, but she suspected that the real reason was his anxiety about her hands.

And he had reason for that.

Meg hadn't lived a soft life, but her hands had never worked so hard. She wasn't accustomed to gripping a heavy piece of metal and holding onto it when harder metal slammed against it. Sometimes, she thought her teeth would rattle loose from the impact.

Then she'd glance at Clay's hand covering hers, and she'd keep her complaints to herself. The wound was still puckered and red as it mended and scarred. She had a strong urge to place a kiss on the scar, which ran across his palm and traveled along the back of his hand.

She imagined that his agonized cry that night had come not so much from the pain, but from the realization that they had killed his dream.

But there were moments when she felt his hand close a little more over hers, when he'd hit the hammer against the chisel and the hand covering hers would react from instinct and tighten its hold.

She relished those moments, held them deep inside her, and longed for the day when her hands could slip away from the chisel and return his to the place where it belonged.

"Why are your hands shaking?" Clay asked.

"I didn't realize they were."

He narrowed his eyes. "Let me see your palms."

"There's nothing wrong with my palms."

He stepped away from the granite, and she loosened her grip on the chisel. As fast as a streak of lightning, he dropped the hammer, plucked the chisel from her grasp, and threw it down. He grabbed her hand before she could react.

"Damn it, Meg, why didn't you tell me about your hands?"

"They're not that bad, and we don't get much time to work as it is. We can't stop every time I'm having a little discomfort."

"A little discomfort? Your hands are raw."

"Doesn't your hand hurt?" she asked.

"Sit in that chair and don't move until I get back."

He stalked from the shed, and she dropped into the chair. He was as distant as the storm that rolled over the hills. She could hear the thunder; she could see the lightning; but she could touch neither. She couldn't reach the essence of the storm.

Clay never smiled. He never teased. He seldom looked at her. He no longer went to church. The masked night riders had reduced his life to the house, the shed, and an occasional walk through the fields. She was here with him every morning, and she'd never felt farther away from him.

He walked in and knelt before her. He set a jar within the crook of his elbow and turned the lid with his good hand.

"What's that?" she asked.

"Some salve my ma made up. It'll make your hands feel better. We won't work tomorrow." He set the jar on the ground and dug his fingers into the thick ointment.

"Place your hands on your lap so the palms are up. Tell me if I hurt you."

Gently, he smoothed the salve over her palm and rubbed it into the raw padding of her hand, then worked his thumb and fingers over her hand, blending the salve into her flesh. "Does that feel better?" he asked.

"Much."

"I'll do the other hand now." He dipped his fingers into the jar, retrieved more balm, and massaged it into her other hand.

"Do you hate me?" she asked quietly.

He stilled his fingers, but didn't lift his gaze. "No," he said in a low voice. He began massaging her hand again.

"Do you know who put the knife through your hand?"

His fingers faltered, then he rubbed her palm with more intensity.

"It was Daniel, wasn't it?" she asked.

"I can't be sure."

Turning her hand, she managed to nestle his between both of hers before he could pull away. She kneaded her fingers over his palm. "Has anyone ever put this salve on your hands?"

"I've used it a time or two."

"Did you put it on yourself?"

"Sure. Just put it on, rub it in. There's no secret to it."

Reaching into the jar between them, she coated her fingers with the ointment, then trailed them down the center of his palm. "The secret is having someone else put it on for you," she said as she worked her thumb between his fingers. "Your hands are so strong. Even when they aren't working, they feel so strong."

"They're so damn big."

"The better to hold me with."

He slid his hand out of hers. "They're not gonna be holding you."

"What about your injured hand? Don't you think the salve would make it feel better?"

He hesitated, and she knew he was fighting with his conscience. Everything for this man was a battle.

"I'll be gentle," she promised.

He squeezed his eyes shut and moaned low in his throat. Gingerly, she lifted his hand off his thigh and placed it in her lap. Lightly, she trailed her fingers over the scar on his palm. "Is it still tender?"

Cautiously, he peered at her. "Not as much."

Creating small circles, she rubbed the balm over his palm. "I go to the swimming hole every night," she said softly. She felt his hand tense and met his gaze. "I keep hoping

I'll see you there."

"It's best if I don't go."

"Why? Because I wouldn't walk out of church with you? I was wrong —"

"No!" He worked his hand free of her grasp. "You were right. We have no future. I was wrong to think otherwise. I was planning to move on because I didn't like the hatred touching my brothers. I don't know why I thought it wouldn't touch you."

"I know you're not a coward —"

"It doesn't matter any more. The twins were right. You should marry Robert."

"I don't love Robert."

He stood. "Your hands need some time to heal. You should probably stay away for a week or so." He walked to the door.

She rose from the chair and clasped her hands before her. "I love you, Clay."

With a sad smile, he glanced at her over his shoulder. "I'm sorry, Meg, but I'm tired of fighting."

Her protest fell on deaf ears as he strode away.

Lying in bed, he studied his hands in the midnight shadows. They didn't look any different, but they sure felt different.

A man could get spoiled having a woman in his life, smiling with the dawn, humming while she cooked breakfast, furrowing her brow while she held the chisel, rubbing salve over his hands. Every day he hated to see the sun rise above the windows on the shed. Late morning would give way to noon, and it would be time for her to leave.

She cooked them another meal and always left a pecan pie sitting on the table before she went to Mama Warner's.

Then Clay would go and watch the corn grow in the afternoon and count the minutes until dawn. He knew the time would come when he'd begin counting the years since he last saw her. He dreaded the coming of that first day when he knew the next day wouldn't bring her back.

She might not love Robert, but loneliness wouldn't agree with her. She seemed to like Robert well enough, and Clay figured the day would come when she'd settle for companionship over love.

He hoped he was long gone by then.

He heard a tapping on the window shutter. He eased out of bed and crept across the room.

"Clay?"

Groaning at the sweet voice on the other side, he opened the shutter slightly. "What?"

"Meet me in the shed."

Before he could respond, she darted away.

Cursing under his breath, then cursing aloud, he jerked on his clothes and headed as quietly as he could toward the shed.

The shutters were down and the door closed when he arrived. He pushed the door open and peered into the building. A solitary lantern rested on his table.

He stepped into the shed and closed the door. "Meg?"

She emerged from behind the granite, wearing her skirt and clutching her blouse to her chest. The pale light reflected off her bare shoulders.

Clay forgot how to breathe, forgot how to move, forgot how to think. "What —" He swallowed. "What do you think you're doing?"

"My shoulders hurt. You got so angry this morning when you found out my hands were hurting that I thought I should tell you about my shoulders and let you rub some salve over them."

His gaze darted over to the table. The jar was sitting there with the lid already removed. He shoved his hands into his pockets, shook his head, took a step back, and bumped against the door. "I can't."

She moved a hand away from her blouse so she could rub her neck. The blouse slipped a little to reveal a fraction of a curve.

He hadn't seen any curves that night by the swimming hole. He'd felt them, but he hadn't seen them. The sight of them could probably bring a man to his knees.

"I thought about asking my father to rub my shoulders, but he doesn't know I come here so I didn't know how to explain why I was hurting." She shrugged slightly, and a little more curve came into view. "Robert knows. I guess I could ask him —"

"No!"

She lowered her hand and clutched her blouse. The curve disappeared.

"I mean —" He plowed his hand through his hair. "How badly do you hurt?"

"I can't sleep."

If he touched her, he didn't think he'd be able to sleep, but then he hadn't been sleeping anyway. "All right."

In her excitement, she rose onto her toes. Lord, her feet were bare.

"Will you spread the quilt?" she asked.

"The quilt?"

She nodded quickly. "I set it on the chair."

He stalked to the chair in the corner, grabbed the quilt, and spread it out on the floor. The sooner he got this over with, the better. He stomped to the table and picked up the jar of salve. "All right. Let's get this done so you can head on home."

She turned a rosy shade of pink that traveled from her cheeks to the valley hidden by her blouse. Demurely, she presented her back to him and knelt on the quilt.

He could have sworn he heard the jar crack in his hand.

She draped her braid over one shoulder. Lord, she had more curves than he imagined: the curve of her side, the curve of her shoulders, the curve of her spine, the nape of her neck. And everything came together so beautifully, it took his breath away. He'd never be able to carve anything that looked as beautiful as she was now.

He dropped to his knees and set the jar beside him on the quilt. "Where exactly do you hurt?"

"Everywhere. My neck, my shoulders, my back. That's why I took off my blouse. I thought it would be easier for you if you didn't have to fight the cloth."

Fight the cloth? Right now he was fighting a raging battle with his own flesh.

Digging into the jar, he coated his fingers, hoping if he used enough salve, he could shield his hand from the silky smoothness of her skin. She tilted her head, and the curve of her nape lengthened. He was grateful he couldn't use his other hand. He took a deep breath. "Tell me if I hurt you."

Tentatively, he placed his hand on her shoulder. She sighed, and he jerked his hand back. "Did I hurt you?"

"Of course not."

He returned his hand to her shoulder and discovered the salve didn't serve as a buffer against the warmth of her flesh. Slowly, he worked his fingers over her shoulders and neck. He carved her curves into his memory as he rubbed the salve into her skin. He had made a mistake. He shouldn't have made love to her in the darkness of midnight. He should have waited until noon when she could have basked in the sunlight, and he could have appreciated all her beauty.

Her narrow back tapered down to her tiny waist. He thought he'd know all there was to carving if he'd been able to study her lines over the years.

He wiped his hand on his trousers. "There. That should take care of your pain," he said more gruffly than he'd intended.

She peered over her shoulder. "Are you in pain?"

He was, but it wasn't any place he could invite her to rub. "No, I'm fine."

She twisted around slightly. "Take off your shirt, and I'll rub your back anyway. I don't imagine anyone has ever rubbed your back for you."

He shook his head vigorously. "I don't like to take my shirt off in the light."

To his astonishment, she rose, retrieved the lantern from the table, set it beside the quilt, and dimmed its flame until it cast more shadows than light.

"There. Now you're not in the light," she said quietly.

But he felt as though he were sitting in the middle of the sun. He spun around and jerked his shirt over his head. He didn't think his back carried any scars above his waist. His hips and upper thighs were another matter. With his back to her, she wouldn't have to stare at the *D* they'd burned into his chest. It was the scar he hated most. "If you're gonna do it, do it," he barked.

"I'm sorry. I was just admiring your back. Even in the shadows I like the way it looks."

She began kneading his shoulders. He stopped breathing. She was using both hands. How was she holding up her blouse? Maybe she was using her mouth —

"How does that feel?" she asked.

Nope. She wasn't using her mouth. "Feels fine, but you're not using the salve."

"I don't like the way it tastes."

Was the woman daft? "Tastes?"

"Tastes," she said in a throaty voice before she placed her mouth between his shoulders.

427

She trailed her mouth and tongue along his spine, and he wished his spine were three times longer than it was. Her mouth traveled back toward his neck. Again, he wondered how she was holding her blouse in place.

Then she pressed her bare breasts against his back, and he forgot all about her damn blouse. Her nipples felt as though they were tiny pebbles buried in soft clay. He smiled inwardly at the thought. He wouldn't mind burying them in his mouth. She nibbled on his neck, then nibbled on his ear.

"I'm not wearing anything beneath my skirt," she whispered.

"Dear Lord," he said hoarsely.

She eased her hands around his waist and nimbly undid the first button on his trousers. "Are you wearing anything beneath your trousers?"

"No —"

She undid another button.

"I didn't know —"

She gave another button its freedom.

"How urgent your need —"

"Very urgent," she assured him as she wrapped her fingers around him.

He bowed his head. "Damn."

She stilled her fingers. "What is it?"

"I was wrong," he said in a strangled voice. "I can't stand up to any torture that's handed out." He twisted around. "Damn you, Meg." He lowered her to the quilt and covered her body with his own. Cradling her face with his good palm, he caressed her cheek with the fingers of his injured hand. "Damn you. Even knowing that hell lies on the other side, I can't resist touching heaven."

He kissed her long and drank deeply as though he'd crossed a desert: she was the well that contained all the things he'd dreamed about as he traveled alone. She was the water, the succulent fruit, the warmth on a cold night, the shade that protected him from the harsh sun.

He worked his hand around her back and fought the buttons on her skirt as she struggled to get him out of his trousers. The solution was simple. Take a moment and stop kissing, but she didn't seem to want to release his mouth any more than he wanted to release hers.

Then they were warmth against warmth, flesh against flesh from their toes to their mouths. Pulling back, Clay leaned over and increased the flame in the lantern.

"I didn't think you liked the light," she said.

"I don't like to be in the light, but I made love to you in the dark and didn't know what

I was missing. I wish I could make love to you in the sunshine." Reverently, he skimmed his hand along every curve she possessed. "You're so beautiful. Every line is perfect."

She pressed her hand to the center of his chest. Tears welled in her eyes. "I'm so sorry they hurt you. I'm so sorry I hurt you."

Shaking his head, he placed his hand over hers and brought it to his lips. "No past, Meg. No future. All I have is now."

"Then let's make the most of it. My shoulders don't hurt anymore —" She took his hand and laid it at the heavenly juncture of her thighs. "But other places long for your touch."

He didn't have to tell her he longed for her touch as well. Having a woman with experience had definite advantages. She knew when to touch him, where to touch him, how to touch him in ways he hadn't dared imagine. She taught him how to touch her. Her moans, sighs, and small spasms pleased him as much as her hands and mouth traveling over his body.

"Come to me, Clay," she whispered, and he plunged into her warm depths.

All the touching they'd done before had shaped the shadows of desire. Now, they moved in a rhythm that revealed the details and carved out an exquisite fulfillment that left them breathless and melded within each other's embrace.

She sighed his name like the soughing of the wind as she trembled in his arms. He kissed the dew from her throat. "How are your shoulders now?" he asked in a low voice.

Laughing quietly, she said, "Better, much better. How are you feeling?"

He lifted his head, gazed into her blue eyes, and smiled tenderly. "I've never felt so good in my whole life."

With an appreciation he hadn't felt in a long time, Clay watched dawn ease over the horizon. The sky had never looked so blue, the fields so green.

Only a few hours of night had remained after he walked Meg home, but he had slept soundly. He thought if it had stormed while he slept, the nightmares would have stayed away.

He heard the rumble of wagon wheels and glanced over his shoulder. The beautiful dawn gave way to the dark clouds of reality. With a deep breath, he stepped off the porch to greet Kirk's father.

The man drew the wagon to a halt and climbed down like a man of younger years.

He removed his hat. His hair had turned pale blond since Clay had last seen him. He supposed losing a son could do that to a man. Mr. Warner studied the hat he was turning in his hands before he met Clay's eyes. "My mother passed away in her sleep last night."

Clay wished the man had just punched him in the gut. It would have hurt less than hearing the words thrown at him as though he wouldn't give a damn. "I'm sorry."

"I gave her my word that I'd mark her place with the headstone you made for her."

"I can't . . ." — Clay winced as he shoved his injured hand into his pocket — "I can't carve the date, but everything else is done the way she wanted. It's in the shed. I'll get it for you."

He strode past the man who'd once welcomed him into his home as he might welcome his son. Entering the shed, he walked to the table where he'd carved Mama Warner's headstone. He trailed his fingers over the lettering that he'd cut as deeply as he could. People would still be able to read her words long after Clay was gone.

He bowed his head. Grieving was unbearable when one did it alone.

"Dear Lord," a deep voice whispered in awe behind him.

Spinning around, Clay stared at Kirk's father as he slowly approached the granite.

"That's my son," he said in a raw voice.

"Yes, sir. Mrs. Warner asked me to make a memorial in honor of those who gave their lives —"

"My wife?" His face showed disbelief.

"No, sir. Meg."

With reverence, he stepped up onto the stool and touched his son's face, carved in stone. "Don't tell me this is what you were talking to her about in church."

"No, sir. I'd misunderstood something. She was setting me straight."

Kirk's father slowly nodded his head. "My son and I fought the morning he left. Did you know that?"

"No, sir."

"Well, we did. We fathers were so damn proud of our boys enlisting the way they did. You were a blight on our honor. We'd planned to lynch you that evening if you didn't leave with them. Kirk found out. Told me if he heard you'd been hanged, he'd desert. I told him if he deserted, I'd hunt him down and shoot him for being a coward."

He dropped his chin to his chest. "He told me I wouldn't have to hunt him because he'd come straight to my door. My boy was going off to face death, and my final words to him were spoken in anger. I didn't tell him I loved him, didn't tell him how proud I was of him. All the words a father should say to his son, I let pass. Now, I can't tell him anything."

Wiping his eyes, he stepped down from the stool. "I talked them out of lynching you because I couldn't bear the thought of shooting my own son."

The man stood with slumped shoulders and a bowed head. Clay didn't know if Kirk's father expected him to drop to his knees and thank him for sparing his life. He didn't know what to say, couldn't think of anything appropriate to say. "Here's the marker."

Kirk's father hefted it off the table. "I appreciate it." He headed for the door and stopped. "I was here that night."

Most of his life, Clay had paid a great deal of attention to silhouettes and shapes. The flour sacks had hidden their faces the night of the attack, but the midnight shadows had revealed their identities. "Yes, sir, I know."

"Kirk told me you weren't a coward, and I called him a damn fool. I was wrong. It'd mean a lot to my ma if you'd come to her funeral tomorrow."

The steady rain began at sunset. The thick branches laden with their autumn leaves shielded Clay from the force of the storm. All he felt was an occasional raindrop as it traveled along a leaf and fell to the earth.

His arms shielded Meg as she pressed her back against his chest. She hadn't come to see him today, but then he hadn't expected her to. He knew she'd be helping the Warners deal with their loss, would be grieving herself. She'd been as close to Mama Warner as he'd been.

But he'd also known he'd find her here this evening, waiting on him. They had shared their deepest emotions at the swimming hole. In spite of the rain, they had felt a need to come here to grieve. They'd wept, held each other close, and now they watched the rain fall.

"Did she go peacefully?" he asked quietly.

"Yes. It was as though she just went to sleep."

"I'm glad, but I sure do feel her loss."

"Mr. Warner showed me the headstone. It's beautiful with the buffalo grass carved in it, so simple and down-to-earth like she was."

"I couldn't carve the date."

"Maybe in time —"

"Maybe."

The lightning flashed and its brilliance revealed the place where they'd first made love.

"Will you go to her funeral?" Meg asked.

"Haven't decided. She doesn't deserve to have hatred surrounding her when she's laid to rest."

"She'd want you there."

"I don't know, Meg."

Turning in his arms, she laid her head against his chest. "We could go together."

"No," he said gruffly.

"I thought after last night —"

"Last night didn't change anything, Meg. Just like the night we spent together here didn't change anything. I'm still the coward of Cedar Grove. That's all these people will ever see. I've been fighting their opinions and hatred for years now. It hasn't made a damn bit of difference, and it won't make a damn bit of difference tomorrow. It's best to just surrender. Hurts less that way. Hurts those I love a lot less, too. When we finish the monument, I'll be moving on . . . alone. If you were smart, you'd start spending your mornings with Robert."

"Do you love me?" she asked softly.

"More than my life."

Nineteen

Meg's hands trembled as she played the organ. She thought she'd released all her tears last night as she stood within Clay's arms. But she was wrong.

Now, she yearned for his compassionate embrace more than she longed for Reverend Baxter's words of solace.

Her tears increased as she unexpectedly pressed the wrong keys. The resounding chords more closely resembled the wail of a lost child who suddenly realizes she's alone than the comforting strains of "Amazing Grace," which she was supposed to be playing in memory of Mama Warner.

The last notes lingered as she clasped her hands in her lap and bowed her head. Tears clung to her eyelashes. She remembered the touch of Mama Warner's gnarled fingers as she gathered Meg's tears the day she cried because Kirk had grown a beard. She remembered the woman's smile as Clay lifted her into his arms, and the peace that radiated through her as she trailed her hands over Kirk's features carved in stone. She held the remembrance of Mama Warner even closer to her heart because woven throughout the memories were moments shared with Clay.

Quietly, the minister eulogized a woman who had touched the hearts of many and helped to shape the destiny of Texas.

Glancing toward the back of the church, Meg saw the door open slightly. Clay slipped in as quietly as a snowflake falls to the ground. With his hat in his hand, he slid into the last pew and bent his head until his hair fell forward and obscured his eyes.

She had little doubt that he had closed his eyes and fought his tears and grief as strongly as she did. When the final words of the eulogy drifted into silence, Meg would receive comfort from Kirk's father and Robert, from her father and Daniel, from Helen, and Sally and every other person to whom she'd ever given comfort.

Who would comfort Clay?

With his large scarred hands, he had cut the names of their children, their parents, and their loved ones into wood or stone so they would be remembered. He'd rescued their slain sons from a mass grave and buried them with dignity.

The monument she'd asked him to carve paled in comparison to the testimony of his love that he'd already given them, that he continued to give them. He had touched the people of this town in a way more profound than the sculpting of any monument, and yet none of them knew of his actions, and if they had known, their hatred would not have allowed them to acknowledge the gift.

Just as her hatred had prevented her from daring to reach beyond the wall of despair to grasp another chance at happiness.

She knew Clay would leave after the closing prayer, before she played the final hymn. He held within his breast a deep respect for people, a respect that had been denied him.

Searching the mournful faces of the congregation, she wondered how many men believed in anything as strongly as Clay believed in his convictions. How many would stand alone?

How many women believed strongly enough in the man sitting by their side to stand beside him when the whole town stood against him?

These women had surrounded her, their fingers working as busily as hers, to sew gray uniforms for their husbands and sons. They had ripped the seams on silk gowns they'd worn on happy occasions to make a flag honoring the most terrifying day of their lives. In the lamplight, they'd gazed into each other's eyes and known that none of them wanted their men to leave.

With meticulous stitches and perfect seams they'd sewn their doubts into the cloth, so that when they met the gazes of their soldiers that final morning, nothing was visible but their love and their belief in that love.

Clay was right. Meg didn't know what had driven Kirk to enlist. She knew only that he believed in what he was doing, and his belief was all she had needed to stand at his side.

The bench scraped across the floor as she moved back. The reverend stopped speaking and snapped his head around to stare at her. Meg took a deep shaky breath, gave him a tremulous smile, and rose from the hardwood bench.

If possible, the congregation became quieter, and she felt their silence wrap around her like a heavy suffocating shroud. Her legs trembled and her knees felt as though they'd turned into the sandy bottom of the swimming hole in which she swam at midnight.

Skirting the bench, she somehow managed to descend the stairs without tripping. Each step she took echoed off the rafters and vibrated against the stained-glass windows as she walked down the center aisle. She halted beside the last pew, and she could have sworn she heard necks pop as people strained to see what she was doing.

Clay stared at a knothole on the back of the bench in front of him.

"I'd be honored to sit with you," Meg said in a voice that rang through the building.

The brown depths of his eyes pleaded with her as eloquently as his words. "Don't," he rasped with raw emotion. "Don't do this, Meg. Not here. Not now."

"I said those same words to you once. I was wrong to say them then. You're wrong to say them now. I love you, Clayton Holland."

Gasps sounded, hymnals thudded to the floor, groans, moans, and sighs rose from the crowd like a psalm thrown toward the heavens.

Clay sprang to his feet. "You're grieving today. You don't know what you're saying." He strode past her to the door.

"I know exactly what I'm saying," she called out, but he closed the door on her final words. She rushed through the door after him, with the disbelief of the congregation echoing in her ears.

She staggered across the porch as someone pushed past her. She glanced over her shoulder. "Daniel!"

"I'll take care of it, Meg!" he called as he stalked toward the waiting wagons.

Meg felt a moment of panic and then relaxed. They never brought rifles or guns with them to church. Clay was striding toward the muddy road that went past the church and through the center of town.

Meg stepped off the porch. With a force that caused her to bite her tongue, she found herself jerked back and held in her father's ironclad grasp.

"What the hell is going on here, girl?" he bellowed as people gathered around them.

She twisted but couldn't break free of her father's hold.

"Meg, are you crazy?" Helen asked. "The town coward —"

"He's not a coward." Stretching her neck, she peered over her father's shoulder to the road. She was afraid she'd see Daniel attacking Clay, but Daniel was nowhere in sight. Clay was trudging away . . . alone once again.

"Clay! You've never run away from anything in your life! Don't run away from me now! Don't run away from our love!"

He came to a dead halt in the middle of the road and hung his head.

"I won't have you running after a coward," her father growled, tightening his grip on her arm, and giving her a small shake as though he could shake some good sense into her.

The voices and words swarmed around

Meg as people surrounded her, blocking her view.

"He wouldn't fight —"

"Coward's what he is —"

"Why's she chasing him?"

"Yellow streak a mile long —"

"Didn't enlist —"

"Coward —"

Through the ragged gaps left between elbows and shoulders, she saw Clay raise his hand, and although his back was to her, she knew he'd slipped his fingers between the buttons on his shirt and was rubbing the "D" they'd burned into his chest.

"I love you!" she cried over the reminders of his cowardice that people continued to throw at her.

He spun around. His voice, deep with pain, carried his words across the churchyard even though he didn't yell. "I have nothing to offer you, Meg, but loneliness, and I love you too much to give you that."

His words effectively parted the crowd, and Meg had a clear view of him standing in the road. She wanted desperately to be at his side. "I'd rather spend my life with one man surrounded by love than the ignorance and hatred surrounding me now."

Slowly, he shook his head. "You can't imagine how much it hurts to be ignored by people . . . you respect. You don't know how loud the silence is or how deeply it cuts. It's bad enough watching the hatred touch my brothers. I'd rather die than see it touch you."

Thunder rolled in the distance. People turned their attention toward the sound. Standing in the wagon, Daniel urged the horses through the water-logged road toward Clay.

"Daniel, no!" Meg screamed as she jerked free of her father's grasp only to be caught by someone else.

For a brief moment, indecision crossed Clay's face, and then he began running toward the barreling wagon, toward Helen's daughter, Melissa, as she played in the muddy road, oblivious to the approaching danger.

Meg heard a scream and didn't know if it was hers or someone else's. Clay flung himself over the child as the wagon neared.

She heard other screams and wails as Clay and Melissa disappeared beneath the hooves of the horses and the wheels of the wagon. When the wagon passed, all she could see was Clay lying facedown in the mud.

Fear gave her the strength to break free of the man holding her.

Fear drove her to rush to Clay's side and

drop into the mud beside him.

"Don't move him!" Dr. Martin cried as he threaded his way through the silent crowd easing to the center of the road.

Helen knelt beside Meg. "Oh, God, my baby."

Dr. Martin worked his way to the ground. Gingerly, he rolled Clay over to reveal Melissa's tiny mud-covered body. She started blinking her eyes and turned her mouth down before she released her first wail. Helen lifted her from the mud and pressed her against her breast, rocking and cooing to her daughter.

Using her skirt, Meg gently wiped the mud from Clay's face. "He's bleeding," she whispered as she watched the blood mingle with the mud.

"Looks like the mud shielded him somewhat so nothing's broken, but he took a blow to the head," Dr. Martin said, his hands busily looking for signs of injury.

"How bad?" Meg asked.

"I don't know."

"Did I kill him?" Daniel yelled as he ran toward the crowd. "Did I kill the yellow-bellied —"

Meg rose to her feet, spun around, and slapped Daniel across the face with a force strong enough to send him staggering back.

"How dare you!" she hissed. "How dare you judge this man and condemn him to death!"

Daniel regained his balance, squared his jaw, and took a step toward her, his blue eyes blazing. "How dare *you* defend him!"

She angled her chin. "Who better than the woman who loves him?"

He jerked back as though she'd hit him again. "You don't mean that, Meg. You can't fall in love with a man by watching him sit in the back of the church."

"No, you can't," she admitted softly. Her stomach tightened, and her mouth went dry. How often had Clay felt this slight trembling of nerves and continued on, standing his ground? "I fell in love with him by spending my days in his company. I asked him to carve a monument to honor our heroes. I thought the task would serve as a punishment for him. I thought it would make him face his cowardice. Instead it made me face my own.

"Every day, I went to his farm and watched him work, waiting for that moment when he'd drop to his knees and ask for forgiveness." Sighing deeply, she glanced at the still figure lying in the mud. "Eventually, I realized there was nothing to forgive."

"My brothers are turning in their graves," Daniel said vehemently.

446

"No, they aren't, not in the graves Clay dug for them. He got to Gettysburg after the battle. The Yankees were dropping the Southern soldiers into mass graves. Clay buried every man from Cedar Grove in a separate grave away from the battlefield."

"I swear, Meg, if you're telling the truth, if he touched my brothers, I'll shoot him dead before the sun sets."

"Why?" she asked softly.

"Why?" He took a step toward her. "Why? Because he's a coward, and I know they'd rather lie in a mass grave than have his hands touch them."

"I don't think so, Daniel." She placed her hand on his arm, and he wrenched free. So much bitterness, so much anger, so much hatred. "Mama Warner left me a letter that Kirk wrote her. He told her that he wrote Jefferson Davis asking that he exempt Clay from serving the Confederacy. He said every man in his company signed the letter. Every man, Daniel. That includes our brothers. They knew Clay wasn't a coward."

"That's a goddamn lie! He didn't fight!"

"He did fight, but he fought for what he believed in, not what they believed in. And he fought as bravely as they did."

Meg swept her gaze over the gathered people. "When was the last time any of you talked with Clay? Who among us asked him why he didn't enlist? I know I didn't. I assumed he was a coward because he didn't follow my husband and my brothers. Like your sons, they were soldiers, yet they saw honor where we didn't. Clay would lay down his life for any one of us. He just won't kill for us."

Meg didn't think it was possible for the crowd to become more somber. People shifted their gazes as though they didn't know whom or what to look at.

"Father, forgive them for they know not what they do," Dr. Martin said in reverence. He twisted in the mud and planted his arm across his thigh, leveling his gaze on the silent crowd. "Those were the words Clay spoke as he stood awaiting his execution. Funny thing, though. After he said his prayer, they couldn't find a soldier willing to shoot him."

Meg knelt in the mud as Clay's eyes fluttered open. Dr. Martin held up two fingers. "What do you see, Clay?"

Clay shook his head slightly. "Nothing. It's too dark, but I want to thank you for coming, Doc."

Dr. Martin's worried gaze met Meg's before he turned his attention back to Clay. "It's always a pleasure treating you, you know that."

"I don't want to die," Clay said quietly.

"I don't think you're gonna die."

"One might miss, maybe two, but not all six. Not six Southern boys with rifles." He closed his eyes. His face grew ashen, and Meg felt the icy fingers of death wander slowly along her spine.

Pulling himself free of the mud, Dr. Martin stood. "I need someone to carry him to my office."

"I'll carry him," Robert said.

"He's always been like a son to me. I'll help you," Kirk's father said.

Meg watched Robert slip his arm beneath Clay's knees as Kirk's father took Clay's shoulders. Together, they carefully lifted Clay out of the mud.

She glanced one last time at the somber faces surrounding her, then followed Clay in silence . . . alone.

Sitting beside the bed in Dr. Martin's office, Meg made herself loosen her grip on Clay's hand. He'd lose use of it as well if she continued to hold it so tightly.

"Meg?" a quiet voice asked behind her.

She twisted and looked toward the door. "Hello, Tom."

Uncertainly, he stepped into the room, holding a bundle. "Sally sent me with some

449

clothes. We thought you might want to get Clay out of those muddy clothes."

Rising, Meg took the clothes from him. "Thank you. That was very thoughtful."

Blushing, Tom cleared his throat.

"Since you said you'd been watching Clay work, I was wondering if you knew anything about our little girl's marker . . . his pa didn't make it, did he?"

Meg hesitated, wondering how Clay would feel about their knowing the truth. She hoped if these people came to know him as she did, perhaps the hatred would melt away. "No, his father didn't make the marker."

"Didn't think so. I was walking through the cemetery, lookin' at the markers his pa made, the ones he made. The ones Clay made look different. I can't explain it, but it's as if he put his soul into it."

"Carving is very special to him."

Nodding solemnly, he settled his hat on his head. "Tell Clay that when it's time to harvest, I'll help him with his fields. It's the least I can do to pay him back for the marker."

"Would you do me a favor?" Meg asked.

"Sure."

"Would you run out to the Holland farm and let Lucian know what happened?"

"I'd be happy to, but John and Caroline Wright already went. Caroline said she'd watch the twins if Lucian wanted to come in." He smiled and shrugged. "Reckon some of us are startin' to see things a little different."

He left, and Meg returned to Clay's side. She brushed the hair off his brow. The bloody and bruised knot near his temple frightened her. She had a feeling it frightened Dr. Martin as well.

Leaning over, Meg combed her fingers through Clay's hair again and again. "Please, Clay, I know you're tired of fighting, but please fight once more for me. Wake up so we can go home."

The pounding in Clay's head increased as he opened his eyes. Yesterday was a haze. He remembered Meg kept prodding him to wake up. Every time he did, she kissed him and told him to go back to sleep.

Her actions made no sense.

When Dr. Martin woke him, he'd ask Clay how many fingers he was holding up. Clay figured that as a doctor, the man would be smart enough to know how many fingers he was shoving in Clay's face.

He preferred for Meg to wake him.

He eased his legs off the bed and pressed

his hands to his temples. He didn't remember coming home, but home he was.

He stood and walked to the chair where someone had left his carefully folded clothes. He worked his way into them, fighting the nagging ache in his head.

He opened the door to his room and gazed into the living area. A small smile crept across his face. Meg was bending before the hearth, humming.

He thought he could enjoy waking to the sight of her every morning for the rest of his life. The pain in his head increased. He needed to talk to her about that. He had reasons why he couldn't marry her, but he couldn't remember what they were.

Turning, she saw him. A beautiful smile eased onto her face. None of the reasons he had could have been strong enough to fight the lure of that smile.

She crossed the room, wrapped her arms around his neck, and kissed him tenderly.

"How are you feeling this morning?" she asked.

"My head hurts a little."

"You should sit down." Taking his hand, she led him to the table and pulled out a chair.

He eased down. "Something smells good."

"Mr. Tucker from the general store brought over a box of supplies this morning. He said when you feel up to it, to come see him, and he'll extend you credit."

The pain in his head increased as he furrowed his brow. "Why'd he do that?"

She sat in a chair and folded her hands around his. "Maybe because you saved his granddaughter's life yesterday."

"His granddaughter?"

"The little girl you threw yourself over yesterday was Helen's daughter, his granddaughter."

"I didn't know Helen had a daughter."

"I imagine there's a lot about these people you don't know, and some of them are anxious to change that."

Clay rubbed his brow. "What's that infernal pounding? I thought it was in my head —"

Laughing, Meg rose from the chair and pulled him to his feet. "Come outside and I'll show you."

They stepped onto the porch, and Clay stared at a sight he'd never expected to see again. People were milling about on his land.

His old barn had been torn down. A new frame had already been put up. He recognized Sam Johnson, Tom Graham, and John Wright as they pounded boards into place.

He saw Robert Warner. And then he heard Kirk's father issuing orders, and he felt a lump form in his throat.

Women were setting food on a table beneath the shade of a tree. Children were laughing, playing, and carrying water to the men who were working.

He wondered briefly if they thought he had died and had come to celebrate. "Why are they here?" he asked.

"To welcome you home. Mr. Lang brought some lumber from the mill this morning, and they came to help put up a new barn," she said.

"I can't pay for the lumber."

"Mr. Lang said not to worry about it. Your credit is good with him. Besides, he figures it won't be much longer until you're family anyway."

He snapped his head around and glared at her. His head rebelled at the movement. "What does he mean by that?"

She smiled, and the pain in his head eased. "He gave Lucian his blessing to marry Taffy."

Clay pressed the heel of his hand against his forehead. "Meg, what happened yesterday? Or have I been sleeping longer than that?"

Her smile increased. "Nope. Just one day."

Dr. Martin ambled over and held two fingers in front of Clay's face. "How many fingers do you see?"

"Two. Doc, what's going on?"

Dr. Martin shoved his hands into his pocket and looked toward the barn. "Amazing, ain't it? Meg said some things yesterday that got these good people to thinking. You putting that little girl before yourself got them to understanding." Dr. Martin laid his hand on Clay's shoulder. "Between you and me, Clay, you weren't the only one who could have gotten to her in time, but you were the only one who tried." He dropped his hand. "Reckon I'd best go look for Pru. Seems she found out how the fire in Johnson's field got started, and that wild boy of hers was behind it. She's decided she needs me after all. Hope I can adjust to married life."

Clay watched him walk away. Everything had happened too quickly to be true. He couldn't believe —

He heard tiny footsteps patter across the porch. He looked down to find a small girl wrapping her tiny hands around his large one. She looked up at him and smiled. "You're my hero."

Clay shook his head. "I'm not a hero."

"You saved Melissa's life," Helen said quietly as she came up behind her daughter.

"That makes you a hero."

"I'm shellin' pecans so Miz Meg can make you a pie," Melissa said.

"No, she ain't," Josh said. "She's eatin' 'em. Me and Joe are shelling 'em."

"I don't mind if she eats the ones I shell," Joe said. "I think she's got the prettiest eyes I ever did see." He took her hand. "Come on, Melissa. You can finish helpin' me with the pecans."

"Will you be my hero, too?" she asked as she followed Joe.

"Yes, ma'am, if you want."

Clay looked toward the barn and studied all the activity. "Is your father here, Meg?"

"No, but it doesn't matter."

"It does matter."

"Not to me. You're all that matters to me now."

Holding Taffy's hand, Lucian walked over to the porch. Clay didn't know his brother could produce a smile that big.

"Ain't this something?" Lucian said as he brought Taffy against his side.

"Who raised the shutters on the shed?" Clay asked.

Lucian turned red. "Kirk's father asked if he could raise the shutters so people could see the monument. Meg said it would be all right."

Meg slipped her arms around Clay's waist. "You might as well get used to it. People are going to be looking at your monument for a long time."

"It was never meant to be mine, Meg. Yours, theirs, but not mine."

"God damn it!" Lucian growled. "I can't believe he had the nerve to show up here!"

Clay followed the direction of Lucian's heated gaze. Daniel drew his horse to a halt beside the barn. Meg tightened her hold on Clay's waist.

Daniel walked toward the barn. All the working men stopped pounding their hammers and walked to the other side of the barn, leaving him standing alone, facing a partially completed wall.

Meg sighed. "I guess it is true. You reap what you sow."

"I could tie a rope around him and drag him off," Lucian said.

"Why would you do that?" Clay asked.

Lucian released his hold on Taffy and jerked his hat off his head. "He nearly killed you yesterday. He tore down your wall of the barn at the Wrights'. Hell, he was probably here the night they attacked you."

"Is that true?" Josh asked as he sidled up to Clay. " 'Cuz if it is, me and Joe got a plan."

"What's your plan?" Lucian asked.

"We wait until he's built his side of the barn, then we tear it down."

Clay eased Meg's arms away from his waist. "Nope," Clay said. "That won't do."

"How come?" Joe asked.

"Because this matter needs to be dealt with right now."

"What are you going to do?" Meg asked.

He touched his fingers to her cheek. "See if I can build one wall while tearing down another."

Walking toward the barn, he could smell the scent of freshly cut lumber. She rushed to his side and slipped her hand into his. "I'll go with you."

"You don't have to," he said.

"Yes, I do. I need you, my brother, and everyone in this town to know that whatever . . . whatever you decided regarding Daniel . . . I'm standing beside you."

Slowly, he nodded. "All right."

Daniel had just carried a piece of lumber to the side of the barn by the time Clay arrived with Meg beside him. Daniel placed the board against the frame before meeting Clay's gaze. "Heard they were gonna build you a barn," he said quietly. "Thought I ought to help."

"I'd like to help, too, but I can't hold a

nail." Clay jerked Daniel's hammer out of his grasp. "But I can hold a hammer. I just need to find someone willing to hold the nail for me."

Daniel's gaze darted over to Meg, then came back to Clay. "Reckon I could hold the nail for you."

"I was hoping you'd say that," Clay said. "You realize, of course, that years of pounding on rocks has given me a powerful swing. I miss the nail, I'll break your hand."

Daniel's Adam's apple slowly slid up and down. "Reckon you know I'm the one who put the knife through your hand so I won't hold it against you if you do end up hitting my hand," he said in a quivering voice.

Clay smiled. "I'm glad to hear that." He tilted his head toward the unfinished barn. "Shall we?"

Daniel took a nail out of his pocket, knelt beside the board, and positioned the nail.

"Hold the nail tight and don't move your hand," Clay said.

"Clay," Meg said quietly.

He glanced at her. "Don't distract me, Meg. I need to keep my attention focused on my task because I know exactly how much courage it took for your brother to come here today."

Clay brought his arm back. Daniel took a

deep breath, turned his head toward the board, and closed his eyes. Meg balled her fists and pressed her lips tightly together to keep from crying out. Clay swung the hammer, and the frame rattled as he drove the nail home.

Daniel stared at the nail that was now halfway embedded in the wood. In disbelief, he looked at Clay. "I thought . . ."

"You thought what?" Clay asked.

"I thought you'd hit my hand."

"Why would I do that? I love Meg. I'd like to marry her, but I won't unless you and your father give us your blessing. Think you could talk your father into giving us his blessing?"

Nodding, Daniel wiped the back of his hand across his moist eyes.

Stepping away from the wall, Clay staggered. Meg and Daniel reached for him at the same time, grabbing his arms to steady him.

"You tore down your wall," Meg said with tears in her eyes. "Now, let Daniel finish building this one. You need to rest."

"Not yet. I have one more thing to do," Clay said.

Daniel released his hold on Clay, but Meg kept her fingers wrapped around Clay's arm. Clay lifted his brown gaze to the blue heavens. Then he lowered his gaze to the corn-flower blue eyes of the woman he loved.

"Will you marry me?" he asked.

She smiled tenderly. "I'll marry you in the center of town with everyone watching." Wrapping her arms around his neck, she kissed him long and deeply.

In front of her brother.

In front of her friends.

Her mouth was hot and moist, and he drank of her sweetness.

He felt her breath, as gentle as the wind, caress his face.

He heard her quiet sigh as soft as the leaves rustling in the nearby trees.

And the promise of a night filled with the scent of honeysuckle wafted around him.

Epilogue

Summer, 1870

Sitting on the bench, Clay studied the monument.

The dappled moonlight filtered through the abundant leaves and danced along the stone.

He'd regained full use of his hand by the time he was ready to carve the finishing details. Sometimes, his hand ached, and it still cramped if he worked too long, but the pain was worth the accomplishment.

He'd given Kirk what he'd asked for: Meg as she was the last time he gazed upon her . . . for eternity.

He heard the scattering of leaves and the snap of twigs as someone neared.

"I thought I'd find you here," Meg said softly as she sat beside him.

He draped his arm around her and drew her into the nook of his shoulder. "I like it best at night. I can't see all the mistakes."

"You're the only one who sees the mistakes. The people around here think it's perfect. That's why they wanted the monument in a special place where they could come and reflect on the past and remember their sons."

"So you suggested the land surrounding our swimming hole."

"It seemed appropriate, since their sons came here to discuss 'men' things. Besides, we won't be using it anymore."

He kissed her cheek. "We might if we come back."

"Will we come back?" she asked quietly.

"I don't know, Meg. I got into the habit a few years back of not thinking past today, but I'll need a place to work once I've learned all I can at the university in Germany. Besides, I like Texas granite."

She nuzzled his neck. "I've grown rather fond of it myself."

"And fond of me?" he asked.

"Especially fond of you." She kissed him slow and leisurely to prove her words. Then she nibbled on his ear. "Why don't we finish this at home? My shoulders are beginning to ache."

He laughed. "I have an ache myself."

"I'll be happy to rub it."

Giving him a smile that promised heaven when they got home, she rose from the bench and walked to the monument. "Come along, Kirk. It's time to go home now."

The little boy hunkered down before the monument shook his head vigorously and ran his hand over the carved letters. He was only two years old, but already his hands were becoming as rough as his father's. He loved the feel of stone and carried broken pieces in his pockets.

"Weed," he said.

"Didn't your father read it to you when he brought you here?"

He shook his head, and Meg looked at Clay. He shrugged. "We knew you'd be along eventually, and he likes your voice better than mine."

She held out her hand. "All right, then. Let's start at the beginning."

She led their son to the front of the monument, and Clay heard his small voice ring out, "My name."

"That's right. Kirk. Kirk Warner is the man on the horse."

Clay listened as she filled the night with the names of those with whom he'd played as a boy. They'd leapt into manhood with courage. War had denied them the sweet rewards of a long life.

Clay stood and walked to the monument as Meg and Kirk walked around the corner. He knelt beside his son and together they trailed their fingers over the letters. Clay cleared his throat as he did every night before he read these words to his son. "Within the shadows of honor, courage often walks in silence."

Beneath the words, he'd inscribed the names of Will Herkimer, the man they'd tortured beside him, and Franz Schultz, whom they'd hanged because he wanted to work a stone quarry and didn't believe in the war. Every name on the monument represented a man who had given his life standing for what he believed in.

Lifting his son into his arms, Clay unfolded his body and wrapped his hand around Meg's. Slowly, they walked away from the monument. He felt his son's head grow heavy on his shoulder and knew he'd fallen asleep as he did every night. Clay wasn't even certain if the boy knew how to fall asleep in bed. He always drifted to sleep on Clay's shoulder, and Clay would tuck him into bed in the room he shared with the twins.

Tomorrow, Joe and Josh would leave with them. Lucian and Taffy would stay behind to manage the farm and raise their own family.

Stopping, he drew Meg against his side. They turned to look one last time at the monument they'd created together. Like their love, it would survive the storms that swept over it.

"We'll come back, Meg."

Reaching up, she caressed his face. "Wherever your dreams take you, Clay, that's where I'll go."

"They'll bring us back here."

With his arm around her, he led her into the shadows where their dreams waited.